MARGARET STORM JAMESON

was born in Whitby, Yorkshire, on 8 January 1891. Her forebears had lived in Whitby, then a small fishing and shipbuilding port, for uncounted generations: her grandfather was a shipowner, her father a sea-captain. She was educated at a private school, followed by one year at the Municipal School in Scarborough. Awarded one of the only three County Scholarships available in the North Riding of Yorkshire at that time, she took an honours degree in English Language and Literature at Leeds University in 1912 and was given a one-year research scholarship, to be held at University College, London: she found University College dull, and transferred herself to King's College. Her thesis, on Modern Drama in Europe, finally approved by Leeds University, was rewarded by the Degree of Master of Arts; it was published in 1920, by the firm of William Collins. In the meantime she had married and had a son.

In 1919 she returned to London, becoming for a year a copywriter in a large advertising agency. She published her first novel, and began a two-year editorship of an obscure weekly magazine, *New Commonwealth*. From 1923 to 1925 she acted as the English representative of the American publisher Alfred A. Knopf, and later, for two and a half years, was co-manager, with her second husband, Guy Patterson Chapman, of the short-lived publishing house of Alfred A. Knopf in London. She married Guy Chapman in 1925, a deeply happy marriage, broken in 1972 by his death, after a distinguished career beginning with the publication in 1933 of *A Passionate Prodigality*, his classic account of trench warfare in France, and ending in a study of the politics and history of the Third Republic of France.

Between the years of 1919 and 1979 Storm Jameson published a total of forty-five novels. She has also written short stories, literary essays, criticism, and a two-volume autobiography. In 1939 she became the first woman president of the British section of International PEN, where she was an outspoken liberal and anti-Nazi, and a friend and helper of refugee writers. In 1952 she was a delegate to the UNESCO Congress of the Arts, held in Venice. She was awarded a D.Litt. from Leeds University in 1943, and is a member of the American Academy and Institute of Arts and Letters. With her husband, she has been an inveterate traveller, mostly in Europe. She now lives in Cambridge.

Of her fiction Virago publish *Women Against Men*, *Company Parade*, *Love in Winter* and *None Turn Back*; they also publish her autobiography *Journey From the North*.

LOVE IN WINTER

STORM JAMESON

With a New Introduction by Elaine Feinstein

Published by VIRAGO PRESS Limited 1984
41 William IV Street, London WC2N 4DB

First published in Great Britain by Cassell & Co. Ltd 1935

Copyright © Storm Jameson 1935
Introduction copyright © Elaine Feinstein 1984

Virago edition offset from Cassell 1935 edition

British Library Cataloguing in Publication Data

Jameson, Storm
  Love in winter. – (Virago modern classics)
  I. Title
  823'.912[F]   PR6019.A67
  ISBN 0-86068-315-X

Printed in Finland by Werner Söderström Oy, a member of Finnprint

INTRODUCTION

The world in 1924 has become too complicated . . . I dream of a vast
railway junction seen at night, hundreds of steel tracks interlaced and
crossing; they vanish into the darkness and as your train rushes on you hope
the signalmen are awake . . . The whole thing has grown too vast and
crazy with power, to be carried on in the old way. The next head-on crash
might finish us.

The wintry landscape of this second novel in Storm Jameson's
sequence *The Mirror in Darkness* portrays, with delicacy and
bitterness, the spiritually depleted London of the twenties. It is a
more ambitious novel than *Company Parade* (1934) in which Storm
Jameson drew mainly on material from the years before and during
the Great War. *Love in Winter* (1935), takes Hervey Russell into a
literary world she now understands with assurance. The force of her
heroine's name is still there to recall generations of Yorkshire
shipowning families from Storm Jameson's earlier trilogy, *The
Triumph of Time*, but the balance of the novel has tilted.

Hervey herself, though still easily hurt, has become as tough and
strong as a tree. She no longer resents a resemblance to her Grandmother (who had once owned the shipowning firm of Gartons) now
the old, merciless woman is dead. When Penn, her unfaithful first
husband, hectors her about her own new passion for Nicholas Roxby,
she is tugged more by compassion for him than pain. 'I should be
less responsible for him if he made a success of something.' She has
moments of tenderness towards him, and even, occasionally, a sense
of failing him, as though she had almost forgotten the brutality of
his earlier behaviour. Some bonds are hard to break.

One bond that remains as tight as in *Company Parade* is the love
Hervey feels for her son Richard, to whom she still keeps her word
against all other needs. It is a relationship touched with the guilt of
early separation; and even though Hervey is able now to afford to
have him with her, difficulties remain between them.

Characters who survive from earlier novels are more fully
developed. Ridley, the novelist whose energy and push brought
him such easy success, has gained in moral stature. It is to him Storm

Jameson gives the voice and authority to deal with Julian Swan, the upper-class layabout, expounding Mussolini's political creed with relish.

The lines of bitterness in the portrait of Hervey's mother deepen as she becomes more harsh and unforgiving than ever towards her retired sea-captain husband. Even Hervey feels a touch of pity towards the slovenly dejection of Captain Russell.

And underneath an Eliot-like chapter heading, which suggests rats gnawing away at a collapsing civilization, Storm Jameson shows a clear-headed view of Marcel Cohen, financier and newspaper proprietor. He is always shrewder than the men who try to use him, if only because he distrusts White Russian diplomats quite as much as the Régime in power in Russia.

Love in Winter is far from a bleak novel. It is filled with companionable friendship among people whose married love has been unhappy. Most importantly, *Love in Winter* draws the growth of a love that had all the virtues of such friendship, and was to bring Hervey the most lasting happiness of her life.

In her portrait of Nicholas Roxby, Storm Jameson continues to use material from her own experience; but in this novel, the act of writing fiction allows her to tell more, rather than less, than she does in her fine autobiography *Journey From the North*. Between 1923 and 1925 Storm Jameson was acting as the English representative of the American publisher Alfred A. Knopf; and it was in the course of these duties that she came to meet Guy Chapman; and make a deeply happy second marriage with him, which lasted until his death in 1972.

In *Journey From the North* a natural reticence prevented her from speaking of little more than the undoubted distinction of Guy Chapman's mind, and the severity of his judgements of her early novels. In *Love in Winter*, Nicholas Roxby emerges as an altogether more rounded character.

It must be one of the most honest portraits ever drawn with passion, yet the accuracy is in no way at odds with the love. Hervey can encompass the knowledge that carefulness, or cowardice, or even the lack of warmth could lead Nicholas to throw away all possibility of their happiness together. If Nicholas cannot offer to take responsibility for Hervey, she is undeterred. She perceives the difficulty he has in making up his mind and respects it, even though she knows it has weakness as well as nobility in it. Nor does she imagine him without egotism, as he lies awake thinking about his ruined life. She understands how inexorably mixed with the pity he feels for his treacherous wife is the memory of all that remained of his younger self that had survived the war. She can even see the streak of vanity in his generosity towards a woman who had betrayed him many times. All that puzzles her is the simplicity with which he is cheated in the operation of his own business. She learns that she will have to be precise in such matters for both of them, since his upbringing has unfitted him for calculation.

What Hervey owes to Nicholas is akin to the spiritual deepening that Storm Jameson speaks of in relationship to her own second husband, 'a happy difficult second marriage, part of the nervous system of my mind.' It is in her description of that enrichment that the novel flows most deeply. That richness includes a love for Villon as one who has truly inhabited that Waste Land Eliot appropriates as his own.

> Qui n'a couché à vent et la pluye
> Il n'est digne d'aller en companie.

'My second marriage was a slow education, in many things. In trust first. Very slow, this—it was many years, a great many, before I even had the courage to say frankly that I wanted to do this or have that. I was so used to going by tortuous paths to avoid being seen, and perhaps mocked.' Nothing fine comes easy and to help her, she recalled a passage at the end of one of Chekhov's tales, which she had not once understood, in which he speaks of bitterness and pity as part of 'being properly in love' and concludes: 'Any marriage worth the name is no better than a series of beginnings, many of them abortive.'

Guy turned Storm Jameson outward, towards Europe; although she remained Yorkshire to the bone. As she said of the church in Whitby, where a memorial service was held annually to commemorate those (like her brother) who had died in the War: 'It speaks to my skeleton, which remembers clearly the worn places in the stairs, the grain of old wood.' She never forgot the pains of her childhood, the beatings she sustained, and the longing that remained in her to please her bitter Mother. 'I have two countries, the Whitby of my birth, and France; the first secreted like a salt in my blood, bone marrow and cells of my brain, the other nursed by my foolish heart.'

In the same way, love for her mother continues to shrivel Hervey's heart with pity, whenever she tries to show it. But her brother, dead in the war, is never out of her mother's mind; whatever blessings come they are too late, since he is not there to enjoy them with her.

In turning to Europe, with Guy, Storm Jameson brought her own first-class mind, and a passion for European literature which had taken her off the path to a safe academic career many years before. She respected Guy's work as a historian far more than her own as a novelist. When I last spoke to her, early in 1983, she was still maintaining that she had 'only written novels because it was the easiest way to earn money'.

She knows well enough that such contempt is unreasonable.

Rationally, I consider that the novel is one of the great arts, and I revere Tolstoy, Proust, Dostoevsky, Stendhal as I revere Mozart and Beethoven . . . but an irrational contempt persists in murmuring in my ear: 'Only an artist without the wit to become a poet (or a sculptor, musician, painter) turns to writing novels.'

With the next volume, *None Turn Back*, Storm Jameson was to abandon *The Mirror in Darkness* sequence altogether. It is hard not to feel that this present volume represents the core of the series, and that when she decided that she was 'working against the grain of my talent' this volume was not the part she had in mind.

Perhaps because she was at her happiest out of England, and travelling with Guy, her portraits of women in *Love in Winter* are unusually generous. Even the lady literary editor seems more a victim of her own desires, than a manipulator of others.

No doubt the political strands which run through the novel gain greatly from the hindsight which permitted her to view the growing menace of fascism in the twenties from its brutal realisation in the thirties; but Storm Jameson was rational and humane enough to have suspected it early. Marriage with Guy Chapman took her to the very centre of the deepening European nightmare. The Continent was already tugged apart by conflicting ideals and as the two of them travelled through France and Germany, she learnt there were enemies even in France itself, (which she always loved); as surely as England was in danger from the machinations of Julian Swan and his thug friends.

Some of her best books were yet to be written, among them *Cousin Honoré*, which shows the forces at work undermining European civilization in microcosm in the province of Alsace. And another, later, novel *Europe to Let* was not only prescient in 1940, but has a stronger sense of the realities of central Europe than many novels written since.

It is easy to see why Storm Jameson was chosen to become President of the British section of International PEN. Never very interested in promoting her own fame, she used her office wholeheartedly to help refugees first from Nazi Germany; and then after the Second World War from the Soviet dominated countries.

Storm Jameson's lifelong carelessness over her own health which has nevertheless brought her to her ninety-third year, has depended upon an extraordinary resilience of spirit as much a physical stamina. Slight and unstooping, she still goes up and down three flights of stairs to welcome visitors. Although she disowns all interest in the domestic, her own flat is immaculately kept. Once there, she probes patiently and persistently into other people's troubles and will only discuss her own life with reluctance. She takes some pride in once having mastered a few meals which met the taste of her late husband whose standards were extremely high. Since his death, she takes no more than an austere interest in food—'boiled eggs, toast'—, though she is a frequent guest at the table of her friends George and Zara Steiner. Early in 1982 when she attended the first night of George Steiner's play *The Portage to San Cristobal of A.H.*, she was very much part of the discussion and disquiet that followed.

If Storm Jameson formed the intention, under Guy's severe eye, of learning to write in another manner, it was decisively not the manner of modernism. On the contrary, she saw the dislocations encouraged by experiments with syntax and language as morally dangerous. In *Journey From the North* she declared:

Today I am much nearer seeing Joyce as a purely disintegrating force, a sacred monster, uprooting established forms to create a waste land, a great anti-humanist, the destroyer by his devilish skill and persistence of the thin walls against barbarism. Writers are innocent of the impulse to destroy civilization. But the roots of the impulse run underground a long way, to the point where the smoke from burning books becomes the smoke issuing from the ovens of death camps.

In this she may have been quite wrong (she would be the first to say as much) but the assertion bears witness to her deepest instinct, which was to see human beings as much more important than books, and human feelings as truer than literature.

Elaine Feinstein, Cambridge, 1983

THE MIRROR IN DARKNESS

II

LOVE IN WINTER

CHAPTER I

THAT year began with Hervey living near London in rooms. Her eight-year-old son lived with her. In the morning she took him as far as the gates of his school and watched him walk slowly up the drive. He walked keeping his head down, as if he did not want to go in. She always waited to see whether he would look round. When he turned out of sight without looking she ran on to the station and caught the nine o'clock train to town.

In the train she read her letters. There might be one from her husband, from Oxford. He never wrote about his work but he described meetings with people, one man had invited him to breakfast, another had been rude—it was not all easy becoming a student again at thirty-three. One morning, opening a letter in an unfamiliar hand, she read: ' Dear Hervey, if you have not forgotten our one meeting I wish you would allow me to give you lunch next week. Choose your own day. It is ridiculous that we are not friends. Nicholas Roxby.' At once she felt that something would happen from this. It was the feeling an artist must have before a new canvas, energy springing from a deep source to his fingers. She had a sense of power and expectancy.

This Nicholas Roxby's face, as she had seen it during moments of sharp humiliation for herself, was as near her mind as her own hand grasping his letter. He doesn't speak here of his wife, she thought. Her thoughts checked and drew back. Why pretend that a married cousin is as interesting as an unmarried one? The pleasure of a new equation

is in its unknown factors. Too much is already known
about a married young man. Now from somewhere she
had the impression that all was not right with Nicholas's
marriage, and at once her mind, which loved conspiracies,
began wondering how to find out. His mother would talk
to me, she thought, remembering Clara Roxby's face, creased
with humour and grief. But she was ashamed to call on an
old lady whom she had neglected for years.

The train slowed into the station. She was alone in the
carriage and could stare into the mirror. (She did not like
to be seen looking at herself, as if that were some disgrace.)
The glass showed her the face no one else saw—and she
had not the wit to see how everything else in it, the wide
guarded eyes, domineering forehead, harsh chin, was con-
tradicted by the long mouth and fine impudent nose.

She walked quickly across Waterloo Bridge, watching how
the January sun moved coldly on the water. The office of
the *London Review* was old and shabby, but the accident
that it had been a private house gave it two staircases, built
for grandeur and used by editors. Hervey's room, scarcely
large enough to hold a desk and her chair, had two doors.
One opened from her employer's room and the other on to
a landing and the side staircase. By that door Evelyn Lamb
could escape, leaving her troubles in Hervey's arms.

One of these troubles was seated in Evelyn's room, waiting
for her. Hervey sighed. She knew there was no hope that
Evelyn would deal with it herself. 'Good morning.' She
sat down facing him, weak at the knees. 'Miss Lamb has
asked me to see you. She can't be here yet.'

'What sort of a Literary Editor is she? This is twice
she hasn't been in when I called. Do you think I want
to come here?'

Hervey looked at him with wary eyes. This man in a
dirty macintosh was, for the time, but nothing lasts, famous
in three capitals for his savage criticism. Evelyn had a
written promise from him for the *London Review* of his
new book. Now, in the way of very intelligent writers,

in whom conscience is generally in inverse ratio to intelligence, he had sold it to another weekly. He had the temper and manners of a Prussian and Evelyn preferred not to risk her dignity in a meeting. Hervey had none to lose.

' Miss Lamb is ill. I am her secretary. I have to tell you how startled and disappointed she was by the announcement about your book. The *London Review* certainly expected to have it.'

' Blast her soul, then,' roared the great man, ' she hasn't said a word about it to me for six months. How was I to know she wanted it ? '

Loud voices frightened Hervey more than a danger. ' But you realise how important any book of yours is,' she said carefully.

' Why the devil didn't the woman write to me ? '

' We were anxious not to vex you by knocking too often at your door,' Hervey said. Suddenly she could feel his mind at the end of her own. She looked at him with a smile. ' You are so much more important than anyone writing for us—you can understand the care we took. Why, the advertisements to announce the series have been rewritten twenty times.' This was a lie. She watched his face as she spoke. ' With another writer we should have waited until the manuscript was in the office. But a Wilde Jones is a responsibility. We owed it to New York and Paris as well as to you to see that everyone knew what was coming.'

The angry little eyes staring at her shifted a point. Something uneasy came into them. ' I suppose you do have some sale in New York and Paris.'

' We have our own agents,' Hervey said in a serious voice. She was rigid with excitement. At the same time she felt like laughing at him. Beside this, a drop was forming at the end of his nose. ' Can nothing be done ? ' she asked gently. ' Have you still the manuscript in your hands ? '

' I'll see what I can do.' He sprang up and began tying the greasy belt of his macintosh. A dirty handkerchief fell out, and he picked it up and blew dangerously into it. Hervey walked with him to the stairs. Spiritually, she felt, they were now arm in arm.

In her own room she drew the breath of thankfulness. That was a near-run thing, she murmured. She felt no surprise that a great intelligence is accessible to flattery. In her short life she had learned quickly. What was not learned had been given her.

She heard Evelyn Lamb come in. After a time there was a visitor and voices, then Evelyn came into her room, opening and shutting the door suddenly. 'That's D. Nash,' she said rapidly. 'It seems she's a young woman, not a man at all. A young countrified creature, without a word to say for herself. She stares at me. You must get rid of her.'

'You asked her to lunch.'

'Don't I know it?' Evelyn answered. 'She can lunch with you.' Half smiling, she went to the other door and hurried away into safety. Hervey stood up slowly. She had discovered long since that Evelyn Lamb's smooth elegance was the cover for an hysterical temper. The reputation she had as a cultivated assured woman, patron of talented youth, was more and more, as she aged, at the mercy of her nerves. Hervey's duty was to spare these delicate strings by offering her own to be played on.

She went with shrinking into Evelyn's room and saw a young woman her own age, as awkward, wearing the same clothes, her eyes watching the door. A sharp pity seized her. As the young woman started up Hervey spoke to her with a warm smile.

'Are you D. Nash? I have longed to meet you. I am Hervey Russell.'

'I've read your novels,' the other said. She was so nervous that her tongue stood in the way of her words. Her eyes rolled; she was like a nervous horse.

'When I wrote them I didn't know how bad they were,' Hervey said, like a friend. 'A dreadful thing has happened. Miss Lamb has been taken off by the editor and heaven knows when she will be released. I suppose you—would you lunch with me?'

She could feel the creature quieting under her hand. Soon she was at ease and talked with a great hurry of words to Hervey's listening face. Did Miss Lamb mean to print any more of her sketches? If you had stayed away, Hervey thought. 'You know how it is with a weekly,' she said, nodding to D. Nash. 'We're not allowed to use the same people too often.'

The other flushed. 'I've written a novel,' she muttered. 'It's here. I don't know what to do with it. Would she, do you think, read it and tell me?'

How can you give yourself away like this? Hervey cried. She was sorry for her. In the same breath she groaned at the thought of giving up hours of her own time to help this young stuttering woman. Sighing, she said:

'Will you let me read it? I believe I know more about publishers than Miss Lamb herself.'

When she went back to the office Evelyn sent her flying out again to buy orchids and grapes and to carry them for her to her house.

She was walking away from the house and saw Evelyn's husband, T. S. Heywood, coming towards her. At once she felt happy. He was her great friend, they were friends before the War. Her life—since her husband left her to go up to Oxford—was solitary. Thanks to Evelyn she knew a great many people, and loved none of them.

'What are you doing here?' T. S. asked. He turned to walk with her.

'Flowers for your dinner party to-night,' she answered.

'Not mine,' T. S. grinned. 'My dear wife has quite given up asking me to dinner. Thank God!' He took Hervey's arm. 'Do you know what? for a happy marriage there's nothing like having an unfaithful wife. She takes care to give no trouble. Those dinner parties of clever people were too much for me, I can tell you.' He looked at her with his big head on one side, and smiled until she looked away. He was very fond of her but he enjoyed the sight of her embarrassment. 'By the way,' he added, still looking at her, 'do you know that Evelyn and your absentee husband are bosoms? Yes.'

'Penn has been reviewing for the paper,' Hervey said.

'Yes, he was dining in the house last week.'

'I know.'

T. S. shook her arm. 'That's a lie,' he said, laughing. 'You certainly didn't know it, and you're vexed. Why do you tell so many lies? My little dear Hervey, I know you too well.'

'Then you ought to know that my vanity is hurt,' Hervey said. 'Penn doesn't come up to see me during term. It's true I don't ask him.'

She caught the four o'clock train home. A familiar restlessness had seized her. She tried to quiet her mind but it had been parted between too many people, between Evelyn, between the furious great critic, and between D. Nash, whose book, long and badly copied, was under her hand. I waste my time, she thought, turning this way and that in hope of peace. Admit, she said, that you grudge Penn his easy life. Her mind remembered wrongs more sharply than a kindness. She did not want Penn to be responsible for their son, yet despised him that he was not. When he was unfaithful she forgave him, and she remembered it against him. He spent half his vacations with her and did not pay for his food: she would not ask him for money, but be sure the sum was chalked up in her mind—yes, you can be sure.

The truth is I lead a disorderly life, she thought. She flattened her nose on the window, trying to see through the thickening darkness. She saw a fat respectable sort of bird, scratching himself, which made her laugh out. The train ran slowly into her station. She jumped out before it stopped and ran home at the heels of her mind.

Richard had begun his tea. Not for the first time she

wondered how it felt to a little boy to come in, to see no one but a landlady, the rooms tidy and unlived in, without warmth, the feeling of a place hired. Can he feel safe? She felt guilty, as if it were her fault that nothing here was his.

' What did you do to-day, my one? '

' Nothing,' Richard said.

' No lessons? ' she laughed.

' Yes, I had lessons.'

' Do you like this school? '

' It's all right.'

' Do you like it better than living with Miss Holland? '

' Yes,' Richard said. He was indifferent.

He could not tell her what he did during the day—partly because the repetition bored him, and because he had a deep dislike of answering questions. He answered as shortly as he could, hoping there were no more to come.

Hervey could not help a feeling of anxiety. Was it natural for a child to be so silent? Yet when she tried to remember her own childhood, a merry-go-round of scenes rushed past; the stone; the double hawthorn tree; the café in Antwerp; the cabin, its air warm and stagnant, of a ship; but from none of them did she hear her voice.

She put Richard to bed. He slept in her room. When she was going out he said in a gentle voice: ' Leave the door open.'

' Don't you like the dark? ' she asked.

' Yes.'

' You'll be in a draught if I leave it open.'

He did not speak. She waited a moment, then pulled the door almost shut and went away. Now, if she were not too restless, she had a few hours in which to add another page or only a few lines to her fourth novel. There were times when she thought that it was better than the others, because it was about a woman she knew as closely as she knew her own skeleton. This was her grandmother, whom she half hated for her unkindness and arrogant heart, and loved, yes, with passion.   A few days after the old woman died she thought, Now that she is dead I have her.   The book rose from these few bones, clothed itself in flesh and walked about her mind.   As she watched she saw that there wanted more books than one to satisfy this great shade. Now her courage failed.   She was so stubborn that she could do without courage.   She noted down the shape of the book and began writing it, giving it time when she would have slept.   She wanted a great deal of sleep; sleep took her quickly and sped her forth as soon as she lay down.

Must I read D. Nash? she thought, sighing.   It was almost too much.   There was a book lying on her table, which she had been reading the night before.   She opened it and forgot where she was.   Soon she was as still as a stone lying at the roots of a tree.   She came to the words— '*Allone, withouten any companye*,' and the happiness she felt was so quick that she could scarcely help tears.   She repeated the words and closing the book, opened D. Nash's manuscript and began to read it with patience.

CHAPTER II

She felt shy and awkward before Nicholas Roxby. He had told her that he was a dealer in antiques, and the shop, when she found it in St. James's Street, was much grander than she had expected. She went in, asked in a stiff voice for Mr. Roxby, and was taken into a small room behind the showroom. She noticed a great many things at once; he was good looking; his clothes were better than her own; when he smiled his face became kinder and very charming. An inexplicable emotion seized her. She could only say a few words. A woman, his secretary, coming in laid some books on his table. Hervey saw that he thanked this woman with the same warm quick smile. She felt dejected by this. Her hat, a new one, seemed to her to be resting on the bridge of her nose and her coat was long and too heavy. To give herself confidence she made a show of examining an eighteenth-century table at one side of the room.

'Where would you like to lunch?' her cousin said.

'Where you like,' she answered politely.

They went to the Café Royal. By this time she felt certain that he found her uncouth and dull. For her own part she thought him so attractive that she stared, an unconscious bad habit. He is intelligent, she said to herself, stubborn, perhaps selfish. She was so sunk that he had to repeat a question. She grew very red, and stayed so for the rest of the meal.

'Secretary to Evelyn Lamb,' she answered.

Nicholas laughed. 'That fake! But I thought you wrote novels.'

'My third novel is coming out next week. It is very dull.'

'Do forgive me,' he said, smiling, 'I couldn't read the others. They were too emotional. Do you mind?'

'I can't write.'

'Unfortunately you can. The kind of writing I like is short and hard. Everything has been over-written. A writer ought to use the fewest and simplest words, without fuss.'

At another time, and spoken by anyone else, this criticism would have made little impression on her. She was never good at taking advice. It fell on a mind charged with emotion. From now on it was her gospel and no ascetic lived more tormented by visions than she henceforth by words.

She nodded at him, stolid and unsmiling. He was afraid he had offended her. 'It seems ridiculous that this is only the second time I have seen you. I ought to have written to you years ago. What with the War, and I married during the War, and afterwards trying to earn a living—I've always regretted that I didn't know your brother.'

'He was killed.'

'I know. He must have been very brave.'

'He was very young,' Hervey said.

Nicholas made a sudden gesture, pressing his hand on the table. 'Tell me something. Why wasn't your mother reconciled with *her* mother? I'm certain the old lady wanted it.'

'It went on too long,' Hervey said after a moment. 'My grandmother ought to have made some move.' She felt anger like a hand on her. 'She let my mother work like a servant all her life till now when she's old. She did everything for you and nothing for my brother.' Half choked, she put her hand over her mouth, alarmed by the bitterness she had thought cured. Nicholas was looking at her kindly.

'It wouldn't surprise me if you hate us,' he said. 'She

was a hard old woman, but in the end she was beaten. All her life was in her ships.' He watched her as he was saying this. 'You knew I refused to carry on the firm? It was after this she sold out of Garton's.'

'Who bought the firm, then?' She knew.

'Thomas Harben.'

'Why did you refuse?' *I* would never have refused, she thought, with self-pride.

A look of fatigue or impatience crossed his face. To her staring he seemed older. 'At the time I was sure. Now I am not sure. It doesn't matter. One of these days I'll tell you about it if you want to hear.' His smile confused and pleased her. 'Talk to me about yourself, Hervey. You're married, aren't you?' He had a vague belief that her husband was not a credit to her.

'Yes. I have a nine-year-old son.'

'Thank God I haven't any children,' he said with energy. 'My wife lives in one house and I have rooms in another— probably you knew.'

Her mind warned her sharply not to betray surprise. She looked away. 'Is that a good arrangement?'

'Oh, excellent. We see each other only when we care to and that's less likely to become boring to either of us.' He laughed.

'Penn—my husband—is at Oxford.'

'A don?'

'Oh dear no. He wanted to take another degree. He's in his second year.' With a smile she hurried Penn out of the way. An impulse she would not look close to made her wish to be, at this turn of her ways, as if unmarried. Beside that to be questioned offended her, as if she lost by it. 'Your shop is so fine as I didn't expect,' she said quickly. 'Do you like selling antiques?'

'It isn't my own shop, I manage it. It belongs to a Frenchman called Beauvier. He has now ruined himself buying and selling francs. We're being sold up next month.' She looked at him. 'It's true, I assure you.'

'What are you going to do?' Hervey asked. She was ashamed of her red face and rested her elbows on the table so that she could hide part of it between her hands.

Nicholas jumped. 'You said that like Mary Hervey— that was her voice.'

'You've heard it oftener than I have,' Hervey answered.

Her cousin touched her arm. 'Never mind that,' he said, smiling into her face. 'Do you really want to know what my plans are? I haven't told anyone yet. You're the first. How much do you know about our grandmother's will?'

'She left my mother five hundred a year for the rest of her life,' Hervey said. Her mouth twitched.

Now it was as if the grim old woman made a third at the table. Her blue eyes, as far-looking as a sailor's, watched them with knowledge and hard pride. She neither awaited their judgment nor needed it. Those who could have spoken for her had died first. She was the last, and much she cared whether anyone praised or reviled her. A spent wave moved now against the wall of her first ship-yard. The wind bent the grass over the rusty girders. Perhaps a stone still lay where her impatient foot had thrust it out of her path.

'Not very much to do for her own daughter, is it?' Nicholas said.

'It was her money, she could do as she liked with it,' Hervey said; these words were forced from her by her self-knowledge.

'Well, she left me the same income, five hundred—and what surprised me, five thousand pounds and part of her furniture. Do you know what I'm going to do? I'm going into business on my own. I've been working out the details for weeks. I thought of furnishing a moderate-sized house in Chelsea, living in it and running the whole place as a showroom for old furniture.' He pushed his cup aside and began drawing chairs and a cupboard on the cloth. Hervey saw that his life was in the scheme. His face became animated; an enthusiasm that made him laugh and gesticulate like a boy got the better of him. She was surprised and moved. She felt a longing to help him.

' As soon as you're ready I'll bring Evelyn Lamb to look at it. She knows everyone.'

' Bless you,' Nicholas said.

She grew warmer with pleasure. He began to talk to her about his sister: ' Georgina ordered me to say that she must know you at once. I think you'll like her, Hervey. She must be your age, she's about twenty-nine. She's very pretty, and I'm told that she's a less beautiful copy of your mother as a girl. What else can I tell you about her? She's too much alive, too much for me—I can't dance all night now. Now when will you go and see her? '

' She'd better come to see me,' Hervey said without expecting any good to come of it. She would run a mile rather than know more people. The effort was each time new and double—to defend herself and to be liked. In one of the many endless fantastic stories she told herself when she was bored, or at night before she fell asleep, she had made a doll which was her double and went everywhere while the real Hervey stayed safe at home. Once, at a trying dinner party, she pretended that she was this doll and succeeded so well that she grew frightened and pricked herself with a knife to make sure.

She was half convinced that by taking thought she could do anything. Her mind was capable of unheard-of persistence and energy. She kept it busy for an hour or more answering questions. Tell me, what did I say? What did I seem like? My voice? Did I say too much? She did not ask, Why are you so anxious to make a good impression? When she was in the train going home the thought of Penn came to her mind. Ah, she thought swiftly, if only I could arrange that he had never existed. She could think calmly and reasonably now about his mistress. The grief she had felt, which made her cry every night for more than a year, was gone. To recall it was like listening to music which used to stir the heart and now says nothing to it.

She was not especially truthful, but to one person, herself, she was never willing to lie. The question, Why did you not leave him at that time, when it would have been simple? she answered honestly: He was my memories and my youth; I had not enough courage to begin again alone.

Just as she was leaving the train she put her hand to her pocket and found her purse gone. The shock rushed through her body. She went back to the carriage and looked everywhere. Nothing. Hiding her panic, she turned home. She tried to remember the last time she had had it. In the office of the *Review*? In a bus? In Nicholas Roxby's showroom? Half of her money for the month was in it, besides her wedding ring, which was so large she rarely wore it. Her fingers had been rounder at nineteen when she married. At the thought of what the loss meant she became very pale. With anger and no patience she thought, In less than a month I shall be thirty and I am not yet rich or famous.

The conviction that she had lost it in the street grew. In that case it was lost for good, and with the instinct to make at least a small profit she seized the excuse it gave her to write to Nicholas. In a letter she could be frank, pleasing, witty—letter-writing was one of the ways in which she could actually send the doll out to play the part of the real Hervey.

His answer pleased her so much that she carried it about with her and read it twenty or more times. 'There is no purse here, and no ring—and worst of all, no Hervey. I send you a luck penny with this so that you may never want money again.'

She turned the George Third guinea over in her palm. It gave her a curious feeling of triumph. A happiness, as sudden and irrational as that of a very young girl, filled her . . . she sat a long time idle, thinking and dreaming of nothing very much. She began to think of the letter she would write to thank him. During the morning she looked up his telephone number but it was several minutes before she felt the courage to speak to him. She was afraid of vexing him if she interrupted his work. At last, making a gambler's effort, she gave the number. She waited with a leaping heart. As she had feared, he spoke in an irritable voice. She took one deep breath and said: 'This is Hervey.' Now he spoke in quite another way and she felt a little confidence.

CHAPTER III

SHE climbed six flights of stairs to her aunt's flat. The elderly woman who opened the door told her that Mrs. Roxby was out—'Miss Georgina is in the sitting-room.' She led the way. Hervey walked behind her with a bright smile; her friend T. S. Heywood would have recognised it at once as only an imitation.

Georgina Roxby was thin, with a modish and very lively beauty, and as soon as she saw Hervey she ran to her and kissed her. This pleased and disconcerted Hervey Russell. To be liked, that is encouraging, but to be liked a great deal has all the air of an obligation. She did not know what to do with unexpected offers of friendship. Usually she treated them as she did the pair of expensive gloves she had bought in a reckless moment—she had laid them up lovingly in a silk handkerchief, and never wore them. Without losing her doubt she felt a quick gratitude towards Georgina. At once, before she could save herself, she was in the flagged yard behind the school. There was the high wall, the trees, and in the corner a bush of some strong weed, like the edge of a jungle. She was the centre of a group of girls. They were her age—at thirteen, with thin long legs and hair combed back from her forehead, she was already unlike them—they were quicker and more assured. You could see that she did not know yet how to dress her hair or manage her legs and arms. Two of the girls were pulling the ends of a rope they had tied round her ankles, all the others were in fits of laughter. Hervey begged them not to make her fall. She was humiliated. She trembled with rage. When she escaped, walking away to the front of the house, and the harbour, the ship-yard, the white gulls, blurred into each other before her eyes, she thought of tortures she would inflict on them if she were not helpless.

Standing beside Georgina, she tried to see the wretched child. It was no use; she could only feel what had been: when she thought of these moments, her mature detachment vanished and she had no comfort to offer to her younger self. Why was I tormented by them? she wondered: I did nothing. Was there something that provoked them? my voice? in my looks? If for a single moment she could *see* the child standing stiffly in the yard she would know the answer to these questions.

' I've wanted to know you for years,' Georgina said.

' It's years since I first came to London to work,' Hervey said. Her face flushed a little. She was afraid that it sounded like a reproach. Turning her head, she looked fiercely at Georgina Roxby. If she, if any one of these Roxbys, supposed that Hervey Russell had been anxious to know them at any time, she would keep out of their sight now and for ever. Her eyes started.

Georgina looked back at her with a smile. ' You ought to have sent for me. You might have known I should feel afraid to write to you. First because of our grandmother treating you so badly, and then when you had written a book and your name was in newspapers and reviews—I was a little afraid of being snubbed.' She had seen Hervey's thoughts and she wanted to help her through an awkward moment. Now she knew what Nicholas meant when he said: ' You may not like her, I don't think she's conceited but she's not at all easy to know.' He had gone on to say that Hervey dressed badly and was very awkward. As she listened to him, Georgina thought that he had liked Hervey: it was in his voice. She hid her surprise from him, and a little anxiety. It is the first time, she thought, since his detestable wife left him—and perhaps it means nothing . . .

or it may be too late. She thought with contempt and anger of Nicholas's wife. It is her fault that he looks old, that he trusts no one: he overworks; he lives only in his office and his club; perhaps a man he scarcely knows comes in and before you can say knife they are both talking quickly about the War—'that winter we were sent down south of Arras '—' he was killed afterwards at Givenchy, and when the letters kept coming for him I sent them back and at last wrote '—' we were in support that week; it rained the whole time, the ground sodden, and the men up to their knees cursing.'

Under cover of giving Hervey her tea she looked steadily at her. Is she kind? Will she be kind to him? But what nonsense, she thought, laughing at herself; I know nothing about her life: if I go too quickly with her she will begin to despise me. 'Don't think me a fool,' she exclaimed smiling. 'I can talk sensibly when you want me to. I'm much too pleased you're here.'

Hervey admired her with a touch of envy—She has everything I have not, good looks, quickness, lively charming manners. She wanted to please Georgina because she was Nicholas's sister, because it was an approach to him. But another impulse had taken possession of her, something less simple and gentler, which she had not yet felt for a woman. She watched Georgina stooping to lift the heavy old-fashioned brass kettle, and thought, She is a little like me, perhaps after all I shall not need to pretend.

Talking in her deep voice, Georgina took a sliding step that brought her against the gramophone. 'Do you like music?'

'I like the Brandenburg Concertos and Mozart,' Hervey said, a little nervous.

'Everyone likes those. Don't you like modern music?'

'But I have never heard it.'

'This is new. A young Frenchman, who uses eight grand pianos. Listen.'

'One would have been quite enough,' Hervey said after

a pause. She looked shrewdly at the other young woman. Clearly Georgina was keeping back something she wanted to say. It was in her mind the whole time, taking the colour out of everything else. She is wondering whether to tell me or to leave it, Hervey thought. She had better leave it—there is no time now to think of the correct answers. Thinking about Richard, she glanced quickly and stealthily at her watch. She liked her cousin more than—now that she was no longer a girl—she had expected to like any new person. Of her two friends one, T. S. Heywood, had changed so much since the War that she no longer knew how to talk to him. The other had been dead more than two years; when she thought of him she saw a room in which they had stayed talking, the corner of a garden, a street and the rain running, seized by the light, along the edge of his hat; but during these two years he had slowly become completely silent. She could not now remember the tones of his voice or anything he had said that was in the least important.

Looking at Georgina, she felt happy and at ease. It was time to go. She stood up, forgot what she had meant to say, blushed, and smiled warmly. There was really warmth in her heart, and not the distrust she would have felt towards a stranger, and which she would have hidden under a too friendly air.

When she was going Georgina took out a handful of violets from a bowl, dried the stalks on her handkerchief and gave them to her. ' Will you come again ? ' she said.

' Yes. Of course.'

' But do you mean it ? I am sure you tell people lies to keep them quiet.'

' I shan't tell you any lies,' Hervey said firmly.

' Is that a promise ? '

' Yes—it is a promise.'

CHAPTER IV

FEBRUARY. A sky without colour or depths. The trees of the small wood through which she and Richard walked each morning ran with moisture. The thin reddish stems of a bush shone transparent in the weak sunlight like the fingers of a hand held before a light.

A fog had extinguished London. People moved about in it half choked, looking to each other like maggots. It was as thick as pitch in north London and Hervey groped her way up the unlit staircase of Nicholas's mother's flat. She felt exasperated and dirty—London is perhaps fit for human beings ten days in the year, not more.

Clara Roxby's skin had faded the colour of an old document. It would be hard to say whether grief or humour had written the greater number of the items. The story was full of contradictions. She was awkward and lively; there was nobody whom she reverenced as she had reverenced her own mother, and it was to defy her that she had turned socialist and gave away her money; she loved and deeply admired her only sister, Hervey's mother—but none of the blows that fell on Mrs. Russell had been cruel enough to satisfy Clara Roxby's jealousy. She clung to her daughter, loving and what was better trusting her. And both knew that if it were to save her son's life she would sacrifice Georgina without hesitation. She was generous, selfish, erratic, kind and unscrupulous. She had a conscience.

She had liked Hervey from the first. Something warm and dependable in the younger woman came to meet her. She felt that she could count on it, and she found it easy and simple to confide in Hervey feelings she kept even from her children.

Hervey took up the photograph of Nicholas's wife and laid it down again without speaking.

' I don't know why I keep it! ' Mrs. Roxby exclaimed. ' It is my Christian duty to forgive her, and I hate her with all my might and main. I wish Nicholas had never set eyes on her.'

' I don't know anything about his wife.'

It gave Clara Roxby a deep joy to tell her that when Nicholas was at the War his wife had amused herself with men, with one man in particular. A year after the War she left him, to go to this man. ' If you believe me, Hervey, not content with ruining the boy's life, she made him promise to pretend that he was guilty, so that she could divorce him. Do you call that fair? '

' No,' Hervey said. Her knees shook. Now I am hearing everything, she thought.

' In the end it seemed the man she ran away with didn't want her. I'm not surprised! Very well. Back she runs to Nicholas—she wouldn't live with him again, she wanted money. Yes, money. Like a fool he gives her half his income. Why, I don't know, except that he always did anything she wanted. Now Beauvier, who is mad too, has gone bankrupt, and so Nicholas loses his salary. Very well. He asks Jenny to do with less money for a short time. She ought to be glad to do anything for him, after ruining his life! Hervey, you never saw such a change in a boy in a few years. What was I saying? But not she! She simply said that she couldn't live on less—and he the fool, instead of saying Damn you, you *shall* take less money, smiles and says, Very well. I suppose he didn't want to seem poverty-stricken. She used to laugh at him when they were living together, and tell him he would never make any money. S-s-s! Why can't he despise and ignore her, the wretch? '

' That isn't easy,' Hervey said. ' You feel obliged to the person you've married.'

Clara's face expressed only scepticism and triumph. 'I was taught that marriage is a sacrament, and the Church, especially my Church, declares it is one. But nowadays young people don't believe anything of the sort—so why should Nicholas behave as if he did? I call it ridiculous.'

Hervey was satisfied to know the story. She was already at work weighing and judging it in her mind to have the truth of it. She felt certain there were turns in it that Nicholas's mother, in her blind dislike for his wife, could not see. What old person, talking about a love affair or a marriage, remembers why the young behave as they do? He may still, Hervey thought, be in love with her, very likely he is unhappy. Until she knew she would not rest.

She was dining with Nicholas that evening. She went home, put Richard to bed nearly an hour before his time, changed her dress and returned to town. They dined in a small restaurant in Greek Street. She wanted to please him and all she could think of was to ask him about his new business. He was only too happy to talk about it. He had been looking at houses in Chelsea to find one that he could turn into a showroom. If only he would ask me to look at them with him, she thought. He did not do so and she felt saddened. If he wanted to see me he would take this chance. Suddenly she said: 'Is your wife helping you with the house?'

Nicholas looked at her with a smile. 'I shouldn't think of asking her. She is too certain that I shall make a failure of anything I do by myself.'

'Will she come and live in the house, and help you?'

'To be truthful, I asked her to do that. Without feeling any obligation to act as a wife, of course. I thought we could live more economically that way.'

'She refused?'

'Not at all unkindly. She was right to refuse. I might as well tell you now—she has no more interest in me and she finds me impossible to live with. And so I daresay

I am,' he laughed. ' I was annoyed at the time because of the money. Nothing else.'

She closed her eyes to jump, as one does. ' I don't believe that anyone finds you impossible to live with.'

Something sprang between them, a trembling of the air, intoxicating. Afraid, Hervey drew back and said in a rough matter-of-fact voice:

' You were going to tell me why you refused to go into Garton's. You were the heir, weren't you? I should like to have built ships.'

' To begin with, the shipbuilding would scarcely have come into my hands. Mary Hervey visited the yards less than a dozen times a year. Things have changed since she began. In those days she walked out of the side door of her house into the yard. She watched a ship from its laying-down to the launch. That was something you could feel under your hand. By the time I came into Garton's it was already inhuman. I had no interest in being chairman of a board of directors.'

' Even though it was your own firm.'

' Oh, I'm not proud of myself,' Nicholas exclaimed. ' It was partly weakness. If it hadn't been for the War. . . . Do you know, the War made everything else unreal and a burden. I lost the energy to face Garton's. I had no ambition to become very rich. The only thing I felt any interest in at the end was aeroplanes. In 1919 I tried to get into the Air Force.'

' They wouldn't take you? '

' Good heavens, no. A used-up infantry officer! They told me to run away and take a holiday. It turned out I'd thrown up Garton's for nothing. And I had a wife to keep in the station to which she'd been looking forward. She would have been better off if I'd been killed. If that had come off my grandmother would have made her an allowance.' He spoke with a lightness that made her wince. It was insincere. He is running away, she thought. It came to her—a young woman would have to be very deeply in love to forgive him for throwing away the Garton money and importance. She was surprised by a pang of sympathy for Jenny Roxby. As if he saw her thought, he said gravely: ' My wife, poor girl, was knocked out. She would have enjoyed spending a great deal of money. I warned her before the end of the War. I don't know in the least why she didn't leave me then.' He knew very well. She had her own good reasons for waiting, he thought, now without any bitter feeling.

Hervey was shocked by his indifference to money and security. If he had ever been poor or hungry he would have known better, she thought. It is because he had everything without struggling for it—Eton, Oxford, he has had an easy life. Not like my life. She felt, she could not help it, a contempt for his want of hardness.

The next day was Sunday. She took Richard to walk in their wood. At one side the trees were being felled to make room for a house. There was a board advertising freehold plots for the ' erection of residences. Sitting-room, dining-room, four bedrooms. All services.' We no longer build. Half a dozen thin silver birches lay across the path, as pale as death. It is a pity that human beings take up so much room with their dining-rooms and separate w.c.'s. The pond on which Richard sailed his boats was already choked up. He looked sadly at the ruin. ' This place gets worse every day,' he said.

' Would you rather be in Danesacre ? ' Hervey said. The thought that she would be freer to spend time with Nicholas crossed another: Danesacre is healthier for a little boy. She looked at him. He was thinner than when he was living there. With his wide forehead, his fairness, the bright blue of his eyes, he seemed to her an extraordinary being. He ordered her to tell him a story and she began the one which had pleased her when she was a child. ' *How cold it is, how very cold, said the little lamb, as she crept nearer to the shelter of the hedge. . . .*' What is Nicholas about at this moment, she wondered. Is Sunday that day of the week he visits his wife? Did he enjoy his visits? It was a strange way of living, and there must be more in it than he would tell—I shall never know the truth, she thought. Her mind, as full as this wood of locked gates and paths which led nowhere, suspected all kinds of deceit in his. In her experience people were never straight-forward about their emotions. They disguised them, dressing them up to look finer or simpler or bolder. 'Does he get back to his mother in the end?' Richard interrupted. He sounded anxious. 'Yes, it ends happily—*But she was not so completely alone as she thought. . . .*'

She thought day and night of Nicholas. Her mind had fastened on her thought of him with all its force. No one knew the extraordinary tenacity with which she could wish for something or for an event. It was as if the order were given to rush all available troops to one point. But it was not deliberate. She was obeying a spirit which drove her before it.

Instead of writing her book that evening she wrote to Nicholas. 'I intend not to ring you up again until I have a serious excuse. Is the idea that you should review a book on furniture for us a good excuse? You asked me if I enjoyed changes. All my life I have enjoyed nothing else, and I feel in my bones that I am coming to another corner. Is it likely that I shall find anything at the other side so pleasant as dining with you? No. Still, I hope you are happy, as this leaves me, wishing for nothing except a very large club sandwich and company, neither of which I have. Yours, Hervey.'

She had a letter from her husband, the first for more than a month. He told her that he had been hard at work. He was finding time to write a novel, unlike any other novel. (It will be about his Miss Hammond, she said.) Then he described a humiliating experience. He wanted sympathy. A young man whom he expected to tea did not come—he had waited, an hour, two hours, and at last he walked to the man's rooms. He met there only coldness and evasion.

It was very strange. 'I felt humiliated. I had prepared everything carefully. He had accepted the invitation and I waited.'

She was sharply angry with the uncivil young man. She did not like Penn to be snubbed. She would write instantly, comforting and reassuring. As she wrote, she thought that if it had happened to her she would have told no one. She wished Penn would not ask her so easily to pity him. It made him a little ridiculous. The moment she had written her letter she forgot him. She threw his in the fire, since she would not want to read it again.

She was so deeply in love that she had no vanity and no self-confidence. She could not think reasonably about Nicholas. She saw him two or three times the week, and he wrote to her as often. But she had neither the courage nor the assurance to suppose from this that he was not quite indifferent. If she had been less deeply in love she could have weighed glances and words. She could have believed, if it were only for a few moments, that she was succeeding with him. As it was she was not able even to hope. When she was not with him her vivid imagination invented for her all kinds of ways in which she could interest and attract him, but the moment she saw him all these seemed useless and ridiculous. Her imagination was too deeply involved. She became diffident, humble, sceptical in everything to do with herself.

Sunk as she was she had no longer the wit to perceive that their intimacy could not have grown so quickly if Nicholas had not wanted to see her.

One day she was having tea with him in the little room behind the showroom. He began to talk to her about the War. She listened without being able to avoid seeing the changes in him when he thought himself back into that time. His face became happier and smoother, softened by a reminiscent smile. She saw that certain names of places, Bapaume, Gommecourt, Arras, Bucquoy, had for him more

than the significance of poetry. With them was involved
depths of an emotion into which she could not enter, by
any effort, or by fasting, or by love. It was occupied
territory. With despair she understood that the War had
taken the fullness of his life and energy. Less than a whole
man survived. She saw that women have more than one
reason to fear war.

'The companies went into rest for a fortnight . . . there
were changes and in April Gary was sent off to another
battalion. I didn't see him for six months.'

'What happened to him?'

'He was wounded—in a bad way,' Nicholas said.

Staring at him she heard the change in his voice when
he was speaking of his friend. He was unconscious of it.
She felt sharply her ignorance and inexperience. He was
looking over her head with a half-absent gaze, as if he had
forgotten that she existed. Unable to bear it she jumped
up and began to look along a shelf of books. She opened
one with a pretence of interest. Nicholas turned round and
said: 'When Gary comes back next month I should like
you to meet him. I'll ask him to dinner with us.'

He was smiling at her with so much liking that she felt
a confused joy. Then at once she thought that the liking
was for Gary. She looked at him and said in a warm voice:
'That is very kind of you. I should like it.'

The same week they dined again at the *Gallia*. He had
decided on his house and he described it to her, room by
room. She had under her arm a copy of a paper in which
was a review of her new novel. The reviewer praised it in
an absurd extravagant way. She knew that his words were
foolish, but she had warmed her hands at them. The book
was not going to sell. She felt ashamed and even so indifferent.

Leaving the *Gallia* they stepped into one of those evenings
when London seems the gentlest of cities. The darkness
overhead was transparent, as if there were light a great way
off—one could suppose the earth navigating a vast sea, with
its riding light and lighted portholes and figures running

from darkness to light and vanishing again on the far side.
Nicholas walked very slowly, as if he were uncertain what
to do next.   'What time is your train?'

'There is more than one,' Hervey said.

'Then let's walk to the station, Hervey.'

'Wouldn't you rather go as you always do to your club?'

'I go there because I have nothing to do and nowhere
better to go.   I'd much rather spend the time with you.'

This answer confused Hervey.   She felt an actual con-
striction over her heart.   In her anxiety to seem natural
she spoke in a cold stiff voice.   'We can walk towards
Waterloo.'

Nicholas did not seem to notice her want of warmth.
They strolled down the Haymarket and along Whitehall
to the Embankment.   Hervey kept her review pressed to
her side under her elbow.   Her book had been out a month
and so far as she knew Nicholas had never noticed it.   She
was too ashamed of it to ask.

The air down by the river was cool and soft, as if it were
not so long since the Thames had been in the country.
Perhaps it had brought back a few weeds or a plait of grass.
They leaned for a few moments on the parapet.   'If you
could choose what would you do, how would you live?'
Nicholas asked.

'In the country with Richard.   I should travel abroad.'

'That's existing, not living.   To live one needs a career
or an interest which absorbs every ounce of energy and
time."

'Then you would have no personal life.'

'Thank heaven my personal life is finished,' Nicholas
said.   'The only satisfaction in ceasing to be young is that
you cease at the same time to want anything but impersonal
pleasures.   To work until you can't stand.   A bottle of good
wine.   To read what you like.   I'm perfectly content with
that life.'

'Is that why you spend every evening at your club?'
Hervey asked.

Nicholas smiled into her face. 'Come along,' he said softly. 'You're shivering. It's too cold to stand.' He called a cab over and they drove the rest of the way to the station. He has had enough of me, Hervey thought. She said good-bye to him at the barrier, smiling to hide her anguish. In the train she thought of a dozen clever and witty remarks she might have made.

During this time she wrote nothing, but she made several notes which she put away for future use.

'The three kinds of love are—sensual—intellectual— imaginative. In *Chartreuse de Parme*, Stendhal describes imaginative love throughout. The first is the simplest and least manageable. At one time in my life, when I had the misfortune to fall in love with an American flying officer, of bad character, I understood it. It is even easy for a woman to be attracted to a man whom neither her intellect nor her heart approve for a moment. The notion of marrying the American only alarmed me, and I had too much stiffness and caution to be the mistress of a man of that nature. One can learn even from avoiding an experience. I learned that one should surrender to sensual love at once, or never. At first it is a physical crisis. To delay, to weigh consequences, to plan, to make terms and stipulations, to admit scruples, changes its nature for the worse. Since I was too proud or too fastidious or too timid or too vain or too shrewd, or even too upright, to give way at once to an impulse, I ought to have run away—with my fingers in my ears. I behaved badly. It is bad behaviour to think about what is a pure pleasure of the senses. The images to which it gives birth are monsters. Do I know anything of intellectual love? No. Is it possible that N. is capable of nothing more?' She could not bring herself to write the name out in full. That would have seemed to her unlucky, as well as able to make what she was writing true. 'Yes it is possible. Love of this kind is easy for men and women in whom quick minds are joined to a low bodily vitality. (N. wants only impersonal pleasures.)   Such people are charming companions, sensitive, witty, sympathetic.   To be happy they need nothing but the good fortune to fall in love with one of their own sort.   *Chacune sa guerre*—I could perhaps in time sergeant-major myself into becoming of this sort.

'The third kind is sufficiently rare.   This is doubtless a good thing, since either it ends badly (as for Abélard) or it never ends (Héloïse).   Perhaps it is impossible to cure. (By imagination I mean the whole self and not only that fraction of it which most human beings intend when they say " I myself."   It is a degree of love in which the whole self is involved, so that it is impossible to pull on one's shoes without its being in some sense an act of devotion. One commits oneself to the last farthing, to uphold, to approve, with what is necessary, it may be for nothing. One can be sure of nothing in this life—the only thing of which one can be sure!   Here for the first time in my life I have no doubts.   To be wholly committed is certainly something.   It is the same impulse whether one is a great poet, or a dock hand, or only Hervey Russell.   What a pity I did not understand anything until I am almost thirty. It may be too late.   That is worse than the rest—you spend years and years discovering one satisfying idea and in the end all you want is to be allowed to begin again.   It is like the songs we listened to during the War.   They were all worthless—what they had they borrowed from us—but I shall never hear anything so clearly again.   It's not enough to have been happy, and to cry and strike your head on the wall.   What one wants is to be young again—and then the time comes when you cry in the same way!   But there are some things I should have altered if I could begin again. There must not have been the War.   My brother who was killed must be alive again.   My mother must have had everything she has wanted and still has not, a large garden, trees of her own, beautiful rooms, success.'

CHAPTER V

THE ANATOMY OF A WORLD

ONE day early in March Hervey walked along the streets between the office and Covent Garden. Ahead of her was a café into which a number of people like herself were passing. It was as uninviting as it well could be—that is, it was a café like the rest. She, too, went in, and when it was too late to draw back she saw that she knew the man at the nearest table.

David Renn was thinner than ever. He was so thin that you could think he had happened to leave his body at home and come out in his bones. He looked up as she hesitated between going and staying, and smiled at her warmly. She sat down, resting her elbows on the brown marbled slab with an air of ease, but she did not know what to say to him.

'It's exactly a year since you were so angry with me.' Renn smiled.

'I wasn't angry. Or you needn't have taken notice of it. I haven't enough pride to keep up a quarrel.'

'So much the better,' Renn said.

Hervey looked at him carefully. 'What are you doing? You don't look well.'

He laughed. 'Do you know, I tried to get taken on as a bill-sticker last week? I hadn't the required technique. It seems it's an expert's job, otherwise you wind yourself into a cocoon and fall off the ladder. I am sure you would have been given the job at once—but I haven't your false air of competence. It's extraordinary the number of people there are in the world for whom the world has no use.

39

What is even more extraordinary is the first moment in which you suspect that you, I mean myself, are one of them. There ought to be delousing stations for society to rid itself of us.'

'I can lend you some money,' Harvey said simply.

'You may be as well off as well—though in that case why are you eating in this hole?—you'll very soon be poor if you go about holding your purse open to your War comrades. Thanks all the same,' Renn said in a light voice. 'As a matter of fact, I think I'm going to touch a job at last. A friend has just recommended me to a friend. You see there is some use in having friends, after all. You should take more interest in yours. I read part of your last book—it was lying on view in the Bomb Shop. There they still let me read for a quarter of an hour in peace before edging me out. It's considerably better than the other two, if you want to know.'

Hervey shook her head. She had no pride in her three books, since the money they made her was nothing beside the pile of money her grandmother's ships had fetched in. She knew now that they were not even true books. There is only one book worth writing—not to cheat, but to record every item in the tale of mistakes, joys, cruelties, and simple meannesses that make up our dealings one with others, then to write down the total, hand it in, and clear off without making a fuss. She knew that she had not the head for this. Even the book she was now writing was false. She kept at it from obstinacy and a sort of pride. And to have something to show her mother.

'I know what you meant when you said I must put everything into my novels—this room, that fat greedy woman, you, Thomas Harben who owns my grandmother's firm, myself—do you know I am a fool and a coward?' she said suddenly—'unfortunately I can't do it. Or not yet.'

'That was what we quarrelled about,' Renn said.

'Yes. Are you still a Socialist?'

' If you want to call me one.'

' Do you believe that things will be better now that we
have a Labour Government?'

' No,' Renn smiled.

' Then what will have been the good of telling poor
women that they must have faith in us—unless something
is done for them *now*?' Hervey said with vehemence. 'The
present only is what matters. No, no, you are wrong,
David. I've been in the movement '—she liked saying that,
it made her know that she had friends—' a long time, and
I know the power in it. You are too mistrustful. The
leaders are honest men.'

The delicacy and bitterness of Renn's smile had not
changed. 'What difference would that make?' he asked
lightly, almost merrily. 'I know an honest man in the
Government—my friend Louis Earlham: he went into
Parliament this year, as a Labour member for one of the
London seats. I have supplied him with information touching
your friend Thomas Harben——'

' I don't know Harben, I've never seen him,' Hervey
interrupted.

' A pity. If you'll come and have supper with me in my
room this evening I'll show him to you.'

She could not see Nicholas, and she was pleased that she
would not have to sit at home with her unmanageable mind.
She put Richard to bed, wrote a letter to D. Nash to encourage her—the novel was crazy but it was better than
any novel of her own: it knew something about the life
of human beings that most of us have forgotten (it was like
a folk tale)—and she had taken on herself to find a publisher
for it. Then she caught a train to town and went out to
Renn's lodging.

She had brought cheese and a pound of apples, and with
bread and friendship it was a meal. They had enough of
everything in common already, their dead friend Philip,
months of wasted work, an illusion or two, even an ideal
not yet too clearly the worse for wear. Philip sat with

them for a moment or two, but when he saw that they went together very well he slipped away.

After supper Renn took a long roll of thick yellow paper from a cupboard and spread it over the floor. 'Now for the Private View,' he said. Unrolled, it covered half the space between the fireplace and the door. 'Design for a portrait of Thomas James Harben.'

The figure of a naked man, erect, arms raised from his sides, fingers splayed out, stretched from top to bottom of the paper. You saw the skeleton, the muscles, and the strong net of nerves. Above, below, and on each side of him were roads, mountains, massive buildings, the sea, rivers, a sky, aeroplanes in formation—a landscape as fantastic as a nightmare. Hervey knelt to look at it. The man was buried to his knees in the earth. His feet were the galleries of a coal mine, with shafts rising through the veins to his knees. At the knee vast slag heaps and buildings covered the ground as far as the first river: they were written over in Renn's small exquisite writing with the names of fourteen companies—Ling Steel & Iron Works, Teeside Iron & Coal Company, Don Bridge Builders. . . . The great muscles of the thighs and belly became without changing their anatomy a web of railways. The oil from a hidden source sprang between the thighs. Nerves ran to the ends of the fingers of the left hand and issued in ways from which five fine ships took the water: to the right—the fingers of the right hand were the long snouts of guns, strong and ugly, like the reddened right hand of Jupiter. From the eye-pits mechanics signalled to the aeroplanes. Other men ran about the passages of the brain seizing the slips of paper as these poured from the calculating machines. Looking closer into the cortex you saw the strong weft of cables, and the delicate masts of wireless stations. There was a close-stool behind the man, in which he had just been making a new world. The shadow cast by him formed a lifelike Crucifixion, and many women were standing by, some weeping and others laughing and waving toy flags.

' Thomas Harben to the life,' Renn said in a satisfied voice.

' I don't like it,' Hervey said.

' I didn't draw it to please you,' he retorted.

' If you gave it to me I should burn it—I find it blasphemous.'

Renn took his pen out and wrote along the edge of the paper, ' Thine be the Kingdom, the Power and the Glory.' He thanked her for giving him a name for his work. Then he rolled it up and put it away. You could see that he was a little disappointed in the reception of his Private View. After Hervey had gone he cleared the table and spread the drawing over it again. He looked at it for some minutes. ' After all, the details are absolutely correct,' he said firmly. He went to bed.

In the morning he dressed himself with particular care and set off to walk to Piccadilly. He had an appointment at eleven o'clock with the man to whom he had been recommended. At first he walked through streets precisely like the one in which he lived; the houses had the same air of cut-down prisons, the walls covered with sores, front doors standing open into the ill-smelling passage. The women were at work in them, using rags, worn-down brushes, and tongues, with the same haphazard impulse. The only men in sight were from the shabby regiments of the workless, who burrowed in their pockets for the half-a-fag they remembered leaving there: if their memory had deceived them they did not give up hope at once—it might be on the end of the mantelpiece, when you could get in to look for it.

For a few streets he had the company of his landlady's eight-year-old grandson. Clive had been kept from school because his sister had just come down with scarlet fever. He looked to Renn as though a degree or two of fever would burn him out in a flash, like a too thin match. The basement he shared with his grandmother and the cockroaches suited them much better than it did him—the old woman had a tough heart and the cockroaches were natives of the place.

Clive had been born gay and the smile with which he greeted Renn in the mornings was made up equally of love and good fellowship. He had an ambition to fly—nothing less—and he cut pictures of aeroplanes from the newspapers Renn bought and gave him. His grandmother had assured Renn that he could save himself any trouble since the boy was certainly marked to die young! But one must love something, and Renn was willing to risk losing a tolerable sum of affection on a poor life.

'Are you going to buy a paper to-day?' Clive asked as he turned to go home again.

'Don't depend on it,' Renn said. 'If I find what I'm looking for this morning I'll buy you something safer than a newspaper—a book of aeroplane pictures. But if I don't find it I shan't be able to bring home even a paper.' He talked to Clive as if the boy were his age—really it would be useless to do anything else. To wait for him to grow up?

Clive turned a cart-wheel on the edge of the pavement for good faith. When Renn looked back he was running along the street, balancing from side to side on his bones of legs.

Through a lane between houses Renn came into a narrow main street. Shops stuffed with food and clothes, all of inferior grades, were divided by two lines of traffic. The best-looking places were branch shops of the great dairies. Renn had an impulse to go in and ask them to send any spare bottles of milk to Clive's basement. It might fortify him for his unceasing war on the cockroaches, in which he was always defeated and always hopeful.

He walked along a number of streets, and came into a different part of the world. For all practical purposes this street was on another planet. Neither the shops nor the people entering them were the same nationality as those he had lately left. Here everything witnessed to the delicacy, taste and acute senses of a civilised race. A shop-window solved, in the manner of a still life, the arrangement of a scarf, a hat, and a single bottle of scent. 'Very nice, but is it art?' Renn murmured as he passed it. In this part of the world even the seasons were different: there were summer roses and strawberries in a window, and the man stepping in to buy had a face as brown as Clive's was livid white.

Renn walked on, passing discreetly fine houses. He was not the only immigrant. Another, wheeling a gramophone on a home-made barrow, was just being moved on by the police when Renn caught sight of him.

He had reached the end of his journey. A building like a vast hotel stood in front of him. The entrance hall was so wide and with an almost eloquent richness, as if the panelling and the electric fittings might begin at any moment telling you what they had cost, that he thought it well to take from his pocket and hold in full view the letter from the man he had come to see. He read the name to the lift boy. 'Mr. William Gary.'

'Mr. Gary,' said the boy.

He took Renn up to the ninth floor, led him along an endless corridor, and left him outside the door of a flat. The door was of figured walnut and Renn looked at it for a moment before touching the bell. As soon as he saw William Gary he knew him.

Gary came across the room with his hand out, saying— he, too: 'Hollebeke, August '17. You had a match.'

'Yes,' Renn said.

'What happened to the third?'

'Oh he died after the War,' Renn said, nodding.

'Pity.'

'Not very.'

'Well—you and I are still half alive,' Gary answered. Renn looked at him again. The other seemed perfectly healthy—nothing wrong there, no artificial limb, not a scar, scarcely even a mark. There were heavy pouches under his eyes, but they went with his features, which were those of an eighteenth-century statesman, a Walpole, perhaps. Renn did not speak.

'You know what I want?' the other said.

Now Renn must put his best foot forward. He stiffened involuntarily—and summoned the phrases he had rehearsed on the way. None of them reported present and correct. You cannot boast of your accomplishments to a man with whom you shared an infested dugout and the seasonal diarrhoea of the district.

'I need a secretary to read foreign newspapers and reports for me. I never was a linguist—now I can't remember even a little Spanish I used to know. Why should I? Let the remnant learn English is my feeling.'

'I read and speak French, German, Swedish, Italian, and a very little Spanish,' Renn said grudgingly.

'Splendid! What more could I want? If any other dago writes to us you can have it translated. I have two other secretaries and one of them reads Russian. Do you know anything about me? Through no fault of my own, I inherited them, I own mines and ironworks, chiefly in Scotland. I took no interest in them until a year ago. Now I've started, I intend to do the thing properly. I was running to seed. . . .'

He looked at Renn quickly and amiably, but with an unmoving face, as if he meant him to understand that this almost intimate talk did not signify anything; least of all it signified a wish to be reminded further of Hollebeke and the day and night of August tenth, 1917. His hand, with its long noticeably strong fingers, tapped the edge of the table. Renn rose to go. 'When do you want me to begin?' he asked quietly.

'At once—is that possible? I shall pay you four hundred and fifty a year. I may want you to travel for me and then I shall pay your expenses. Does that strike you as fair?'

'Very fair,' Renn said.

It took him some time to find his way back to the lift.

He wandered down several wrong corridors, between polished doors and electric lights let into the mouldings in the shape of arrows, and turned a great many corners before turning the right one. I should indent for a map, he said to himself. An under-porter hurried to hold open the door. Renn smiled warmly at him.

Now for Clive's book, he thought.

CHAPTER VI

THE MAN WITHOUT A FUTURE

As soon as Renn had gone, Gary began to regret having engaged him. Now he was trying to live as though he had been born, fully grown, on the day in 1920 when he was told that he had recovered completely from his wounds. He determined then to cut himself off from the War, leaving his dead to their fate, with their questions unanswered. Sometimes he seemed to himself to be succeeding—and at other times, usually when he was asleep, he found himself at the frontier of that country and with pain and delight he took back his *carte d'idéntité* and passed in. He went here and there, now floating easily in the green waters of a river, now sunk in the familiar frowst of a dugout, now ' in rest ' watching, as if it were the only one of its kind, a tree coming slowly to life. Awake, he could avoid these excursions, with a little ease. It was no pleasure to him, when the door opened, to see Renn step towards him from the night obscurity of a trench. He resented the impulse he had obeyed in engaging him. It was not kindness—not more than if Renn had been hit that night and he had been forced to see to him. In the moment Renn stepped into the room he had noticed the worn edges of his jacket and the glaze of hunger, unmistakable if you have seen it once, on the skin of his face. Well, he thought at last, I can keep the fellow at his distance—he has been disciplined.

He thrust Renn out of his mind. There were a great many papers and letters on his desk, sent from the Glasgow office. For some hours he read and re-read. With patience and tireless energy he was learning his business as owner of

48

the mines and works from which he had been content only to draw money in another life. Already he felt less like a young and inexperienced spider dropped suddenly on to a web the size of England. The threads of his web crossed seas.

At five o'clock he went down to the gymnasium and boxed with the instructor until he had exhausted himself. After the bath he stood for a moment at the glass and looked quickly at his body. He was very strong. It is strange I don't become so used to it that I forget it, he thought. Yes, you can place guards on a thought—and that leaves you nothing to think about, except the guards. He would be talking to someone, and all at once think of it. His hands jerked up, fingers fluttering, as if he had been shot.

He began to dry himself with rough haste. As he dressed he was thinking of something the instructor had said to him. Suddenly he thought: Does the man know? He took hold of the rail.

When he reached his rooms he remembered that he had to dine with Thomas Harben. He telephoned to the garage for his car. He drove himself, giving up his mind to it with a feeling of pleasure. He thought a little of the man he was going to see. He respected Harben as a divisional commander who knew his job—very necessary when your mistakes cannot be buried. Patience, he said to himself— in a few years I shall be able to defeat him at his own *Wehrsport*.

He found that there were two other guests. He had known one of them for years—the day must have been favourable for ghosts. George Ling looked old, and he had shrunk a little since the evening in 1916. Then he was discussing military strategy in Gary's own club, and Gary had crept out, feeling that a happy soldier on leave was out of place in these groves dedicated to war.

The third guest was a middle-aged Jew, Mr. Marcel Cohen. He looked at Gary with smiling brown eyes. Before coming he had looked up Gary's war record—his

way was always to know something about the private tastes
and deeds of his business associates: it gave him the footing
he needed. ' My son was in your regiment,' he said. His
eyes searched Gary's face with an avid pride.

Gary looked at him. ' Indeed.'

' He was wounded in 1916.'

Gary made no answer to this and Cohen had to step past
the dead boy to keep his place in the conversation. There
were only the four of them at table, brought together there
by Thomas Harben's sardonic humour. The dinner was
in celebration of George Ling's retirement from active life—
he thought of it as having been active. Now he had sold
to Gary and Thomas Harben the remainder of his shares in
the Ling Steel & Iron Works—it was a family firm, which
his grandfather had taken over in simpler safer times from
Mary Hervey. He kept a seat on the board of the new
firm, and since his control had been nominal all his life,
you would not think he felt a change. But in fact he was
feeling most miserable. He sat between Harben and Gary,
his rosy cheeks paling, and looked from one to the other
with a pitiful weak smile. He had never understood the
details of the transaction. All he knew was that he had
sold his shares for a great sum and reinvested part of it in
preference shares of the new Harben Ling Company. Now
he felt that he had taken a fatal step in selling at all. He
had done it because he was so frightened. It was the terrible
complexity of modern business frightened him—he believed
that it meant the end of the world. What with the revolution
in Russia and the collapse of morals everywhere he did not
think the end could be far off. And sometimes when he
looked at Thomas Harben he thought that Harben was
Anti-Christ.

William Gary, too, was looking at Harben. He noted
the fingers, long, rapacious, with blunted tips, the big fleshy
nose, the body, powerful, heavy, but only sparely covered
in flesh. This was the first time Gary had been in his
house, and he was impressed by the fact that Harben was

more formidable when he was taking the trouble to seem a genial host than when he did business. To keep himself in countenance Gary thought, But after all he needed my coal mines in Lanark. The negotiations with Harben had taught him more than a year's reading of reports and figures. He had watched a respectable bourgeois firm, the Ling Works, give birth to the swollen Harben Ling Company. That the birth might be propitious, Harben had given the care of it to the financial house of Thomas Harben & Company, which handled the issue, placing it through Lloyds Bank, of which Thomas Harben was a director. This Thomas Harben multiplied on the face of the earth. Harben knew Harben, and Harben conceived and bare Harben. There was Harben who owned shares in William Gary's Lanarkshire coal mines, Harben who had his own collieries in Yorkshire; Harben who controlled the Clyde Iron Works, the Harben Ling Company, the Don Iron Company, with five other steel works, and plate mills, blast furnaces, engineering works, and bridge-building works, and who burned Harben's coal; Harben who controlled five passenger and cargo lines, and two or three yards and marine works as well as the great Garton's Shipbuilding & Marine Engineering Works, and placed orders with Harben for his fine steel; Harben who owned the Stokes Chemical Works; Harben the director of a railway; Harben the chairman of the financial house of Harben; Harben the chairman of an Insurance Company, which invested in Harben; Harben the director of a bank, which at need obliged Harben with credits on the excellent security of Harben's interests. It was fantastic, almost frightening—like a nightmare in which at every turn you meet the man from whom you are struggling to escape.

'This,' Harben was saying, 'is a still champagne which is only——'

He was interrupted by the noise of a scuffle outside the door of the room. It was so unlikely a noise to hear in this house that it startled. A man called out twice in an urgent voice. George Ling half rose, then sank back in his chair.

Harben looked at the servant pouring the wine and he went out of the room. In a moment he came back. ' It was the person who got in on Monday, sir. Mr. Dennis had the front door open for a minute and he took his chance to slip in. Mr. Dennis turned him out.'

' Next time let it be the police,' Harben said. He looked down his nose at the table and said: ' An old madman— I've had nine or ten letters from him. He lost all his money in the Northern Counties Shipping Company, four years ago. Now he's been reading about the trouble in the World Line in some newspaper, perhaps one of yours, my dear Cohen, and it's started him off. In some lunatic way he confuses the two firms, and holds me responsible for his losses. He wants me to give him his money back. Well, he'll have to be locked up—though he's not the only fool in the world.' He lifted his glass, looking to George Ling. ' To your happiness, my dear fellow. And to Harben Ling & Company.'

' To Harben Ling & Company,' George Ling repeated, in a trembling voice. At the age of fifty-nine he was already a shaken old man, while at sixty Harben was still in his middle age.

' At least that part of your money is safe,' Harben said smiling. It amused him to play on Ling's fear of losing his money—not from cruelty, but because he thought the man was a canting humbug. ' I shouldn't like to say as much for your shipping shares. Prospects are worse this year than ever.'

George Ling looked at him without being able to speak. I am all alone in the world, he said to himself. There was so much noise in his head that he never heard the question Marcel Cohen asked, only out of pity for him, or Harben's reply: ' Garton's? Sound as a bell, my dear Cohen. Who knows it better than you do ? '

Cohen's only reply was an amiable gesture. Certainly he

knew everything about Garton's. He knew the names of
the five passenger and cargo lines, the value of the blast
furnaces, the three yards, and the engineering works Garton's
had added to itself since Harben bought it—at such a price
—from Mary Hervey. He knew that an issue of bonus
shares in 1920 had doubled the ordinary share capital.
Without waiting to see what would happen, he had sold
his. And in the next year, when Harben & Company
issued four million pounds debentures for Garton's, he felt
it prudent to become a debenture holder at seven per cent,
and hold fewer shares drawing, this year, ten per cent.
They had paid him thirty on the dazzling peaks of the
War. He knew all this and a great deal that was quite as
important about Thomas Harben. He looked with curiosity
at Gary, about whom he did not yet know enough. In
a day or two he would find out more. His mind, a rat
with strong cruelly sharp teeth, would very quickly be at
the heart of anything there was to know. He watched the
servant lift up a decanter so that the light glowed in it.
He felt well and lively, his body warmed with food and
good wine. The yellowed skin of his face gleamed as if
polished and his eyes sparkled.

Suddenly he heard George Ling speaking to him in a
quiet anxious voice, as if he had seized a moment when the
other two were absorbed, to tell him something secret.

'What is it, what is it, I didn't hear you,' Cohen
murmured.

'I was asking you if you knew my son-in-law, Nicholas
Roxby,' Ling said again. He leaned towards Cohen, his
head drooping, with a look of reproach on his face. Cohen
should have listened to him before. It was too late now.

'Are you talking about Nicholas?' William Gary asked.
He had stopped in the middle of what he was saying, to
look politely at George Ling. 'I had dinner with him last
night,' he added in a voice that, for the sake of his host, he
tried to make amiable. He fully shared Nicholas's distaste
for his father-in-law. Moreover he disliked Nicholas's wife.

George Ling made a serious effort. His eyes strained and he became crimson in the face, but he refused to be kept quiet about what was, after all, a matter of morals. 'Since you are his friend—his greatest friend—I hope you will try to do what you can for him. The unnatural life he lives——"

'I thought he seemed busy and very happy,' Gary interrupted him calmly.

'He wrote to my daughter that he had lost money,' Ling said, as if that at least were inexcusable.

'But surely she knew?' Gary asked, with a cold smile.

'My daughter——' Ling began, and stopped. The other had turned quite away from him to continue his conversation with Thomas Harben. Ling's glance shifted from him helplessly to the little cluster of glasses near his hand, and then to the fingers of his hand—he examined them with deep care, trying to overcome his anguish. The words, 'my daughter,' had started Marcel Cohen off on an account of the dinner party given by his own only daughter Fanny, at her house in Bruton Street. In an eager voice he told Ling everything, every detail, the names of the most distinguished guests, the cost of the wines, and he described the decorations of the table and Fanny's looks and dress. He forgot to say—perhaps he was not even thinking of it—that since her marriage (she had married a Gentile) Fanny had never invited her father and mother to one dinner party.

Ling listened with a dazed air, trying, since he was naturally polite, to understand why the other man was so anxious to impress him with all these details. He could not understand it. He felt exhausted. It's awful, he thought, awful, thinking all the time of his lonely days and how he was certain to end them in poverty, without a soul caring whether he lived or died.

Cohen stopped speaking. He looked at his watch and said quickly to Harben: 'Will you forgive me? I have an appointment at the House of Commons.'

He rose to go. But now it seemed to Ling that his one friend was leaving him, and he too stood up. At the door he took Cohen's arm, stooping over it as if he could scarcely stand. He shuffled his feet, convinced that he had no longer the strength to lift them. At the door Cohen waved his free arm in farewell, but Ling, the old weak man, did not even turn his head. Gary was left alone with Thomas Harben.

The room they sat in was small, panelled in waxed light woods. It was actually a strip of the large room next to it and had been planned especially for these small dinner parties, of men only, which Harben gave not more than nine times a year. It kept an air of quiet reserve, as if it had a mind of its own, and he liked to spend the whole evening here with his guests, sitting at the small oval table, the liqueurs at his hand, and the thin fluted coffee cups, and the centrepiece of Chelsea figures which had once belonged to his mother. It was out of place in the room and he liked it as well for that reason as for the other.

He said nothing for a moment. Just as he was about to speak he saw Gary's hands jerk against the edge of the table. Harben glanced quickly upwards, but the other's face was expressionless. It was a heavy face, although the features were delicate, pouched under the eyes, over which the lids dropped quickly when he was talking.

A curious intimacy—without warmth—had sprung between them during the past weeks. Harben's mind was never within miles of the thought, He could have been my son. But he was conscious of a vague interest, such as he had not felt for any man, not for any person, since he was a boy at school. This had the strangest effect on him. He felt an impulse to talk to the younger man—not on any special subject, just to talk, to interest him. Even he himself did not recognise that the weight on his tongue was due to shyness.

' Who is Cohen, then ? ' Gary said.

' He owns the *Daily Post* and the *Evening Post*,' Harben said quickly.

' Is that all ? '

' Isn't it enough ?   One can't do business without a press,' Harben smiled.   ' He's also a director of Garton's, and he has large interests in a number of steel firms.'

' But the *Daily Post* is almost a Socialist paper.'

Harben looked up at the ceiling.   ' Don't you think that one needs to keep in touch with those papers more even than with the others ?   Cohen knows where to draw a line. Now for instance '—he began to speak with an unusual animation, looking into Gary's face as if he must convince him—' this business of the World Shipping Company.   Do you know the details ?   They're highly interesting.   In 1919—you were still in the army, I dare say—the World Shipping Company decided to buy twenty-five steamers from two other lines, the Thomas Line and the Grosmount Line.   I happen to be on the board of the World Company. They asked my advice.   At that time freights and profits were very high, and I advised them to buy the ships at the best price they could—and they paid £23 10s. a ton.   A stiff price, but it was the market price at the time——'

' The two other lines, the Thomas and the Grosmount, belong to Garton's, to you ? ' Gary interrupted.   He shut his eyes quickly and opened them, once, twice.   It was a habit.

' They came under my control there in 1918,' Harben said coolly.   ' With two other lines.   Very fine ships.   If freights hadn't crashed after the War they would have earned their price.   The World Company issued, to buy them, nearly £2,000,000 ordinary shares and £1,500,000 debentures.'   Harben shrugged his shoulders lightly.   ' You know what happened to freights.   They fell like rockets. The World is not the only shipping firm to go down.   They did their best to meet it—last August ten steamers were sold by auction.   They fetched about a seventh of the purchase price.   January this year Garton's bought back another eight—very cheap.   A fair deal in the circumstances.   When the World Company collapsed—eight weeks ago—a proper howl went up, just as in 1920 over the Northern Counties crash. In that affair, too, a few of the shareholders wanted a public inquiry, but it was quickly suppressed. This time something different is happening— a young Labour member called Earlham has taken it up and is pressing it. And here's the point—this fellow earns his living by writing for the *Evening Post*!' He struck his hands lightly together and looked at Gary with a smile, half grim, half expectant. ' Neat—eh ? '

' Cohen is going to dismiss him ? '

' When he has hanged himself thoroughly,' Harben said.

' I wonder '—Gary hesitated, then he plunged quickly— ' I've often thought—we ought to get to know these Labour people. It's like keeping a Radical press,' he smiled.

' Begin with this Earlham ! '

' Well,' Gary said softly. He stared at the wall for a minute. ' Let me try,' he said.

' Try.'

' You want to prevent the inquiry ? '

' That's quite simple,' Harben said. ' Of course,' he added, ' there mustn't be an inquiry. Everything is above board and clear—there's been nothing irregular in any of the transactions. Here it's only a principle. . . . You can see it's inadvisable to have the names of firms—Garton's, for instance—being bandied about in the papers.' He looked smilingly at Gary. ' But do this your own way.'

' If I make a hash of it, you can still suppress him.'

' Yes.'

There was a silence. Suddenly Harben said: ' How old are you ? ' Concealing his surprise, Gary answered: ' Thirty-two.' Harben nodded, as if it confirmed something he was thinking. He rose at once, as soon as Gary said that he must go, and himself went with the young man across the hall to the door. Gary could not help a slight feeling of nervousness. It was almost as though the big wicked-looking vulture at the Zoo had shown a wish to become friendly.

It had been raining and the pavements were wet. A soft misty glow came from the street lamps. The street was silent. The fresh smell of earth rose from a garden at the side of the house. Farther along the street a man stood close to the railings; as Gary came up he started out, holding both hands forward in front of him. He was tall, old, and his hands were trembling. He stepped straight in front of Gary and in a low voice, gently and without haste, he said:

'For the sake of our Lord and His blessed saints—I am penniless—give me back part of the money you took from me.'

Gary understood that this was the madman who had been annoying Harben. There was such a look of patience on the man's face as you see on the faces of workmen. That he was no workman was plain from his hands. Long, slender, and bony, they shook violently from side to side as he held them towards Gary.

'Your loss . . . I have nothing to do with your money,' Gary said quietly. He drew his note case from its pocket and began to unfold a note. The other man took a step backward.

'Then you are not Thomas Harben, the shipowner?'

'No,' Gary answered. 'I am not.'

'I thank you from my heart for your courtesy and kindness,' said the other quickly, in his old man's weak reserved voice, with gentle self-possession, and without a trace of lunacy. 'Even if you had been, I could not have taken this money. I have lost a great deal—all my savings—an immense sum. I only ask for justice.' He seemed satisfied by having said this. Turning, he went slowly away, holding his shabby overcoat together with his hand, crossed the wide street, and after a time disappeared into the darkness.

CHAPTER VII

THE least tolerable side of war is not its horror but its
pleasures. There is a satisfaction in prolonged dangerous
effort which is paid for—if not immediately, with one's life
—with years of spiritual and bodily exhaustion. In 1924
all the War countries were filled with still-young men whose
energies just carried them to the end of a normal day. Any
extra effort was too much. For most, they had no idea
what had happened to them. Brimming with enthusiasm,
they took up ideas, they began this plan and that—and
suddenly their enthusiasm vanished. Their cup was dry
and empty. But why? They did not know why.

Nicholas Roxby did not know. He wrote the beginnings
of four books before he felt that he would never finish one.
He made new friends. He could not spend a second evening
with any of them. Very soon he wrote nothing, not even
letters. He read—but added to nothing except his pre-
judices. His life was becoming fatally like the life of any
stiff careful Roxby in his line. He was afraid to know
how empty he was

Now to see Hervey and to talk to her surprised him with
the offer and threat of fresh life. If she had not written
to him, and telephoned, and made the excuses for their
meetings, he would have done nothing. From dryness, he
would have let her go. To each his fear. He found that
to be with her rested him. He spent fewer nights half asleep
and half awake adding column after dusty column of figures
—instead he fell asleep and dreamed that he was a child
living in his grandmother's house. Sometimes he believed

59

that he was a little in love with her, and then he thought,
If I had only known her ten years earlier, before I was as
dull and tired as I am; if I had fallen in love with her
instead of Jenny. This was as foolish as wishing to be
young over again. And how foolish everyone is.

When he thought of it, Nicholas supposed Hervey would
be certain to make demands on him, on his body and spirit,
which he would not be able to meet. Beside he had not
forgotten Jenny's telling him after the War that he was a
failure as a lover. He did not wish to hear that again. He
was simpler than Hervey, with none of her tortuous ways
of thinking, and he knew that she was in love with him.
Then why didn't he run away from her, why when his
telephone bell rang did he think first that it might be Hervey?
What a thing to ask! It is because after all life is an en-
chantment. If anyone wishes to die he dies. Nicholas, for
all he had blocked up as many windows as he could to avoid
paying the tax on glass, loved the heat of the sun. He
answered Hervey's letters; he did not telephone to her, but
he waited, with a pleasure that was half the memory of
pleasures, for the moment when leaning his ear to the
telephone on his desk he heard her speaking his name.

He made a great trouble of the dinner to which he invited
her and Gary—so much that his landlady, who liked him,
quite losing her patience told him that she had been a cook
when he was in his cradle. 'That's impossible, you were in
your own,' he said smiling, and retreated.

On the evening Gary came early. He walked in and
took up a book and began reading it as if he were in his
own room. Nicholas watched him with a half smile. He
knew that Gary was exasperated by the thought of spending
an evening making polite talk with a young woman. 'A
novelist,' he had grumbled when Nicholas asked him, 'you
know I never read a novel. What on earth can I talk to
her about?'

'That's settled then, you'll be here at eight o'clock,'
Nicholas said, smiling, and without a change of voice they

began to talk over the battalion dinner, for which he
was responsible.   They were so much at ease in each
other's minds that sometimes a stranger had an impression
that the one who talked was only saving the other one the
trouble.

Before his friend came Nicholas had been moved to take
out his Spanish maps, not touched since he put them away
in 1913.   He left them lying on the floor: when Gary
looked at them he pointed to the names of certain villages
in northern Spain.   Both young men smiled.   'We didn't
know what was good for us,' Gary said, but the cynicism
was meant to be consoling.   If you had told them that this
moment was the last in which each would feel as certain of
the other as of his own breathing, neither would have understood you, so used was he to this life in which the thought
of doing without his friend had not entered.

Mrs. Dick opened the door of the room, and Hervey
Russell came in with her air of minding no one.   She
glanced from one young man to the other; Gary heavy and
quick-moving, and Nicholas, fine-drawn, slighter and less
formidable than his friend, giving her back a kind quick
smile.   It was either their evening uniform, or the way
they were standing side by side, made her feel that she was
a foreign visitor.   They are both very attractive, she thought,
sighing.   A familiar confusion had seized her mind at the
sight of Nicholas, so that her head was an empty shell, all
her senses gone away to listen and stare.   She sat down on
the couch Nicholas drew forward for her and waited helplessly
for him to speak.

When she came in Gary had remembered instantly a
luncheon party in Nicholas's rooms in Oxford the year
before the War.   Nicholas had invited him with two other
young men (they were both killed) to help him to entertain
his grandmother, Mrs. Hervey: half closing his eyes Gary
saw the sunlight dazzling the quad outside, the shadowy
room, and the old woman's fierce sunken face, half smiling,
the older for being set among wavering immature lines.

The sudden moment vanished with its dead. He was looking at a young woman clumsier and less confident than Mary Hervey, but so like that she drew on herself all the distrust and resentment he had felt for her grandmother.

During dinner he saw that she was in love with Nicholas, and watching Nicholas he fancied that he was not quite so far gone. He's going quickly though, he thought, listening to his friend's quiet voice. An unreasonable anger seized him, but whether against the War, that had sapped his friend's vitality, or against Hervey for being too close to the domineering old woman, he could not have said. He knew too sharply that Nicholas was not a match for this tongue-tied young woman, unwearied by any war, obstinate and persistent. He wished ardently that he could get rid of her before the mischief was done.

Nicholas was talking about flying. ' I tried to get him into flying before the War,' Gary said suddenly. ' He'd have come, but for his grandmother. By now we should have been Air Marshals—or the heads of an aeroplane firm.'

' Or dead,' Nicholas smiled.

'Was that before you left Garton's?' Hervey asked quickly. Talk, she said to herself, you must talk—they'll think you are a fool. And perhaps you are, she finished. Her head still felt light and empty, filled like a shell with murmurs close to her ear.

' Yes,' Nicholas said. ' I was very keen to fly.' He looked at Gary.

' Then why——?' began Hervey.

' I thought I couldn't disappoint my grandmother. She wanted me in the firm,' Nicholas said quietly. ' I tried to persuade her to build aeroplanes and put me in charge, and she thought I was mad.'

' And then you disappointed her in the end,' Gary said. There was so much bitterness in his voice that the other two looked at him.

' It was an end of everything,' said Nicholas, with a

smile. 'Of her, of me, and I suspect of Garton's as she made it.' He spoke to Hervey. 'Do you know, I told you a lot of nonsense the other evening? The real reason I left Garton's was because I wanted to be free—chiefly of my grandmother. She put me in the place of her son, that is, she decided my school, my allowance, my work, my whole future for me. It was the greatest kindness and generosity and I was not in the least afraid of her as almost everyone else was, and yet it was too much. I had to clear out—just as in fact her son did.'

'She was an autocrat,' Hervey said. She smiled. She could recall with no trace of the old shame that her grandmother had laughed at her when she asked to be given work. When Mary Hervey died she took with her, as well as the infinite succession of her own memories, the sting of that one. The dead cannot laugh at the living.

'A tyrannical old woman, she ruined your life for you,' Gary said, looking with a calm anger at Nicholas. 'You could have been selling aeroplanes at this moment—instead of chairs and tables.'

'Don't despise my chairs,' Nicholas said smiling. 'At least they can't be used to drop poison gas.' What's the matter with you? he thought, looking at Gary with love and patience. He thought he knew how much of his own defeat Gary was resenting in his. Don't worry, it doesn't matter nearly so much as you think, he said, consoling himself in this silent argument.

'I am sure you would not have given up a shipbuilding firm and a fortune,' Gary said, smiling politely at Hervey. Surely, you fool, you can see that she is every whit as bad as Mary Hervey, his mind shouted.

Hervey gave him a startled glance, opening her eyes wide. For the first time she was aware of his hostility and dislike. She felt ashamed but not in the least surprised. She put it down to her silence and stupidity. Naturally he resents wasting an evening on me, she thought. But he had asked her a question. 'No, I should not have given them up,' she answered. 'I always wanted to build ships.'

'You're extraordinarily like Mary Hervey,' he said.

'I can't see any likeness at all,' Nicholas exclaimed.

'I have no desire to be like her,' Hervey said simply. Seeking desperately for something to talk about that would please both men, she asked Nicholas a question about the War. He began to describe the look of a trench at night and then without meaning to he told her something that had taken place one night. Gary interrupted him to add forgotten details and now both were launched. Their faces altered, becoming younger and merrier, even their voices lost the polite smoothness of a social occasion. Wine glasses were pushed out of the way or used to make a position, and suddenly Gary saw the expression on Hervey's face. She was listening closely, with a faint smile, outside it all, and content. With something like despair he recognised the adroitness with which she had turned the conversation to a subject that left her free of responsibility. After all she is clever, he thought, scarcely able to pull himself out of the trap. Nicholas had fallen silent, his eyes fixed on a point no farther in the past than his young days and already as far out of imagination as the days before the Flood. Before he could check it Gary had thought, Nothing will ever equal that time. He was astonished to hear Hervey's voice; she had said nothing for an age.

'The women of my generation will never catch up with their men who went through the War.'

So you can be humble as well as domineering and adroit, Gary thought. A feeling almost of affection for her surprised him, with the belief that she would be kind to Nicholas if he trusted himself to her. But would Nicholas trust anyone again, after all that had happened to him since the War? He felt sorry for Hervey because coming late there was nothing left for her. Between them, the War and Jenny had had all, or almost all. You don't know that yet, but you will—my poor dear, he thought, you had better give up thinking of him and find someone of your own sort, an ambitious Yorkshireman would do. He leaned forward and said quietly:

'I shouldn't think of the War and all that if I were you. You'll only become confused and unhappy. It's all over.'

'Not for you—or Nicholas,' Hervey said.

That's true, but how did you know? he thought. He smiled at her. In a few minutes a change had come over all of them, they had a new feeling of security, sprung from the effort Hervey had made to sink herself. It was a reward she had not expected. Nicholas was only aware, with relief and joy, that the other two, his friend and Hervey, were beginning to get on. For Hervey everything took on a charmed beauty, the square of darkness in the window, the fiery coals, the room, light falling from above on to their faces and hands—the look of Nicholas's hands clasped round his knee filled her with happiness, which mounted until it was as though she had banners waving in her. But it was time for her to go to her train. She went with reluctance, half knowing that this quiet friendliness was too good to last and perhaps after this it would never again happen to them to have anything together.

Nicholas walked with her to the end of the street to find a cab. He asked her as soon as they were outside the house what she thought of Gary. In her fervent praise of his friend he could detect nothing that was not perfectly right and just.

She said good night to him with the last flicker of her airy triumph. Leaning back in the cab, with closed eyes she called up his image and made it live through the whole evening again. He stood here, he smiled, he looked so, he said that. She did not believe, the gulf between their experience of life was too wide, that he could ever love her, and at the moment it was unimportant. What was important was to fix every moment she had had, so that none could escape her in the future; and that she was doing.

Hervey writes. 'When I was a child we used to travel to London to meet my father's ship. My mother hated ships and the sea, and a young child is no help but a trouble on a long journey—they were longer in those days—but for a time she went each voyage. London is much too large to give any dreams to a child, and for a long time I thought that Fenchurch Street (where the Line had an office) was the fashionable part of London. We went up as far as Hyde Park, but in spite of the dreary length of the journey between them, I joined Tidal Basin, Fenchurch Street and the Park together in my mind and made one image of them. It was better when we left London for Antwerp. After the last sight of flat green fields, with only a few houses and a public house with the name ' Adam & Eve,' there was only the sea, the saloon with its swinging lamps, my bunk and the aged magazines under a cushion in my mother's berth. Long before we reached Antwerp I was as tired of the sea as she was. But then entering the river, between fields dotted here and there with Noah's Ark trees, and at last the docks and the quay. Each morning we drove into the town in an open cab in the sunshine. I remember a street of tall old yellow houses, and the flower women in the Place, gathering the foreign brightness round their petticoats, and a shop we knew as the bazaar, a place more opulent than anything in London. But on one visit we went out to the ramparts and there, drowsing in a field of long coarse grass in which were blue flowers, I had such a sense of the strangeness and wonder of this world that my heart swelled and if I had been alone I should have cried for joy. After that day, two or three years passed before the same emotion filled me—this time one morning in Danesacre where I had run in playing into a short street above the harbour. It was a double row of small faded houses, and it was laid with cobblestones through which here and there grass was growing. Again, just as in the Antwerp field, I felt my whole being transported with bliss, and each time I visited the street in these years the sense of strangeness and beauty returned.   I believe that the two moments, separated by years, were parts of a secret I have not understood—as when, passing along a street, we hear spoken a few words, too few to grasp the meaning of the sentence, only enough to seize its unmistakable importance for us, so that we can never rest this side of understanding.   Meaning or no meaning, time or no time.'

CHAPTER VIII

BEGINNING THE POLITICAL AND SOCIAL ODYSSEY OF LOUIS EARLHAM

THERE were days (two or three in the year) when Earlham left the House with feelings of happiness and exhilaration comparable, but only slightly comparable, with his feelings on the day of his election—these days could be recognised as belonging to the same family, poor relations. Much likelier he walked home in a mood of despair or shame, at best uncertain. He was twenty-eight years old and for half those years he had drawn a wage. Before his election he had supposed he knew every twist and trick that may be forced on a man who is poor and intelligent. He had the good fortune to know many things about life that many men never discover, only because they are fortunate. It took him less than a week of rubbing minds with the other members of his Party in the House to realise his inexperience and dire ignorance, not indeed of its creed and doctrines, but of the means of applying them in the long deathly serious game of parliamentary forfeits. To-day he was bewildered. He walked very slowly through St. James's Park and half his mind was busy with his need of a warmer overcoat while the other half struggled with a conversation that had just taken place. His half-ironical wish to cut a figure in politics made him doubly nervous about it.

His thin face, its features marked and delicate, was drawn with fatigue. The dossier of the World Shipping Company, once he took it from Renn, had led him into a warren of enquiries. Burning with hatred of the persons involved—their callousness and self-interest disgusted him—he had

68

thought he could make use of this one instance to discredit the whole shape of a society in which a few men through their interlocking directorates become usurers to the nation, feeding, or foreclosing and ruining, with the strokes of a pen. At the same time he hoped to credit himself with enthusiasm in the cause of justice. He felt it, in any case.

The farther he went with this business the more anxious he became to do it and himself justice. Other members of his Party began to show an interest. A few words, dropped as if by an afterthought, exasperated him because he was unable to decide whether he was being warned or encouraged. In the end, and after days of heart searching, he plucked up courage to ask the leader of the Party to see him. And the more—huddled in his thin overcoat against the wind in St. James's Park—he glossed the interview, the less he made of it. You could make anything of it.

It began with his walking, at the appointed hour, eager and nervous, into the leader's room and finding him at work. He waited. For the hundredth time he experienced the familiar feeling of awe and doubt. In his tussle of a life he had come across many men who were capable, charming, and ambitious, and he had tests that he applied to them— but he had met no other person who could spread a distance between himself and his friends, and so implacably, as this man. At the very moment in which he rested a hand on your shoulder you saw his back going away. There were some members of the Party to whom he never spoke and seemed unable to recall their faces. Earlham was astounded to meet smiles and kind words. Flattered, he tried to discover a reason for them. There seemed to be no reason.

In a few moments, still writing hard, the older man said: ' Please begin, my dear Earlham. You don't mind if I go on working, do you ? '

' It will be a little difficult to explain,' Earlham said. He was faintly exasperated.

Another moment, and then the leader put down his pen,

and passed slowly his hand over his face and hair. 'Oh I am so tired, so tired,' he said gently.

'Shall I come back at another time?' Earlham asked.

A grave smile altered the other's looks. 'No, no, my dear fellow. Get on with your story. I want to hear it.'

Warmed and already faintly excited, Earlham plunged into the case of the World Shipping Company. It was brother to a deliberate fraud. 'The Thomas and Grosmount lines were actually under Thomas Harben's control in the Garton group when, as a director of the World Company, he advised their purchase. In 1919 the World paid over £23 a ton for the ships, and this year have resold them at £4. But to whom? To Garton's. Garton's even held a mortgage for part of the purchase money. The whole of the ordinary capital has vanished—two and a half millions. Clearly things had been tumbling from bad to worse for a year, yet at no stage were the shareholders called together to discuss ——'

'Why do you want to follow this up?'

A muted note in the deep, flexible voice halted Earlham in mid-stream. Suddenly he found it awkward to give his reasons. They savoured of enthusiasm—genuine, but a little ridiculous in an argument.

'You can see, my dear Earlham, that there is no profound reason why one of our useful young men should take up the cause of a great many middle-class shareholders—not one of whom would support us at any time.' He sent an indulgent glance over Earlham's face. 'Oh I know what you're going to say—it's the rottenness of it all. Of the system. Of all it touches. Yes, an infection. Yes, yes, I agree with you.'

'It is because I am in a difficulty about the—the relevance —that I'm here now,' Earlham murmured.

'No doubt, no doubt, I agree with you, yes, with my whole heart. And yet we're so few here, my dear fellow, few, weak. A company against a great army. We need to conserve our strength. We need to look very closely where we are going—lest we stray from the direct road. And in putting one foot forward we must never lose sight of the fact that the other foot is behind still. Now I want you, my dear Earlham, to promise—yes, as a favour to me—that you will think very carefully and deeply—deeply—before you express yourself on any matter. By all means go into the windings of this rotten business, acquaint yourself well with them, wrestle with them—and then come back to the everyday world and its problems strengthened and refreshed for the fight which is before us. A long fight. Yes, yes, a long long fight. And now, my dear boy—look at this desk—look at me—I'm no longer a young man. You young men with your untarnished energies—I envy you. I envy your strength, and above all I envy you your illusions. Wonderful, wonderful!'

The long slow gesture of hand and arm that pushed Earlham across the room and out of the door remained with him. He rehearsed it, furtively, glancing round to see whether anyone had followed him across the Park. He was alone on an empty path.

Slowly, from his need, and his habit of irony, he began to arrange things in his mind. Once again I have let my feelings carry me away, he said wryly. After all, the scandals of capitalism have less to do with us than—he hesitated—we have to overthrow the system. That's an answer. He felt a quick gratitude. I have been praised, encouraged, he thought warmly: my need now is to get experience. *Then* will be the time to advance plans of attack: one can't advance singly.

Now he felt happier. His self-assurance awoke. After all, I have learned a great deal, I am learning, he cried. A sudden cold shower spattered him from a tree. He glanced at the bare stems with a laugh. The sky was cold and transparent, and the buildings south of the Park hung in it like ships. An impulse of love moved him for this city. It could not be said to have nurtured him, since in his early years it had done its best to starve him out. He felt the passion of an artist to remodel it, that a child should never again suffer as he had suffered.

Now he began to imagine telling Rachel about the interview. He hurried, thinking with a soft excitement of the flame that would start to her cheeks and the leaning curve of her body as she listened. She would follow every word as well with her eyes.

They had rented the lower half of a house, near Victoria Station, in a street which clung to its respectability by a narrow ledge. He was taken aback to find David Renn in their room. An acute embarrassment seized him. He was so used to talk freely with Renn that when he had something to keep back he did not know in the least what to say. But what have I to hide? he thought quickly. Renn was his best friend.

‘ Have you brought me news of a fresh scandal? ’ he said, smiling.

‘ I came to see my god-daughter.’

‘ Well, how do you find her? ’

Rachel, speaking from the kitchen, said: ‘ What do you think, Louis! He helped me to bath her. She’s so good with him as you never saw.’

She came in carrying a tray. The apron she had wrapped round herself was much too large for her. Renn stood up to go. ‘ Oh, stay to supper, David,’ she begged.

He shook his head. The conviction that his friend wanted him out of the way was too strong. Earlham walked with him to the front door. ‘ I’m going on with the Harben scandal,’ he said lightly. ‘ At the moment I don’t see clearly the precise way to handle it for the best. You know that a minority Government is not in the easiest situation in the world. We have to pick our way. A public enquiry might give us more trouble than it was worth. I shall do everything I can. Don’t give up faith in me, Davy.’

‘ If I did that I should have to give up everything,’ Renn said smiling.

On the step he turned, holding the door. ' You're still writing for the *Evening Post* ? '

' Yes, we need the money,' answered Earlham.

' Well—I thought that Cohen had no connection with Garton's after he sold his ordinary shares, but I was mistaken. I find now that he is a large debenture holder. You'd better think of that.'

Earlham closed the door. He went back to Rachel quickly, with relief. At least with her all was simple and kind. With her he had only to pour out his thoughts and, with the grave look of a child, she listened and approved. In the moment it took him to walk from the door to the table he had put his friend's words far out of his way. If death were an act of will most of us would remain alive only by the instinct to postpone an unpleasant decision.

Rachel listened. Her eyes, dark and clear, watched him the whole time as he talked. She had to remind him to eat. If you had said to her any time, ' What is your religion ? ' she would have answered, ' I am a Socialist.' But from the moment, in her eighteenth year, when she met Louis her religion had its altar. Her steadfast Jewish heart offered its perpetual sacrifice there. It was easy, in their poorest days, to pretend that she had eaten before he came in. At night she protected his young and thin body in her arms. Suppose he were to die of the cold! Nowadays she had other anxieties. He was overworking; late nights became imperceptibly mornings in which he sat writing for his newspaper. One week she added up his hours of sleep. They were fewer than fifteen.

' Eat, Louis, eat,' she said gently.

' If I eat another mouthful I shall explode,' he answered, ' the Tory press will announce it, Another anarchist blows himself up! '

She cleared the table and went upstairs. Soon he followed. She was in their bedroom, holding a dress to the light. ' How can I go to a reception ? ' she demanded. ' I have nothing.'

'Oh my little love, you're so pretty,' Earlham said.
'Listen. You're twenty-three. Before you are thirty you
shall have a dress for every day in the week.'

'Then I don't want them,' she said, smiling. 'Socialists
can't be fine.' She took hold of his arm. 'Come and see
your daughter asleep. She's only perfect.'

Obediently Earlham looked at the sleeping child. She
was dark like her mother, and with the same air of patience
and delicacy on her tiny features. His arm round Rachel
moved gently, to turn her towards their bed.

CHAPTER IX

EPISODE AT WATERLOO STATION

NICHOLAS lowered his voice until she could scarcely hear him. She had to lean forward against the table. Fortunately they were alone in the upper room of the *Gallia*, or she would have imagined that the others must all be looking at them. ' The battalion went back into rest and I went on leave. That was in October. I thought that London had changed, or I had. In fact it was London. *We* were still in the wood of 1914 and England had gone forward, so that we were in some sense, perhaps only in some lights, your ghosts. I nearly met you during that leave. You were in London visiting your publisher. Georgina knew Charles Frome well, I rather think too well, and he invited me to dine one evening when you were to be there.'

' What happened then ? '

' I forget,' Nicholas said. He remembered clearly the means his wife had taken to keep him with her that evening, only to gratify her vanity. It was the beginning of a long humiliation that he wanted to forget as thoroughly as possible. ' If I had only known you in time,' he exclaimed.

Hervey did not speak. It means nothing, she thought. Her bones seemed to have become smoke, light and wavering.

They left the *Gallia* a little later than usual and took a cab to the station. The nine-thirty train had left exactly two minutes ago. Looking at the board they saw that the next train was not due for another hour. ' You must go and leave me,' Hervey said, smiling. There were benches set round a showcase, in the centre of the wide deserted space in front of the platforms. Without meaning it they

75

sat down there to wait. Hervey held her purse in her hand.
It came open suddenly and the money spilled over the
ground. Nicholas picked it up. In the end a shilling was
missing, and she hunted for it with so much anxiety that he
asked, ' Is this all the money you have ? '

' Until the end of the month. It's enough,' Hervey
said. ' See, there's my shilling.' Holding it in his hand,
Nicholas said:

' Hervey, you are adorable.'

Now I have stopped breathing, she thought. Her mind
became perfectly still. She was not confused and not afraid.
' You too,' she said.

' I love you.'

' I love you, Nicholas.'

There was a silence while they looked at one another,
then Nicholas said, smiling slightly: ' You knew this was
coming.' Hervey shook her head: ' No, how could I ? '
' But you must have known it would happen.' ' I knew
that I loved you very much,' she answered, speaking slowly
to give herself time to speak the exact truth: ' I hoped you
loved me a little, but I didn't think, it didn't seem likely,
that I was good enough to be of very much importance
to you.'

' You're far too good,' Nicholas said. Again she had to
listen closely to hear what he said. It would ruin her to
lose a word. ' There is so much that you don't know.'

To her tortuous mind, prober of thoughts, this could
mean only that he had not told her the truth about his wife.
He was her lover still—why had he told her he was not?
Ah, but I know, she thought. She no longer expected
truth. Nevertheless the words were a shock to her, but so
far below the surface of her life that she felt only an indescribable confusion. It was after all easy to accept them.
An abyss had opened at her feet but she shut her eyes and
jumped, speaking (she could not help it that her voice rose)
a little wildly.

' Never mind. Doesn't it make you happy, a little happy,

that you're being given everything with both hands and asked for nothing?'

'I shall never ask anything from you, Hervey.' Nicholas looked at her with a curious smile. I had begun to shout, she thought, ashamed. She lowered her voice and said quietly:

'It doesn't matter. It doesn't matter in the least. I love you very much.'

'When I first saw you I thought you were hard and conceited—a second Mary Hervey.'

'I know you did.'

'Since then I have given way to you—do you know that for a fortnight I have gone about saying to myself "Hervey," and carrying your letters?'

In silence she showed him his own five or six, worn from being rubbed together in her pocket with keys and pencils and a provident knot of string. Nicholas reddened as though he had been much younger, and said: 'Oh my dear Hervey.'

They could see the platform at which her train was now standing: a few people, infinitely remote, walked up and down. 'I must go,' Hervey sighed. They went towards it slowly, with reluctance, but when she was seated in the train she felt what was almost relief, as though she had been carrying something that was too heavy and too valuable. A stumble would have spoiled it. She let her arms fall at her sides, and as the train moved she leaned back thankfully, out of sight. For once she was not anxious whether she had behaved well. Her mind was for a time not her own. It was an empty place into which she could summon Nicholas. She was content with simple repetition: the reality was much finer than anything her imagination could supply. Her mind was like a child which falls asleep over the handful of weeds it has pulled.

The next day was Sunday. She wrote to Nicholas, then took Richard for his walk. They walked in their wood. A light rain earlier in the day had covered everything, moss, naked trees, the coarse last year's grass, with a film of bright drops. These glittered in the cold spring wind. Richard ran wildly about, shaking the low branches so that they showered over his face. His cheeks were scarlet on white, and his eyes shone, wide and astonishingly brilliant. He was not usually so noisy. Hervey followed him about, ready to smile and to answer when he shouted to her, but her mind was away—so he looked, so he smiled, so spoke. She had made no plans for her future. The whole of the scheming practical side of her mind had fallen asleep, leaving her to think peacefully of her great happiness. There was nothing she wanted from Nicholas that she had not already got. She did not know what would come of this new turn, she, the wise forward-looking Ulysses. Thinking of Nicholas, she felt quietly contented and a little timid, afraid she would not be fine enough. My life has made me rough, she thought. There seemed no absurdity in thinking of herself as harder and rougher than a man of thirty-two who has spent four years soldiering. As she knew it, her hardness was given to her, with her patience and her remembering mind.

At last I am at peace, she thought. With the thought she felt her life, that had been pouring from side to side like the leaves of a tree in wind, fold into deep shade. She felt a boundless confidence and security. ' No, I'm coming,' she said to Richard. Holding her dress aside, she began to run. Despite her happiness, she recalled at this moment that Nicholas had warned her against taking him too easily for granted. But I shall have my own way, she thought: I need only patience.

CHAPTER X

A YOUNG MAN WITH A WHIP AT HIS HEELS

ONE morning Evelyn Lamb did not come to the office and sent for Hervey to wait on her at her house. Hervey went there and found her with a very red face, which paled slowly in about an hour—the effect of a new lotion Evelyn had used that morning. She gave Hervey letters to write and manuscripts to read, and kept her to lunch. The delicacy with which Evelyn ate a small salad and drank black coffee took away Hervey's satisfaction. She felt gross. So much she had advanced, however, that the room they sat in, made austere at great cost, did not impress her. I would have it different, she thought. Evelyn startled her by saying:

'You were dining at the *Gallia* last night. Who was the man?'

'My cousin, Nicholas Roxby.' She wanted to talk about Nicholas, to say anything, no matter what, so long as she could speak of him, but she could not begin. She sat and gaped at Evelyn like a fool, her lips parted. Evelyn watched her with sudden envy, thinking: Does she even know how fortunate she is to be able to feel like that about any man? Hervey's inexperience, her awkward hands, her slowness, filled the older woman with an exasperated liking. She smiled with much kindness.

The colour ran to Hervey's cheeks. 'He has taken a house in Chelsea—near this one—where he sells old furniture. Will you go to look at it and take other people?'

'Yes,' Evelyn said. Her smile persisted. 'Are you going to be lovers?'

Hervey shook her head. ' But I don't know,' she mumbled.
' He has a wife, though he doesn't live with her.'

' Have you thought about it ? ' Evelyn smiled.

' No.   Not at all.'

Again Evelyn felt unwilling envy. She felt that Hervey
was speaking only the truth and it was almost more than
she could bear, to look on at a love so fortunate that it took
an age to come to the point. ' You will have to before
long,' she said drily, ' and if you take my advice you won't
rush into all that pother of divorce. If you want to live
a civilised life you'll keep your own place and let Nicholas
visit you in it. In such a way both of you will keep your
identity, and you'll enjoy each other all the more, for a
longer time. You don't believe me—but I assure you I'm
explaining the difference between romance and monotony.
Marriage between two people who could afford to live
properly is partly laziness and partly greed.'

' I don't know,' Hervey said again vaguely. She looked
at Evelyn and began to describe Nicholas to her—he was
tall, he had dark hair and a short mouth, he exaggerated
small things, so that he was always laughing or groaning,
cold or hot, never merely calm.

' Oh but I know that, I know,' Evelyn interrupted.
She waved her hand before Hervey's face: ' they're all
alike, all young men. Your Nicholas is quite ordinary, it's
you who think that no one ever smiled or groaned until
he did.' She then added with great calm: ' Don't tell me
too much about it, Hervey. I might easily use it to
harm you.'

' Why should you ? ' Hervey asked, taking care not to
show surprise.

' Think that I might lose patience with it one day and
try to punish you for looking happy. I'm forty-two and
that makes infatuation ridiculous and irritating when it isn't
sad.' She was unpractised in telling the truth about herself
and the effort saddened her. In a moment she saw that
Hervey was not interested, not even embarrassed. She was

just going to send her off as a servant came into the room to give her a letter. The young man was waiting, who had brought it from Mrs. Thomas Harben, Lucy Harben, ' to ask you to be kind to my young friend and (distant) relative, Julian Swan. He has a book of poems on which he needs advice.'

' Bring him upstairs,' she said to the servant, and to Hervey: ' Wait. He may be impossible or boring and then you must get rid of him for me. You could take him away and let him read his poems to you.'

Julian Swan entered. He was tall, very well made, fair, and his left foot dragged slightly. As he came towards Evelyn he tried to conceal it by walking as slowly as possible: his smile was remarkably sweet, and his eyes, which he kept on her face from the moment of entering, fine and brilliant. He had barely glanced at Hervey. She was able to sit quietly at one side and scrutinise the young man. He seemed to be her own age; he had the voice and gestures of his caste but with an added and incongruous self-assurance —he is regretting something, she thought, perhaps his foot. The effect he made, despite the dragging foot, was of vitality and arrogance. It came to her: He is cruel and he is used to being admired. She was staring at him with her usual intensity, and after a time he was conscious of it and turned his back. At first he had talked to Evelyn about her essays, which plainly he had read and did not merely agree with. Then he spoke of Italy; he had lived for the past eight months in Rome and he had seen and talked at three times to Mussolini. ' He is a great man, the greatest in Europe, perhaps in the world!' ' Then you speak Italian?' Evelyn said. ' Italian, and Spanish,' Swan said, laughing. ' A few of my poems were written in Spanish.' ' Ah, your poems,' Evelyn said, in her slow gentle way. She looked across at Hervey. ' Go back to the *Review*,' she said, in the same voice: ' if there are any urgent letters you can sign them. I shall come in to-morrow morning.'

As Hervey walked towards the door, Swan was saying to

Evelyn: 'I can assure you that writing verses was only to fill time, after an accident, in which I broke both legs. I don't mean to spend my life in that way. It was to know you that I persuaded Lucy they were good poems. Poor well-meaning Lucy doesn't know any better. . . .' They were laughing together when Hervey shut the door.

CHAPTER XI

NICHOLAS IS NOT EASY

APRIL. Before long Hervey began to think of ways in which she could spend a longer time with Nicholas. In the evening she was often tired, and to put Richard to bed and then to go back to town for two hours or only one, when Nicholas had other people to see, wearied her. Nicholas seemed content, and that troubled her a little. She had begun to wish for some change. Her will could not be kept asleep for long. At last it was Nicholas's sister who helped her.

One afternoon in April Georgina walked into the office of the *Review* and said that she was coming home with Hervey. There was a spare bedroom in the house. Georgina said she wanted to get away from London, and if Hervey did not mind she would stay a week at least. Hervey was pleased. There was already the strong liking between her and Nicholas's sister and now something had been added to it—she did not know what it was, but she knew that the other woman was troubled, and though she must have a great many friends of her own kind she had turned instead to Hervey. This seemed right. By some chance, or it may not have been chance—after all, they were cousins—they knew each at sight so well that Georgina could think of Hervey as awkward and eccentric, and Hervey of her that she was unreliable, without their pleasure in each other clouding for so long as a moment. This was something new for Hervey, but it was already part of her life, so that she could imagine what she had lost by not knowing Georgina earlier.

Georgina made herself comfortable in the small ugly sitting-room. In a few moments she had taken possession of it more thoroughly than Hervey had been able to do in months. Hervey's notion of living in a room began and ended with keeping it tidy. She had nothing to spare to make it live.

As soon as Richard had been taken away to bed Georgina said smiling:

'What are you going to do with Nicholas?'

'Anything he will let me,' Hervey answered. 'Do you mind?'

'No.' She corrected herself quickly: 'Of course I mind. I'm more than a little jealous of you—I've always thought of Nicholas as attractive and liked being seen with him. We used to walk and go to dances together. But first, before the War, there was Jenny who did what she liked with him, and afterwards, after she had left him, he had no time or energy to amuse himself. Do you know, Hervey, that the War changed Nicholas so greatly that you—seeing him for the first time now—know someone completely different. He was charming—unspoiled, very eager.' She stopped speaking. 'I'm sorry, do forgive me,' she said.

Hervey did not answer, and watching her, Georgina's thoughts went on: How well does she know Nicholas? She herself had seen him alter from the pliant and too generous boy into a man turned narrowly on himself, dry, without warmth, and she was deeply sorry for Hervey. Nicholas, she thought, will hurt and disappoint her, and if she shows it openly he will leave her; he is too easily tired. Now if I could I should like to arrange for someone to look after her with kindness. That she needs and should have.

Hervey looked up with a smile and said: 'Don't be too sorry for me, Georgina. I dislike being hurt—I'm ridiculously easily hurt—and I take things very hardly and make a fuss, but under everything I am as tough and strong as a tree. I can't be hurt unbearably. I once thought I could but that was nonsense. It is only if anything happened to Richard that I should be quite done for, no fight left in me.'

She hoped that now Georgina would feel free to talk, but instead Georgina told her stories about her mother. One day Clara Roxby had been invited to the funeral of a poor woman in Hoxton and the priest gabbled the service, so that at last Mrs. Roxby struck her umbrella on the floor and said, 'Not so fast, my good man, not so fast.'

Hervey laughed out. 'That sounds more like Mary Hervey,' she said.

'There was no servility in those people,' Georgina said. 'You and I, who seem freer, are only indifferent, and we could be much more easily silenced if, perhaps, a government wanted to silence us. I should like to have seen anyone, any authority, try to silence Mary Hervey. She would have gone to prison rather than hold her tongue!'

'Well I would too,' Hervey said. She added quickly: 'But not before Richard grows up and is safe.'

Then Georgina laughed at her, kindly, and they gave up talking for that time. Hervey smiled in the instant of falling asleep, at the thought that her friend was asleep in another room in the house. It made it for the first time seem a living cell in the surrounding blackness.

The next day was Saturday. She left Richard with Georgina and went up to London to meet Nicholas and spend the day with him in the country. He was waiting for her on the platform beside their train. She saw him before he turned round, neat and soldierly in his trench macintosh, his head held back. He was remote and cold, as if carrying out a duty, but he warmed when he saw her. He said smiling:

'You won't mind if it rains on us?'

They left the train at Marlow and began to walk to the hills. There was bright sun and a few ragged celandines in the hedges. The air felt of spring, which made Hervey think she had too much energy. It worked in her every-

where, except in her tongue. As usual she kept silence on
what most occupied her, in fear of offending him. She
wanted to know how she stood with him, and whether he
was content to live as they were doing, and whether his
wife knew, but she was afraid to open any of these questions.
When they left the road and began climbing, Nicholas
stopped suddenly and put his arms round her. 'Oh Hervey,
I should like to go away with you for a long time.'

'Why shouldn't we?' Hervey said. She spoke quietly to
hide her emotion. She would have agreed to any plan.

'One day,' Nicholas laughed. He held her for a moment
and kissed her and they walked on. Hervey did not speak.
A minute later, Nicholas said quickly: 'I don't think we
can marry—shall you mind? It sounds brutal. I think—
if we could go away for two or three months——'

'When you like,' Hervey said. She had accepted at once,
without a tremor.

'Have you ever been in a divorce court? It's intolerably
nasty, like an execution. And one has to talk about it to so
many people, some of whom would be hurt.'

'Your wife,' Hervey said.

'Has Georgina described her to you? My mother detests
Jenny and can't be fair to her. The strange thing is that
Jenny depends on me, in spite of thinking of me as a failure.
You mustn't suppose she has no mind. She has a good one,
of an unoriginal sort, which she is too lazy to use. Partly
because she believes that a very pretty woman ought not to
work—even at living. Her ambition used to be a great
house, a salon after the manner of Mrs. Thomas Harben,
and herself as the *amie* of a great many famous men. Actually
men tire of her, she asks for too much homage, at tiresome
length.'

Hervey could not feel contemptuous. She only thought
it strange that there were women left who did not know
that only the fortunate and, so long as it lasted, the very
beautiful, can live an easy life. She held her tongue, not
caring to check Nicholas.

'I was completely in love with her, Hervey, and for years. She wouldn't marry me at first in spite of knowing that I was going to have Garton's—and I don't think she imagined for a moment I'd throw it up! But she wanted something more solid and impressive than a very immature young man. I think she married me when she did because she saw the other eluding her. And of course she liked me, I think as much as she ever liked anyone. When she left me—but it was long after I'd given up Garton's—she supposed she was going to make a better marriage, but the man ran away from her. Then it was a question of my helping or not helping her. My mother of course thought I should hand her over to her father. He is a detestable creature. I didn't. She'd been humiliated enough. . . . You think I'm a fool.'

'No. You had to help her,' Hervey said quietly. She did not think anything of the sort—she had said it to please him. Does he realise that now he is forcing me to help this foolish useless woman? She put the thought quickly out of sight, and in a few moments, because it was the first day of spring, and because Nicholas at least loved her—even if he had no kindness for her—she was happy, with her mind as well as her body, which felt light and gay. For once she was not clumsy. They had lunch, sandwiches and dry figs, on the top of the hill, and she took off her hat to feel the sun. Nicholas touched her hair.

'How fine—like fine soft silk,' he said. He drew his finger down over her cheek. 'Your skin is the smoothest I ever felt.'

Hervey turned to him blindly, speechless. She had not known how much she needed assurance. Nicholas did not seem to notice it, and she kept herself quiet. After a time her body ceased to tremble.

They came back to town in the late afternoon. In the train Nicholas had felt exhausted. These failures of his body made him impatient and angry. He could not understand why, since the War, he grew tired for no reason, too

tired to want anything but to be left alone to finish whatever
he had in hand.   At these times he hated his body.

He had arranged for Hervey to come back with him to
his rooms.   They had tea together.   He felt that she was
troubled but he could not help her, and he was impatient
and bored by so much emotion.   Why not leave things
alone, my dear?   he thought: can't you see my hands are
full?   Not knowing what to say to him, nervous, she asked
him about his house.   He was moving to it from these
rooms in a week's time.   Now I must speak, he thought,
and so he said abruptly:

' It must be a success.   I can't fail again, it's too much.
I don't want success for its own sake, but to prove something—do you see?   If I make another failure it means
that I'm incompetent and a fool, only fit to draw dividends.
I'm risking everything on this effort and not only my
money.'

' And if it succeeds, will you be satisfied ? ' Hervey asked.

' Yes.'   He touched her arm lightly.   ' Work is far more
necessary to me than anything, Hervey.   If you, or Jenny,
were to get in the way now I should have to leave you out,
do you understand ? '

Hervey was dumb because of the pain.   She looked down
at her hand lying on her knee and waited.

' I can't undertake more than one thing at a time,'
Nicholas said.   ' That's all I have the energy for, and I
don't much like being driven.   First it was my grandmother,
then Jenny, then Beauvier—the feeling that I'm being held
down to a set of circumstances always has this effect, it
makes me want to get out quickly—*foutre le camp*, before
it's too late to make any move.   One should be prepared to
move at short notice.'

Hervey felt the skin of her face stiffen so that she thought
it needed an effort to part her lips.   But agony of mind is
less serious than we like to think.   She was able to say in a
calm voice: ' Do I have that effect on you ? '

' I haven't anything to give you, Hervey.'

She had reached the point at which the mind gives its tormentor the slip and even begins to enjoy being lost. She was defeated—except for a vague sense, too vague to convince her, that if she were as unimportant to him as he said he would never take this trouble to tell her. At the moment she was only quick enough to say lightly:

'But I haven't asked you for anything.' She noticed now that he was looking grey, as though any minute he would drop, and she thought, I must go, I can't do anything, he is too far away from me.

'Ah but you will,' he said, with a smile.

'That you must wait to see,' Hervey said. She stood up. 'I must go now.'

He remembered that he ought to keep her to dinner—that had been part of the plan they had made for the day, it was their first day together—but he let her go. He went with her into the street and she walked on without looking to either side, quickly and carelessly, her head poked forward. You would think she had to batter her way with it.

She walked without thinking—on and on—obeying an instinct which had convinced her that the less you think about a defeat at the time the better. It was easy to be pleased with trifles, the comical sharp face of a passer-by; a man begging under an arch with a sorrowful monkey looking from his jacket: then when she reached Trafalgar Square it was the moment for a miracle. The half hour before dusk. Every impurity had been sucked from the light so that the buildings, column, and fountain, sprang in it with a delicate clarity. The sky burned a pure bright blue, brighter towards the west, and the thinnest visible half-circle of moon stood in it over the Haymarket. The pillars before St. Martin-in-the-Fields were as white as bones. Every line and colour was distinct, separate, but the whole was glowing, bathed in the light. I have never seen anything like this, Hervey thought. She stood still to look again and again. Oh stay for ever, she cried to it; it had made her think (you may be sure) of her own eternity.

She was at home hours before Georgina expected her. Nothing was more certain than that Georgina knew what had gone wrong. She glanced up from her book, smiled, and turning over the page said: 'Richard was very good. You've spoiled him, Hervey, at his age he ought to be bathing himself. I had everything to do.' And that was all, but Hervey, sitting down under the light, now tired as if at the end of her strength (but that was not true, she was still stronger than Nicholas, than Georgina, than anyone), felt that enough had been said to keep them friends for a lifetime, no matter what Georgina said or did. Georgina was untruthful; she was shamefully careless; she burned holes in the chair covers with her cigarette; she lived for excitement. So much Hervey knew about her already. But she was brave and generous. She was very gay; she laughed when Hervey was in her gloomy reforming mood—I shall never know anyone like her, Hervey thought. She stood up and walked across the room to straighten the curtain. There was nothing else she could do at the moment to convince Georgina (who never noticed whether the curtains were straight or crooked or had lost a hook) that she loved her and was grateful. As she passed her Georgina looked up and nodded quickly. The intimacy between them was safe, and Hervey could go back to her chair and sit quietly waiting until the moment when Nicholas—but no, not yet, she thought swiftly; it could wait: it must wait; it must cease tossing in her mind before she was fit to look at it to see what could be salvaged. In the meantime she was very hungry, and taking an apple from the cupboard she began to eat it, trying to make as few sounds as possible. Georgina put her book down and said:

'I want to talk to you. You're so sure of yourself—and you despise people. You must help me.'

Hervey looked at her in surprise. Is that how I seem to you? she thought: it's ridiculous and impossible, I despise no one. She turned her chair half round so that Georgina could talk without looking at her.

' I wanted to tell you the first day. But you made me keep my distance and it was only afterwards that I thought, I can trust her. You don't trust anyone, do you? It's your only fault. No, it's only one of them.' She put her head down. 'Nicholas showed William Gary to you— would you believe William used to admire me? That was before the War, when I was a girl, and during the War I fell in love with your publisher Charles Frome and lived with him. I supposed he was going to allow his wife to divorce him and we should be married, but in the end he couldn't face it and I broke with him—not that I minded it very much but I can't endure a coward. I'm not strong enough myself. None of this is important—I'm telling you about it so that you won't think of me as inexperi- enced and romantic. It may be true that I'm romantic. I tell lies to make myself appear interesting, not as you do out of pity for people. I shan't tell you many. How am I going to persuade William Gary that I'm sincere?'

' Do you want to marry him?' Hervey said.

' Of course. I could forgive myself for Charles if he had turned out to be less greedy or less prudent. I could beat myself for having made such a mistake. But there seemed no advantage in *waiting* during the War. Why not live at once? I don't believe that William himself did much waiting at any time when he was a young man. I shouldn't have minded that.' She looked at Hervey with a smile. ' He won't let me talk to him. What am I to do?'

' You're beautiful,' Hervey said, after a moment.

That meant less to Gary than it had done in the past, Georgina said. Ignorant as she was of his mind, she knew that much. He had changed—she tried for a more exact word —It was not, she said, that he was less ardent for life but he lived in different things. There must be something that could take the place of beauty for the self-centred man he had become. ' Oh, tell me,' she cried. ' You must know.'

' Yes, there might be something,' Hervey agreed.

But it was wordless, she thought. It was nothing that

you could say or do, it was a state; it was the being ready
to satisfy a need, but the need changed, it altered from one
person to another, almost from hour to hour.   As this
afternoon I failed completely in my guess, she thought—
almost happy because she had explained it—but another time
I shall not fail. ' You could perhaps wait, listening closely,
until you know what it is he wants.'

' I can't wait! ' Georgina said.   She was laughing at
Hervey now.   ' In less than three months I shall be thirty.
I know that unless something happens to me this year it
will be too late.'

Hervey looked at her in silence.   Her own impatience
was only the whitened edge of a patience as deep as the
sea.   She could not understand such impatience as her
friend's.

When she went upstairs she found on the chair by
Richard's bed the book in which he wrote his ' essays.'
' How you write Books ' was the last.   What does he think
about it, she wondered.   Richard never asked her for any
help with his school work.   But at his age, she thought,
seeing it very clearly (it seemed less than a year ago) I was
getting hundreds of words by heart every day; and my
mother ' heard ' my lessons in the evening.   She read,
holding the book under the feeble gas lamp: ' First you
Write what your book is going to be about, then you send
it somewhere to be printed.   Then if it is a good book it
will be published and charged so much for, if it is a bad
book it is Sent back.   My mother Wrote a book each copy
was so much money it took a very long time to Write—
When it was finished it Was about one inch and $\frac{1}{2}$ thick.'

' Well, thank heaven Richard will never be a writer,'
Hervey murmured.   He said something to her as she stooped
over him, but he was asleep the whole time, his body curled
up in the narrow bed, his lips firmly closed.   She touched
him lightly, straightening the clothes.   Whatever happens
I won't give him up, she thought.   The thought scarcely
reached the surface of her mind.   It was almost as un-

necessary as if she had said, I won't give up my right hand, or my eyes.

As soon as she lay down, the thought of her failure to keep Nicholas returned, and this time found her at home.

At first she was filled by self pity and a truly bitter grief. It is unfair that he surrendered wholly to a mean stupid woman, she thought, unable to think of any other reason for his unkindness. I want very little, only to be allowed to comfort you—why must I be sent away, why must I be hurt? oh Nicholas, I would like it if you loved me better since I love you so much.

But with Hervey, when she had lamented long enough hope would break in. She began to laugh at herself, then to think that all was not lost, then to compose in her head a letter to Nicholas, then to think that he had smiled at her. So with one light stroke after another she drove down the memory of failure, it began to seem bearable, and she fell asleep.

On Monday morning she was saved the trouble of writing to Nicholas by his telephoning to her at the *Review* office instead. He asked her to come with him to see his house. She went and he showed her everything, the rooms in which each chair and table was perfect in its kind. He was restless with pleasure in it and the more she said in praise the more he was pleased and very gay. ' But where will you live? ' she said at last.

There was a strip of a room at the back, with doors into the garden but no window. It held a bed, a double chest and a bookcase. ' Here.'

When he was not looking she laid her hand on the pillow.

In the hall, as she was leaving, he said: ' No, wait a moment,' left her, and came back with an old silver spoon, the silver worn very thin. ' Look, it has your initials, I saw it and got it for you.'

' For me? ' Hervey said. She touched it delicately. To take hold of it gave her confidence. Now I am loved, she

thought. The Garton in her was pleased that it was a
valuable spoon, worth possessing. Nicholas watched her
with a smile. She thanked him eagerly, with her heart,
and went away confused. He had said nothing that showed
he knew she had been unhappy, yet he had made her a fine
present. It was her simplicity made her weigh the two in
her mind to know how she stood.

An evening in the same week she had supper with him
in his house, and afterwards when she was going Nicholas
said: ' I wish you didn't go, Hervey.'

' I should like to stay with you,' Hervey said. ' Shall we
go into the country and stay together ? '

' We'll go in about a month's time—in May,' Nicholas
said.

Now this was better than she had hoped. She was careful
to seem unmoved. ' I should like that.'

' How long can you stay ? '

' Three—or four days,' Hervey said, with a moment's
thought.

' Come back into the drawing-room for a few minutes,'
Nicholas said hurriedly. ' I want to talk to you.' He had
seized her hand and he drew her into the room. She waited.
Nicholas walked up and down. Once he asked her to be
patient. She had gone back to her chair and at last he
seated himself near her and said: ' You remember I told
you that there was a great deal you did not know.'

Now I am to be told, Hervey thought. She placed her
hands together, to help her. She was ready to accept
anything.

' I am no good to you, or to any other woman,' Nicholas
said. ' I don't want to be troubled to make love to anyone,
or—what's worse—to live with anyone so unspoiled, so
good, as you are.' He would have explained to her that the
War had caught him young and had used up in him more
than a young man's energy, but he was determined not
to make excuses for himself. ' I should disappoint you in
every way.'

Hervey had listened with the sharpest care. ' Is this all? ' she said in a quiet voice.

' It seems too much,' Nicholas said.

Hervey recalled what she had thought to hear. I am spoiled, she thought. But this, although it made her ashamed, gave her confidence.

' It was one reason why Jenny couldn't live with me,' Nicholas said. ' It might happen again; with us.'

' No it won't happen, Nicholas,' Hervey said simply. ' I may be unlike other women,' she went on with the same simplicity, ' in finding lovemaking less necessary than love.'

' Does that mean anything? ' Nicholas asked.

' Yes,' Hervey said smiling. ' It means that when we go away together next month I shall expect you to fall asleep in my arms but you need not take the trouble to behave as a lover, unless you change your mind.'

' Aren't you ashamed? ' Nicholas said, beginning to laugh. The air of strain had gone from his face. In another moment he jumped up and kissed her, half shaking her between his arms. ' You would persuade any man that you knew better than he did if you spoke to him in that voice. No other woman in the world is so easy to love as you are, Hervey. Everyone ought to be in love with you. What a fool I was not to look for you ten years ago.'

' It would have been too soon,' Hervey said.

Hervey wrote: ' I remember two things. One is evil and the other good. The year before the War, when I was living with Penn in that squalid room, I tried to poison myself. To punish me for some offence, Penn was refusing to speak, and suddenly the room was too much for me. It was no pleasure to be alive and I took out all the headache tablets T. S. had made for me and swallowed them. I was afraid then and told Penn. He was lying in the bed. He got up quickly, his eyes dulled with anger, dressed, calling me vile names, and went away to find a doctor. Before

he went out he stood at the end of the bed and shouted:
" Do you realise that you may have got me into trouble?
If I can't find a doctor at once I shall bring the police to
you." I begged him with tears not to disgrace me in this
way. The doctor he brought was rough, and he agreed
with Penn that I ought to be well whipped. I was just
nineteen, so that my last whipping was not more than five
years away, and I thought they might do it. For a long
time I could not forget that Penn had threatened to bring
the police. Even though I was ashamed of myself, knowing
I had behaved in an unforgivable way, I thought that he
ought not to have said it.

' The second memory is of walking with Penn in the
country near Liverpool. It is poor country, flat and colourless, but for that very reason, looking back I see it as
charming. It lies behind me in a clear bright air, with
a glow of yellow and green over the fields and white dust
on the leaves. No doubt it is the simplicity of my life then,
hard though it was, which charms me and has been pre-
served in my memory of the country, much as pulling open
a drawer in the Chinese cabinet at home gives me back the
whole of my early life at once and more than that, the life
of Danesacre when it was still alive and lovely, one of the
ports of England and familiar to men living as far away as
Odessa or Archangel and even China. And as well as the
charm of the country in my mind, there is Penn as he
looked at that time. I have neither love nor liking for him
now but I am fast to him by the same nerve joining me to
that country and to the young woman who walked in it,
and was all the time looking away from it. There is no
honesty in denying this. But now what will happen to
Penn if I leave him? He will become a ghost living in the
many places I have known with him.'

CHAPTER XII

EARLHAM HAS REASON TO FEEL AFRAID

ONE day towards the end of April Earlham was sacked from the *Evening Post*. The letter was lying on his desk when he went in. He was to go directly: the terms on which Marcel Cohen employed his staff allowed him to dismiss at a day's notice.

He was alone in the leader-writers' room, and when he had read the letter he had only to leave at once to avoid seeing anyone. But he sat on until a man came in, one of the reporters. Earlham told him. He seemed to be surprised, but from his face Earlham saw that the news was at least expected. He decided to see the managing editor. To his question: 'Why is Cohen getting rid of me?' the other man had no clear answer, but just as Earlham was leaving the room he said abruptly to him: 'I'm very sorry you're going—but you can't have been comfortable here since you were in the House. This is not a Socialist paper, you know.'

'It supports a Labour government,' Earlham said.

'Well—we **shall** miss you,' the other man said, smiling.

Earlham left the office, and walked down to the Embankment. He had come here when he was a child, scuttering across the bridge like a rabbit, from the warrens of Southwark. Hungry, in rags, he had rubbed his thin belly against the parapet for hours, watching the river. He felt happy here. Dreams—what dreams he had then!—he rescued drowning women, was carried off by pirates, chattered with foreign sailors: at the end of the story he often collapsed and died; and when he imagined this, tears raced over his

97

pale cheeks making channels in the grime. As darkness
came, flowing up the river, now with now against the tide,
he turned reluctantly home. The basement where he and
his mother lived was filled with vapours from the river.
His mother would be full, too, of complaints—she complained all the time and yet she laughed and she was gay.
She loved him. The last sound he heard before he fell
asleep was a groan and a laugh; the last thing he felt, her
dry roughened fingers stroking his cheek. She died when
he was thirteen, before he had had time to give her one
single treat of all the treats he had promised her. He came
in one evening and found her laid dead, not a complaint or
a laugh in her.

An extraordinary bitterness seized him with the thought
that all his efforts, his intelligence, his future even were in
the claw of heartless rapacious men, like Cohen. I am
twenty-eight, he thought, too old to be still unknown. He
passed a workman waiting on the curb for a tram. The
sun was full on the man's face, so that Earlham saw it with
the glaze and sharpness of a painting—blue sunken eyes,
hollowed cheeks, a stubble of hair falling over the mouth.
The man was staring in front of him with a look of great
patience. Awkward and scarred, his hands were folded over
the end of a short plank he had with him. Earlham felt an
impulse to speak to him. He saw himself halting before the
man—I promise you the reward of your patience. Trust
me. I am your leader. I will think for you, I will work
day and night. I dedicate myself to you. He saw the
platform of a vast hall, himself almost alone on it—there
were other men, but they were half seen at the back. The
faces of twenty thousand of his followers turned towards
him: he heard their voices, acclaiming, shouting. He
raised his hand. At once, silence. He spoke. The actual
words of the speech sprang in his mind. He moved the
vast crowd where he pleased, to tears, to mirth, to a passion
of loyalty—for him, for the leader. The hour has struck
for which we toiled and sacrificed. You and I have known

dark days. And now, now that power is within our grasp, let us go forward together, in the same trust, the same certainty as in the past. But let us remember in silence for a moment those of our friends and comrades who fell during the fight. Comrades—friends—to our dead!

He had reached the end of the Embankment. A brown haze was thickening slowly the air. The Houses of Parliament loomed through it like the towers of a mediæval tale, certain to end badly. Now the clock struck behind the mist, and he stood still, counting the strokes. Four. Five. He was on the point of beckoning a cab. The thought of his loss struck him full in the throat. He put his head down and gasped. The fear of poverty, closer to him than any other, drenched him in its bitter spray. He stumbled as he walked on.

When he reached the end of his street he broke into a run. He could not wait another minute to tell Rachel. She did not answer him when he ran in calling 'Rachel, Rachel!' He went from room to room, looking for her. Entering the kitchen, with its scrubbed table and the tray set on the table, he remembered that she had gone to her parents' lodging with the baby. Perhaps it would be night before she came home.

He stumbled against a clothes-horse filled with petticoats and frocks. As he gathered them up he thought: What a pity children grow out of their things. The garments were twice as pretty as full-grown ones. He began thinking how Rachel would look at him when he told her that they had only his member's salary. A fourth of it they gave to her parents, old weak creatures who had nothing to live on. He did not grudge them the money, but his senses rose in revolt from the saving and scraping that must begin again. During the last years a hint—the veriest whisper—of luxury had crept into the house. A bottle of eau de cologne stood on their dressing-table upstairs. It had not been opened; it was a symbol. Some impulse of Earlham's nature hungered for ease and fine living. He felt a stifled resentment to know that Rachel would not complain of hardship. She would eat only potatoes and wear her shabby clothes with a good heart. She is too humble-minded, he thought.

He heard steps outside the door. It was David Renn, and almost before he was inside the house Earlham had begun to speak. 'Cohen sacked me this afternoon,' he began heavily, and ended with the hot words: 'How am I to tell Rachel, poor girl?'

'Rachel won't mind very much,' Renn answered. He seemed to be at a loss. His eyes, watching Earlham, were gentle and yet remote.

This quiet scrutiny disconcerted Earlham. Behind his friend's air of kindness he felt the critic, the watcher. It came to him that he was being judged, that Renn had found one of his weak places—and this vexed him unbearably. Now more than before he needed belief and approval. In a kindling voice he began to speak of the future; he had words, tones, a warmth, that could charm the distrust from Renn's thoughts. And at last, only by hearing his own voice, he grew quiet. He felt worn, but upheld. I shall survive this, he thought with certainty. I have survived worse.

CHAPTER XIII

HERVEY DEALS WITH A CRISIS IN HER OWN WAY

In May—it was during the week before Hervey and Nicholas were going away together—Evelyn Lamb wrote to Penn that if he had not done it already he would be wise to ask his wife about her cousin, 'with whom (Evelyn wrote) she spends days and no doubt nights.' She added the sentence at the end of a letter in which she rejected a review he had written for her. It was half to turn his mind from the rejection and half mere speculative mischief.

Hervey came home from work early one afternoon to find Penn at her rooms. She knew from his face there was trouble, and in spite of herself she dreaded it. Penn had an air of sullen dignity, but she saw that he was feeling very pleased with himself. Drawn to his height of six feet, he stood there and glowered down at her. It was all arranged, even to the gestures. There was a touch of triumph in it. What has he done now? she wondered, uneasy and scornful. It was soon out that he had looked for and found the bundle of Nicholas's letters she kept folded among her clothes. They were not many, but they were enough to give him a fair notion of the truth.

'So you were going down to Hampshire together?' he said, smiling.

'For three days,' Hervey said.

'Did you mean to tell me?'

'No.'

'You don't grow less dishonest as you grow older,' Penn smiled.

Hervey did not answer. She had been shaking when he began, but now she was angry at the loss of the letters and afraid of what he would do with them. She could scarcely trust him not to read them aloud to his friends in Oxford. He had no dignity. He would humiliate both of them in this way, almost without knowing what he had done.

'Where have you put my letters?'

'They're not in this house any longer,' Penn said.

'You've sent them away?' Her heart sank.

'Never mind what I've done with them.'

'Richard is just coming in,' said Hervey. 'Please don't talk of it now.'

She ran out and Penn heard her telling the boy that his father had come, but there was no answer from Richard beyond the casual question: 'Did he come in a car?' He came in then and was very friendly, but Penn saw plainly that his son had no affection for him. He was too full of himself to wonder who was to blame for this, himself or Hervey. But he was bitterly offended. For the next two hours Hervey paid no attention to him. She gave Richard his meal, read to him, and at last took him away to bed. She was away close on another hour and when she came back to Penn her face wore the first signs of bewilderment he had seen on it. Actually, she had come to a resolution to get back her letters at any price. Her mind felt tense, as though it were a cord drawn tightly round the bones of her head. She had thought a little about Evelyn's part in the discovery but she attached no importance to Evelyn and was neither shocked nor hurt to know that the other woman had harmed her. At such times her profound contempt for people awoke to release her from them. As she came into the room she felt certain of being able to manage Penn.

Perhaps he guessed this confidence. His mood changed and an overbearing expression she knew well came over his face. In earlier years he would have threatened her with his hands, but now he was a little afraid. Before she could speak he said loudly: 'Don't you think you can twist me,

my girl. I know you too well. I've lost patience with
your persuasive tongue.'

'Where should we be now, without my persuasive tongue?'
Hervey said calmly—'if it is really only my tongue that has
talked you into being able to live like an irresponsible young
man at Oxford, while I earn Richard's living as well as
my own.'

'Are you going to tell me it's my fault you've disgraced
yourself?' Penn shouted.

Hervey looked at him with dislike of his hectoring voice,
and at the same time, seeing how helpless he was to punish
her, she felt sorry for him. 'No!' she said, after a moment.
'No. Except that if you had not run away to Oxford I
should have had no time to spend falling in love. But I was
unhappy with you before then.'

'Thank you!' Penn said. He stared at her. 'I gave
you credit for more pride. You and your Nicholas—
I gather from his letters that *you* were the eager one of
the two. Very pleasant for your husband. A wealthy
cousin, who showed no interest in you until you began to
be known! Really, Hervey, you surprise me.'

'Nicholas is by no means rich. He works for his living.'

'And I suppose I don't,' Penn exclaimed.

'Of course you don't,' she said, with provoking calm.
'An equipment officer in the Air Force in England didn't
work. You're not working now.'

'No?' said Penn. He made an attempt to seem haughty,
but she knew him too well to be impressed. He was
ridiculous in her eyes. Something in her was hurt and
shocked that it was so. She turned aside from him, and
struggled to keep herself quiet. She was surprised that he
could still make her feel impatient and bitter against him.
She did not care now if he had a dozen other women; yet
to think quietly of all that had happened was no easier.
It angered her. She would never forgive him for the way
in which he had spoiled both their lives. She thought of his
bullying of her and Richard, and of the endless lies. Less

excusable than all was his calm assumption that he need do nothing for Richard.

'What would have become of Richard if I had not been able to work for him?' she said bitterly. She felt sick and tired of him. Yet when she saw him standing there, solemn, peevish, posing before her as the dignified husband, she felt a curious sensation of pity, almost of love, for him. He has never grown up, she thought. He understands nothing, neither himself nor what he has done to us both.

'Will you give me back my letters?' she asked him gently.

'Certainly not.'

'Did Evelyn know you were going to take them?'

Penn leaned forward and wagged a finger in her face. 'You can't get at me there. I don't care a hoot for Evelyn Lamb's opinion or for any opinion. I'm completely indifferent. Make as much trouble as you like, it doesn't matter to me what you do. It's your own business if you quarrel with her, and lose your job.'

'Oh I wasn't going to accuse her,' Hervey answered. 'It's not worth it.' Her cynicism was almost that of a child, which does not understand why this and that injustice has been done to him, but accepts them all. 'Please give me back the letters, Penn. I liked them. You never write to me yourself.'

'Why do you want them?'

'They are my dearest possession,' she answered. 'They are almost all I shall have. You know I'm not going to marry Nicholas,' she said, suddenly overcome with grief. She bent her head to hide it from Penn.

'You mean that if I hadn't found you out, you would have lived with him and said nothing. What did you intend to do when I came home?'

'I hadn't thought that far ahead.'

'Am I to believe that?'

'It's the strict truth,' Hervey said, 'not a lie to please you.'

'You admit it might well be?'

Hervey shook her head.   She was in terror that he meant
to use the letters against Nicholas.   She could not face
that, having no certainty that Nicholas would forgive her
for it.

'What did you expect to get out of going away with
your sweet cousin?'

'Three days,' Hervey said.   Realising that she would
have to give these up she began to cry quietly and bitterly.
She was surprised and ashamed.   With a severe effort she
stopped at once.   She sat looking at her hands to calm
herself.

'If you were not—does he want to marry you?' Penn
asked.

'No.'

'Then the visit to Hampshire is an episode?' Penn
exclaimed.   He seemed dumbfounded.   'You can bring
yourself to go with a man who doesn't even pretend—if
you're telling the truth—to think very much of you.   What's
come over you, Hervey?'

'If I knew I would tell you,' Hervey said.   She trembled.
She could not bring herself to say that Nicholas needed her,
because she had no proof of it.   A memory lightened her
heart—*Love, any devil else but you Would, for a given soule,
give something too.*   'I don't want Nicholas to do anything
for me,' she said, looking at Penn seriously.   'Why do you
think that love must always end in a definite act?   There is
more than one kind.'

'Dear me, very philosophic we've grown,' Penn mocked.
'I suppose you keep on that high level with each other
all the time.   Perhaps he prefers it that way?   Well, so
long as you behave yourself, I shan't disturb you, my dear.
But mind—I won't be made a fool of by you.   Not Penn!'

'You can't watch over me from Oxford,' Hervey said
quietly.   'I'll make a bargain with you.   Give me back the
letters, and I promise you that after the three days are over
I won't see Nicholas again.'   She shut her eyes as she spoke,
to avoid seeing what she was doing.   If he would respond

now, she meant to keep the bargain. She would do anything to get the letters out of his hands.

Penn stood still in front of her. ' If you believe I'll make things easy for you, you're much mistaken,' he said, sneering. ' I'm not going to hand my son over to you, to be brought up by you and your cousin—don't think it. Get that into your head.'

' Are you by any chance going to bring him up yourself? ' Hervey said. At this moment she felt only contempt for him.

There was a silence. Penn sat down again and said in a low voice:

' I never thought you were tired of me, Hervey. All this time I've been at Oxford I've looked forward to living with you and the boy again, in a decent place—I was going to work and try to make something of my life. This finishes me. You didn't mean to do it, but it's what you've done, and only you could have done it to me. It's almost funny. You might as well have taken a knife to me and cut my throat. I would never have believed it of you, Hervey.' His face quivered and he put both hands over it.

This sight was too much for Hervey. She began to cry again, partly for Penn and partly for herself. I have no right to be sorry for myself, she thought angrily, but she could not stop her tears. They seemed to force themselves from the centre of her body. She was wrenched by them. They were sharp and burned her cheeks. After a time Penn forgot his own unhappiness in alarm. He knelt down beside her chair and tried to calm her. Scarcely conscious of him, she let him stroke her hands. He took his handkerchief and wiped away the tears, but they flowed on and on. ' Don't, my dear, don't,' he said.

Now I am going to die, Hervey thought. Her will had not died yet, and she said: ' Will you give me my letters back? '

' Very well,' Penn said.

She seemed to hang in space for a moment. Her mind

cleared. She felt the arm of the chair under her arm and stood up. 'Where are they?' she said softly. She spoke softly because she was afraid of waking his resentment.

'In the cloakroom at the station.'

She wiped her face, felt that she could walk, and stroked Penn's cheek. 'Dear kind Penn. Can I have them at once?'

'Do you want me to go there now?'

'I'll come with you.'

They went and Penn drew the parcel out and gave it to her. It was now nine o'clock. Hervey felt exhausted and empty. On the way home she took Penn's arm, making herself as soft and dependent as a child. He began to talk of his work at Oxford, and of the criticisms he was writing for the *London Review*. 'I'm turning out better stuff than any of your big bugs, though I say it as it shouldn't,' he said, with energy.

Again, she felt a strange hot pity for him. His boasting alarmed her. I should be less responsible for him if he made a success of something, she thought. Actually, the criticisms were not good enough, and it was with difficulty she persuaded Evelyn to use them. Hervey disliked the feeling that, but for her, Penn would not have even this trivial satisfaction. It made her ashamed.

'Have you read the newer French critics? I can lend you two or three books,' she said eagerly.

'Thanks, but I don't need to go to school again,' he laughed.

They walked on slowly, in silence. Hervey could scarcely put one foot before the other. She recalled the promise she had made to give up Nicholas. She would never give Richard up. Her softness covered what was as fixed in her as iron—her will to keep her son and without losing the other. She was afraid Penn would ask to stay the night with her, and she would be ashamed to refuse. But he said nothing. He allowed her to make up a bed for him on the sitting-room couch, and she went upstairs and fell asleep at once, first putting the letters in a safe place.

Penn went off early to Oxford. The next morning she had a letter from him, asking her 'to send Nicholas packing. I appeal to your generosity,' he wrote. He has made up his mind that Nicholas is indifferent to me, she thought. She had no intention of losing her three days. Penn's appeal made no sense in her mind and she destroyed his letter and forgot it. She had come to an end of her generosity to him. A certain heavy sense warned her that she had not finished with feeling responsible for him. She was a Calvin to herself, only to herself, and she was certain that she would pay for her happiness. No doubt, she said, there is a Chief Accountant in charge, and the bill will be presented.

For all that she went to stay at Stockbridge, leaving Georgina with Richard. She and Nicholas were the only visitors in the small and curiously solid hotel, everything about it made to last, in an age which believed in the future. They arrived early in the afternoon and Hervey was impatient until she had found a way to take him to Broughton, to the village in which she lived during the War. It slept under the southern edge of the downs. There was a narrow and very steep path leading to the downs and as they climbed, 'I am taking you,' Hervey said, 'to one of the most beautiful single places in the world, my own country of Danesacre not excepted.'

She led him through the trees to the green edge of the downs. Behind them were beeches on which the young leaves were scarcely grown, transparent, as though light ran in their veins, and below, the open valley, the river, and the scattered hamlets. 'This is the most English of the counties,' said Hervey; 'nowhere else is the turf so fine, the hills rounder and plainer, and the trees fresher. I was happier here than anywhere,' she said smiling.

'Happier than you are now?' Nicholas asked.

'Freer,' Hervey said, when she had thought for a minute. She could not even to herself explain better what she had lost.

Nicholas had been watching her. 'There is some trouble in your mind.'

Hervey was surprised and touched. She was unused to so much interest, since if Penn thought she was troubled he took care not to gratify her by asking a question. 'Yes,' she said diffidently, and thinking that he would have to know some time, she told him that Penn had read his letters.

Nicholas listened without seeming disturbed or vexed. 'What does he mean to do?' he asked.

'I'm not sure,' Hervey said. She was still certain of being able to lead Penn, but she delayed, without knowing why, to tell Nicholas this. Perhaps she did not want to make it easy for him. She was not invariably soft with any person, except with her son.

'Did he know you were coming here?'

'Yes,' Hervey said. 'But he hoped I would change my mind.'

'He may decide to divorce you,' Nicholas said quietly. He touched her hand. 'If he does we must be prepared for it. I should ask Jenny to divorce me, and we can marry.'

'It would be a long troublesome business,' Hervey said, watching him.

'It would be unbearable. But we may have no choice.'

'Would it do you harm?'

'In my business? Oh no, I don't think so,' Nicholas said drily.

She was too shrewd, as well as too sensitive, to like the thought of driving him into marriage. Such a bargain is a bad bargain, she told herself grimly. At the same time she felt uncertain and weak. But I must do nothing at all; I must let time arrange it. This was harder for her stubborn will than any subtler plan could be.

'I am certain I can keep Penn quiet,' she said. 'It would be a mistake to have trouble now, when the new business of Nicholas Roxby Ltd. has hardly started.'

'And what if he were to make conditions?' Nicholas

said, half vexed. ' He might want a promise from you not
to see me. Most men would.'

' Should you mind ? '

' I don't think I can do without you.'

Her heart jumped. ' There is no reason why you should.
I can arrange that too,' she said, keeping her voice and face
quiet.

Nicholas sat for a time in silence. ' You make me feel a
coward.'

' Nonsense,' said Hervey lightly. ' You are not a coward,
you are my dear love.'

It was time to go. Hervey turned back once to look.
An emotion—half grief, half exultant joy—flooded her
mind. ' Let me look at you,' said Nicholas. She stood
still obediently. When their hands joined, a sharp ecstasy
filled her. It was like nothing she had experienced, and
she remembered it. Her ecstasies were more often from
the mind. They went back to Stockbridge, crossing the
clear green Test which runs through this valley, Stockbridge
one of the villages strung on its cool thread. Towards dark
Hervey went upstairs; she undressed without lighting the
candles, and waited. Nicholas's room opened into hers.
When he came in he said at once: ' Oh Hervey, are you sure
you want to go on with me ? I'm no good for anything.
I shall hurt and disappoint you.'

This at least was simple enough. ' I have no choice,'
she said smiling. ' I love you so much.'

On the third morning, when she had already filled her
shabby suitcase, Nicholas asked her to stay two more days.
Poor Hervey—the colour ran to her cheeks.

' I should like to stay. I would if it were not for Richard.'

' Why Richard ? '

' He is expecting me,' said Hervey.

Nicholas looked at her with a little surprise. ' Is that
your only reason for going at once ? '

' I haven't another,' she said, in confusion, wishing
strongly that she had had the wit to think of one. She

was unscrupulous in getting her way and yet had a great many scruples—one of them concerned Richard. In all honesty she believed she was not justified in denying him anything. You can say she was a bad mother, but when so many good mothers have bad sons, can you be sure? There may even be another war and then what will have been the worth of severity?

AFTER six o'clock Gary was alone in his flat. He came back from the gymnasium, dressed, and sat down to wait for Nicholas. When the bell rang he opened the door, expecting Nicholas, and it was Georgina who stood there smiling. He led the way to the sitting-room and talked as quickly as though he were pleased to see her. She looked round her at the books, the waxed floor, the chairs, and said: 'One would think you liked to spend money.'

'Why should you suppose I don't?'

'You once told me that all you needed for happiness was a room with a lock, a set of maps and a rucksack. This flat belongs to a rich man.'

'That must have been before the War,' Gary said. 'Shall I get you some tea? Sherry?'

'May I have a whisky and soda?' Georgina said.

He poured it out for her, and one for himself, which he left untasted. 'You didn't send an answer to my message,' Georgina said in a light voice. 'So I've had to come for it myself. Perhaps Nicholas never gave it to you.'

Gary moved slowly across the room to a couch nearer to her. He seated himself heavily, like a sack doubled in the centre, his eyelids twitching as they did when he was intent on some thought. He ended by coming straight at the point. 'But I've given up amusing myself.'

'Riding, dining out, walking—you've given all that up? Even if I ask you to do them with me?'

'I can't stand the tone in which people amuse themselves

now,' Gary said violently. 'London has turned rotten.
What do you expect when the only people with the energy
to amuse themselves are young women, and boys who spent
their last year at school waiting to be called up—and the
wily birds who found safe jobs? Oh I know the suburbs
and the provinces are full of the new growth, but you're
not asking me to meet it, and in any case I couldn't talk
to it. It has a new language as well.'

Georgina looked down at her hands crossed on her knees.
She had pulled her hat off and a shining wing of hair hid
her profile. He was angry with her for coming, yet when
he looked at the fold of hair he remembered touching it.
He even remembered that he had wished passionately to
hold and kiss it. A revulsion of dislike made him jump
up and walk across the room.

'I suppose my life does seem trivial to you,' Georgina
said softly.

'Not at all.'

'I like dancing and running from house to house and
seeing people and talking to them.' She smiled. 'Do you
know I'm convinced that I shall die young? It's quite
necessary for me to enjoy things now. If my life is to be
short, I want it to be a succession of splendid dazzling
scenes.'

Gary controlled a wish to hurt her by making fun of
this nonsense. He halted in front of her. 'Quite a number
of my friends used to feel like that,' he said gravely, 'and
in the end most of them did die young.' He added in a
rougher voice: 'Just as well for them they did. Yesterday
I went down to a police court to see what I could do for a
young man, one of my company commanders. He was
charged with drunken disorder. It came out that he had
had no work since he was demobilised. He begged and
did odd jobs and drank the money. It was no use my
swearing what was true that the boy had been a good and
reliable officer. The old tired ape on the bench said that
made his conduct all the worse. My testimony added a

month to his sentence. They don't realise, these fools of magistrates, that although that boy looked sane he was in fact mad. He went mad during the War.'

' He can never have been strong in his head.'

Gary was irritated by her light voice. 'Nonsense,' he said loudly. ' Every fighting soldier and some civilians went mad during the War. Those who had enough imagination cured themselves. Others, if they had no anchor and no friends—like my young company commander—succumbed. What I can't stand is the abysmal lack of imagination, not to speak of human decency or gratitude, that condemns him to rot away when he is no longer needed to play at heroes with his immature body and mind.' He stopped, ashamed of having lost his temper, and said quietly: ' He should have been killed. So should I.'

Georgina looked at him in surprise and grief. 'Why? Please tell me why, dear dearest Bill. Is there nothing I can do?' She leaned forward, close to him, her eyes filling with tears. ' There is nothing I wouldn't do to help you, if you would let me.'

Gary's hands jerked upwards, fingers spread out—gesture of involuntary rage and pain. His heavy body leaned there unmoved. ' Very kind of you to feel like that,' he said quietly.

At this moment Nicholas walked in. He had found the front door open. Georgina pretended not to notice him.

' We used to be such friends,' she said softly. ' Now since you came home you never come near me. Is it because of Charles Frome?'

' I don't take any interest in Frome,' Gary answered.

Georgina looked at him for a second as though he had stunned her. She recovered at once. She stood up, nodded to Nicholas, and said, ' How simple!' She smiled at Gary. ' Don't think you have finished with me,' she said in a merry voice.

Nicholas picked up her hat.

' Would you like to put that on in here?' Gary said gently. He opened the door of a bedroom.

'No. You shall tell me if it looks all right,' she answered. She stood in front of them with an expectant smile.

'You look lovely—wonderful,' Nicholas said.

When she had gone, he turned to his friend and began to speak about the coal strike in Gary's mines in Lanarkshire. He wanted Gary to make concessions. Gary listened with impatience and in a few moments he lost his temper completely and abused Nicholas without restraint.

'What you're saying is mere sentimental Socialism,' he shouted. 'You've been in bad company lately. I treat the men properly, and if they choose to go on strike they're no better than deserters. Far worse—poor devils of soldiers had an excuse for running. Have you any idea what the miners are like? Overgrown greedy children—savages—louts——'

Nicholas listened in silence. He waited until Gary was out of breath: then he said quietly: 'No, this is no use.'

Gary looked at him with nervously blinking eyelids. His hands, which had been gripping the couch, loosened. He stood up quickly and heavily. Nicholas knew what he would say before he spoke.

'Come along, Nicholas.'

Nicholas fell into line and they moved off together. There seemed nothing in this particular moment to distinguish it from the earlier ones, yet in fact it was completely and irrevocably different.

CHAPTER XV

EARLHAM DINES WITH WILLIAM GARY

EARLHAM was pleased and gently surprised by the letter inviting him to dine with Gary. The two had met less than a week earlier, at the House of Commons. Earlham was walking through the lobby when a Liberal member who knew him slightly seized his arm, with the words: 'Earlham, you can answer this fellow's questions better than I can. My friend William Gary. Louis Earlham. Do forgive me now, I must go.'

Their talk, which lasted less than a quarter of an hour, left in Earlham's mind a vaguely pleasant image. The more he thought about it, the better he was pleased to think of meeting the other man again.

Gary had chosen a restaurant in but not of Soho, new, expensive, discreet. He looked at Earlham with a friendly smile. 'Writers, actresses and the 1912 Young Set, faint but still pursuing,' he said. 'I thought you might prefer not to be seen dining with me. I am, after all, a wicked mine-owner. You and I are enemies. But considering that it is only five or six years since we were on the same side, I thought I might ignore politics and allow myself a human pleasure.'

Earlham felt a warm thrill. It wiped out the curiosity with which he had been waiting to hear why he was asked to dine. He liked William Gary. He was a little diffident about beginning the conversation. Suppose I bore him? he thought anxiously. But Gary had begun to talk of the War. It is the *lingua franca* of a generation. The survivors have only to remember the names of places, and with them certain dates in the years 1914-18. With these they can go anywhere, in an area enclosed between defined ages —which is after all less troublesome than other frontier barriers. Earlham found himself talking without awkwardness. An emotion of gratitude seized him. He began, with vivid impatience, to think how he could return the meal. I shall invite him, he thought, to the House. A vision of his own half-furnished dining-room, Rachel carrying out the used dishes, displeased him.

' Brass hats plagued us during the War, and they plague us now,' Gary said. He began to tell Earlham about a Trades Union official who had forbidden changes which would have lightened the work without affecting any part of the routine. He broke off to say smiling—' I mustn't talk about these things to you. You're forced to support your own particular brass hats. When I trespass on a forbidden area, warn me off, and I'll withdraw at once. In good order.'

Earlham looked at him with a confused smile. ' No one can dislike brass hats as much as I do,' he said.

' The common enemy,' said Gary. He lifted his glass. ' May they be caught by their own shells! '

' My experience in the War was that men are on the whole decent and simple. If they have decent rations, and are not harried by a great many unnecessary orders, they are good children.'

' Exactly.' Gary spoke eagerly, with the smile that had charmed Earlham. Coming and going on a face so heavy as Gary's it had a disarming gentleness. ' It is even possible that you and I want the same kind of world. Without brass hats, and with plenty to eat and good dry quarters for the men. We can meet out of sight of our respective brass hats and exchange views. You know more than I do about certain things. But I may even be some little use to you on occasion. What do you think? '

CHAPTER XVI

GARY was seated in his own library, with Thomas Harben. It was six o'clock. There were wine glasses, two decanters, and a dish of early strawberries at one end of the table. The rest was strewn with papers which Gary began to gather together and insert into folders. 'It's extraordinarily kind of you to help me in this way,' he began.

'Nonsense,' said Harben. 'If we are to be allies, you must see all the necessary information, ground plans, and orders of the day.' He paused. 'I can't remember that I ever had an ally,' he said. 'I shall probably overfeed you in my anxiety.'

This was said with so much simplicity that the younger man was abashed. With the best will in the world it was impossible to feel any human emotion towards Thomas Harben. Can it be possible that he wants to be liked? Gary thought, with horror. 'Who is this fellow, Swan?' he asked quickly.

'Some degree of cousin of my wife's.'

'Do you think he's the man we want?'

Harben looked down his long nose. 'Well connected, poor, ambitious, energetic, intelligent.' He was going to say more when Gary's servant came in, followed by Julian Swan. 'You're five minutes late,' he said instead: he nodded towards Gary. 'This is Swan.'

'Very good of you to come,' Gary said at once. He noticed that the young man was lame, and that the edges of his cuffs were shiny. His clothes had been good when they were made, but it was a long time ago. He was extremely handsome, with reddish fair hair, tall, well built except for his lameness, his head narrow, his mouth small, fine, and too expressive. There may be some Jew in him, Gary thought. Watching him carefully he saw that Swan was taken aback and angered by Harben's deliberate rudeness. The colour in his cheeks heightened, and he was on the point of making a retort. That will do the poor devil no good, Gary thought ironically. He leaned forward. 'Will you sit here?' he said with a smile.

'Thank you,' Julian Swan answered. He sat stiffly in his chair, with folded arms, waiting to be addressed.

'Sherry or a whisky and soda?'

'Neither, thank you,' Swan said. He smiled for the first time. Ah, said Gary, he has thought better of an impulse he can't afford. This poor young devil suffers from vanity—it would be pride if he were not poor.

'Now to come to the point,' Harben said. 'You've read the memorandum I sent you. Do you understand what it's about?'

The young man looked at him with scornful energy and spoke in a low steady voice: 'I understand that you have collected money from a number of industrialists, directors and so on, in order to found a society to protect your interests against the spread of subversive movements and doctrines. Your memorandum speaks of an Economic Council. You intend this Council to issue leaflets and hold meetings; to make use of the press; to keep dossiers of suspected persons, and to watch the activities of movements and societies which threaten the industrial machine. You believe that the State should exercise its authority over the lower orders and inferior nations, while leaving industry and private enterprise alone——'

'Good heavens,' Gary said, smiling, 'there is no need for you to recite the whole of the memorandum. All we want to know is whether your sympathies are with order or revolution. At the same time you might eat a strawberry or two if you won't drink. I'll tell you what—these forced berries don't taste of anything very much—they're improved by dipping in a thin wine. Try it.' He pushed the dish of strawberries over towards Swan as he spoke, and when his servant came in—' Open a bottle of the Niersteiner,' he said to the man. The curiously greedy look on Julian Swan's face amused him. With a slight smile he watched the young man dipping strawberries and eating them until the dish was almost emptied. In the meantime Harben asked several questions, all of which Swan answered with energy and increasing good humour. He spoke Italian and Spanish, he said. He detested Socialism. He was extremely strong. ' And your leg?' asked Harben.

At this abrupt reference to his lameness Swan blushed hotly. He had difficulty in answering, and again Gary interrupted to help him. ' You were in the War?'

' Only for eight months,' Swan said in a sharp voice. ' I was wounded very slightly. I had a motoring accident last year in which I broke both legs. I'm lame in one ankle. It doesn't touch my health. I can still hunt and box—I rode a hundred miles a day for five days in Spain this winter. Do you know Spain?'

Gary lifted his hands, denying and rejecting. ' Yes. Well.'

' It is still a country in which people think more of courage and imagination than of cleverness,' Swan said. ' I detest cleverness.'

' I don't encourage my subordinates to be too clever,' Harben said drily. His eyes shone maliciously and he pressed his long fingers on the table with a brutal vigour. ' My wife does. It is one of many differences between us. I have no doubt she'd prefer to make a poet of you, but if you're going to direct this Council you must decide to give up poetry. Can you do that?'

' With the greatest ease,' Julian said.

Less than five minutes later he was leaving the flat, appointed director of the Economic Council with a salary of five hundred pounds. Before the door of the room closed he had heard Thomas Harben saying: ' Do you agree that he is energetic? ' I might be a well-paid slave, he thought, with a spasm of fury.

In a few moments he had forgotten it in the intoxication of success. Now I am on my way, he thought. Joy seized him. He saw about him in the May-bright evening a new London. Shop windows crammed with riches, endless streams of cabs and buses carrying people to their amusement, even the beggars and match-sellers were caught into the luminous moment and there fixed, as in a painting by Canaletto, so firm, so clear were the shapes and colours of the scene. He made his way east along Piccadilly and at last stepped into a bus and was carried as far as St. Paul's Cathedral before he came to himself. There he stood on the pavement, and debated whether he would go home or spend one of his few notes on a meal. Looking up he saw the great dome of the church like a ball of light spinning in the blue of space. The wish seized him to stand there and look down on the conquered city. He went in, paid his money. The first and longest stage of the climb left him panting and exhausted, his ankle in torment. He paid again and went on.

When he stepped out on to the gallery he met a rush of cool wind. He was alone there. He could lean against the wall, feeling the pressure on his heart loosed and his head becoming light and clear. He looked down over London, over the desert of roofs to the sky line, fringed with trees, with yet more buildings; looking at the bright snake of water, at the docks, the bold lines of bridges, the many spires, domes, factory chimneys, parks. He saw that ships lay between houses, that cliffs of stone and mortar can take on the dignity of *mesas* in a dry country, that the marshes and forests familiar to the Romans and to the men before the Romans have not completely vanished. A familiar excitement possessed him. He felt lifted up before the world—' What a city to sack! ' he murmured. His blood shook in his body. I am the modern *condottiere*, he thought:

hereby I declare war on all spineless snickering intellectuals, blind-at-birth idealists, liberals, pacifists, shopkeepers. I am intoxicated with life, I intend to drink, ride, eat, fight, make love, as much as I please. The white-faced black-coated shopkeepers, for whom carefulness and liberalism were invented, have ruled the world long enough! When they came it was still a tournament, and they have turned it into a dingy market. They said, All men are brothers—so that they could cheat their brothers in peace: they preached Liberalism only to save their miserable sickly skins from being drubbed by some young man with more courage than money; they taught their children to speak of heroic action as violence, they pulled down the altars of the sun and set the golden calf there. Because they feared life, they feared death. Hence the stale and stuffy bethels of democracy— a world safe for shopkeepers. Hear me; it is I, I, Julian Swan, leaning over your ant-heap. If you smother me, at least I shall crush some of you first with my foot. But you won't smother me so quickly and easily! Put your shutters up and crouch in your back rooms with the till, you will hear our shouts in the street, laughing and threatening we shall break in on you; we shall bring back to the world danger and glory, the *élan vital*; all that the sneering lying half-men have destroyed we restore, we, the whole men, the captains in armour.

He saw the Economic Council—a council of shopkeepers! —as a door. He had no clear notion where it would lead him, but he struck it with his foot and passed through. His mind leaped forward to a moment when he would stand in Trafalgar Square, with the phalanxes of his young men— as in Rome he had seen Mussolini stand, and the arms lifted, the flags, the music, the shouts of five thousand as one shout. He raised his own arm. He beckoned. A disciplined wave moved over Whitehall, and the foam of its shouting flew over the whole country, bringing hope and life where it fell. 'Ave, Julian!' After all, it was an Emperor's name.

Two schoolboys had crept out on to the gallery and were watching his gestures with the aloof embarrassed interest of the young. He dropped his arm, and still secure in his dream, strode past them to the low doorway and plunged at the first stairs. Before he reached the ground he had run out of breath and illusions and had begun to think about his dinner.

He lived in a single room, once a servant's bedroom, in Queen Street, Mayfair. After looking into his notecase he decided against dinner: he bought a quarter of a pound of *Leber-wurst* and some fruit and carried them home to his attic. There, he took into his head to ring up Evelyn Lamb. She was alone and she invited him to supper. He put the food he had bought into his cupboard and went off at once. On the way he thought a little about her, but more about the meal he was going to eat. Since she had spoken of supper, it would be cold—perhaps cold chicken, a salad, and a bottle of burgundy. She was alone—that meant a simple meal—but she was well off and from that he hoped for the best and even for some out-of-season delicacy. He enjoyed good food and good drink.

Evelyn had invited him to fill a blank evening. Before he rang up she was lying on her bed, thinking with despair and anger of her life. She was tired of everything, of her work, her reputation, her friends. When she thought that in the morning she would have to dress, to go to the office, to read the proofs of her weekly article—written, as always now, with the last drops of her blood—no, it was too much. She groaned with boredom. There was a dinner party to-night, to which she should have gone, but at the last moment she had telephoned an excuse. She was ill, worn out—actually, she was as well as ever, but it was the thought of seeing the same faces and hearing the same careful and witty remarks made in voices all alike and all, whether slow or hurried, coming to the same pre-arranged end—I can't do it, I can't bear it, she thought.

She rose. She walked to the window and pressed herself

against the glass, looking into the street. Surely something must happen soon. Someone would come. Life, stagnant as a pool cut off from its source, would begin to stir in her— At forty-two I can't be finished, she thought in panic. Something strange has happened to my mind—it is worn out, I can't think; in a short time I shan't be able even to add one word to another: I am ruined. She stroked her cheek, feeling it smooth and unblemished. A thought touched the surface of her mind—The new oil I am using is good—if there were oils to feed the mind. If there were only oil for the dry mind and the dry spirit. I shall go away. I shall leave everything and hide myself in some village.

At this moment the bell rang. She listened to Swan's voice as if it were a reprieve. She ordered the cook to prepare a cold *suprême de volaille* and to bring up a bottle of the Meursault. Then she went into her bedroom, looked at her face, changed her slippers, and waited.

Swan came into the room slowly. When he walked slowly and very deliberately he was not lame. His lameness was always in his mind.

The supper was better than he had hoped—slices of breast of chicken, with cold asparagus tips buried under the cream, excellent wine, coffee, old brandy—he ate and drank with frank enjoyment. Evelyn could not help laughing at him. It was a long time since she had watched a young man so unashamedly and joyfully greedy.

' You know all the wrong young men,' he observed. ' I can live on crusts without grumbling, but when I am given good food I like it. I live in my senses as well as in my mind. The delicate squeaking intellectuals you admire so much have no stomachs, no virility, and no life. Their brains have sucked them dry. Why do you bother with them? They don't give you any pleasure. They feel none themselves.'

' But you don't deny the intellect? ' Evelyn said mildly. She was too used to her reputation as a critic and arbiter of taste to think of defending it.   Lesser women needed defence, she did not.

'The modern intellect is only a morbid growth,' Swan retorted. 'The invention of Jews and liberals. One of these days there will be a rush of clean blood through society, driving them out. Do you know what? The world is tired to death of your contemptible intellectuals—what have they ever done to succour it?—there are fewer free men to-day than in any age. Why, you are tired of them yourself, Evelyn.' He rested his elbows on the table and looked at her with a young charming smile. 'I shall call you Evelyn, it is the right name for you, smooth and yet grave,' he said softly, but with a subdued insolence. His blue eyes gleamed.

'As you please,' Evelyn answered. She could have snubbed him so easily that she would not take the trouble to do it. His admiration soothed her. She listened when he spoke of the need for authority, for a leader—to restore to men their lost confidence in themselves as men and not cogs in a machine.

'Yes, it is true,' she said suddenly. 'It is true, Julian. We do need authority—obedience—life must become simple again!'

The void within her was created only by the disorder in the world. Her strength was used up in finding reasons for this and that impulse. Now if I could rest on something I should be at peace, she thought. But the thought became confused and vanished. She let her gaze move from Swan's lively face to the shape of his body—long, with flattened curves and thin ankles. His fine reddish hair was cut close, like a glossy skin stretched over the bones of his head. A sensual excitement filled her. She imagined herself crouching beside him and her hands moving here and there—there was no one image, but she saw herself making this gesture and that until her head grew light and her mind a blur.

Swan rose to go. It had been clear to him for some minutes that he could do as he pleased. It was not caution that restrained him so much as the streak of cruelty in his nature. Let her think about me for a time, he said to himself. He gripped her hand so strongly that she winced.

When he had gone Evelyn began to prepare herself for the night. After her bath and the oiling and massage of her face, she locked the door of her bedroom and crossed the room quickly to the windows, taking care not to tread on certain marks in the steel floor. She drew the curtains apart, then, moving with the same care, returned to her dressing-table and arranged the candlesticks and other things on it in a definite pattern—it was the shape of a star. To assure herself she glanced round the room. A chair stood out from the wall in its wrong place. Evelyn frowned with vexation. Now it was necessary to begin over again from the start, unlock and lock the door, cross the room, re-draw the curtains, arrange the dressing-table, then walk watchfully to the bed. Here she placed the three pillows so that one lay across the bed in the usual way, with the others at the sides, to form the letter H. It was the initial of her dead sister's Christian name, as well as Hervey Russell's. For an unfathomed reason it gave her a strong feeling of ease and security to lay her head on their names.

It was only within the last year that she had elaborated this ritual, but already it was part of her life. No one must disturb her at it and no change be made in its order. When it was finished she felt relieved and comforted, and could rest.

CHAPTER XVII

NICHOLAS HATES TROUBLE

AT the end of his term at Oxford Penn went into the country, to his mother. He stayed a few hours in London on the way and saw Hervey. It was a warm close day, without wind or sun, and she was listless, tired of Evelyn, of Evelyn's exacting and uncertain temper. She made an effort to talk to Penn.

'Next year at this time you will have taken your Final.'

'Much good it will do me,' Penn said. 'I wish to heaven I hadn't gone to Oxford. We might have been living peacefully together somewhere——'

Hervey looked at him with a curious expression. She felt sorry for him and at the same time indifferent. 'We were never peaceful together,' she said, to console him. 'I was too ambitious and you are much too easily offended and careless. You should have married some quite different person.'

'You make other women seem dull,' Penn said.

'Poor Penn,' Hervey said. She looked through the open door of her room to the landing window. The upper branches of an elm tree in the yard stirred faintly in a current of wandering air . . . at once she remembered a group of trees overhanging a lane near the university where she and Penn were students. They walked here, and it was here when she said she loved him he had answered, ' Poor Hervey,' as if he knew what lay waiting for them. How I have failed you since then, she thought, forgetting his unkindness. And now how I am starving you of love and help. The conviction seized her that she would be punished for her

treachery. She put up a fierce silent prayer. Punish me,
and not Richard. Or Nicholas, she added as an afterthought.

'What are you going to do about me?' her husband said
abruptly. 'What's in the back of your mind? If you ever
look there—my God, it must be a labyrinth of a place.'

'Nothing but tiredness,' Hervey said.

'What's the matter with you?'

'I don't know. Evelyn keeps me until four o'clock, then
I go home—and play with Richard and put him to bed.
Then if I don't come back to town I write until two or
three o'clock. It's all the time I have.'

Penn looked at her with resentment. 'I suppose you
mean I ought to support you, so that you could write your
precious novels.'

'Oh, no,' Hervey said quickly. Why need you suspect
me? she said. From the beginning, even before their
marriage, he had accused her of every wrong motive. In
those days I was simple enough, she thought. She looked
at his face—as smooth as a boy's for all he was thirty-three,
more than three years her senior—in a moment he would
lose his temper with her. 'I write as often as I care to,' she
said soothingly. 'I don't like writing.'

'Then why do it?'

She was going to say: 'For money for Richard,' when
she remembered that this, too, would offend him. She held
her tongue.

'You look tired, Hervey,' he said gently. 'Aren't you
well?'

'I have had that pain.'

'Where is it, I don't know anything about it,' Penn said.

'I've told you about it,' Hervey said smiling. 'It comes
here'—she laid her hand fleetingly on her body, over the
pelvis. 'Like the sharp blade of a knife,' she added, without
much concern. It never occurred to her that she was made
of anything less tough than iron.

'You'd better see a doctor about it,' Penn said indifferently.
He knew she would not. He took her great strength for

granted, as she did. 'And now I must go, Hervey. Are you going to kiss me?'

'Well, why not?' Hervey smiled. She laid an arm on his shoulder. It was impossible that she had loved him and yet—ah, I shall never free myself from him, she thought. This was bitter to her, and yet she was sorry for him and she denied him. There was no warmth, nothing better than kindness in her touch.

'I suppose you're waiting your own time to leave me,' Penn said. 'Let me know what you arrange,' he said coldly. 'You *manager*.'

'I'm not managing this,' Hervey said, with present honesty. 'I can't promise you very much, Penn—but if you'll leave me alone I promise not to do anything without warning you.'

'Oh, I'll leave you alone,' he laughed. 'Thank you for giving me lunch. I can't afford an expensive meal myself. When shall I see you again? God knows. Never mind— I love you and I always shall. You're my dear Hervey, whether you like it or not.'

Two days after he went she had a letter from him accusing her of every shape of deceit. He gave her a week to decide whether she would give Nicholas up completely. 'If you refuse I shall divorce you,' he wrote. He said nothing at all about Richard.

It was Richard's birthday. There were presents for him from her mother, and three from herself but nothing from Penn. He has forgotten, she thought, in real anger. She put five shillings into an envelope, wrote 'With love from Penn' across it, and laid it with the others. Richard *shan't* be disappointed, she said passionately.

She spent the day with Richard, not taking him to school. Under its surface her mind was busy with the new event. She did not always take Penn seriously but there was the chance that he was in earnest. At best he would be dis-agreeable. He has confided in his mother, she thought, seeing clearly Mrs. Vane's innocent shrewd face and clear eyes, and the thought behind them unyielding and simple. Hervey's unmeaning charity towards everyone covered Penn's mother, who did not like her. In Hervey at eighteen, timid, childish, as friendly and awkward as a puppy, she discerned an erratic and wilful temper and she knew that no good would come of the marriage. Penn was her only child.

Next afternoon Hervey made an excuse to leave the *Review* at two o'clock. She went directly to Nicholas's house. He was in the little room where he wrote his letters. His secretary, Mrs. Hughes, smiled at her with a mingling of sympathy and disapproval, and went away.

'What is it?' Nicholas said.

She showed him Penn's letter. Seated at the other side of his desk she watched him while he read it through twice. If he will help me, she thought, looking at him—she felt confused and shy. Nicholas gave the letter back to her.

'What do you want me to do?' he asked quickly.

'Nothing,' Hervey said. 'I thought you should see it,' she added slowly. She felt ashamed.

'I'll do anything you like. But is he—does this letter mean what it says?'

'How do I know?' Hervey said ironically. She saw that he was puzzled and in a nervous irritable mood. For another moment she sat quietly watching him. Her self-confidence had left her and she did not know what to say. Suddenly she could not sit still any longer. She jumped up and said excitedly: 'It doesn't matter. I can arrange it—there will be no need for you to do anything.'

'For goodness sake sit down again and keep quiet,' Nicholas said. His eyes were unkind and over-bright; his face expressed exasperation and bitter doubt. At last he stood up, took hold of her by the shoulders and kissed her lightly.

'Don't answer the letter, let him do his worst.'

She watched him closely. 'You don't want that, Nicholas.'

'It had to come sooner or later,' Nicholas answered. 'It would have been easier a little later, but it can't be helped.'

' I must go,' Hervey said, looking round her. She went away quickly, avoiding Mrs. Hughes, who had been waiting in the hall to stare at her. I was wrong to come here, she thought drily. She saw that Nicholas dreaded the trouble involved in a divorce—he would have to tell his wife and his friends, and he had no energy with which to face it; he was tired with the strain of his new business, and the uncertainty. He had risked all his money in it.

After a time Hervey felt a strange exhilaration. I am alone, I have no one helping me, she thought: it is better.

Next day he rang her up at the office and asked her to dine with him. She saw at once that he had thought himself into a fever. Though she tried hard, she could not reach him. After their meal he told her, using as few words as enough, that they had better not see each other at present. He spoke in jerks. His face was drawn with the effort, and grey. Hervey would have given much* to be allowed to take his body in her arms and rest him. You might as well dream of resting a torrent, she thought with a flash of humour. She could only listen. When he stopped speaking she said quietly, ' Never mind, Nicholas. I can't argue with you about it. I think you're spoiling us both, but you must do as you like.'

' I'm forcing the colour out of my life,' Nicholas said.

Then why do it? Hervey thought. He left his chair and stood close to her for a moment, half leaning on her, as if he were tired to death. Now when if she chose she might hold him, her arms stayed at her side. As soon as she could without haste, she went away. In the train she fell asleep and awoke a moment before it reached her station—she stumbled out, still half asleep. The moon was high and full. It was for a time veiled by clouds so that the light seemed to spring from them. Etched in light, the leaves of the trees floated on darkness. Hervey walked slowly, buoyed up by the exhilaration she had felt before. It is something to have lost all, to be naked as at birth. That is, when one is young—later, body and mind shiver at the thought of loneliness: the time is too short ahead. With new eyes, she noticed the sharp edges of grass, the markings, as fresh as if just made by a pen, on the shell of a benighted snail. All was changed by the experience of loneliness. She had grown hard, self-certain, proud.

This went very well for a time, and she was lying in bed when the first wave of grief caught her. She sat up and broke into a passion of weeping, pressing her hands over her mouth to stifle the sound. She felt as though a weight were crushing her breast. Richard moved slightly in his bed. She became still at once, and now a cold lucid anguish seized her. She got up and felt about in the darkness for a small photograph of Nicholas she had in the pocket of her coat, and held it in her hands. Her pain was direct and simple, a sense of unendurable loss. After a time she fell asleep, but her hands remained clenched, and from time to time she opened her eyes and said, 'Nicholas,' softly and in anguish.

In the morning her mind began at once to think of ways in which she could see him again. She had not let him go. He had given her up but she had not agreed to it. The conviction that beneath his impatience and fatigue Nicholas needed her and loved her was stronger in her than before. It was as if he had spoken to her with two voces and she had heard one only. She had no shame and no pride. Both had been reduced to a handful of dust in the flame. Now her wits were sharpened and her mind quickened in an abnormal degree. There was nothing, no audacity of which she was not able, to get her way. Her mind was bent to one end with all the force of a strong, domineering, subtle nature. It was rarely she was roused to use it in this way— for the most part she was too lazy—but when the occasion arose it was a great deal truer to say that she was possessed than possessive.

She had now the sense to be patient. For five days, five long June days, she did not write to Nicholas. She wrote to Penn, a brief temporising letter, and had no answer.

CHAPTER XVIII

LOVE AT FIRST SIGHT

DURING this time she saw her oldest—and except for Georgina—her best loved friend. This was Evelyn's husband. He looked now older than his wife, and actually he was half a year younger than Hervey, and twelve years younger than Evelyn.

He waited for her outside the office of the *Review* for an hour—he would not come inside. He had quarrelled again with Evelyn that morning, and he did not want to see her. He walked with Hervey to the station, talking without saying anything, and when the train came in he said abruptly:

' I shall come down with you. I have a book for Richard's birthday—I didn't forget it on the day but I was busy.'

How kind he is, Hervey thought, and how plain! She looked at him with her strangely impersonal gaze. Even when she liked people, she could not help a movement of cold curiosity towards them.

T. S. Heywood's head was large and heavy for his body: he had a long arched nose, and a mouth which became severe and sardonic when he smiled—he had delighted in this when he was young but he had almost forgotten it. Only Hervey knew that he was shy, and sensitive to the point of idiocy. He looked at her now with a sharp smile.

' Don't stare, our Hervey. You have no manners— I don't wonder you're not a social success.'

' How do you know I'm not? ' Hervey asked lightly.

' Are you? '

' No,' she answered, with a smile. ' When I am forced

to talk to people I am only anxious to please. That is very well at the time but I forget them too quickly.'

'Penn did you a great deal of harm,' T. S. said.

'I'm very hard. You can see I have lived through it without much damage.'

'The harm isn't apparent, except to me—and I knew you when you were a schoolgirl, afraid of nothing and no one. You were like—like a young merry peasant,' he finished badly.

Hervey blushed. 'An awkward companion in a room,' she said.

'You were splendid.'

There was a long silence. 'So you think I've changed for the worse?' Hervey said at last.

'You've lost your self-confidence, and you mistrust everyone,' T. S. said. 'It was bound to happen—you can't spend years fighting lies and unkindness and not change—do you know what Philip and I said to each other when you told us you had married Penn? We said, And that's the end of our Hervey. It was, too. One day just before Philip died—he was wandering and he must have wandered far into the past, because he began to curse Penn for something that happened so long ago I had forgotten it. Why didn't you get rid of him years since, Hervey? You were nineteen when you married and you weren't happy with him for a year. My God, I'll never forget coming to see you both during the War—I thought seriously of killing Penn.'

'He wasn't always unkind or lying,' Hervey said.

'He ruined your life.'

'Yes—in a way. Only in a way. I should have made other mistakes. I don't think sensibly. When I want a thing I want it so badly that I think nothing except how to get it.'

'Then you didn't want to get rid of Penn? I can't believe it. Why, apart from everything else he was an insufferable bore!'

' I couldn't walk out of the house with a young child only because my husband bored me,' Hervey said, laughing. Nor even because he struck me and lied to me, she thought. She did not feel any bitterness. All that seemed in another life. Beside that she had Nicholas now to draw her mind from the past.

' If you hadn't lost courage you would have done it,' T. S. said.

' Perhaps.' She laughed again at his vexed face. ' You are too simple-minded. The truth is—I thought and felt for years that all I wanted was to be rid of Penn. But my will had not left loose of him. As soon as the moment came—when he was cruel, or when I knew he had a mistress to whom he was giving all his money—my will refused to give him up. And there are always practical difficulties. If I could have walked out of the house with Richard— but there were Richard's clothes and his travelling bath and the cot—and all my books and the silver my mother gave me, and my grandmother's tea service, and a chair I liked very much.'

T. S. broke into a fit of laughter. He laughed holding his sides. ' I never heard such nonsense,' he shouted.

' A woman would know it was not nonsense,' said Hervey smiling.

When T. S. could stop laughing, he said: ' And what about Penn's mistress? Was she one of the things you couldn't leave behind ? '

' No, I didn't like it,' Hervey said. She grew very red. ' I behaved badly,' she said, looking at him with honest eyes, honest and yet perplexed, like a child. ' I asked questions. I cried every night for a year. The truth is one forgets to be sensible and experienced at these times— I behaved as if I were nineteen and just married—when I was crying I *was* nineteen. After a time I returned to my proper age and I remembered then that I had no longer any respect for Penn and not much kindness.' She thought for a moment and said: ' It shocks me when you talk as though

I had done something foolish in not getting rid of Penn quickly. You can't treat human beings like that. A little patience. . . . Marriage is a deliberate act. Do you know what?—even now I have the strongest possible feeling that my duty is to my husband and Richard's father. After all, I have taken as much from Penn's life as he from mine.' She frowned and said with some diffidence: ' If he were younger, I should feel happier about leaving him.'

' He's three years older than you are,' T. S. said roughly. ' You can't be responsible for him all your life.'

' You and I were brought up very awkwardly,' Hervey laughed. ' I still believe that if I do wrong I shall be punished. And what is worse, I don't trust Heaven to punish me fairly. It might strike Richard, or play me any other mean trick——'

' My dear little Hervey,' T. S. began, and stopped. He put his hand on her knee. ' Do you trust anyone—me, for instance ? '

' I trust you not to tell me any lies.'

' But you think you know quite as much about life as I do ? Well, never mind—I *am* your friend. If you murder anyone, come to me at once and I'll get rid of the body. I'm very fond of you.' He sat back in his seat, deeply moved, yet angry with her for her stubbornness. To calm himself he told her a ridiculous story about one of Evelyn's dinner parties, where two well-known novelists, who were critics as well, quarrelled so furiously that one of them shouted, ' At least I don't write balderdash.' On which the other replied in a soft voice, ' My dear chap, that is what I complain of in your books—you won't write the only thing you understand.' ' And each of them is over fifty, and has a wife and family,' T. S. said, grinning, ' and then you tell me that novelists show signs of intelligence. Why, they're scarcely human. An impulse to write novels is the mark of an arrested development. . . .'

When they went into Hervey's rooms they found Georgina there, playing with Richard, who had come home early from school. She was on her hands and knees, her shining hair in disorder, her eyes brilliant. Hervey had never seen her so beautiful. She was startled by it, and half saddened, as we are by coming suddenly on very great beauty—it seems to us first as though we had remembered something and then that what is irreplaceable has been lost. T. S. stood with his mouth half open, gaping at her. When Hervey said: 'This is Georgina Roxby,' he took her hand in a grip that made her draw back.

'Have you been here long?' Hervey asked.

'I was here when Richard came home.'

'Thank heaven,' Hervey said.

The others looked at her, T. S. with his sharp smile. 'You think far too much about Richard,' he said. 'Where he's concerned you're not sane.'

Hervey did not answer. Too many other things were involved in her thoughts of her son—her hard youth, the disappointments, tears, the wasted ambitions, all she had been robbed of and all that she had laid down. It was her own youth that talked with her in Richard, and which she was determined to save in him. A fountain of grief sprang in her. She would not allow anyone to see it. 'Who cares what I am or am not?'

T. S. glanced at Georgina. 'Have you any influence with her?'

'Not I!' Georgina laughed.

When Richard had been put to bed, they went out. There was only one walk—through the spoiled wood. It was cold and a high wind had sprung up, clashing the trees and making it difficult to talk.

T. S. had become rude and dictatorial. He lectured them in a loud voice on their shortcomings. 'Hervey keeps her job by lying to people—in another three or four years her mind will be worth nothing. You don't sharpen a knife by misusing it. Or keep it clean. As for you,' he turned to Georgina, 'I can see you are one of these parasitic young women with nothing to do more useful than dancing and dressing yourselves. Tell me what good you are to the world.'

Hervey was surprised and vexed. She tried to quiet him but he blustered on, as if he were too conceited to know he was making a fool of himself. Georgina laughed. In the end she said indifferently, ' I'm sure you're right, and how tiresome it all is. Tell me what good the War was. What do you do for a living?'

' He experiments with a new poisonous gas,' Hervey said, with deliberate malice.

'No doubt that will be useful in ridding the world of another generation of young men,' Georgina said gravely.

T. S. did not answer them. He looked at Georgina with a puzzled face. He knew that she was laughing at him. He was drunk with misery and apprehension. He dropped behind, and Hervey supposed he was feeling ashamed of himself. Actually he was in his mother's kitchen watching her iron his shirts. He had his school satchel under his arm and he was very hungry. His mother looked round at him with a guilty smile, so that he knew she had forgotten to set his tea. Her face was scarlet with the effort of pressing down the heavy iron and she put her hand up to push the wet straight hairs from her forehead. It left a dark smudge, Her blouse gaped away from her skirt at the sides. He was angry with her for being untidy and unpresentable, so that he would be ashamed to bring another boy home, and at the same time she made his heart ache—she was inefficient and overworked and always kind. His throat swelled. An unmanageable emotion assailed him. He did not know what to do, and so he threw his satchel on the table, and shouted: 'Why isn't my tea ready? I have to go.' His mother smiled still, but now it was as if she had hung the smile on her face badly, so that it was not quite straight. She lifted the iron—a brown triangular patch was left on the front of his shirt. Sixteen years ago!—the smell of singeing cloth was in his nostrils.

CHAPTER XIX

NICHOLAS IS CONTENT WITH WHAT HAPPENS

ONE morning at the end of June Evelyn was in a good
mood. She came into the room smiling; she smiled at her
harassed typist, and gave Hervey two carnations she had.
' I bought them for you on the way,' she said. Hervey
did not believe this, and she never knew how to give thanks
for an unwanted gift. She mumbled a word or two, and
seized the moment to remind Evelyn of her promise to
visit Nicholas's house. Evelyn's expression changed. Closing
the door into Hervey's room, so that no one should overhear,
she said:

' Does Penn know about Nicholas? Have you enlightened
him? '

' Yes,' Hervey said. She turned her face away, afraid
that the older woman would see in it that she knew who
had enlightened Penn first. She despised Evelyn for not
knowing that Penn would give her away. For all her
learning, she is stupid about people, Hervey thought. She
has no judgment. She is as stupid as only a very clever
woman can be.

' He has gone away to think about it,' she said.

' Does this Nicholas Roxby want you to marry him? '

' Perhaps it would be better not to marry,' Hervey said.
' That was your advice, and I have not forgotten it. But
if you were to see Nicholas and talk to him, you would
know how I ought to behave. I wish you would see him.
You have so much judgment.' She looked into Evelyn's
face. Her eyes, deep and yet clear, reflected only hopeful-
ness and affection.

139

Evelyn smiled. 'Very well,' she said, 'but we must make a party of it.' She gave Hervey half a dozen names of rich women who would be useful to Nicholas, and told her to invite them. Five of them accepted. Hervey rang up Nicholas, to warn him what to expect. Hearing him speak, she felt light-headed and gripped the edge of her desk. Her heart shuddered in her like a muffled bell. She was able to seem cool and friendly. When she told him that Evelyn Lamb was bringing five other women to see the furniture, he groaned.

'Aren't you pleased?' Hervey said.

'Yes, yes, of course. My God, how awful!'

'You must have people like that. Who else will buy from you?'

'I know. Bless you for arranging it. Are you coming with them?'

'Do you want me?' Hervey asked.

'If you come, I shall enjoy it,' Nicholas said quietly. 'If you don't——'

'Very well then, I'll come.' She had never meant not to come.

She followed Evelyn, Mrs. Thomas Harben, and the other women into the house. They were all smooth elegance, like expensive walking-sticks. Hervey felt a hedgehog among rolls of silks. She did not go with them through the house but stayed behind talking to Mrs. Hughes. She had more than her grandmother's preference for common men and eccentrics—the other classes bored her and she was profoundly impatient of the burden of social inequality. To be naturally stronger or cleverer than the ordinary is very fine: to be richer, and better educated because you are richer, is only burdensome. Mrs. Hughes was shrewd and experienced, and Hervey enjoyed talking to her. She was anxious, too, to make a good impression on Nicholas's secretary.

Evelyn bought a William and Mary tallboy, and Mrs. Harben chose a set of chairs and four Spanish candlesticks of great beauty. The other women exclaimed and chattered and bought nothing. When they were leaving, Hervey stood a little aside. Nicholas took her arm.

' Will you come this evening ? ' he whispered.

Hervey nodded. She knew that she was going to regain her lost place, and she felt strangely unexcited. It was the release of a spring coiled in her body.

It was late, after nine in the evening, when she returned. She could stay less than half an hour, she said. She was nervous and spoke quickly. Nicholas drew her into the sitting-room and kissed her, dragging her head back, and seeming to need the assurance of his hands. He laid his cheek on her forehead and held her so that she could neither breathe nor see him.

' Are you going to take me back ? ' he asked quietly.

' Is it what you want ? '

' More than anything in the world, Hervey.'

Hervey waited a moment. She felt as though she were alone, with darkness around her. ' You go away from me,' she said in a low voice.

' I know. I'll try not to.'

' When you go it means I have to take a long journey to fetch you back.'

' How long a journey, my darling ? '

' East of the Sun and West of the Moon,' Hervey said smiling. She had just remembered it.

' Oh, love, love, I was a fool to think I could do without you.'

' Try not to go away,' Hervey said. ' I can come to look for you a few more times, but not if it happens too often. I should lose courage.' As often, she was saddened by her own words. ' I have a little shame left,' she said weakly.

Nicholas snatched her to him again. ' Forgive me, Hervey, I've been very unkind.'

She turned her head, and set her lips to his sleeve. A deep sense of fulfilment and peace upheld her. She was tired and her eyes smarted. ' I must go home.'

'Not yet,' Nicholas said.

'I must. I'm very tired.'

'You believe I love you, don't you?'

'Yes, I believe you.'

'You need strength and kindness. Instead of giving them to you I torment you.'

'It's not of the least importance,' Hervey said.

Nicholas went with her to the station and looked after her until the train was out of sight. She was glad to be alone. At the next station the carriage emptied; she lay down on the seat. It is foolish to care so much, she thought; I can't help myself, I must do as I can. I am thirty, and I have learned that nothing lasts. I thought that Penn had humiliated me too much. When I was twenty I thought I should be famous in a few years or never. I know now that people like me can't be humbled to death, we are too near the ground and too strong. And I shall never be famous. Hereby I resign ambition, she thought drowsily.

Georgina was still living with her. She did not ask Hervey what had happened. There was a cupful of milk on the table: Georgina took it and went away into the kitchen. When she brought it back, warmed, and gave it to Hervey, she said: 'All right?'

'All right,' Hervey replied, and added as if to herself: 'for the moment.'

Georgina seated herself against the wall, her head held back. Her throat was long and slender, with a faint swelling, and her chin formed another long straight spare line. 'I never knew how many happy people there were in the world until I became unhappy. This evening when I went into the lane there were lovers in every gateway.'

Hervey did not know what to say. She tried to hear her friend's mind. 'Are you only unhappy?' she said at last.

'No. I'm sometimes very happy. When I am dancing, and on clear nights when I can see all London from my window, the dark houses and the lights—strangely few, after all. But the dissatisfaction and the hunger is still—here——'

She let her hand fall again. ' Just now when you came in, your face was peaceful.'

' I can't comfort you,' Hervey said.

' A stupider person would try,' Georgina said quickly, with a smile. ' I've seen William twice in the past month—the first time I went to his flat, and afterwards I made Nicholas take us both out to dinner '—she struck her head lightly on the wall—' Hervey, if I didn't know in my heart that he is—I must have a simple word—bound to me, and to no one else, I would try to forget him. I think of him the whole time.'

Hervey recognised in this her own blind impulse. ' Do you know that there's something *old* in us,' she cried, ' in you, in me, and in my mother—I suppose in some of the others—those dead Roxbys, Hansykes, Gartons, you don't suppose they were willing to die? I see something that I want, and from that moment I see nothing else. It is as if a cloud blotted out the real world. You are the same. I think it's dangerous—the real world has not vanished because we have been blinded—it is there full of stones and rocks that trip us up or fall on our heads. . . .'

' I'm not nearly so stubborn as you are,' Georgina smiled. ' I shall certainly give up before I break my neck.'

She began to describe William Gary as he was before the War—he and Nicholas were the same age, but where Nicholas was blurred and immature Gary had been self-certain. At nineteen he looked ten years the elder. Hervey listened without speaking. She was vaguely critical of Georgina for keeping nothing back of her weight of love and fear. How can she give herself away like this? She felt no impulse to confide in her turn. There is no doubt I am weak and a fool in loving, she thought grimly; but I needn't speak of it, or ask anyone to help me.

Only by listening to Georgina with her whole mind, she drew closer to her. At last there was no barrier between their minds and she could feel the thought in her friend's as soon as it moved. It was not necessary to say anything.

But when they went upstairs and she gave Georgina a light from her own candle, she felt a new sort of love for her. Leaning forward, she set her lips to Georgina's with a deliberate gentleness in which everything was made plain. It confessed that she understood her friend's state: it said (more intimately and truly than words), I like you, and admire you, and I wish you well; in effect, it was a long speech, a promise. Georgina smiled at her. She held the candle to one side, shielding it with her hand. A thread of light from it wavered across her cheek. ' Good night.'

CHAPTER XX

DEFEAT

THE weeks passed. Half way through July, Hervey began making plans to carry Richard up to Danesacre for his holiday. He had grown pale and soon tired—the flat southern air never suited him, and she half wished she had not brought him away from the north. To please him, she described the days they would spend together on the sands, and the wide scaur, covered with pools which were like dwarf undersea jungles. His eyes shone with excitement.

She told Nicholas she would be away a fortnight. The same evening she was sitting with him in his house. He seemed unwilling to let her go away. Crouching against her chair, he leaned his forehead upon her knees. 'Hervey.'

' Yes ? '

' Don't stay long in Danesacre.'

' I must stay at least two weeks.'

' I want you so much now.'

' Is that true ? ' Hervey asked quietly.

' More than true. When you're not here, I wait for you to ring up, to write. Without you I'm only half alive.'

She trembled with joy. ' I shall come back in August.'

' Don't go, Hervey.

' I must for a few days.' She thought of the promises she had made to Richard.

Nicholas lifted his head to look at her. His eyes were grave and yet bright. ' I began badly. Will you marry me, Hervey ? We can't go on any longer like this. I need you terribly . . . all the time. Will you forgive me for what happened, and let us be married as soon as we can ? '

145

'Yes, I will marry you.' She kept her voice low, even calm, but her hands were trembling. He laid his own over them. 'I'll take care of you,' she said.

'You do that always,' he answered, ashamed.

'Must we live in this house?'

'Why? Don't you like it?'

'It's a museum,' Hervey said, frowning. 'I should never feel certain that you wouldn't sell my bed under me. And I don't like Chelsea. I don't like living in a plain. Couldn't we have two rooms somewhere else? Somewhere on a height.'

Nicholas laughed. He told her that she was no better than a northern barbarian, still unused to civilised ways. 'You want a hilltop so that no one can visit you,' he mocked.

'I want to be able to breathe,' Hervey said seriously.

She felt lighthearted and gloriously happy. She made Nicholas laugh, and laughed herself. A spring of gaiety had been loosed in her, from a source the past had blocked up with stones; once more she was able to speak without thinking, as readily as a much younger Hervey. After a time she remembered the unpleasantness Nicholas would have to face now. Her heart misgave her.

'Will your wife be angry with us?'

Nicholas raised his eyebrows; he seemed older at once. 'I don't expect her to be pleased,' he said drily.

'Is it worth it?' I ought not to ask him, she thought; but I must know. Must.

Nicholas touched her face gently. 'You're worth anything.'

She stroked his hair, laying her fingers on the fine bones of his head. Now I am happy, she thought. Her happiness floated off into a sense of peace, deep and exquisite, so that she was unable to speak. Nicholas looked at her with a softened expression. 'Don't be afraid. I'll try to make you happy,' he said.

'But I don't care about that,' Hervey said gently.

'About what, then?'

'You—only you.'

'You don't realise—I'm too old for you.'

'Two years!' Hervey laughed. 'Is it so great a difference?'

'Do I look only two years older than you? No—look at me. Look at my forehead, at my eyes.'

Hervey looked him full in the face. 'I can't see you coldly,' she said. 'You are the man I love—I shall always love. Do you think I've lived through so much without knowing what it is I want? You are part of my life.'

'I wish we could stay here like this for ever.'

'But I shall come back, Nicholas.'

'Love, my love, my love,' Nicholas said. He took her two hands, laying them against his face. This gave her so much pleasure that she was forced to keep still and to close her eyes.

The next day she wrote to Penn, and asked him to divorce her that she might marry Nicholas. 'There is nothing I can say to make this sound well,' she wrote. 'Don't think kindly of me. Think as unkindly as you please. I could write better if I were not afraid of making many and false words of it. But you know, better than anyone else would' (this surprised her as she wrote it) 'how little I like writing this to you.'

Obeying an obscure impulse she did not post the letter at once. She put it on one side, as if writing it were enough. That done, she gave less than another thought to Penn. She was deeply content and at peace. The future did not yet trouble her: she had not considered what place would be set for Richard when she lived with Nicholas. There will be time for Nicholas now, and then for Richard, she thought, seeing time and her life as a spinning ball, in which divergent lines could lie out in harmony. Her profound contempt for Penn, of which she was scarcely aware, dismissed without further thought the idea that Penn could take Richard himself. Let him try, she said, frowning.

In the morning she had a letter from Penn, in which he told her that he was lonely, living in the country without her, and begged her not to leave him altogether. Reading these sad words, she was a little shaken. She forgot them soon. On her way to the *Review* she took from her bag the letter she had written the day before and sent it off.

She did not see Nicholas that day. The next evening she went to him at his house. She saw at once that his mood had changed again. He was farther from her than ever. He had spoken to his mother about the divorce: Clara Roxby (she was a Roman Catholic) had first wept, and then had reviled his wife. Hervey saw that to Nicholas this was worse than everything. A feeling of loyalty to his wife, mixed with heaven knows what memories of their past, forced him to defend her against his mother's words. Mrs. Roxby had lost her temper and shouted at him in a voice unlike her own, so that he remembered suddenly whose daughter she was. In the end he rushed from the house, and meeting Gary had spent the night with him. They spent it drinking and talking of the War, thought Hervey, looking at his lined face and bloodshot eyes.

She could do nothing with him. The journey East of the Sun and West of the Moon is long and hard, the way stony. She put out all her wits but they were only able to bring her news of defeat. During supper he said abruptly:

' Why have women such a craving to possess ? '

Hervey was struck silent. She saw that he was blaming her for the trouble and unpleasantness the divorce would bring on him. Her throat grew rigid with pain, and she felt cold. After a time she managed to say quietly:

' I don't think they are more possessive than men.'

' Yes, they are more calculating and persistent,' Nicholas said. He glanced at her coldly, with an air of weariness and vexation.

Hervey could not speak, and yet she was able to feel sorry for him. Looking at him, she knew that he was deathly tired, perhaps ill. It was a useless knowledge. She could not touch him. He was sitting a few feet away, but an impassable barrier, raised by his thoughts, lay between them. She sat still, with folded hands.

As soon as the meal was over she said she must go. Nicholas did not try to keep her. On the way to the station he told her once more that he had nothing to give her. ' My whole life is bound up with my work. You won't find what is not there.'

' That is not what is troubling you,' Hervey said quickly. ' You are only afraid of hurting your mother by the divorce. And your wife,' she added, in a calm voice.

Nicholas looked at her without kindness. ' Yes, that's true,' he said. ' I don't enjoy hurting people. Did you imagine I should?'

Hervey lost control of herself for a moment. ' I seem to be the only person you don't mind hurting,' she cried suddenly. She knew that it was an unwise speech. But the words were out before she could check them. Nicholas seized the chance.

' That's altogether unfair,' he said: ' I warned you a long time ago that work, and the freedom to work as long and hard as I please, come first. I won't have my life torn up by the roots for the second time.'

' You make me realise that I am nothing,' Hervey said softly. These other people, she thought, his wife, his mother, are closer to him than I am.

Nicholas did not answer. They reached the station. Hervey saw that she had forty minutes to wait for the train. She had no strength left to try further.

' You had better leave me,' she said to him. On other evenings they had walked up and down this platform, engrossed, so unwilling to make an end that leaving one train go they waited carelessly for the next.

' Very well,' Nicholas said.

He held her hand for a moment; he turned away and walked off. Hervey watched him go, stiff and soldierly. She touched now the depths of her agony. During the time she waited for her train, she sat staring about her, unable to think. Her mind sent up foolish petitions: Don't take him from me; I can't live. Those other people and other things have defeated me, she thought; I can't reach him.

The train came in and she took her place in it, still without thinking clearly. Why is there nothing for me? she asked herself. Why was another woman, who did not value it, given all his loyalty and courage—so that although he needs me he has no energy to face the unpleasantness?

When the train moved, she stood up to look at herself in the glass. She believed that she had aged in the last hour—but look as she might there were no lines on her face, and no marks of a tragic lot. Her eyes, wide and grey-blue, the colour of a northern lake, smiled of themselves. You are a foolish woman, she said, blushing. No sooner did she turn away from the glass than her mind showed her image after image of Nicholas, walking away from her, without looking back. Tears came suddenly into her eyes. She sat down, bowed over her hands, to ease the pain. This time I am really beaten, she thought. This is the second time Nicholas has driven me away. I should never have come back; this time I cannot.

She shuddered. I am making myself ill, she thought vaguely. She looked at her watch, and saw that they must be nearing her station. Wiping her face, she began to repeat all she could remember of *Comus*. ' *The star, that bids the shepherd fold* . . .' It helped, certainly.

In the morning she had Penn's answer to her letter. ' I was expecting to get this some time, but now it has come —my God, it's awful. Yesterday I caught a chill, and the doctor has ordered me to bed. And there are some things we ought to settle. I'd like to see you again, too—my mother says she will be pleased to see you whenever you will come. Oh, Hervey, my Hervey, how can you leave me for ever? How can you? I shall always be crying for you in the dark. How awful. Never able to come to you again. What am I to do? But there, you don't know and don't care what I do. I can't believe it.'

She read this pitiful letter almost without emotion. Perhaps she did not believe it. Penn had appealed to her foolish heart so many times that, insensibly, she had come to the end of pity. Time and again, if he had behaved badly, or had ill-treated her, afterwards she had felt sorry for him— looking young and tired he would speak to her in a soft voice, and at once she became his kind mother. This time she could not. She was sorry for him now, but without much warmth, as if he were a stranger who had asked her to take pity on him.

She put the letter away without answering it. I must have time, she thought. For what?

She wrote to Georgina and asked her to come down and to stay with her on Saturday and Sunday. When Georgina had agreed she rang up Nicholas. She felt calm, even reckless. She was obeying a strong impulse in acting in this way, and without any reason for it her spirits rose, and her courage had returned. Since everything had gone wrong, she could as well please herself what she did.

Nicholas spoke to her in a gentle voice. Immediately she said that she meant to be in London on Sunday—' Can we go out of London, again? We can talk better that way.' To her relief and joy, he agreed at once. He told her at what hour to meet him on Sunday morning, and began to say something else but she cut him short. ' I shall see you to-morrow,' she said, in a distinct voice. To her grave surprise, she felt indifferent and calm.

She rose early on Sunday morning and came up to London, to make it seem that she had spent the night in town. She would not let Nicholas think she had come up on purpose. When she saw him, her heart turned in her side. It is no use, she thought; I shall never get over it. But she greeted him with a composed smile, and in the train on their way to Goring, she was able to talk of this and that, as if nothing were wrong.

At Goring they walked to the river and stood for a few minutes looking at the sunlight, which poured into the water and flowed with it, away, between green meadows and gardens, out of sight.

'You'd like to climb to the top of a hill, wouldn't you?' Nicholas said, smiling.

They walked along country roads, white with summer dust lying thickly on leaves and grass, and crossed one field into another. It rose steeply against the blue sky. The ground was chalk, and its knuckles showed white through the dry wrinkled skin. The earth here was frail and exposed, like the skull bones of an old man. A holly bush stood alone half way up the hill, as if planted there for some festivity, and forgotten. There were thick-grown trees on the far side running down into another valley. Nicholas flung himself on the ground, in the full sun. The shadow of a tree fell to his shoulder and Hervey seated herself there. Her delicate skin would not bear the sun.

For a time they were silent. Nicholas had taken off his coat, and she looked at the bones of his shoulders beneath his shirt. He is very thin, she said to herself. This seemed to her a proof that he was less able than she was to deal with the rough of life.

'What have you decided?' she said abruptly, without giving him any warning.

Nicholas did not look up. He sat with bent head and after a moment he began to talk about his life with Jenny: he said that she had grown impatient with his bodily exhaustion after the War and distrusted his attempts to become successful. There were words she had used which he had not forgotten. He repeated some of them, and with an unbelievable bitterness he added that they were more than half just.

'It is true that I am finished as a man,' he said. He had found a loose fragment of chalk in the grass and was turning it between his hands. Hervey could not look away from it. She stared at his hands while he was speaking and saw the sharp edges of the chalk, gleaming between his fingers. Nicholas Roxby's fingers were unlike him—short, quick, practical. As long as she lived she would remember that sunlight on chalk turns it green, violet, or yellow, by the angle at which the light enters it.

'Well?' she said at last. 'Well, Nicholas?'

Nicholas looked at her for the first time. He was not happy. 'What am I to do?' he said, half inaudibly.

'What do you want to do?' asked Hervey softly. 'If you tell me that, I will tell you what to do.'

He had turned his face from her again. 'I don't want the divorce to go forward,' he said. His voice was scarcely articulate, as if he found a difficulty in pronouncing the words. 'I can't face it—it destroys my work by drawing away half my strength—and then——' he hesitated, and at last said: 'I can't tell Jenny. She will be hurt by it, and I feel responsible for her still. . . .'

And not for me, Hervey thought. She was not offended, and not in the least surprised. In the whole of her life, no one, except her mother, had ever felt responsible for her. She did not invite help, though she was often in need of it. She looked curiously at Nicholas. She did not understand him—When I am behaving badly, I know what I am doing, and the reason, she thought; but these romantics confuse everything.

'Have you forgotten, Nicholas, that on Monday evening we arranged I should write to Penn and ask him to divorce me?'

'Did you write?'

'Of course,' she answered, without change of tone. 'I posted the letter on Wednesday. I have had an answer.'

'Well?'

Already she was sorry for making him see the edge. Why ask other people to be honest? she thought sharply; that is not your business.

'You have not yet told me what you want done,' she said gently. 'You must do *that*, Nicholas—and you must know that you can trust me.' When he was still silent, she persisted, ' Tell me what you would like me to do.'

To hear him, she had to lean forward until her cheek was almost touching his own. He spoke below his breath— (what a phrase that is, to be sure).

' Can you stop this thing going any further ? '

' Yes. I can do that for you.'

' How ? '

' I can see Penn and tell him I have changed my mind, I don't want to be free.'

' Will he——'

' If I say it in the right way, he will certainly be willing to—forgive me.'

' That's unbearable,' Nicholas muttered.

She had to stifle her swift and merciless humour. It was like a salt wave which washed over her mind and drew back, leaving it smooth and without marks. She now saw nothing except Nicholas. It was not even that she loved him or was sorry for him. Simply he had taken the place of her own fears and weakness in her mind; she thought only of helping him. Without needing to think about it, she knew that she must give him back his pride at all costs. A man entirely without self-respect is a dry husk; one might as well give him up. Strange to say, she had not yet given up Nicholas. What can you do with a woman stubborn and mulish as that ?

Her habit of deception helped her. ' Please listen to me, Nicholas. I won't live with Penn again. If he expects it I shall find some way to escape it.'

She did not believe for a moment that it would be possible to escape.

Nicholas looked at her. ' If he wanted you to live with him again—we should have to—then we must go through with the divorce.'

To go through all this again ? thought Hervey grimly. Not I. ' It won't be necessary. I shall stop the divorce, and without promising to live with him.' After all, he will be at Oxford for one more year, she thought. It came to her—but from what unvisited region?—that Nicholas was making a great deal too much fuss about the acts of her body and not enough about her soul. Her soul had fainted within her at the thought of returning to Penn.

'You're sure you can manage it?'

'Yes, yes.' She had never felt less sure of anything, no, never in her life.

'He has done you enough damage,' said Nicholas. 'And now I——' He did not finish, but made an oddly frustrated gesture with his arm.

Hervey had begun to feel tired. But she could not give way yet. Her task was only half done—she felt the full weight of Nicholas's unhappiness on her mind. He was bitterly ashamed of himself, and yet—how clearly she saw it—he was too disillusioned, the War (and Jenny) had used him too hard: he could not feel that anything was worth the risk of struggling for it. She could not leave him feeling ashamed.

'I might take a flat in London in the autumn,' she said, slowly. The idea was scarcely formed in her mind—she had stumbled on it in looking round there for something to give him, as one gives a coloured toy to a child to distract him. 'You could have one room in it for your own, keep some of your books there, come to it when you like.' Nicholas did not answer, and glancing at him she said softly: 'Would you like that?'

'Yes.'

He had spoken in a dry voice, and she thought, No, I've done enough; I'm finished. She sat still, looking at the sky, a high blue arch in which one cloud moved lazily, as white as the chalk itself, but dazzling and alive. It was less fragile-looking than the earth.

'You will be making plans to clear up this and arrange that, five minutes after the Last Trump has sounded,' said Nicholas.

Why, so I shall, she thought, amused. But she was not much comforted. His interest in her plan had been too

brief and uncertain. 'Shall we go now?' she said, as if she
were not a hundred years old, an old tired woman creeping
over the dry earth.

They walked down between the trees to a road over
which cars moved past their eyes like brightly-coloured
shuttles, to this end and that, weaving dear knows what
pattern, into which the trees, the meadows, the sleek distant
river, were rudely subdued. It was now very hot, and
Hervey was thankful to reach Pangbourne, and to enter
one of those hotels that keep the airs of a decayed country
house, and within are as genteel, inefficient and agreeable
as you could hope.

There was a stifling hot room, and a garden into which
they went and sat down. Nicholas ordered tea. In the
middle of the lawn a large ancient cedar sprang unmoving,
like a frozen fountain of shadows. Coolness dropped from
it. Hervey tilted her head back and relaxed. That was
the wrong thing to do. A curious desolation seized her.
For the first time she felt that she had been abandoned.
How unkind Nicholas was to send her away! It was not an
easy feeling, and she shivered a little. Her heart nipped her
suddenly, as though to remind her it was there—'Here,
you, I am not yet a stone. Feel me.' She was afraid—just
as a girl approached them from the house with a laden
tray—that she might cry. That would be a disgrace, and
in front of a stranger.

The girl set the tray down, smiled, and went away.
Hervey looked into the teapot. She seized a spoon and
began absently to stir it.

'After all, it's a queer feeling,' she said.

'What?'

'Being given up.'

Nicholas glanced at her. Perhaps the lightness and
coolness of her voice actually deceived him, or perhaps he
was unable to face such a thought now. He said something
she did not catch, but that it was not worth asking him to
repeat it she knew. She handed him his tea, and asked:

'What did your mother say of me, Nicholas? Was she vexed?'

'Oh, no. Not in the least. I think she is sorry for us—but you know what she is like—her mind flies at a tangent from the least touch; all she would talk of was the sin of divorce and Jenny's evil nature. She spoke of your mother too. She seems afraid of her—and then she had been reading somewhere that the children of first cousins are always idiots, or criminals——' Nicholas broke off, biting his lip. Hervey said nothing. She was thinking that one son is enough: she did not want to bear another child. At the same time something cried in her, with the bitterness of death itself.

They stayed in the garden until some coolness worked its way into the air, stealthily and lightly, like the fine edge of a knife. There was a train to London at six o'clock. At one moment during the journey Nicholas touched her hand and said: 'I should like to be lying beside you to-night. I am horribly tired, and you rest me.'

'Well——' Hervey hesitated. 'Shall we ever go away again?' she said brusquely.

Nicholas was taken aback. After a pause he said: 'I think it might be unwise. In all the circumstances.'

So much carefulness was too much for Hervey. She felt that she could not breathe and laid her hand on her throat. Her face gave her away. At this moment the train had stopped, and several people came into the carriage. Nicholas spoke quickly to her, gripping her arm, but she would not speak. No, I am too hurt, she thought sternly. She was past deceiving him to help him. At Paddington he hurried her across the platform, into a cab.

'I'm sorry, I hurt you,' he said urgently.

'No, it's too much,' Hervey exclaimed. 'I have a dreadful day in front of me with Penn.'

'Oh, my love, my poor love. You *shall* have something. We'll go away whenever you like—every week—forgive me again, Hervey, I'm no good to you even when I love you.'

' I must go home now,' Hervey said wearily.

She said it again as soon as they were in his house, but she stayed an hour longer, and slowly she began to feel happy, even joyous. She could not doubt that Nicholas loved her. He held her until they were both exhausted and looked at each other with eyes strained and aching, sunk in their sockets. ' I shall hurt you all my life,' Nicholas whispered.

' No,' Hervey said.

' Yes, because I am a coward.'

' Why are you afraid ? '

' Of failure.'

' You shan't fail, Nicholas,' Hervey said, with a smile.

' Hold me, then, my love—if you let me go it is the end of me.'

' You go so far when you go away from me,' Hervey said.

' I'll never do it again.'

' Never—to go—again,' Hervey repeated. Her lips felt dry. I have done my best, she thought. If from carefulness or cowardice or lack of warmth he takes away what life we might have together, I can do nothing. I have tried to give him back his pride, she thought steadily; I have endured betrayal and loneliness: with both hands I am offering him love—greater than anyone will offer him again. If it is no use, I can't do any more. And perhaps I have failed.

' Now I must go,' she said aloud.

She would not let Nicholas go with her to the station. She told him that she must be alone, and because he was tired he gave way. She meant to think about Penn on the way home—she would have to face him the next day—but her thoughts wandered, weak and lost, so that the more she said: ' Let me think,' and pulled at the corners of her mouth, the farther they led her, and she stumbling— until all at once she knew where she was, and lightly, joyously, she ran down the narrow street and swung the gate open. All old Danesacre houses have the same bleached look—it is the salt sea in the air—but the child holding the gate was used to it: she looked not at the house but at the laburnum above her head, gazing upwards until the pure yellow of the flowers swam together into one flame. Her heart beat quickly with happiness. I shall never forget it, she thought —never, never.

CHAPTER XXI

PUTTING OFF THE EVIL DAY

SHE did not think about Penn until she was on her way to him, the next afternoon. His mother had taken a small house in the country to the north of London: it was three miles from the station, and when Hervey had asked her way twice she found the right road and walked slowly in the strip of shadow cast by a hedge. She was in no hurry to reach the end. What lay in front of her was not easy. As she walked, she tried to arrange what she must say to Penn, but her thoughts kept straying—to Nicholas, to her need of new shoes, to even such trifles as a bird scuffling along the hedge—and at last she gave all up and decided to trust to the moment. She felt humiliated by her errand, and yet a little excited.

Mrs. Vane met her at the door of the house, looking gravely. I knew that she would ruin Penn, thought the poor woman, shaking; she remembered that her husband had hated Hervey from the first and prophesied some bad end—Oh, she cried, if he were only alive and here now. She was more than a little afraid of Hervey.

To another eye, Hervey would have seemed harmless enough. She looked at Mrs. Vane with a propitiatory smile and said meekly:

' How is Penn? '

' He's better,' Mrs. Vane said. Two patches of colour came into her cheeks. Her eyes, fixed on Hervey, had the simplicity and innocent cunning of a child. ' The boy's wretched, Hervey. Think what you're doing. What right have you to spoil his life? '

' He has spoiled mine,' Hervey said mildly. She wondered how much his mother knew of Penn's way of life. The contemptuous thought crossed her mind: he can think himself safe; she'll never hear of it from me.

Mrs. Vane wrung her hands. ' That's neither here nor there. I don't believe it. . . . Penn is careless—I do know that—but he has a good heart, and if you had had more patience with him—it's a wife's duty to be patient and to think more of her husband and children than of herself.'

Certainly you did *your* duty, Hervey thought swiftly. Not Penn himself saw what this hated daughter-in-law had seen and heard at once—the voice and gestures of young Aggie Vane living on defiantly in the body of an ageing woman. Hervey felt sorry for her, and unmoved. The days when she had been deeply anxious to find favour in the eyes of Penn's mother were long past.

' I should like to see Penn at once,' she said gently. ' I must go back again to-night.'

' Think of Richard,' Mrs. Vane cried. In her agitation she seized Hervey's hand, but dropped it again at once as if it stung her. ' You have no right, for the sake of your own selfish wicked pleasures, to deprive Richard of his father. Do you think you're fit to have the child ? '

The last sentence turned Hervey to stone. She looked Mrs. Vane full in the face. ' Don't encourage Penn to take Richard from me,' she said in a harsh voice. ' If you try to do that, I shall tell everything I know about Penn, and that will ruin him, so far as getting a post in a school is concerned. Moreover, nothing—nothing in this world— is more important to me than Richard. Please understand what I mean.'

Mrs. Vane fell back against the wall. She did not under- stand Hervey's words, but she felt with horror the implacable enmity in her tone. ' Oh, poor Penn, my poor boy! ' she cried. ' What can become of him ? '

' Your poor boy is thirty-three years old and well used to thinking of himself,' Hervey said lightly, almost merrily.

But she was ashamed that she had lost self-control. ' Perhaps things are not so bad,' she went on in a gentle voice. ' Let me go up to see Penn—I can promise you not to make him angry. I'm sorry I spoke in that way. . . . Won't you believe me ? '

Mrs. Vane could not bring herself to take her son's wife into his room. She sat down. ' He's at the back—the end door.' If she had been looking at Hervey she might have seen the change in her face, from a young softened air to fear.

Hervey walked upstairs slowly. She was thinking, I should like a good cup of tea. Penn, wearing a dressing-gown and shawl, was seated in the open window, his long thin fingers drooping over the arms of the chair. It was an appeal to her sympathy. She went over to him and took his hand: it lay limp in hers.

' Do you remember coming to see me when I was ill— when we were engaged ? ' he asked mournfully.

' You don't look very ill now.'

' I'm getting better,' Penn agreed. ' I was in a bad way last week. I can't say that I really want to die—but there doesn't seem much else for me to do.'

' You're talking the most dreadful nonsense,' Hervey said.

' I haven't realised yet that you're leaving me. I suppose one day I shall realise it—and then I shall wish you'd cut my throat first.'

Hervey was silent. Under her resentment of this familiar habit of playing on her feelings—in earlier years it had always succeeded—she felt only shame. I am to ask Penn mercifully to forgive me—to let me off the divorce—why ? So that Nicholas is left in peace and I can do everything for him, as now, without any trouble to himself. Nicholas gets everything from this arrangement, she thought, and Penn nothing. Except the lies I am going to tell him. And although she believed that if Penn's treachery and ceaseless lying were taken into the account they would affect the balance, she was still only deeply ashamed. I am a wicked

heartless woman, she thought. She tried for a few moments
—while Penn went on talking and talking—to comfort
herself with the thought, After all, I have only a little
pleasure in loving Nicholas; there is more pain in it than
happiness. But this could not cloud her mind. At last she
thought: I shall tell him only the truth: he may punish
me; but there it is, I can't help myself.

'I have changed my mind,' she said abruptly. 'I hope
you won't divorce me.'

Penn's mouth fell a little open. He was immensely
surprised. Then at once malice took the place of surprise—
he wagged his head and smiled, with an air of knowing all.

'So that's it, is it?' he laughed. 'You wrote to me
without consulting your precious Nicholas? Well, well,
who'd have thought it of you, Hervey. Upon my word,
I'm shocked.'

Hervey had half turned away from him. Doubling her
hands together and blushing, she listened with bent head.
At last when he had talked himself out she began in a hurry
to say that she thought to move into London, where, if
Penn forgave her, he might stay during his vacations and
make friends with such as William Ridley—and with any
other writers who were (she said faintly) important. Here
she could not help an inward pang. If, thought she, anything can be worse than living again with Penn it must be
to have a great many writers always in the house. She felt
an involuntary contempt for her fellow novelists. They
haven't a mind above their books, she had cried.

Penn heard all this with a meditative smile, but he was
sharply caught. His smile became boyish and sweet. Half
absently he leaned forward and stroked her arm. 'I daresay
I shall surprise a few of them,' he said gaily. 'Probably
your friends think you have a poor sort of a husband. Very
well. We shall see what we shall see.' And forgetting that
he was too weak to move, he threw off his shawl and began
to walk up and down the room. 'So the divorce is off,' he
said, looking at her from the side, with the same knowing

smile, and now it was as well friendly. 'All this emotion doesn't suit you,' he exclaimed. 'You look thinner and pinched and I swear there are the first lines under your eyes. You should have known better than to involve yourself with these damned Roxbys. They're all crooks, of course, out for what they can make—*I* could see that. My dear girl—you can't teach me much about the world. Well, well. Perhaps it won't do you any harm to have the conceit knocked out of you—and you can count on your poor despised Penn not to remind you of it too often.' He laughed, and with great good humour kissed her on both cheeks and her mouth.

'You'd better stay the night. Room here for two,' he smiled.

'No, no—but thank you very much,' Hervey cried. 'I must go now,' she said anxiously. Out of all heart, she leaned her body and hot face against the window, trying to grow calm. And in the end I have not been honest, she thought. I have not told him that I love Nicholas and must still be allowed to see him. Truly I told no lies, but neither have I told the truth. She had the steadiness not to voice these thoughts—afterwards she said to herself, How could I have felt like confessing to Penn, to a man who betrays a confidence as soon as it is made? And she was surprised that even now she could not shake off her weakness for him, as if, knowing him so well, she was forced to say, He is this, he is that, but he is not cruel or vicious.

An hour later she was in the train and, thirsty and worn out, she reflected that Penn's mother had not so much as offered her one cup of tea, and this seemed to her a more shocking lapse from decency and right living than anything in Penn's nature and conduct.

CHAPTER XXII

HERVEY THROWS AWAY MONEY
AND A SAFE JOB

HERVEY had been at work a full hour when Evelyn came in. She heard her voice in the outer room and busy as she was she did not go out to her. On the next day she was going to Danesacre with Richard and she wanted to leave nothing undone with which Evelyn could reproach her on her return. Her work was of a special order—she was Evelyn's whipping boy, her *alter ego*, the thick curtain between Evelyn and the trouble of living.

In a few minutes she heard Evelyn scolding her other secretary, an elderly woman, for a number of crimes. Hervey had noticed during the last four or five months a curious change in Evelyn. Always very careful, in her writing, to check every fact and quotation, she had become obsessed with the desire for order and neatness in her room. It was not merely order she desired, but the same order—the ink here, her pens there, books of reference to the left, unsigned letters to the right. A fraction of an inch difference in the position of her crystal and silver ink bottles now sent her into a paroxysm of anger. She stormed, scolded, or was cruelly sarcastic, until the bewildered woman burst into tears, apologised, and was after proper interval forgiven.

Suddenly the scolding ceased. Hervey listened. The editor himself had come into the room and was talking to Evelyn in a low voice. The bell on Hervey's desk rang— it rang in the pit of her stomach, she could not endure loud noises. She jumped up and ran into the next room. At once the editor began to speak to her in a severe voice. He held up a page of the current issue of the *Review*, pointing his finger at an inexcusable error, which was going to bring an action for libel on them. Hervey was thrown into confusion by the harshness of his voice. She took a step forward, quaking, and peered at the lines. Alarmed as she was, she looked only stolid and gloomy.

'But I didn't pass that,' she exclaimed. She turned to Evelyn. 'You remember I asked you, in the proof, if that had better be struck out, and you took it from me——' She broke off, in a sudden panic. The editor's loud voice had so scattered her wits that the truth sprang out of her before she had had time to think. Of course it was her place to take the blame, Evelyn's blame. She had committed a frightful crime.

'A deliberate lie,' Evelyn said calmly.

There was a moment's silence. Hervey waited. She felt guilty, as guilty as if she had really been responsible for the libel. When she was in trouble—if she had made a mistake or if she had offended anyone—she became at once the child who will be beaten. Her knees shook and her mouth dried up. At these moments she was a coward.

The editor glanced from one to the other, dropped the page on Evelyn's desk, and walked away without another word. His back looked, Hervey thought, as though he were running away. At the door he glanced over his shoulder at his literary editor and said: 'I must see you about this again, Miss Lamb.'

As soon as the door closed Hervey said humbly: 'I'm very sorry—it took me by surprise. I——'

Evelyn cut her short. She was beside herself with annoyance, and her delicate face had become suffused and swollen. For several moments she talked to Hervey as if the younger woman were a thief caught redhanded. She insisted, too, that Hervey had been lying to the editor. 'You must go in and tell him so, and apologise,' she finished, in a low voice. She sat down in her chair and closed her eyes. Her fingers were turned over like claws, resting on her knees. She is mad, **Hervey** thought.

She had had time to recover herself. The thought of explaining to the editor that she had forgotten, or had deliberately lied, was very unpleasant. But she was so used to guarding Evelyn—it was for this she was paid—that she fell at once to thinking of the words she would use. At that a change took place in her. It was not she who changed, but some impulse that split the husk of her mind, in a moment, as if all had been ready, only waiting for the moment. She was not less a coward or less anxious with any cost to please, but a part of her drew off from the coward. She grew calm. No, I shan't do it, she thought. Evelyn had opened her eyes and was looking at her with dislike.

'Either you tell the truth now and apologise, or out you go,' she observed. 'I can't employ a liar.'

'On the contrary—you employed me in order to tell your lies for you,' Hervey said grimly.

She was no longer confused. In a short space she had grown at least a year. She thought with steadiness and great clearness that it would be awkward to do without the money Evelyn paid her. Then why not apologise? There was still time—time to smile and to arrange words in such an order that the editor would guess the truth. This thought pleased her.

She looked through the open door into her own room. Something rough and careless woke in her, and observed Evelyn with gross derision. 'I'll see you damned first,' she said with a loud laugh, and went out.

An hour later she was drinking coffee and covering an envelope with figures. I was foolish, she thought, without too much conviction. She was still young enough to be exhilarated by any change. Beside that she had forty-five pounds, enough, if she stayed quiet in the country, to let her finish her novel. Her heart felt light. The heavy burden of knowing a great many people, of sending and answering letters, of listening, of taking care to please, fell from her and rolled away. She was strong, but Evelyn had often worn her out. When she found that Hervey was clever with people in much the way that some people are clever with horses or wild animals, she used her mercilessly. In one day Hervey would borrow a dozen shapes—to please, to cozen, to soothe. She had often to soothe Evelyn herself. One day going home after an exhausting morning, she stood still and pressed her fingers over her eyes, thinking: Who am I? To be Evelyn's obedient dog and go through stale tricks—it was humiliating: Now I am losing myself, she thought in fear.

Looking at the envelope on her knee, she drew a thick line under the £45. 'At least I shall have peace,' she said. It was useless. The idea of making a change exhilarated, but not the thought of passing long solitary months in the country. However often she abused London, and dreamed of leaving the place for ever, of living a peaceful life, speaking to no one but of simple indifferent things, she was still caught by it. Her unfulfilled ambitions nagged and girned at her. Suddenly it began to seem to her that she had managed everything as badly as possible. She gave up drinking her coffee, paid, and went out, looking if anything stolider than before.

She was to see Nicholas in the evening, the last time before her holiday, but now she felt unable to face him in her shabby dress and thick winter shoes. Her thin shoes were at the cobbler's to be mended. After the visit to Penn she had written Nicholas a short letter, extremely careful (and for her, too) in which every word was meant to reassure and reproach him in the same breath. There had not yet been time for him to send an answer. Probably, in any case, he would not have answered—he preferred to leave difficult letters to settle themselves. That was Nicholas.

For all these reasons, but most of all, perhaps, because of the shoes, she decided to telephone instead from the station.

'Is that you, Nicholas?' she asked softly. Before he

could speak, she went on, ' After all, I can't come this evening, and since we are catching the first train from King's Cross in the morning I shall not see you to say good-bye.'

There was a silence long enough for her to hear her heart beating more quickly and loudly. ' Why aren't you coming ? ' he asked.

' I have a great deal to do,' she said vaguely. Standing sideways to the telephone, she could see the platform through the glass of the door. Over there, she thought, is the very seat where Nicholas said, I love you. It seemed to her that the words had been spoken in another life, to another person: too much had happened since then—simple feelings had been clouded and her happiness of that evening turned to uncertainty and effort. It is a pity, she thought, that it had to be altered and spoiled; but she did not blame anyone, least of all Nicholas. He was now speaking to her in a low voice, and listening carefully she felt that he was sorry and a little relieved.

' Did you have a wretched time at . . . ? ' He broke off without saying the name of the place.

' I told you,' Hervey said. She remembered a phrase from a rejected draft (one of half a dozen) of her letter, ' My sense of justice suffered the worst.'

' I don't understand . . .'

' Don't you, Nicholas ? Suppose it were the other way round—suppose you had asked Jenny to divorce you and had then begged her to let you off, but with the full intention to see me as often as you chose ? Wouldn't you feel that you had behaved unfairly ? '

' Yes, I see,' Nicholas said slowly. It was very strange, listening to the few slow words, as though the intensity of her thought were drawing them from the depths of air outside the world.

' Don't mind about anything,' she cried. ' It doesn't make the least difference.'

' I think it does,' answered Nicholas. ' It has made a

difference to you.   You feel you have treated Penn
badly.'

Hervey lifted her eyes and saw the face of a woman who
was passing the door, slowly, as if without any strength.
She was young, not thirty, but her shoulders drooped, lines
ran from the corners of her mouth, pulling it down, and her
eyes stared round her without, it seemed, noticing anything.
They met Hervey's; she received from them such a sensation
of darkness and emptiness that she felt dizzy, as if, leaning
from the edge of a cliff, she saw nothing beneath.   All this
passed into her mind in less than a moment, before the
woman had moved out of sight; and now Hervey felt that
Nicholas and she were not alone, each between walls, but
were standing together in an open place under a vast sky,
while men and women, as the sands of the sea for number,
passed and repassed incessantly, so that she became afraid of
losing herself in them.   Now Nicholas's voice began to
seem unreal, as if she had only imagined it, and she called
out—' Nicholas! '—in fear.

' Yes, I'm still alive,' he answered.   She could hear that
he was smiling.

' I shall come back as soon as I can.'

' Without you, London is a desert,' Nicholas said softly.

' Don't hide yourself in it then. . . . If you do I can't
come to look for you.'

' Why not ? '

Hervey did not answer for a moment, and he answered
himself.   ' Because of Penn.   Because of your sense of
justice.   Oh, my poor Hervey—I've done you a great deal
of harm.   My loving you doesn't seem much use, does
it ? '

' It's all I want,' Hervey answered, smiling.   She imagined
for a breath that he could see her.

' Are you happy ? ' asked Nicholas.

' Yes.   Good-bye.'

' I shall miss you.'

Well, I'll write to you.   Good-bye.'

' Good-bye, Hervey, and bless you.'

' Good-bye.'

She listened another moment, with a half smile, and hearing nothing, put back the receiver very gently, and left the booth. Her face, as she stepped out, took on a serious preoccupied air, as if she had been discussing some grave matter. She felt the light and the scarcely moving air on her eyelids with joy.

CHAPTER XXIII

RICHARD TAKES A PHOTOGRAPH

THE hay was down in the field opposite Mrs. Russell's house, and in the garden of the farm at the back the farmer's wife had planted bright red and white poppies, in ranks. A light breeze was blowing. Scarlet and white petals covered the path, and the scent of hay stole into every room in the house. In the marvellously clear air even the loose stone fences four miles away, dividing field from moor, were visible, rough and yellow-grey against the russet moor. The warmth and the stillness made themselves felt in Hervey's mind before she was fully awake. Opening her eyes, she watched the light waver across the ceiling. She could hear Richard's voice in the house. She thought that he must be speaking to her young sister, and in a moment Carlin shouted back to him, her voice the childish copy of Mrs. Russell's— she was like her mother in looks and temper, and neither did she fear her.

Rousing herself, Hervey went over to the window and leaned out. On such a day in summer the light striking the sea is flung back in a myriad broken arrows, so that the whole air is threaded through with a soft glitter. The streets are awash with it, and to walk abroad is an adventure, like going ashore in a new country.

She dressed quickly and ran downstairs. Her mother meeting her in the hall said: 'Your breakfast has been set on a tray in the other room.' Through the half-open door of the breakfast-room Hervey saw her father seated at the table. He took almost all his meals alone. He walked abroad alone, or he sat alone in the breakfast-room or his bedroom, a stranger in his own house. He never set foot in the other rooms; if he was driven to speak to his wife he would poke his head round the door of her room and call to her from there. Sometimes for days he did not speak. Now and then he dropped a few words that were clearly the end of a long confused thought—perhaps he had been pursuing it for many days.

Mrs. Russell had no more patience left for him. She spoke to him sometimes as if he were a servant, her voice harsher and more arrogant than had been Mary Hervey's at her worst. The past was still living in her, and now she did not forgive him for it. She blamed him for her hard life and for her own mistakes. Her worst enemy could not have planned for her a more disappointing life.

This morning, when she watched Hervey at her breakfast, her mouth was shut in a firm bitter line. A letter had come from Vera Cruz for Captain Russell. Mrs. Russell had seen the stamp and the neat handwriting, like a clerk's.

' He must have been writing one of his lying letters to the agent in Vera Cruz,' she said in a loud voice. ' When you got your degree he wrote this same man a long yarning letter about sacrifices he had made for you. I saw the post-card the fool sent him in reply.' She laughed scornfully. ' Hah. He to make sacrifices! He never lifted a finger for any one of you. If I hadn't insisted—and if you hadn't earned scholarships for yourself—you might have had no better education than the board school. Much *he* cared.'

Hervey's heart ached for her mother. Since she was a child, and years before she understood it, she had been made to know that Sylvia Russell resented her husband. At times Mrs. Russell's bitterness came up in her too strongly to be put by: then she told her things Hervey never forgot. When William Russell was at home between voyages there was always the feeling of strain and suspense in the house, and bitter quarrels, in which the children were forced to take their mother's side. Jake, by being the younger and a boy, was able to keep apart from the worst of the conflict, but Hervey escaped nothing.

She became, where her mother was concerned, dangerously sensitive. One summer, when Hervey was fourteen, Captain Russell spent three long months at home—that year was the year before Carlin was born—and from some words her mother said in anger she came to believe he was cruel to her. She was seized with anxiety for her mother, and spent two or three hours every night crouched on the landing outside her door, ready to rush in at a cry for help. Shortly before daylight she crept back to her bed, and was still heavily asleep when she should have been up and dressed. Her mother had to bend over her and shake her, every morning, until she was thoroughly awake.

Hervey's longing to save her mother persisted under everything in her life. She could not bear it that her mother was old and finished. When Mrs. Russell spoke of the past, she listened with awful grief, saying in her heart, Why aren't you young? why aren't you happy? She saved money to give her presents. But her mother's bitterness was older than Hervey, and nothing Hervey could do was any good. She could not, by her loving and suffering and bringing gifts, make it that Sylvia Russell was not old, and not ruined by her own will, and nothing less was the least use.

She looked down at her hands and mumbled:

'It doesn't matter what he writes to people as far away as Vera Cruz. And probably the man doesn't believe him.'

'Hah, I don't care what he writes, or doesn't write,' Mrs. Russell said sharply. 'Let him do as he likes.' She was silent for a few moments. Her blue eyes were fixed and remote: a sailor, from long watching, has that look always. Of her children, Jake and Carlin had it, but not Hervey: even when she was most sunk and distant she left someone on guard.

In a different voice Mrs. Russell was saying: 'Richard is too thin in the face, Hervey. He's quite pale, too. You are thin and pale yourself. You know, the south doesn't suit Danesacre people.'

For a moment Hervey felt panic-stricken. Any thought of danger to Richard threw her mind off its balance at once. She hid her alarm quickly, afraid of being laughed at.

' I don't know,' she said vaguely; and without having thought about it clearly, she went on: ' I wondered whether I would leave him in Danesacre when I go back to London. He might go to the new preparatory school . . .' She kept her eyes on her mother's face the whole time, feeling her way in both their minds at once. ' Perhaps he could live here with you. He's no trouble, now that he can bath and dress himself '—she forgot to say that she still did both for him—' and I don't see why I should pay Miss Holland two pounds a week . . . I'd rather pay it to you——' She broke off, afraid that she had said too much. Until this moment the thought of leaving Richard again had remained hidden below the surface of her mind. Now it emerged fully grown. At once she felt a familiar grief, as sharp as a knife—why leave him, why not stay here with him? And she thought of Nicholas. And again her ambitions turned uneasily in their cage.

Nothing of this old conflict—so old now that it seemed her own age—appeared in her face, which was more stubborn than usual.

' I have given up my job,' she said absently.

' What did you say? ' Mrs. Russell exclaimed.

Hervey roused herself to improve the bad start she had made. ' You know I was only supposed to work half the day—but almost every day Evelyn Lamb kept me until four o'clock. It meant that Richard came home to find no one there. And then '—she cast round in her mind for the reason that would impress her mother most of all—' the last thing was that she made a bad mistake, for which I was to take the blame—it meant telling a deliberate lie to the editor. I felt I couldn't do it.'

Mrs. Russell turned red with anger. ' I should think

not indeed! Tell lies for her! I never heard of anything
more shameful. And as for taking her blame on your
shoulders—I wouldn't do such a thing was it ever so.'

How little you know of the world nowadays, Hervey
thought, sighing. She felt glad her mother was on her
side.

'Have you any money left?' asked Mrs. Russell.

'I have about forty pounds. When I finish the novel,
I shall have another hundred at once from Charles Frome
and five hundred dollars from the American publisher.'
She looked at her mother with an uncertain smile. 'I
thought I might stay here to finish the novel—it will take
me about a month—and then try to get work in London.
I don't like to rely on writing for a living. It scarcely
feels safe.'

Mrs. Russell nodded at that. She, too, felt something
untrustworthy and raffish in it. At the same time she was
proud of Harvey's cleverness. 'You must do what you
think best,' she said slowly. 'You know this is your home,
where you can be.'

No, no, it is your home, and Carlin's, Harvey thought
swiftly. She gave her mother an awkward smile. Neither of
them spoke of Penn—perhaps only Mrs. Russell thought of
him, and with a helpless anger—since Hervey had long since
given up expecting him to help her. Now as well she had
her own reasons for not expecting anything from him.

In the afternoon she was walking back from the sands
with Richard when he said: 'I should like a camera.'

He had stopped before the window of a chemist's shop.
'Look,' he said. 'That is the camera I want. The small
one.' He delighted in small-sized objects, and he had a
dozen miniature books, a Bible, a *Paradise Lost*, an atlas,
and others, which he never opened, but cherished for their
smallness.

'But you can't take photographs,' Hervey protested.

'Oh yes I can,' said Richard. He looked calmly at her.
'When you were away Georgina showed me how to use her

camera, and so I know about it.   Please buy that one for me.'

Hervey knew that she ought not to spend the money. But she had not the strength of mind to refuse him anything, when she had any money at all in her pocket.   If he had asked her for the moon her first impulse would be to find something that looked as much like it as possible.   They went together into the shop, Richard pretending to be careless. How well she knew that air!   The camera was more expensive than she had feared.   The man then showed her a cheaper one, much larger, which, said he, was also more suitable.   Glancing at Richard, she saw his face change.   He said nothing, only stared at the small camera in his hand.

'No, I'll take the first one,' Hervey said.   Sighing, she handed over the money.   Richard looked at her with one of his dazzling smiles.   His eyes were brilliant and wide open with excitement.   My little love, Hervey thought.   She felt a sharp pleasure in giving him what he had wanted.   It was as if a living creature moved in her, softly, stretching out its arms and laughing with joy.   She, too, was excited.   The pleasure a woman is said to feel in conceiving a child she had begun to feel only when she could give him something he needed or liked.

As soon as they were at home Richard hurried in to show off his camera.   Carlin Russell looked at it with an air of indifference.   She was jealous of Richard—and she felt vexed that she had not thought of asking for one for herself.

'Hah, you'll soon break that,' she said.

'No, I shall not.'

'He won't know how to use it,' Carlin said fiercely to Hervey.

Hervey wanted to quiet both of them.   In another moment Carlin would be angry, and then Hervey would have to take her son's part against her wild young sister.   Both children were stubborn; Carlin, five years the elder, had the less self-control.   Hervey was ashamed of feeling angry with her. She felt an unwilling sympathy for the little girl.   I am her sister, as well as Richard's mother, she thought, and I know her too well—she would be kind to Richard if he were docile and admired her.   At the same time she felt herself losing patience with Carlin.   She was dancing round Richard, singing in a jeering voice: 'Baby Richard found a camera, Baby Richard broke it!'

Richard looked expectantly at his mother.

'Stop that now, Carlin!' she said angrily.

'Baby Richard broke it!' sang Carlin.

At this moment Captain Russell came out of the house, shuffling towards them in his stocking feet.   He was wearing a shabby reefer and carrying the garden shears.   His grey hair stood up over his head in wisps, and he had not shaved. He halted near them and stretched a large hand, as brown and wrinkled as the bark of a tree, towards the camera.

'Hey, boy, what have you got there?' he demanded.

Richard backed away in silence.   He had every reason to be alarmed.   His bedroom was next his grandfather's, and between malice and curiosity the old man could not keep his hands off the boy's things.   He had broken one toy already and hidden others.   Richard had told no one about these raids.   So far as possible he ignored the habits and deeds of older persons.   He felt this to be the safe way of dealing with them.   But his grandfather confused him by acting in a way that was not merely queer but wicked.   I shall hide my camera, he thought.

'Is it your own?   Hey?' Captain Russell said, drawing closer.

Suddenly Carlin rushed forward.   'Don't touch it!' she said fiercely.   'Do you hear?   You're not to touch it.'

Startled and offended, Captain Russell dropped his hand. 'I don't want to touch it,' he muttered.   He glanced quickly round, afraid that Carlin's voice would carry to her mother's ears.   Hearing nothing, he raised his own voice.   'I was only going to look at it.   I've had dozens of better cameras through my hands. . . . Yes, dozens,' he repeated.   He looked at their faces.   He was now completely at a loss.   No one answered him; he turned and shuffled in a great hurry across the lawn. Keeping his back to them, he began clipping the hedge, handling the shears as if they were scissors.

Carlin stared after him with a look of scorn and dislike. Her lips curled. ' He'll make a rare mess of that hedge,' she remarked.

Seen from the back, Captain Russell had a slovenly dejected air. Hervey could not help feeling a little sorry for him, but it was only because she knew what was passing in his mind. She had no affection for him. Carlin touched her arm and smiled. All three stood in silence, watching the uncouth old man slashing at the hedge as if he were possessed.

' I shall tell mother,' Carlin said. She skipped away.

Later in the afternoon Richard took a photograph of Hervey, Mrs. Russell and Carlin. He fussed about, grouping them to please himself, Mrs. Russell seated, Carlin kneeling down on the grass at her feet. Hervey waited a moment to help him with the camera. He can really use it, she thought. She was overjoyed by this proof of his cleverness, as if it were a miracle that he had hands, and fingers that moved. The moment sank into her mind, taking with it the sunlit wall and the boughs of the lilac. Mrs. Russell was looking at the boy with a familiar smile, half shrewd, half ironical: Carlin partly closed her eyes to show that she disbelieved and despised the whole thing. What Hervey did not see was the unashamed pride in her own face; it shone forth as soon as she took her place in the group. As well for her that she was standing behind Mrs. Russell, and not in her sight.

She did not escape entirely. In the evening, after Richard had been put to bed, Mrs. Russell told her she spoiled him.

' You're bringing him up to think he can ask for anything he wants,' she said.

' He can ask,' Hervey laughed.

' Aye, and you give it to him,' her mother retorted. ' You'll ruin him, Hervey.'

Hervey did not answer. Why not give him everything? she thought. Life is too uncertain. There might be another war, and then what good would strictness have been to him? She thought of her brother, killed before he was nineteen. How few things Jake had in his short life! No, no, she cried, everything has changed, everything is uncertain; it is no good believing in the future. The only thing I can do for Richard is to make him strong and well, and give him everything I can reach. If he is happy, he will be good. She thought for a moment of her own childhood. What has my mother's severity done for me, she thought, except make me afraid and mistrustful?

She glanced at her mother, who was staring stiffly in front of her—at what? Her heart contracted with the old feeling of helplessness. A hard life you have had of it, she thought, and with no reward, but only your son taken from you and killed. She began to think, what can I give her?

After dark she went out and walked along the cliff top, looking at the lights of ships passing a long way out, and at the black shoulder of the coast. Far below her, in the darkness she could see the white edge of the sea. All was still. She knew this crumbling path of old, and walked carefully, avoiding the places where the earth had cracked and fallen away. There was the scent of a privet hedge in flower, but there were no gardens near—it must have drifted a long distance to reach the edge of the sea. It will reach one of the ships, she thought; for some reason this thought gave her intense joy. She strained her eyes to see to the farthest ship, and thought, Oh that I could go freely over the whole earth all the days of my life.

Now Saint Mary's on the east cliff struck the hour, the wind blowing from that side. Hervey counted the strokes. So late? she thought anxiously. She hurried back, afraid of her mother's displeasure, but the house was in darkness. She let herself in without a sound and went to her room, quiet as a shadow. Her pen was still across the page, where she had dropped it, without waiting to finish the sentence. She wrote the end of the sentence.

She wrote to Nicholas. Opening her book again, she

began to write, with extreme slowness, altering and crossing out a great many words. Her room looked east. When she came in, there was already a change in the darkness, and before she stopped writing and began to move her stiff fingers up and down, the day had come.

CHAPTER XXIV

ONCE or twice in the year Thomas Harben and his wife dined alone. It would happen accidentally—but it was an accident his wife would have declined to avert. Completely without affection for her husband, she had too much dignity to make this an excuse for avoiding him in hurried or clumsy ways. To-night a dinner party to which she had been going was cancelled at the last moment: it turned out that her husband was dining at home; and here she was, listening with an air of attention to anything he had to say.

She had married out of gratitude—and not without the feeling that she had done a wise thing in the circumstances. These were the sudden death of her father, a vast unprofitable estate, and two younger sisters to be thought for and married. Thomas Harben, who had had some dealings with her father, came to her help at once, settled old debts, cleared up the accounts, and showed her that she could either sell the estate in lots or try to let it. A third way would be to marry a man able to spend money on it. She had few hesitations in choosing to marry. At that time she respected Thomas Harben.

It was perhaps the marriage itself which destroyed respect. Either Harben knew that he was unloved and thought of it as a bargain, his success against her breeding. Or he deceived himself. The last thought made him a fool, and the first—a good business man. Perhaps both thoughts occurred to her. She had, too, to guard herself from feeling ashamed of her own part in the bargain.

There were no children.

This morning she had noticed—it was another accident—that she had been married exactly twenty-three years. She did not look at herself longer in the glass, but during the afternoon something made her say to a friend:

'I am not sorry I have no son or daughter.'

'Why?' asked her friend.

'Because the world is falling to pieces.'

'Your son—if you had one—might have known how to help it!'

Lucy Harben shook her head gently. She thought it a foolish speech. There is no helping a world which refuses to respect what ought to be respected. At one time, she thought—more than a hundred years ago—her own family had helped to rule the country, which began to sink as soon as money grew stronger than land. The whole story was told when a Thomas Harben had to be called in to save the landowner from ruin.

She had dressed for this meal as if it were a ceremony. Her husband had given her so much jewellery in the first year of her marriage that she had difficulty in deciding which of these gifts was the most valuable. In the end she took the diamonds to wear with her black frock.

She was a handsome woman. She looked her full age (she was fifty), but it was as if she were a different woman rather than an older one than the young woman who had accepted Harben out of gratitude—and policy. Her grey hair had its own beauty and her shoulders, full and white, were smoother than they had been in youth. She had a habit of half closing her eyes as she listened.

'Your young second cousin, if that's what he is, has not done badly,' Thomas Harben said. He set his glass down empty; it was refilled, and he took it up and drank with an obvious pleasure. He is becoming greedy in age, thought his wife.

'Julian?' she said, smiling. 'But he's extremely intelligent.'

' Intelligence can't always be brought to market,' her husband said.

' And is the market value the only one?' she asked, without a trace of irony. Her voice was polite and pleasant. She would not allow herself to use irony against her husband.

' The only one I can make use of,' Harben said. He spoke with a brutal shortness, which did not belong to what he was saying. He did not believe that an intelligence is no use until it has been fatted for market. But he resented in his wife the politeness with which she supported the difference between them. There was scarcely one thing in their lives on which he and she did not put a different price. Her notion of a successful life was not his—in her heart, he knew, she despised even the purpose of his life. And yet she makes use of my money, he thought: what does she want? What kind of man does she respect? He did not think it possible that she could respect Julian Swan, for instance. He felt strongly irritated. Where would you be without me? he wanted to shout at her. Who would pay for your music? Where would your musicians be and your painters and writers if I did not give you the money to pay them? What would your reading books do for you?

At the same time he noticed that she was dressed as if for a party, and wearing his diamonds.

' You're looking very well,' he exclaimed.

After a slight pause Lucy said: ' Do you know that it is twenty-three years to-day since——' She broke off, smiling.

' Upon my word, is it?' Harben said. He had only a vague notion of what she had been about to say. Clearly it was an important occasion—perhaps their marriage. But why speak of that?

For no apparent reason a feeling of triumph invaded his mind. I don't understand women, he told himself; why should I? What, after all, is there in a woman to understand worth the trouble they make of it? It was many years since he had felt a sensual impulse towards his wife, but now he began looking at her shoulders and arms. She rose to leave him at a moment when there was no servant in the room, and as she passed he ran his hand over her breast.

Her body winced of itself. She recovered instantly, and went on as if nothing had happened. But in the instant something very ignominious for Harben had taken place: when he closed the door after her and returned to his chair his face looked sour. He turned his head from side to side, so that his long nose was more than ever like a strong fleshy beak. All at once he jumped up. Walking over to the sideboard he touched its corners one after the other, furtively and quickly. A servant came into the room and asked him whether he would take his coffee here or in the drawing-room.

' Here, you fool,' he said.

He was scarcely angry with his wife. His resentment of her went as far beyond what had just happened as if it had happened between strangers. He hardly knew even what he resented, unless it was that she did not respect him. It's intolerable, he thought vaguely—intolerable, damnable. His head was throbbing, he had drunk too much burgundy during the meal—he was going to have a poor night. The idea came to him to go out at once to see Lise. She would quiet him and give him a cup of lime tea for his head—and in any case he must see her.

Lise's house was at the farther end of Chelsea. He was sure to find her alone, since she had a few acquaintances and no friends. He approved that. Her reserve, and her admirable good sense, attached him to her as firmly now as when he first knew her. She had every quality a man needed in a mistress, discretion, self-respect, an even temper, and one secret attraction for him to which he had never put a name, but he had felt it at their first meeting. She was standing at a window, holding the curtain aside with one hand and at once he had seen himself, a small heavy child, walking along a street in a foreign city: his mother had said, ' Look at their shutters, how they hate the sun '; and a vision of long rooms in which the light was the colour of water came into his mind. Lise was half German.

She was brown-haired and brown-eyed, with soft heavy arms. All her gestures were slow, like her speech, and there was always a moment, before she moved or spoke, in which one saw the new word or gesture forming itself like a leaf. She was a good cook and felt a quiet pride in her house. She knew the recipes for a great many herb teas, which were not German but French—she had learned them in Strasbourg, where she was brought up. Harben had known her for three years before he heard from her that she had lived in Strasbourg. She never talked about herself, a reserve he found pleasant and soothing. It was like walking in a forest of which one knows only the shape without having explored yet any of the paths and valleys.

She was reading when he came in, and looked at him with her light smile. He told her as he was taking off overcoat and gloves that he had a headache, but when she was moving towards her kitchen, to prepare his tea, he stopped her. ' No,' he said, looking down at her.

He was not an inconsiderate lover but he could not pretend to any of what he called 'sentimental ballast' in his love-making. In his manner towards her, his caresses, there was always a trace of brutality, the coarse patronage of a man whose sensuality has never outgrown its satisfactions. Lise existed to be made use of—he was no more inclined to consult her feelings than to use her in any way roughly. On this occasion the violence in his mind changed immediately into an excitement which started a dozen incongruous images there. He saw his room at Garton's, his wife's shoulders, the backs of Julian Swan's hands, covered with reddish hair, and the page of a book written closely in rows of figures. A sensation of gratified pride swelled in him. He realised that he was conferring a serious honour on Lise, and the idea that she too felt this gave him merited pleasure.

Leaning back in a chair, he allowed her to bring him the tea, though his headache had vanished.

She watched him lift the cup in his strong fingers and thrust his nose into it. Like a vulture, she said to herself again. She was too sensible to allow herself to feel hurt by his indifference, but she could not help actively disliking his old man's vigour: it seemed to her unnatural. When he glanced at her she smiled, with a faint irony. She had nevertheless a respect for him. He was a rich man with no desire to waste money. She had been very careful not to give him the idea that she might try to exploit him.

When Harben left her, at eleven o'clock, he took a cab to his house. The man stopped at the wrong number, and getting out he walked the short distance. A man was waiting against the railings of the house. As Harben approached him the man stepped forward, holding his hat with both hands, as if it supported him.

'Pray forgive me for troubling you,' he said softly, ' but you are Mr. Thomas Harben, I think?'

Harben recognised by his voice the old lunatic who had been twice to the house. 'I am Thomas Harben,' he said. 'What do you want?'

'I would put up with getting back only a part of my money—if it's not convenient for you to pay me the whole of it,' said the man, in a firm, anxious voice. His head drooped forward. He was bald, except for a few white hairs over the ears, and the light from the street lamp fell on his bare head and on the shoulders of a jacket shiny with age and going into holes at the seams.

Harben felt a touch of compassion for him. 'Take this and get away,' he said, holding out a ten-shilling note.

The other drew back against the railings.

'Allow me to remind you that I have lost the whole of my savings,' he answered, with a little dignity.

'That has nothing to do with me,' Harben said, irritated. He walked past the old fellow and drew his key from the pocket into which he put back the rejected note.

'For the love of God——' the other man began, now terribly agitated. 'I am starving——'

'Try the police,' Harben said. He went in, shutting the door gently. His head was throbbing again and he felt angry

and quite exhausted.   An impulse to telephone to the police-
station seized him, but he did not trouble himself.   The
wretched creature would certainly go away before morning—
if not, he could be given in charge.   Pressing his fingers along
his forehead, above the temples, and panting, Harben went
slowly upstairs.   He regretted having gone out at the end of
a hard day.   When he entered his room and saw the turned
down covers and the tray with the decanters at the side, he
gave a sigh of relief and lay down on the bed for a moment.

CHAPTER XXV

AT the same moment, but on the north-east edge of England, in Danesacre, Hervey Russell had lifted her pen to begin writing; and in another part of London William Gary read over for the third time a letter he had written, signed it, and locked it away into his desk. He stood up, stretched himself —he had been writing since dinner—and walked over to the window. The letter would not be posted to any man or woman.

The window of this room looked towards the Green Park. Now nothing could be seen, except a row of lights and where the light touched them strange spectral trees, like undersea plants drawn upright by the current. There were lights in the windows of hotels and in the street, and a thread of light ran over the centre of the road like a direction sign. The wheels of cabs crossed and recrossed it, weaving the bold many-hued pattern of a city. Gary thought: I am that thread. The wheels go over my body, carrying Nicholas who is thinking of his young woman; Georgina who wants me to love her without knowing what has changed in me; and that severe, powerful and heavy image, Thomas Harben. I had better think of Harben.

He and I will be allies for a time. When he dies (he is sixty and I am thirty-two) I shall take his place. Already I am sharing with him decision and deed. My Lanarkshire coal. lifted from mines that belonged to my father and grand-father, feeds the furnaces in his iron works and steel mills. Together we own coalfields in Yorkshire, and iron works on the Don. He is an ironmaster on the north bank of the

Clyde and I again in Ayrshire. I now have a foot firmly in the Harben Ling Company which has swallowed up not merely the steady-going firm that belonged to old George Ling's father, but a steel works in Doncaster, another on the Tyne, another on the Tees, with plate mills, blast furnaces, coke ovens, ironstone mines, and foundries: between us we deliver a mountain of steel girders, steel sheets, steel rails, blast furnace coke, pig-iron, oil-pipe lines, the scaffolding for a world. Heaped together the chimneys of our several furnaces and works would make a city and their smoke turn day into perpetual night. In a few weeks I shall set my other foot in the firm which once belonged wholly to Nicholas's grandmother, to that Mary Hervey whom I hated, because she had sacrificed (as I thought) his whole life to an idea she had. I was very ignorant in those days. Now I can smile, thinking what the old woman might say if she knew that her successor had added three yards, two marine engineering works, and four shipping lines, to her cherished and once orderly and compact Garton's. Let us hope it can stand the strain! Thomas Harben himself is a portent. He is a pyramid whose shadow falls across a million sweating slaves. He has done and will do deeds that I am ashamed to copy. He has no imagination and yet he has made a new world. The world *I* shall make will be cleaner and better. He is all-powerful in his, but he suffers the indignities of a weak stomach and he has not left children.

Neither have I any sons, nor shall, since my wounds made me impotent; I remember the doctor's face and his hands. When I remember my mutilation I see in the same moment a noon in Spain, the sky a burning blue flame, the motionless white mountains of cloud, and an old crone gathering up sticks by the side of the road; and then night, the next night or any night, and that woman who waited for me—I shudder, my hands jerk upwards, I am filled with disgust and a useless anger. I have remade my life. I am reborn, I live to fulfil my own purpose; I have new desires; my mind is pleasantly clear; I know, as they say, what to do. Poor Georgina, poor child.

Nicholas knows. I shall lose Nicholas to his young woman. Do I mind this? A part of me feels intolerable bitterness and rage, but it is a small part only: it belongs to the past which I have given to the past. The time will come when I shall think of Nicholas as seldom as of that boy I found dead by the side of the trench, with no mark on him. But not yet, my dear, not yet. Go with your young woman. Soon we shall have in common only the accident that we were at Hannescamps together: you will have turned that way and I this: you to your new wife and your unquiet thoughts, and I to my few certainties. I shall not lie awake at night oftener than you will. You will discuss what ought to be done to restore order to the world, *I* shall restore it. You will invent schemes, and talk about them with your new friends, anxious and hard-working men and women gathered in conference halls and secret shabby rooms; my schemes will take precedence over yours. Remembering the War—of which you have remembered only the voices of young men (the excitement, the irrecoverable friendships) and the look of a trench, a road, and a wood—I shall give the men what they want. None of them want what you would give them, ideas are nothing, responsibility is nothing, freedom is a burden; they want clean dry quarters, the rations coming up at night and divided fairly, they want security, they want coals by the side of the fireplace, and a piano for Winifred. In their minds your talk will make the noises of wind in an empty chimney. They will rather choose mine.

I shall use this man and that: one I shall promote and another I shall despatch to take over a difficult position. I shall become more respected as you fail; yet you will ask me for nothing. I shall walk here and there, not as we walked in Spain the year before the War, but as a spy in the enemy's lines. I shall have extra cables laid under the sea, roads built in the mountains, young men will fly my aeroplanes over deserts, over temples, over forgotten villages; I shall sit at the centre of this, the roads and the cables will run through my brain, the aeroplanes will take off and land there; I shall be grass, scorched earth, air, water; in the morning I shall clothe this body, glancing at it from habit, and in the evening I shall take care to give it hard exercise. Men in my state—did you see it? My hand jerked, the fingers sprawling: my imagination is not yet under control.

The thread is still there. At night, I approach the frontiers of an occupied territory. I remember the pass-word. In the pocket of my tunic I carry my passport and an identity card. Shall I use them? Shall I turn back? It is of no importance except to myself. I am already tired. I have learned to seem easy when I am not. My life has not turned out as I planned. I am less intelligent than I thought; I have missed what I expected to find: my discipline has been inadequate. I remember rooms, shabby and uncomfortable, where I have been transported with happiness, sunlight that has made me close my eyes, the taste of bread and wine in a dry noon, wind on naked limbs, voices, words (it does not matter that they were afterwards proved to be lies), a touch. I am not content. I am not resigned. I would rather be young and obscure than old and known.

CHAPTER XXVI

DAVID RENN MAKES AN ENEMY AND MEETS
A YOUNG WOMAN WHO KNOWS HER MIND

THE next morning Gary arranged to send Renn to Italy, to
Trieste, where he was to rebuke their agent, a clerk in a
shipping office, for the inadequacy of his reports. It was
not a pleasant nor a particularly easy task, but Renn had
proved himself tactful, and for some unsought reason his
employer found a satisfaction in setting him awkward tasks.

As he finished giving Renn his instructions, Julian Swan
arrived. 'Yes, send him in,' Gary ordered. He said to
Renn: 'You'd better stay. You'll be pulling in with
him when you come back.'

He amused himself, while he looked out the notes he had
prepared for Swan, by watching the two younger men take
stock. They were as unlike as possible and yet there was
a likeness. Renn, only three years older than Swan, looked
middle-aged by contrast. Swan's skin was a reddish-brown,
a shade darker than his hair, and he stood with the military
stiffness he affected, his hands by his sides, fingers clenched.
His eyes were gleaming with vitality. He was a fine animal.
Renn lounged against his desk, the one he used when Gary
kept him working in that room. He looked better, better
fed, than he had looked when Gary engaged him, but his
eyes were bloodshot and his face had the lines that four
years' soldiering had placed there, deep in the fine skin.
You could see the skull behind them.

He listened without seeming, to the orders Gary was
repeating to Swan. The Economic Council must tackle its
first important job. All this chatter about nationalising the

mines—bunkum, but dangerous bunkum. It must be cut
short at once. Counter arguments, figures, proofs of one
state of affairs, denials, the right use of the press—how
easily he can plan an attack, Renn thought. A feeling of
helplessness came over him. Why not accept the Garys and
the Harbens? Why struggle? Obedience is rewarded.
You take wages from them to keep life in your own body,
he said to himself: how I despise you for that! You ought
to have starved quietly. But that sounds simpler than it is:
it takes months, and in the meantime there is one's poor
devil of a landlady. And there is my mother. I am not
complaining—but why arrange the sum so that another war
is the only answer?

Gary dismissed both of them together. In the other room
Swan turned with an air of eagerness.

'So you're off to Italy. My God, I wish I were going
with you. Since the War it's the only country—I mean
since Mussolini took hold of it, of course. Have you been?'

'No,' Renn said. He was moved to add: 'I'm not a
Fascist.'

'You will be when you come back,' Swan laughed.

'I don't think so.'

Swan looked at him with some disfavour in his eye.
'Wait till you've seen what it can do for a country. I was
in Italy just after the War, and it was going downhill fast,
nothing but swinish incompetence and corruption everywhere. All that's gone now—Mussolini and his grim young
men are cleaning up the mess faster than the swine made it.'
He stood with his head held back, flushed, staring, arrogant.
'You'll see for yourself.'

'I suppose that pouring castor oil into an elderly professor
must be a pretty grim business,' Renn said—'even when
your pals are holding him down.'

Swan had been going away. He turned back. From
his greater height he could look down at Renn. 'You'll
be whimpering about violence in a moment. Meaning
you'd rather not risk your skin.'

' As to that,' Renn said quietly, ' I think I've seen too much violence. I had four years in France, you know. I think you were luckier ? '

Swan went on looking at him with contempt and hatred. Renn stared back for a moment and went out, not elated by cheap victory. He felt very much ashamed of himself. You really ought to know better, he said severely; that was a shocking lapse.

His passport needed renewal. He had already filled in the necessary papers and he presented himself at the office, handed over papers and passport, and sat down to wait. In repose, the unusual delicacy of his face was more marked. His skin and even his lips were almost colourless; he had fine rather thin lips, fine arched eyebrows, and bright eyes. The habitual expression of his face was one of light irony: this was a defence more than thought. In a group of people he might pass unnoticed, but once you had become aware of him none of the other faces were of any interest—much as if the masterpiece of a Chinese artist were set down among the portraits in the year's Royal Academy.

He became interested in one of the other applicants. She was, he thought, a schoolgirl, very neatly dressed. Do they, then, issue passports to children ? he wondered.

She seated herself at the end of his row of chairs, and since there was no one seated between them he could look at her without trouble. She had taken off her hat and he saw that she was wearing small gold rings in her ears. She had black straight hair, cut short: seen from the side her face had one peculiarity; whereas most noses, however prominent, follow the line of the face downwards, hers, which was small and very fine and thin, jutted out—it made Renn think of a ship's bows. She turned full towards him, and he thought that she was enchanting—her face narrow and pointed, eyes as clear as brown water, pitch-black eyebrows, a fine mouth and a long throat. She was sunburned and unpowdered. Still thinking her a child, he smiled to encourage her. She gave him a shrewd glance, then slid quickly over the chairs to one next his.

'This is my first time,' she said. 'Will they take long? I'm dying for a cup of tea.' She had not thought to lower her voice, which was astonishingly clear and loud.

'I don't think so,' said Renn. 'Are you going abroad to school?'

'My goodness, no.' She laughed as she talked; it was a pleasant sound, but a loud one, and heads were turned towards her. She either did not see them or did not care. 'I'm going to Paris with our buyer. I suppose she wants someone to run her errands. I know French and she doesn't, see? Fancy a dressmaker not knowing French—I suppose she points and snatches.' Pointing and snatching with a thin brown hand, she laughed again.

'You mustn't laugh here,' said Renn.

'It's not forbidden, is it?' She put her hand over her mouth and looked hopefully at Renn, and he realised that she was expecting him to make another joke. He was saved by hearing his name called. He went up to the counter, took his passport, and came back.

'About that cup of tea,' he said. 'Shall we drink it together?'

'Markham,' the passport official said.

'Why not?' she answered, smiling at him frankly.

'Markham.'

'Goodness, it's me.' She jumped up and ran to the counter calling out: 'I'm coming, I'm coming.' Everyone stared at her as she walked back to Renn.

Outside in the street, she hastened on, talking all the time. Renn glanced anxiously about him until he saw a small modestly-begging café. They went in. 'I'm starving,' Miss Markham said, with a smile. 'All this morning I was running about the town like a hare, too quickly to eat. I'm not the woman described in my passport; I'm a void, an ache.'

'How old are you?' asked Renn.

'Nineteen. How old did you think?'

'About fifteen. I'm twenty-nine myself.' He watched her face as he said it.

'You look older,' she said. 'But never mind, I like you. As a rule I don't care for men. They never take me seriously and I'm a serious person. I intend to succeed.' She looked at Renn with suspicion: his expression satisfied her; she laughed again in her clear ringing way and asked him his name.

'David Renn.'

'Mine is Hannah. Hannah Markham, and I design clothes —I mean that my father paid a hundred pounds for me to work in Baring's in Wigmore Street, but I know more now than they could teach me. If I ever get a chance I can dress anyone. Look,'—she took an envelope from her bag—'I'll design a coat for our skinny waitress.'

Renn watched her as she stooped over the sketch. The eagerness of her nose seemed to him pathetic and exquisite. Each time he looked at it he felt the same deep pang of joy. She finished off her sketch, signed it in a sprawling hand, 'Hannah,' and handed it to him.

'That's charming,' Renn said, looking at it carefully. He folded the envelope into his pocket-book.

'No, but it's good,' the young woman persisted.

'Very good.'

'I didn't mean you to keep it, you know. But of course if you want it for your wife——'

Renn shook his head. 'I haven't a wife.'

'Your girl, then.'

'Until this afternoon I hadn't even that,' he said.

'Now you're growing cheeky,' she said. She took her hat from the chair and drew it over her eyes. 'Is that right? I must go at once, or I shall be in trouble.'

Outside the shop Renn said: 'When can I see you?' He was surprised by the intense anxiety he felt. This had never happened to him until now.

'Do you make a habit of this, young man?' When she frowned, her eyebrows met in a double arch.

'No, certainly not,' Renn answered. He looked at her. 'Please believe me.'

To his relief she said, smiling: 'It doesn't sound true, but I'll believe you.'

'It is true,' said Renn. 'I have been in love before, but it was not—not serious.' He took her arm and walked her swiftly along the street. 'I don't know that I enjoy what is happening to me, but there you are, it can't be helped, and we must just make the best of it. When do you finish work?'

Miss Markham drew her arm away and looked at him with narrowed eyes, but she was struggling not to laugh. 'Why should I make the best of you?' she cried. 'You're quite mad. Very well—in the evening I leave Baring's at half past six or seven. But don't come this evening. Now I shall have to take a cab—you're to blame. Here, come here,' she called. She waved her arms at the driver of the taxi, and ran after it.

Renn watched her out of sight, with an intent hard look on his face, as though he had remembered something not very pleasant. Despite it he was filled with an amazing sense of exhilaration. It passed slowly, leaving him restless and uncertain.

CHAPTER XXVII

HE THAT IS LOW NEED FEAR NO FALL

LONDON south of the river is a huddle of towns and villages, one running into another, yet each distinct souls. Thus Tulse Hill is late genteel Victorian, and Brixton rubs against it with the familiar air of a coster jammed against some disconcerted clerk in the six-thirty. Farther east, the districts have kept a flavour that has been crushed out on the northern side of the river. A grim slum has some memory, foreign shells ranged along a sill, a fuschia in a cracked pot in the window. Here and there a shop flaunts a hand-painted sign, crude, flat, defiantly individual. Beyond Greenwich a wooded cliff rises some hundred feet above the marshes of the river; Bostall Wood is green in spring; and Plumstead has every air of a forgotten seaside town but only the sea. Greenwich, neighbour to Blackheath (colonel retired on half pay), runs from the dignified, salted with memory, to the horrible and the drab. In 1924 a street of small new houses sprang up on a piece of waste ground below the railway. They could scarcely have been worse built, the abrupt enterprise of a local builder, no worse and no more ignorant than any other. He sold two of them: the rest, after a mournful interval, were let at twelve and sixpence a week with rates to men in steady jobs.

When Frank Rigden, ex-soldier, moved into London from the country, he lived first at the other side of the river, in Hackney, in two rooms in a street of older and much less shoddy houses. His wife was country bred and that wilderness of bricks and all-pervading dirt sickened her. Her father had come with them, and he and the baby slept in the sitting-room and she with Frank in the small bedroom. The window of this room looked on to the yards of worse houses and Sally's country reserve was affronted by the traffic to and from the row of earth closets.

They endured this place for six months, until Frank had a stroke of luck exceeding all hope. His only relative was friendly and good tempered, a Trades Union official in London: this man, Joe Bradford (because he was a northerner he was called Bradford Joe), now helped him to a job in the Stokes Chemical Works. Here his wages were sixty shillings a week—not enough to excuse Sally for going into the new house. But her heart leaped so at the sight of it. She even knew that it was nastily built, of poor stuff—but it was clean; from the bedroom window she saw the river and the funnels of small steamers; and by some grace there was a boiler in the kitchen giving hot water.

Her conscience smote her hardest on Friday, when Frank pushed over to her all but the money for his dues, one sixpence for tobacco, and the threepence he gave the local Labour Party. If they spent less on rent Frank could have more for himself—this ' if ' went upstairs and downstairs with her, into the shops where she looked at both sides of a penny before parting with it, and invaded often her dreams. Sally Rigden pondered her dreams: the religious faith which had nourished her mother failed and dwindled in her, until the dry ground split to reveal older roots. All that part of her which craved a mystery fed itself on dreams and the broken vague memory of some few country spells of which her mother remembered only fragments from her mother: Sally received them at the same time and in the same spirit with her grandmother's recipe for bog beer, a safe cure for warts, and the neat way to turn the heel of a sock. Thus she was afraid to see the new moon through glass, wore a new pair of stockings on Easter Sunday, and if she broke one object knew that she would break two more before the week was out.

On the night of the 22nd August she dreamed that she

was walking with Frank in a town at once familiar and strange. The streets were narrow; it was evening; there were factories, crowds in the streets: she and Frank stood before a door into some building, and at once, without a word, Frank had left her. He passed through the door and she knew she would never see him again. Within there, they would kill him; it was not known, no one smote, but there were accidents—always accidents, and first one man and then another vanished into the vast building, to be seen no more. There were young men with sly cruel faces standing outside the door, and she shouted to them to help her and beat with her hands on the door. They laughed at her. She became frantic with fear, running here and there, looking for Frank and knowing that it was useless. There was nothing you could see: she shouted that there was danger, they were killing her husband, but there was nothing to see, all was behind doors and walls—only she knew that men were snatched away and in a hidden place, with machinery at the sides, they died. 'Frank!' she called. Her voice cracked. 'Frank! Why have you left me alone?' She woke with tears in the half light and lay for a long minute trembling: even the reality, Frank safely asleep with her, could not at once dissolve the terror of her dream.

She remembered it the next day, faintly, as she did her work, and again in the evening. Frank's cousin had come in to supper, and afterwards, while she patched Frank's shirt, the men argued, Joe Bradford blowing out clouds of smoke, until his large smiling face looked at them through the clouds, like in a picture, thought Sally. She trusted Joe without liking him. He was kind to them; he was sensible and generous and never once lost his temper, however wildly Frank spoke, and yet—she could not think what it was about him, and she felt ashamed, too—he vexed her with his great face and shrewd twinkling grey eyes. His eyes are small, he is like a pig, she thought. Something sharp, jeering, flickered in Joe Bradford's gaze, behind the good humour.

She stood up and asked him in an eager voice, kind and soft: Did he find the draught from the window too much? She would close it; the evenings were colder already—even in August——.

'Now don't you trouble yourself, my lass,' Joe said. He lumbered from his chair and closed the window himself. 'Si'tha—you shouldn't be dragging at awkward things now.'

Sally blushed and sat down again. She was a sight, she knew: it seemed as if her second child must be twice the size of the first. At least it was taking up twice the room. She felt burdened and clumsy, and longed for it to be born.

Now she thought she heard her son calling her and she rose and went softly out of the room. But the child was sleeping peacefully in his bed. His nightshirt was up round his neck: she drew it down and smoothed the blanket. 'Sleep, love. Sleep.'

When she came into the room again Frank was talking in a low voice. He was excited and upset. She could tell by the small muscle in his cheek; when he was vexed it moved quickly under his skin. She went over and stood beside him. Joe was listening to it with a faint smile, humorous, sensible, sly. She leaned with her hand on Frank's shoulder.

'My idea is, there's more to it than just our wages,' Frank said. 'Trade's good, is it? Right, you ask them for higher wages. They agree—well, anyhow, they give you half what you asked, see? Fine. Everyone's pleased, I'm pleased, Sally's pleased, the boss is pleased at getting off with half, *you're* pleased—it was you argued with them and made the terms—of course you're pleased. Next year— trade's bad. Why? No one knows. I don't know, the boss don't know, you don't know. All *he* knows is his profits are down, all *I* know is I'm to take less wage—and all *you* know is it's no use trying to get what isn't any longer there. So you argues—compromise, compromise, compromise—come to an agreement—capital and labour have much, you says, in common—oh, have they? Well, they haven't, see? Times are good—I may go up a bob. Times are bad—take two bob less and get out of here, see? Well, what's in common about that? You tell me. You only tell me.' He paused. 'Well, them's my views,' he finished, in a still lower voice. He felt Sally's hand on him.

'Do you credit,' Joe said, smiling. 'Mark you, I agree with them. And mark you again, *my* job is hours and wages, and regulations. I'm no politician. I'm not in Parliament—no, no, Frank my lad, it's Mr. Louis Earlham you want here now, not Joe Bradford. He's the member, isn't he? And same as you, he's a Socialist. You tell him what you want. One fine day he'll get it for you—if you can wait that long.'

His voice had in it the scraping jeering sound that Frank feared. It was because of Earlham. Joe Bradford disliked Earlham: he would never admit it; at meetings or in committee he talked familiarly to Earlham and made his sharp jokes—but Frank was not deceived by them. You cannot deceive the hearing of a lover. And what, if it was not love, did Frank have for Earlham? He believed in every word Earlham said; in election time he followed him from meeting to meeting, he stood for hours in the cold, he gave out leaflets; he could nearly—if it were not for Sally, he would willingly be shot dead for him. If none of this is love, the word is the poorer for it.

He had not thought all this. He felt only that Joe's sneer—oh, without a word—was bad; it was like the stones and the dirt thrown at Earlham that night he spoke in the street. It made Frank itch to send his hand against the other man's eyes.

And at once, like Sally—and perhaps because she was leaning on him with all her weight—he felt ashamed and sorry. Who knows better than me what a good chap Joe is? He had been kind: he was good and decent all round; in his soft Yorkshire voice he spoke words that put the heart back into tired men: women (all but Sally) liked him, the children came up to him in the street. That was Joe—good if ever there was a good man. A good friend.

' It's easy for a man like me to give off about how things ought to be and aren't,' he said, smoothing it all over, apologising. ' You chaps has the trouble of dealing with them as they are.'

Even as he said it, he felt the old disappointment. You heard a man speak at street corners, or in half-lighted rooms; you listened, the words striking down, like a hammer, like rods—' the workers must stand together, they must fight, they must——' yes, yes, he said to himself, and then what happens? when shall we stand? where? who was it spoke? He clenched his fist; he believed, his hand felt in his pocket for the threepence. *England, arise, the long long night is over*—His heart jumped. Something will come of it.

' Ay, that's so,' Joe said seriously.

All this time Sally kept her hand on her husband's shoulder. His face was turned from her, so that she saw an ear, a cheek, flat where hers was round, stiff short hair. One Sunday, years ago when she was going with Frank, they went to church—she wanted people to see her with him—and the text that day was, ' Behold a miracle.' It came to her that moment, and there was a flash of light from a window. What miracle could be more than the shape of Frank's head, how it had come from nothing, the bones, the flesh covering the bones? She could scarcely wait for the end of the service, thinking she had to tell him, but when she came to it, as usual there was nothing in her mind. They never found much to say to each other. Time and again she had the feeling, not understanding, and no words for it. It made her feel that she could do anything, move wardrobes, run up and down stairs, scrub, mend, sand the hearth, all without effort as if she were dreaming and would wake and find it all to do.

She wished Joe would think to leave soon. Tired, she rested her other hand on the chair back. The wood was worn smooth. She had two such chairs, which had been her mother's, and with a bed, a painting of a cottage, the large chest of drawers, an iron preserving pan, and four blue and red vases, were her pride and her good. She had enough of everything: all the rooms were furnished; in the sitting-room there was barely room to move round. She felt protected and safe.

So she stood, her hands on that she valued, and felt the child. She moved slowly, stooping to right a mat, and went out to the kitchen. Her father was busy there—he mended chairs and such for their neighbours—but she did not look at him. She stood with her head bent, waiting; her mind was full, heavy like a tree with its leaves in full sunlight, but there was no sound in it, no movement, only a sense of warmth and fullness, as if she had gathered all she could and must lie down and sleep.

CHAPTER XXVIII

EARLHAM THINKS OF THE FUTURE

EARLHAM looked fixedly at the wall opposite his chair. He wanted to avoid seeing the faces of the men and one woman in the room. He liked a very large audience, in which one pair of eyes was like another. A Divisional committee meeting bored him because there were only a few faces; he was forced to look at every one of them, and to listen to speeches so familiar that he considered they ought to be indexed and then, instead of speaking, each delegate to the committee could hold up a disc bearing the number of his favourite speech. He knew already which man would make the sensible and unavoidable comment on a proposal, and which would return at long length to what was said in 1912 when the identical proposal came before the Party. He knew that at some moment, Mrs. Harrowing would complain that not enough care was given to the forthcoming elections for the Co-operative, and another member would counter with the bad arrangements at open-air meetings, and a third draw out how in the neighbouring Division, where formerly he had worked, these arrangements (left solely to him) went, without exaggeration, like a clock. There were as many desperate ideals in the room as heads, and nearly as many good-tempered jealousies, which no one was willing to push to extremes. To understand why the English are the salt of the earth, as well as the most patient and the most exasperating people in the whole world, it is not necessary either to read what they write or to know the men who direct policy. The committee of any unimportant Divisional Labour Party—consisting it may be of two railwaymen, a local builder, an electrician, the foreman of a works, two women who in order to come have put off their ironing until the next day, a schoolmaster, an old journalist, a still older man who knew Keir Hardie, and a well-to-do man or woman whose Socialism is an affair of his nerves or his head and not of his bones—will serve to discover every virtue and weakness of our subtle stubborn race.

Earlham had become a Socialist with the same impulse that kept him dry-eyed when his mother, who died of under-nourishment, was buried at the charge of the Southwark ratepayers. It is true that it cost less to bury her than it would have cost to keep her alive, but her son missed her.

At each stage in his growth—when he left school before he had begun to satisfy his hunger for knowledge, and when he ran messages for a printer, without an overcoat and with shoes which blistered his heels and let in the rain, and when he fell asleep at his night school, and when, in the first years of their marriage, Rachel pretended to eat her evening meal before he came in—the impulse was fed by some fresh rage. He had no comforting beliefs. He did not believe that to be born poor is to be born fit for nothing except for hard work begun at the earliest age allowed. He did not enjoy coarse food, cheap and badly cut clothes, rough sheets (if any) on his bed. His skin was not thickened to enable him to do without warmth; bad air and tainted meat did him fully as much harm as if he had not been used to them from his first years. He did not discover Socialism. It discovered him, one evening when, to get a little warm, he worked his thin body into the very middle of an open-air meeting of the Southwark Labour Party.

His feelings about the delegate who had been talking for five minutes without being able to bring out what was in his mind were a blend of all these memories, of cold, hunger, tears shed at night, for his mother and because his heel hurt him, useless desires and rebellion, ambitions he might as well have resigned at birth, every throb in him of longing

for a life as different from the one given to him as if he had
wanted to have three heads.

He was exasperated by the speaker's slowness, by his
repetitions, and his windings back and forth without coming
anywhere. At the same time he felt a burning pity for the
man. He would give anything to be able to help him.
Waiting for him to find words was as painful as watching
the effort to walk of a man whose limbs are twisted. And
the limbs could have been straight, he thought, with fresh
anger. He stiffened the muscles of his throat to hide a yawn.

The room was airless. Its single window was kept
closed to shut out the noise from the street. There was a
smell of over-worn clothes and rotting wood. On one
painted wall was a network of cracks, and it was these kept
Earlham awake. With half his brain he pretended that
he was commanding a besieged city, set observation posts
protected his stores and his ammunition dumps, fastened red
flags to the public buildings; with the other half he listened,
nodded, answered questions and spoke about the situation of
the Party in the House. He said it reminded him of an
incident during the War when with a waiter from the
Carlton Hotel he found himself holding a long section of the
line. This started smiles.

Leaving the place, he had to walk through a bad part
of Deptford. In the narrow street every kind of smell was
sucked up and distilled by the August sun, petrol, air from
the sewers, sweat on unwashed bodies, the bye-products of
civilisation. A man about his own age and build had been
waiting for him in the next street. He came forward shyly,
with the words:

'We give out them leaflets th' other night, Mr. Earlham.'

Earlham stopped and gave him a friendly smile. 'Why,
that's splendid,' he said.

He could not remember anything about leaflets, nor the
man's name. He knew him by sight as one of his helpers
during the last election. He used to come straight from his
work to the Committee Rooms. Earlham could remember

about him nothing else, except that he hardly seemed to rest. He might be one of twenty other helpers with the shoulders of a working man, the blunt fingers, and the eyes blurred by their look of distance and patience. In spite of the heat, he wore a muffler—it was to appear tidy.

'Yes. Every last one of them,' he said. 'Most down by the docks.' He laughed shortly and looked at his hands.

Only anxious not to let the man see that he had been forgotten, Earlham walked the length of the street with him. He talked about the Party. When they reached the bus stop, he shook hands. 'Keep it up,' he said warmly.

'Trust us for that, Mr. Earlham.'

Earlham glanced aside when the bus started, and saw the man withdrawn about a stone's cast, looking after him. Frowning, he thought, What the devil is his name now? He sought in his mind among patient ghosts, unknown soldiers. Never had he felt a greater confidence in himself. He forgot his exasperation during the meeting. His heart leaped with pleasure in feeling himself able to repay the trust of humble men.

He was leaning forward, knees crossed, his head on his hand. Now he raised his eyes a short way, to the face of the woman seated opposite him in the bus. She was old: her skin was so closely covered with fine lines that it was like a worn rag; her eyes were sunken and still bright. She was dressed in the black coat she had worn each time she went out for the past fifteen years. Her hands, scored like her face with the story of her life, were folded idly in her skirt. At that moment the bus stopped; a few bars of music floated up from the street. Her hands unclasped themselves and her old fingers, like discoloured bones, tapped out the rhythm on her knee. Clearly she noticed nothing— it was some spring, as deep in her as her childhood perhaps, that welled up for a moment through the dead roots, and in a moment, as the bus started ahead, vanished.

Earlham was strangely moved. Here in these streets, he thought, life—choked back and sullied—runs clear at the source. He saw from the bus a narrow alley-way between houses, and doors opening into a squalid court. He imagined the heat and the stench. I'll rebuild it, he said, raging: I'll pull down the foul bricks, return them to the fire, kill all the rats, and raise up tall airy blocks—I'll build *upwards*, and the space saved shall be gardens. Why not? There are enough hands, enough bricks, enough heads.

The old woman got out, surprising him by her quickness. On the pavement she looked like a heap of old clothes. This heap still had some vanity—it paused at a shop window to arrange its hat before moving away.

Earlham looked at his watch. He was dining out: Gary had said he would come for him to his house, and he would be there now. Earlham felt restless and uneasy, wondering what impression he would take away from the shabby rooms. Now the journey, with its long waits, was endless. The heat inside the bus grew unbearable: not a breath of air moved in it until they were crossing Westminster Bridge.

Earlham reached the house to find Gary with Rachel, waiting for him. He looked quickly at Rachel to know her thought. For once he could read nothing in her face. She was unusually serious, but that might be only her feeling of responsibility for the visitor. She had even an air of watching him. Earlham was annoyed. Did she think Gary would steal the spoons?

' Have you waited long? ' he stammered.

' Less than half an hour,' Gary said, smiling. ' Your wife said I was not in the way.'

Rachel smiled slightly. ' He asked for you, Louis. When I said you were out, he asked for Mrs. Earlham. I told him that I was Mrs. Earlham, and he looked at me puzzled. It's very vexing, Louis. What can I do to look old enough to be a married woman—wear a cap, as my mother did as soon as she married? ' She shook her head, gravely. ' And now if you will both please go away. I had just bathed your daughter, Louis, and her clothes are still on the floor——'

Earlham caught an ironical gleam in her eyes. He did not understand her.

They dined in Gary's flat. It was the first time Earlham had been in the place, and he was half alarmed by everything, the huge entrance hall, the glitter of crystal and polished wood, the bronze lift, a room in itself. All this richness, he said to himself, and in Deptford children trying to sleep in rat-infested houses. He was ashamed to find himself here.

Gary's flat soothed him by its simplicity. He saw well enough that it was a simplicity which costs money, a great deal of money—and yet he liked it. Some impulse in himself craved just that ease and space. Especially he admired a Chinese rug and a desk which had been fitted to Gary's needs.

Their meal was a plain one, and the silver he handled thin, through age. He felt its lightness and smoothness. For no reason he recalled the hands of the old woman in the bus.

During dinner Gary for the first time talked openly about the Labour Party. He began by asking a question, and then as if absently he said: 'How I wish I understood your point of view.'

Earlham looked at him. 'Do you mean—my political views?' He spoke in a dry voice. It was on his tongue to say: Have you ever been hungry?

'No, no——' Gary said. He brushed politics out of the way. 'Your lasting views. What you hope for this country. Not to happen this year or next, but as an end.'

'I should like to pull down the houses I saw this afternoon, for a start.'

'Of course. And after that?'

'Social justice—to every child an equal chance in life, on his merits. Birth is not a test of fitness for one life rather than another. I know a Conservative member of Parliament, the son of a rich father, who has never had one thought in his life. Why is he there? Because a "safe" Conservative borough chose to elect him on his party label, his yellow hair, and his money.'

'All that means nothing,' Gary said calmly. 'What is important is to have a blue print of your just State, and a plan of campaign, marking the stages—this year's advance, next year's, and so on. Everything else is fairy-tales, written for the children.' He smiled. 'What would you do if to-morrow you were Labour Prime Minister, with a majority in the House?'

Earlham could answer this, and he did, tumbling one project after another on to the table among the plates and the used glasses. When he paused, Gary's heavy face had become mocking and affectionate.

'Yes, very fine,' he answered. 'And now shall I tell you who will defeat you? Your own followers. Tell me, tell me honestly'—he looked at Earlham as though he were depending on him for the answer—'how many of them have the knowledge—are competent to understand and control our extraordinarily complicated society? Industry? Finance? My dear chap, I can tell you that for two years after I began to interest myself in my own business, I was as much at sea as if I'd been brought up in a convent.'

He spread one hand on the table, and Earlham noticed almost with fear the unusual length and thickness of his fingers. He must be able to crack nuts with those hands, he thought, confused.

'The answer is—education.' He remembered the night school, and his uneasy sleep. That was awful, awful. 'You must educate every child as a responsible human being,' he said bitterly.

'And a responsible financier and director of industry? And in the meantime?' Gary's face quivered with laughter. 'No, no, Louis—unless you snub me, I shall use your name—we must be sensible. There will be a stage, a long and arduous stage, in which everything is done to improve the lives of workers——' He stopped, and said smiling: 'You admit that workers are necessary?'

Earlham put his hand to his head. Rigden, he thought suddenly. That chap's name is Rigden. Frank (or something) Rigden—he saw the man's face, with its look of expectant simplicity.

He felt hemmed in by Gary's mockery. It was all in the friendliest kind. He did not resent it.

'Work is necessary—but not poverty. Not maimed starved colourless lives.'

'I had something to suggest to you,' Gary said, with his curiously sweet smile. 'We don't agree in everything, but we are agreed on the next stage, at least. Why don't we pool our experience? Don't take me too seriously—and don't mistake me. I don't mean an alliance! I am a mine-owner—and as long as possible I shall remain one. You, my dear Louis, are a Socialist, charged to get rid of me! In the meantime we both want decency and order. The comparison is with America, where both sides shoot, lie, cheat, and murder. The American capitalist—like the American labour leader—is a dirty fighter. Do you believe sincerely that we can't do better than that?'

He went on talking for some time—and Earlham listened with a vague yet keen pleasure. He enjoyed being consulted. He enjoyed giving advice, and with every word he felt that he was entering Gary's mind. Come to think of it, there was as little to understand in William Gary as in Frank Rigden. He stayed until midnight, and told Gary about his boyhood, his mother's death, Rachel, the *Evening Post*—once Renn's name was on the end of his tongue, but for some reason he held it back.

He walked home. His heart was leaping; he was greatly exhilarated and aroused; vague brilliant images floated through his brain. At one moment the thought came, Have I been flattered or made use of? He stood still. At once he was strongly certain of himself. Well, let him make use of me, he thought, with a smile. I know exactly where I stand—I can look after myself; and no doubt, one day I shall use *him*! He quickened his steps. The darkness

round him—he was walking at the back of Victoria—and
the August night sky, pale, but not so pale that the stars
were invisible, made him want to throw his arms about.
He felt the senseless happiness of a very young man.   Perhaps
it was owing to him; his real youth had been hard.

Rachel was asleep.   If he spoke to her she would wake
as lightly and suddenly as a child.   Before she had moved
her head her wide dark eyes would be questioning him.
Did you enjoy yourself?   Are you tired?

He lit a candle, to save gas, and set it some way from
the bed.   Her body took up little room, and her thick black
hair, cut short as it was, hid one side of her face.   One
hand lay relaxed, above the sheet, the fingers held slightly
apart: she had thin supple fingers.   Even in sleep she had
the serious docile air of a well-mannered child.   That there
were fires in her thin body, he knew well.   She could be
moved to hot anger in defence of her faith—to Rachel
Socialism was not an idea, it was a rushing torrent, fed by
her racial memories of cruelty and oppression.   The occasion
past, she was again, at once, his calm loving Rachel, so wise
and thoughtful he forgot always that she was still very
young.

' Rachel,' he said.

Her eyes were open, watching him.   An instant before,
they had been closed.   He stooped over her, half kneeling,
and blurted out: ' What did you think of him?   You liked
him, didn't you? '

Rachel stroked his arm for a moment.   ' He is pleasant.
Intelligent—polite—handsome.'

' Is that all you thought of him? '

' He is not one of us,' Rachel said.   She looked at him and
sighed.

Earlham did not speak.   He was unreasonably hurt and
disappointed.   It was as if someone had told him that the
meal he had just enjoyed was meant for another guest.   He
was humiliated.   His hand lay still in Rachel's: he would
not, by withdrawing it, give away his disappointment and—

yes—anger. It had seized him, like a hand thrust against his ribs, in the instant she spoke. Not one of us. A foolish romantic phrase—and what did it mean?'

'David Renn came to see you this evening,' Rachel said slowly. 'I told him you were out and he stayed and helped me with the typing. He is good, is David.'

That was another grievance—that she should type notices and envelopes half the night for the local secretary. Let him write out his own notices.

'Renn's notions were always impracticable,' he exclaimed.

Rachel lifted herself on one elbow. She stretched her other arm round him and pressed gently against his head. He touched her small breast. 'Oh, my poor Louis, poor darling Louis,' she said softly. Her fingers caressed his hair. She could not have known why she felt this sudden pity for him: her heart became light with it; she felt she must protect him, from some person or danger. But from what?

'Come to bed, Louis,' she entreated him. 'It must be midnight. You will be tired.'

'Yes, yes, I am tired,' Earlham said quickly. He thought he said it simply to agree with her and to avoid having to talk any more, but when he got into bed he felt himself tired out. Leaning over against her for comfort, he fell asleep at once, and slept almost without stirring until Rachel awoke him at nine o'clock. She had been up and moving about as quietly as her cat Habakkuk since early in the morning.

CHAPTER XXIX

NICHOLAS was dining with Gary in his flat. They were together much more since Hervey was in Yorkshire, but something was missing from their intimacy. Nicholas was quieter and Gary more talkative than before. He asked Nicholas about his new work, and when that failed he tried to provoke argument by saying what he knew Nicholas would contradict. This evening he accused Nicholas suddenly of turning socialist.

'Nothing of the sort,' Nicholas answered. 'I dislike labels,' he added with vehemence.

'All the same, you are becoming what I call a social sentimentalist,' Gary said. 'You were talking yesterday of rich people as if they are somehow to blame for others being poor. You must know that's all my eye. It's a strict question of social and natural adjustments. Everyone can't be well off any more than everyone can paint or write. And it would be a hell of a world if they could.'

'It's a hell of a world as it is,' said Nicholas. 'How many half-starved and half-clothed children do you suppose there are within a mile of this building? I don't mind people being rich. What I mind is their frightful complacence about poor people's children. That shocks me. It ought to shock you quite as much. You used to feel these things.'

He did not look at his friend as he said this. After a moment Gary said: 'Sentiment is no use, Nicholas; you can have sane readjustments or you can have a bloody revolution. The Labour Party thinks you can have a

216

revolution without blood. That's one good reason why I despise them. They're woolly-minded. A logical Socialist would be a Communist.'

'And I suppose a logical Tory would be a Fascist,' Nicholas said swiftly.

'Do listen to me,' Gary said in a quiet voice. 'We can drop the labels. They don't matter, since no Englishman who is worth anything wants to splitarse about the streets in a uniform, bawling *Giovinezza* and administering castor oil to Ramsay MacDonald. Leave that to the idle. But I've thought this out to the last sandbag, or as far as I can see at this time—and you're the only person I'm going to talk to about it. I want your help.' As he said it, he knew it was no use asking Nicholas to help him. This was the first time such a thing had happened. He and Nicholas had been friends all their lives—that is about thirty years. He went on speaking in the same low voice.

'The world in 1924 has become too complicated. There are too many terribly powerful engines loose in it. I dream of a vast railway junction seen at night, hundreds of steel tracks interlaced and crossing; they vanish into the darkness and as your train rushes on you hope the signalmen are awake. The trouble nowadays is that the signalmen and the rest obey scores of competing companies, each with their own time-tables and wayleaves—result, accidents, confusion, loss, men dying and lost. The whole thing has grown too vast and crazy with power, to be carried on in the old way. The next head-on crash might finish us.'

He paused to fill Nicholas's glass. The meal was served from the dining-room downstairs and Gary's own servant waited on them. When the coffee came Gary sent him out. He was a Scot, an ex-soldier whom Gary had saved from jail for peddling without a licence, and he would certainly murder anyone if Gary gave him an order. As a servant he was less efficient.

'Well, what do you suggest?' asked Nicholas.

'There must be a plan,' Gary said. 'We must have

order—to avert the most frightful disorder. And because of the complexity, and the explosives lying about, we shall need strict discipline. You can't run a world in which aeroplanes and power stations and plague germs and our late unlamented Divisional Commanders are all present, as if it were only a little noisier than in 1824. And you can't run it on goodwill, as your Socialist friends seem to think. Why, Nick, I know one of the Labour men, Louis Earlham —a well-meaning pleasant good sort of a fellow—I like him immensely and I wouldn't trust him to manage an orderly room at the Base. No, no, that's no use now—we need knowledge and responsibility above and obedience below. The General Staff must know its job and the men must be decently fed and housed. . . .' Gary looked at Nicholas for a moment with an intense anxiety. He felt what he was saying. His eyelids twitched once or twice, a nervous habit which Nicholas remembered he had as a boy.

'Can't you see what I'm after?' Gary said. 'It would be a new world.'

After a few moments Nicholas said: 'I don't think I like your new world.'

'What's wrong with it?'

'I think I—a General Staff is always inhuman,' Nicholas said. He spoke badly—frowning and making a false start with each sentence. His mind was confused. He felt as though it had been churned; it was bursting with words but none of them were in place.

'You want to say—I——' he stammered. 'Oh my God I can't think—your mind is so much quicker than mine——' It was always quicker, he thought, seeing himself running after Gary in the past. *Come along, Nick.* He obeyed. For years and years he answered, *Coming*, as if no other answer were possible. No other had occurred to him. I suppose I never had a mind of my own until now, he thought, startled. The effort he was making became painful.

' Generals live too far from the front line,' he said. ' Look what a mess they made of Loos. And you've been talking as if we were at war still——'

' We are,' Gary said.

' Oh, nonsense.' Nicholas turned red. ' Any way, I loathe the idea of a world divided for ever into brass hats and other ranks—all the authority on one side and all the obedience on the other. Why can't you teach people to respect each other?' A blinding light came to him in his confusion. It lasted less than a minute, as if it were a search-light turned on and off by the same impulse. ' Here's where we split,' he exclaimed. ' You'd get us out of our mess with guardians and well-treated slaves. The Platonic city. Leave me outside. I couldn't stand it, Bill.' He stammered. ' Men should respect each other,' he repeated. ' They would. If they were properly taught.'

' Who's going to teach them?' Gary said. He was being very patient. His heavy shoulders were drawn up and forward, so that his head drooped.

' I might do that,' Nicholas laughed.

There was another silence. Nicholas felt strangely excited.

The movement of Gary's arm was like something giving way. It crashed down on the table and sent a knife flying against a glass. The noise of the glass breaking jarred Nicholas's nerves. He gripped the edge of his chair.

' This isn't one of the arguments we had in your old room,' Gary said. He dropped as he spoke a whole lifetime of memories on to Nicholas's hand—with all their skies, suns, fields yellow with flowers, and acrid-smelling dugouts. ' This is serious. I want your help, my dear.'

That now was too much for Nicholas. He made a gesture of denial.

He was obstinate in a curious way. Yielding and lazy, he became intractable at the moment when his deep emotions were involved. Some grudge, or some fear, started up to warn him not to give himself away. At these times it was best to leave him alone to quiet down of himself. Gary knew this. If he seemed to forget it, it was because he knew that nothing now was any use.

Nicholas did not look up. In his usual voice he said: ' You've taken over a part of Thomas Harben's shares in Garton's, haven't you ? '

' Yes,' Gary said, wondering a little. He had some experience of his friend's occasional malice, but it was always unexpected and it always stabbed him.

' You'll be a director.'

' Shortly,' Gary said.

' Well, I don't mind your taking the seat I kicked over,' said Nicholas. ' But Garton's and the rest ought to keep you busy, without wanting to play Follow my Leader—with yourself as leader.'

Gary's patience and his good humour gave way together. ' You're as weak as water,' he said. He raised his hand and brought it down on the table. ' You can't make up your mind—you don't know what you want until it's too late and then you lie awake thinking about your ruined life. I asked you to come into the Air Force with me before the War. You wanted to fly, but you didn't want to hurt your grandmother by leaving Garton's. Then you did leave it—when it was no use. You married a worthless young woman and you let her ruin you. I suppose in revenge you'll ruin your next wife with your scruples and your bad moods——' He broke off, as abruptly as if his throat had closed up. He looked exhausted and unhappy. ' I'm very sorry,' he said.

' It doesn't matter. You're quite right,' Nicholas said quietly.

' Let me give you some more brandy.'

Nicholas pushed forward his glass. The servant came into the room and said: ' Excuse me, sir, Mr. Renn has been waiting for twenty minutes. He said you asked him to call at ten o'clock.'

' So I did. I'd forgotten him,' Gary said. ' Just a

moment, Nick. I have some papers and letters for this fellow, he's off to Germany in the morning.'

Renn came in and stood near the table while Gary looked through the letters. Nicholas made some remark, which Renn answered as shortly as he could: without looking round Gary said: 'Oh, Renn—this is Mr. Roxby.' Renn smiled very slightly. Gary did not ask him to sit down, and he went away in a few moments with the papers.

'Who is that?' Nicholas asked.

'My secretary.'

'I thought for a moment I knew him.'

'You may have seen him here,' Gary said. His manner expressed his complete indifference to the idea.

Nicholas left early. Gary came down with him, and they sauntered towards Chelsea together as they had done a score of times. The streets and squares on the south of Hyde Park were as empty and cloister quiet as in time of war, so that one knew with pleasure that they were open to the sky. Gary had recovered his usual air of heavy and sleepy good-temper. They passed George Ling's town house, and he made a comment so apt and improper that Nicholas laughed until he cried. Gary walked almost the whole distance with him.

A few days later Nicholas saw Renn looking into a book-shop in Piccadilly. He went up to him and said: 'I thought you were in Germany.'

'Oh, I only flew to Berlin and stayed one night there,' Renn said.

They stood talking for a moment, and Nicholas invited Renn into his club to drink a glass of sherry before dinner. He had liked him at once, but it was because Renn had been ignored the other evening that he was taking so much trouble. But for that, he would have avoided him rather than make an effort. Nowadays he found that other people bored him more than they stimulated. I must be getting very dull myself, he thought.

They sat in the window looking at the Green Park,

which belied its name.   The hot August sun had dried up
the sap in the trees.   Nicholas loved the heat of the sun.
It renewed his youth and he became gayer and less nervous
or moody while it lasted.

In a rather hesitating manner Renn said:

' We have one friend—Hervey Russell.   I taught her to
write advertisements, and afterwards she was my assistant on
a weekly paper we wrote and published.   She even dusted
the office sometimes.'

' Of course,' said Nicholas.   ' I ought to have remembered
your name.'   He laughed.   ' Was she a good sub-editor ? '

' She worked very hard,' Renn said seriously.   ' She
wanted *The Week* to be a success—the one thing it couldn't
be.   I think she was disappointed.'

' Does Hervey want success ? '

' She did at that time,' Renn answered.   ' I rather think
she is changing.'

He had a review of Hervey's latest book in his pocket;
he had been carrying it about him for several weeks, meaning
to send it to her.   Searching for it, he drew out a thin book
of poems.   Nicholas noticed that many of the margins were
written over in a fine and clear handwriting.   He looked at
the title of the book.

' Do you like Eliot's poem ? ' he asked.

' No,' Renn said.   ' He doesn't enjoy his Waste Land.
He doesn't hate it either.   He has never lived there.'   And
as if the words were familiar on his tongue, he repeated:

> ' *Qui n'a couché à vent et à la pluye,*
> *Il n'est digne d'aller en compagnie.*

I think that's a proper comment.   It's not the whole comment, of course—that would be another poem.'

' Oh, you like Villon better,' said Nicholas.   He was
delighted and felt that he knew Renn.

' He is really and truthfully post-War,' Renn said, with
his curious smile.

' I began to write about the War,' Nicholas confessed.

He was surprised to hear himself saying this; he had told no one else.

'What happened?'

'I gave it up. The events were too close—or I was too sluggish a writer. I couldn't find the right words.'

'You'll finish it some day,' Renn laughed. 'Our friend Hervey will see to that.' Afraid he might have annoyed Nicholas, he said quickly: 'I began my own comment on *The Waste Land* some time before it was written. It's not finished yet. A long poem I call *London*, into which I'm trying to compress all I've learned from sleeping in the wind and rain.' He frowned. Nicholas saw that he regretted having talked so much of himself. But the account of Renn's unfinished poem excited him and he determined to know more in time.

Renn had seen an evening paper brought into the room. He asked Nicholas to forgive him for looking through it; he explained that he had written an article for this paper— it was the *Evening Post*—about the condition of the shipping companies. A friend of his, Louis Earlham, occasionally wrote for it and he had arranged with the editor to print the article, on the understanding that he was the author.

'Do you mean that Louis Earlham has signed it?' asked Nicholas. He was surprised and flattered that Renn had told him all this.

Renn nodded. 'You mustn't give me away,' he said absently. 'I know you won't.' He smiled slightly. 'And so actually I'm **not** indiscreet.'

'Is your article there?'

'No,' said Renn. 'In its place there is an article in the financial column, congratulating the Labour Government on refusing an inquiry into the loss of two and a half million pounds in the World Shipping Company. It was a flagrant case of fraud, by the way.' He put the paper down. It was impossible to know what he felt. In a few minutes he left, saying he must find Louis Earlham at once. Nicholas invited him to dine with him at home another evening, and he seemed surprised and pleased. When he had gone Nicholas found his copy of *The Waste Land* laid at the side of his chair. He could not help looking at one of the pages. The pencilled entries seemed to have nothing to do with the poem. One of them was dated July 30th 1924:

> *Mon enfant, ma soeur*
> *Songe à la douceur*
> *D'aller là-bas vivre ensemble.*

He knew that he was trespassing, and shut the book.

CHAPTER XXX

WHAT do I think about this man? Renn wondered. He
had been listening to Earlham for an hour, and so far Earlham
had said nothing that was not insincere or meaningless. And
this change in him—if change it was, and not the peeling
off of another skin—shocked Renn much less than did
his own indifference. He thought he must have caught
from Hervey Russell her naïve cynicism—the instinct (it
was not want of heart) that made her distrust all men, so
that no alteration and no treachery surprised her. It was
not simply because he loved Earlham that he found it easy to
forgive him for lying. Then why is it? he thought. Why am
I not angry nor contemptuous? Is it because I still hope?

He looked closely at this friend, and could not believe
that he had changed within. Louis is tired to death, he
overworks, Rachel had said. It is true, Renn thought,
Earlham looked as though fatigue had become part of him—
as he used to look during the War. Renn found himself on
a road he had no wish to follow; he drew back. A soldier
has no respect for politicians, he thought: in those days
Louis was also free.

He smiled at Earlham. 'Tell me why you found it
necessary to drop all idea of an inquiry into the shipping
scandal, and I'll believe you,' he said softly.

They were drinking coffee in an A.B.C. Outside, in
the gully of the Strand, the sun blazed on a welter of traffic
and struck from the pavement as fiercely as a gong.

'It was taking time and energy I couldn't spare,' Earlham said. 'You don't realise the difficulties in our way in the House. I consulted people, the chief himself. You can't tilt at windmills from the Left—it costs too much, and brings in nothing at all. Why worry because a number of middle-class shareholders have lost their money in a capitalist swindle? Who—except themselves—cares? And what business is it of ours?'

'We discussed this before,' Renn said, gently. 'Neither you nor I care about the lost money—lost in any case. But an inquiry—or if that was impracticable—an article, a series of articles . . . the shipping firms, with their inflated capital, their bank mortgages, and the rest of it, are the system itself. Expose them, and you expose the whole. The whole of the rottenness underneath, the money game, the instability, the unchecked greed—all. Moreover, the day is coming for England, for English ships, when you will be able to turn round and point to your written words and say: I warned you: in 1924 I warned you.'

He felt himself becoming excited and passionate. He stopped. Enthusiasm was out of place—and no use.

'Who would publish the articles?' Earlham asked.

'You arranged with Cohen to print one in the *Evening Post*. . . .'

'He read it and turned it down.'

There was a long silence between them. That was not new, but this time both of them felt uneasy. 'Tell me one thing,' Renn said at last. He was smiling. 'It's a foolish question—I am curious, that's all—do you remember writing the words *Socialism in our time O Lord* across an army order and posting it to me, the day you were demobilised?'

'Of course I do!' Earlham exclaimed.

'Do you still believe that?'

'I? . . . believe what?'

'That it will come in our time.'

Earlham shrugged his shoulders. 'It will come some time,' he answered. 'I don't know when. Who does

know? As MacDonald says himself—one should take only
one step at a time——'

'Or one step forward and two to the right,' Renn laughed.
'Does he really say that kind of thing? How—inspiring.
I'll tell you what, my dear,' he said gaily, 'and it is very
serious—I'm not laughing about it or you—one step at a
time is all very well for children—when we still were children
—but now it's too slow and barren. Safety first and socialism
in the millenium is not faith. It's not even fear. It's dryness.
The sap doesn't run in you; you're too well placed, you're
becoming bureaucrats and officials. Your reasonable attitude,
or whatever you like to call it, is your defence. You know
it as well as I do. But take care. Something lively and
violent is abroad. Impatient. I warn you that you will be
defeated by this—impatience. Call it so. In the end it is
you yourself who will defeat your own ends.' He leaned
forward and shook his friend's arm gently. 'Do you
remember? *Here comes a candle to light you to bed, And
here comes a chopper* TO CHOP OFF YOUR HEAD!'

He laughed again, looked at his watch, and jumped up.
'I have to go, Louis. I have an appointment at three.
Not in the least political.'

He paid their bill and hurried away. A Saturday afternoon
somnolence had fallen on the side streets through which he
walked to reach the British Museum. Miss Markham was
not yet there when he arrived, and he sat down under the
columns to wait for her. The pigeons circled as slowly as
dowagers. In the air there was a scent of burning leaves;
here, in the shade, it was very pleasant. He was within
a breath of falling asleep, when she touched his shoulder.

'You were asleep,' she said loudly, like a child.

'I wasn't—and you must not shout when you get in
there,' answered Renn. He spoke in a rush: his heart was
beating violently, as though he were out of breath.

'It's all "must not" with you,' Hannah cried. 'Mustn't
shout, mustn't laugh—what must I do, then?'

'Only remain exactly as you are, for ever and ever,' said

Renn. He now noted that when she laughed she held her head back so that her throat strained like a bird's—and he thought this as adorable as her hair, her tiny gold earrings, and her black eyebrows: he could not take his eyes from her.

Inside, in the great hall, she put her arm through his, and sank her voice to a penetrating whisper. She had a pencil and notebook in her hand; she was going to steal designs from the Greek vases. ' I shall change it—look— so,' she whispered.

' Now it's no more Grecian than you are,' Renn smiled.

' It's more amusing this way. Who wants to be an ancient Greek in 1924? And of course don't you know that I'm a Phœnician? I was born in that part of Cornwall where they landed to sell their silks and buy tin. One voyage they had a sick captain on board, and they left him behind, and when they came back for him next year he was married—to my ancestor. At least that's my father's story. Do you know my father? Henry Markham. He's an historian, and religious. You could say of him what Mrs. Slammekin said of the Jews—*and bating their religion, to Women they are a good sort of people*. He loves my mother, and to me, too, he gives money to live in London, and plagues us to death with his church funds and his collecting money to build more churches. As if there weren't more than enough of the dark dank places!—do you know, they remind me of shells at low tide . . .'

' What are you doing at Baring's? ' Renn asked. He enjoyed the sound of her voice, subdued now, but still clear and full. He scarcely heard what she was saying.

' I told you—studying to become famous.'

' Will your father pay for that too ? ' murmured Renn.

' I shall find a way,' Hannah said calmly. She closed her book. ' And now, let us look at the jade tortoise. I hope you mean to give me tea. I have forgotten to ask you— have you enough money? We have been twice to the theatre and once to a concert. I shouldn't like to ruin you.'

' My very dear and very kind Hannah——' he began.

Now he loved her so madly that he could not keep up a pretence of irony. His legs shook under him. 'You can ruin me if it would give you any pleasure,' he said, trying to laugh.

'Nonsense,' said Hannah. 'Are you earning good money?'

'Four hundred and fifty pounds a year!'

'Not bad. And you have no wife? No one depending on you?'

'My mother.'

'What is she like?'

'Kind. She's simple-minded but not simple. She looks after my father, who had a stroke and won't talk now, although he could very well.'

'But what does she look like?' Hannah said, smiling and impatient. 'I think with my eyes, young man.'

Renn saw his mother plainly—light and small, with the rosy skin of a north-countrywoman, finely arched nose, eyes clear and clear-sighted. He could not describe her. 'She is old and pretty,' he said lightly.

'He is half an idiot,' Hannah said with a sigh. 'Shall I design a dress for her, your mother?'

'Good heavens, no!'

'Tell me much more. Have you any friends?'

Renn hesitated a moment. 'Three, no, two—one, the best, is dead.'

'Were you a soldier? Were you ever wounded?'

'Yes.'

'Badly?'

'Shrapnel, in my leg. Enough for a lifetime.' He made a face at her. 'Here's your tortoise. He is really a beauty.'

They stood side by side to examine it. In her joy Hannah had forgotten her curiosity about Renn. She gazed at the tortoise intently and radiantly, her head a little on one side. Into the clear, always changing brilliance of her eyes, there came something disquieting, something cold, as it were a reflection from the creature's green smooth cold back.

'Oh my lovely monster,' she said softly. 'Do you know what'—she glanced at Renn—'my notions of beauty are embodied in this tortoise; I want my life to become as smooth and elegant. And it will—you'll see.'

After one glance at the tortoise Renn had taken a step backwards, to watch her. He had discovered that her hair was cut a little shorter at this side than at the other, and the discovery delighted him. 'I am sure you will get what you want,' he said.

'Of course,' she answered. On their way out, she told him exactly how she would manage her business—when she had one of her own: she displayed an astonishing grasp of detail and knowledge of the world. Renn was surprised and not surprised. He was torn between the wish to talk of his feelings and the certainty that she would laugh at him. He kept his voice steady only with difficulty. When she left him it was actually a relief, since without her he could give himself up to sensations and hopes of which he was half ashamed, so well he had schooled himself to expect nothing of life. Another hour like the last and I shall go out of my mind, he thought. A gulf opened at his feet. And far from dreading the fall into it, he felt a tremor of joy through his body. What would be the use of trying to describe it?—it is either indescribable or too familiar.

CHAPTER XXXI

HERVEY LEAVES RICHARD. THIS IS THE SECOND
TIME: THE FIRST, SHE LEFT HIM TO MAKE
THEIR FORTUNE.

At the end of August Hervey had written less than the
half of her novel, but what she had written was already the
length of a long book. She decided to make the best of this
misfortune. With a little trouble the second part could be
stretched to make not one only but two more books. And,
thought she, a trilogy is considered very respectable—as well
that it will bring in three times the profit of one book.
Satisfied with this Yorkshire reckoning, she wrote to her
publisher that she had finished her novel and would send it
to him as soon as it was typed.

She would be forced to type it out herself, partly to save
money and partly because she altered and revised each
sentence as she went, so that many pages could not be made
out but by her own eye. With all this care, she had no
pleasure in what she had written, and thought at times how
she could escape from this necessity of writing.

Now that the book was finished she became restless. In
two weeks, she had made her plans—to find work in London,
and to leave Richard with her mother until she felt ground
under her feet. So much for her ambitions. She was now
thirty and seemed tireless.

Nicholas had written that he wanted her, and that alone
would have drawn her to London, to try fortune again.

Danesacre in September is very lovely. The wind blows
most often from the south-west; light mists, gone before
noon, shroud the hills in the morning; in the clear air the

sky appears as frail and transparent as a bubble, stretched
to breaking point. As I grow older, she thought, I grow
closer to this earth: in time I may not be able to leave it.

She felt her mother's disappointment so keenly that it
was not easy to leave her. ' I hate going away,' she said
awkwardly.

' I'm sure I hate to see anyone go,' Mrs. Russell said.
She looked at Hervey with a softened air, and with doubt.
' When you were a little girl you were restless and patient—
I used to think, how can she be both ? You live now as if
you were made of iron, and there is an end to that.'

' I haven't reached it yet,' Hervey said easily.

Leaving Richard was a harder grief. She suffered as
much now as at the first; this pain seems to be incurable
by time or familiarity. She put spurs in herself to run from
it, and that was no use. She sat with clenched hands in the
train and wept bitter unseen tears. ' Why am I going ?
No good will come of it.' At one station she bought a cup
of tea, but she was not able to swallow it. She began to
think of turning back. Towards the end of the journey
she took Nicholas's last letter from her pocket, and read it
through again. She knew it by heart.

She had written to her old lodgings in St. John's Wood.
By return she had a letter signed ' Vera Wood (Mrs.).'
This woman, who was unknown to her, had just bought
the house. She offered Hervey a room on the second floor,
at a rent no higher than she used to pay to live in the attic.
Rents, like wages and hopes, had fallen since 1919.

In the few minutes when she was showing Hervey her
room, Mrs. Wood had told her that she was a War widow;
had sunk all her money in this house. ' Shoot m'self if
it sinks,' she whispered, smiling and nodding. She had
once meant, she said, to have a small house of her own.
But the War, and so on. You could wonder whether she
recalled at moments (perhaps at night) the image of a young
woman with her husband, or whether that had become
simply unreal, a story told of another woman. You could

wonder—but she would never tell you. She was thin and lively, with a reckless face and voice. Hervey liked her, as she liked all adventurers.

' Does a Mrs. Hunt still live here ? ' she asked idly. ' She had the first floor.'

' Has it now.' Her landlady looked at her with an inquisitive smile, sizing her up. ' D'you like her, then ? '

' Yes,' Hervey said.

' Well, I do, too. She's as bold as brass, y'know.'

She went away. After ten minutes there was a knock on the door. Hervey opened it, and there was Mrs. Hunt, truly as bold as brass, her gross merry face freshly painted vermilion and white. She invited Hervey to drink tea with her.

' Do you remember coming into my room five years ago ? ' she said in her strong voice. ' I declare you're not a pin less dowdy than you were. Why didn't you take the job I offered you ? '

' I didn't care for it,' Hervey said, smiling at her. Delia Hunt lived—and lived well—by tricking their money out of foolish unhappy women. It is the oldest business in the world and pays the safest dividends.

' You've changed,' Delia Hunt said drily. ' Five years ago you wouldn't have said it to my face. I see you can still smile in that way—as if I was your nearest and dearest,' she grumbled. ' Where's your husband ? Have you got rid of him yet ? '

' No,' Hervey said softly. ' I've thought of it.' She looked at Delia with a smile half embarrassed half ironical.

' Take my advice then, and be quit of him *and don't take another*. Freedom—and a little of what you fancy—that's life if you can bear it. If you can't—so much the worse for you. It comes to the same place in the end.' She jumped up, and walked across the room as if she were balancing her body on a tight rope. She seemed to beckon with her big coarse thighs as she walked. It was extraordinary—so much vigour with such a weight of flesh.

And she must be long past fifty, Hervey thought, watching her. There was something in Delia, in her very grossness and lively cynicism, that woke its like in the young woman, as if in both the life were the same in grain, of the same wood. But the one stem sank itself deeply in the earth, and the other sprang away from it.

To be with Delia added fuel to Hervey's restlessness. She felt strong and confident enough to do anything. The sense of youth, courage, and life grew stronger in her every moment: her cheeks burned; her eyes, her whole face, became eager and triumphant. And this was the young woman who, less than an hour before, was too wretched to drink tea and had thoughts of going back.

She was beginning to explain her plans to Mrs. Hunt when a step sounded on the landing. ' My husband,' Delia said. She looked at Hervey with her bold smile, and half closed her eyes, smoothing her dress over her body.

' I'll go back to my room,' Hervey whispered. One Hunt is enough, she thought—she had no wish to know a second.

' No hurry.'

Delia's husband was as Hervey dimly remembered him— a big man, hard and fleshy, with an arrogant face, good-looking without any grace or kindliness. He had a noticeable jaw, a prominent nose, and a long shapely mouth. When he opened his eyes widely, which he did seldom, there was something mischievous, something nearly engaging, in his expression. They were oftener half-closed, the line of the eyelids drooping at the outer corner; this gave to his whole face a guarded air.

' Tim, this is Miss Russell,' Delia said, with a jerk of her elbow towards Hervey.

The dislike Hervey felt for this man was instinctive. She was too arrogant herself to tolerate arrogance in a man. She felt that he had a contempt for women, and the accident that she understood why he despised women (because they gave way to him) did not make it palatable. Violent and eccentric (in her heart), she revolted against violence—in the strife now sharpening between reason and violence her word would always be for reason.

Smiling politely at Tim Hunt, she thought—exactly in the words she used as a child—I must take care, this is one of our enemies. She went away at once, not hindered by Delia. Delia's husband held the door open with a respectful air, which vexed Hervey again.

When she reached her room she ran to the window and opened it. A barrel organ below in the street was playing the *Missouri* waltz. At once she remembered the American flying officer with whom she had been in love during the War; and the doubts, the passion, the extraordinary excitement of those days. She remembered everything, every turn, stone, and bush on the road between the aerodrome and the farm where she was living. She had something then which she had lost, a sense of lightness, youth, life without end; the expectance of life to come. She expected —what? to become famous? to travel the world? to be free? Yes, all that, but something more, and more impersonal —that life would be sharper and swifter, needing less of this awful patience. In those days, she thought suddenly, I *was* free.

She spread her arms apart, and said gently: 'What will happen to me?' There was no gentleness in her mind. She felt lifted up and fierce, ready to strike. Happiness, ecstasy—she had had both, a full due. I have never been happier than I am at this moment, she thought. She felt giddy with it.

What, she cried, shall I do with my evening? To stay in (and to write to Richard), as she meant before talking to Delia and hearing that worthless memorable tune—that had become unbearable. She would write to Richard, and afterwards she would go out. But I must talk, I must have news of the world. Nicholas did not expect her until to-morrow and—how little she trusted him—she was afraid to telephone to him. If it should be the wrong moment!

Her first thought was of her friend, T. S. Heywood.
She spoke to him on the telephone and an hour later she
was seated with him in Gatti's restaurant in the Strand.
' Why Gatti's ? ' she asked him.   Whoever came to Gatti's ?

' For old time's sake,' T. S. said ridiculously.   His eyelids
flickered.   He was extraordinarily pleased to see her.

' And why have you come up ?   Did you come to be
reconciled with my wife, with Evelyn ? '

' No, never,' Hervey said bluntly.   ' I came up to find
myself some work.'

T. S. lifted his eyebrows.

' Tired of writing novels ? '

' That was not *safe*,' Hervey said.   He laughed at that,
and asked her what sort of a job she wanted.

' A decent one,' Hervey said swiftly.   It did not matter
what she said to T. S.—they were friends since too many
years.   ' Not one like yours—inventing poison gases for
another war.   You ought to be ashamed.'

' Why ? ' he said mildly.   ' Look round this room.   How
many of them are worth preserving ?   Think of the underfed
millions.   Why care about the future of a nation which wastes
its human resources so callously ?   And then if we are such
fools as to need another war, to cure us of our folly, we
deserve what we shall get.   There are still people, our
Hervey, who talk of war with respect.   It will be a shock
to them to discover that war has become the filthiest of
filthy sports.   Dropping my gas bombs from four miles above
a city is scarcely heroic—no more heroic, at least, than
hiding from them and trying to hide your children.   From
my end the snag in the whole business is that so many of
them won't survive the shock, to hear me say I told you so.
I hope sincerely that I shall be about when the Prime Minister
and the two slipperiest of his colleagues emerge from their
cellars and are promptly lynched by the remnant.'

Hervey was seized with anger, familiar and useless.   She
clenched her hands under the table and saw herself running
away carrying Richard.   When he was older she would not

be able to save him. He would be killed as her brother had been—cruelly, uselessly, because there were men who prepared war and fools who allowed it. T. S. knew what she was thinking. He smiled sweetly.

'Don't listen to me, Hervey. I'm a crabbed old man '— he was not yet thirty—' there'll never be another war. We'll warn people in time what to expect.'

'Well,' Hervey began. She sighed. She was touched by his kindness: she liked him; she understood him better than anyone in the world, better than Nicholas (whom she loved). She and T. S. were more intimate than falling in love would have allowed them to be. And yet there were things she could not say to him. She was on the point of asking him, Was he happy? had he made it up yet with Evelyn? She looked at him—he was forbidding, the lines round his mouth warned off sympathy and curiosity: she held her tongue. He is very unhappy, she thought.

He asked her abruptly: ' Are you going to see Georgina Roxby ? '

'Yes, of course,' she said. She was surprised, and took instant care not to show it.

'Then tell her——' he stopped, and glanced at her as if he hoped she would finish the sentence for him; a queer air of mockery and exasperation crossed his face. ' No, what's the good ? ' he said, with a smile.

'Did you like her ? ' Hervey ventured.

'No, I fell in love with her,' T. S. said, without bitterness. He was ashamed, but not angry. ' I'm well aware it's useless and to be honest it had nothing to do with me. It's like having had a stroke—except that I can't have another and pass out. Queer, ain't it ? ' He looked at her with a wide smile. ' People talk to you about themselves—heaven knows why. You're not interested, are you ? '

'Not especially.' She hesitated. ' I'm not interested in you, what I feel isn't interest, it's love of a kind—I wish I were some use to you. You live alone too much.'

'I'm not entirely celibate,' T. S. observed. ' As for

living alone, I never knew anyone I could live with the whole time, except you or Philip. I shouldn't want to marry Georgina, only '—he paused, and added in a dry voice—' only to keep her to myself. Oh my God, Hervey, what fools we are—I, you, all of us—the fools of our bodies.'

Hervey did not answer. She was thinking now less of him than of herself, of the folly—call it a passion, an obsession —that forced her to waste hours thinking about Nicholas when she should have been at work or writing her book. No doubt it was weak and she must be ashamed of it, but— she half smiled—why so serious? Even a great passion will become manageable in time. Looking at her friend, at his old-young face, and nervously twitching eyelids, at the stains on his fingers, at his slovenly clothes, she was moved to pity for him, and because she could remember him very distinctly as a dogmatic young student she exclaimed:

' How happy you and Philip and I were when we were young and very poor, living together in those wretched rooms, and we thought we were going to change everything.'

T. S. laughed. ' Tell me what you expect to do for yourself now, Hervey love. Can I help you at all ? '

' I shall be all right,' Hervey said. She was supremely confident. ' I can always get work.'

' What it is to be young! ' T. S. mocked her.

Hervey blushed—not because he was laughing at her, but because of the warm kindness in his voice. She felt the warmth in her veins, running to her heart, and thought: If I could help him. But there was nothing she could say or do or be that was any use to him in his hard need. She was shaken by grief and pride: the final and terrible loneliness of man is less than his courage, and both are at once in- voluntary and an act of his will.

CHAPTER XXXII

END OF A STAGE

Before setting out to meet Nicholas on Sunday morning she swore to herself she would say nothing that sounded as though she hoped he would change his mind. If he wanted to drift, she would herself drift with him. This would be hard for her practical and managing mind, but she needed the lesson. She had learned more self-discipline in the last eight months than in the rest of her life.

It did not occur to her that Nicholas might have changed or have been learning.

They met at Paddington and took train to Henley. As they walked through the town she remembered an evening three years ago: she had learned that Penn brought his mistress here and to torment herself she made the journey to Henley to look at the hotel and to imagine them together. With Nicholas she passed the very door. No tremor of all that foolish agony survived. She thought, I shall never feel so deeply again. This thought, and her escape and new lightness of heart, lifted the moment clear out of time. Sunlight and the shadows cast by the houses were sharpened now to last forever—that is, for so long as her mind lasted. She felt a joyful relief, and walked now quickly to keep up with Nicholas. He walked always at such a pace that unless she protested he would weary her in the first mile. He was too impatient to loiter.

' Did you have a good journey yesterday ? '

Hervey hesitated—an inconvenient scruple drove her to answer: ' I didn't come yesterday. I came up on Friday.'

239

Nicholas stood still. 'Then why did you wait until last night before ringing me up?' He was frowning, puzzled.

'You expected me yesterday.'

'What has that to do with it?'

'I thought,' Hervey muttered, 'you might not want to see me earlier—you weren't expecting me.'

She broke down in confusion. Nicholas walked on slowly without speaking. 'Are you angry?' she asked timidly.

'With myself,' Nicholas said.

'Oh why, Nicholas? You've done nothing—it was my foolishness——'

Nicholas turned to look her in the face. 'It was my proved unreliability,' he said quietly. 'You didn't trust me—why should you? I've let you down too many times.'

'I don't think of you in that way,' Hervey replied. She controlled the excitement his words roused in her.

Nicholas smiled at her with love. 'You are too good to me, my dear, and very bad for me. Better than forgiving me both times when I behaved like a cowardly fool, you should have turned away and left me to come to my senses——'

'But how could I believe you would come to your senses?' Hervey smiled. 'You were far more likely to forget me in a month.'

'If you left me now I couldn't forget you . . . I hope you will never go away again, Hervey, unless I go with you. We'll go sometimes. I used to walk about Spain with Bill, before the War.' He was speaking with visible difficulty, in a low voice. 'If you're still willing to live with me, that is.'

'Yes, that is what I should like,' Hervey said at once.

'Absolutely sure?'

'Yes I am sure.'

'You are the best person I know, the most honest, and the dearest,' Nicholas said quickly. They were still walking along the road. He halted her with his hands on her shoulders, and kissed her mouth. She was surprised and touched to feel that he was trembling. As so often happened to her in supreme joy, she was unmoved and calm. It came to her at once as soon as she had promised to live with him that they must marry—because of Richard and because nothing else would reconcile her mother. She decided this in silence. To her sudden relief, Nicholas said:

'We shall have to marry, because of my mother.'

'And Richard.'

'Yes—and Richard,' Nicholas said. He had some idea —he was to discover how weak it had been—of Hervey's concern for her son.

'But the divorce, Nicholas?' She was feeling her way. 'Talking about it—with the lawyers.' And with your wife, she thought, unable to bring herself to speak of Jenny Roxby.

'I shall dislike it very much,' Nicholas said. 'And so will you. I shall lose my temper at least once and behave badly. Will you forgive me for it?'

'You had better ask at the time,' Hervey said drily. To cover one roughness by another, she added: 'Will your mother and Jenny go on giving trouble?'

'My mother, no,' Nicholas said slowly. 'As for Jenny— she never realises how relieved I should be to throw away all the cards in my hand and clear out, for good.'

'Yes. Don't forget that I'm in your hand,' Hervey said.

'Oh, you're clever,' Nicholas exclaimed. 'You always know what to say, to leave a mark.'

Hervey did not answer. She was still, in some north-east quarter of her mind, sceptical and uncertain. After all, we have said this twice already, she thought. Yet at the end of their day she was certain. What had happened? Something so prosaic, so devoid of romance that she scarcely liked to think about it. She thought of it all the more. During lunch she had said: 'I must buy some things for my room—a tea-service . . .'

'But I'll bring you a silver teapot and the other things,' Nicholas interrupted. 'All the Queen Anne silver Mary

Hervey left me is still in my bank—I had no use for it. You might as well have what you need of it, now.'

'It's very kind of you,' Hervey said gently. Nicholas had offered it as a matter of course, and she would take it in that spirit, without seeming impressed. But the whole balance of her life was altered. Her mind became perfectly still—like an orchestra in the instant before an arm, raised and then lowered, lets spring forth a jet of sound. It was as if he had said: 'Here is my life, which you can use as you please.' She was lifted up, grasping the handle of a silver teapot.

They were blissfully happy—like old friends or like young lovers—at home in each other's mind and yet timid and strange, with all to learn. Although nothing had been settled about their future, and all that was only beginning, they were confident and easy. On their way home, Nicholas said abruptly: 'I wish you would arrange for me to see Penn, before he goes up to Oxford.' He did not give her time to answer, but put his arms round her and held her closely. 'My love, my dear, my pretty one. I swear I'll be kind to you my whole life.'

In her room, when she was alone, Hervey took her manuscript book and wrote: 'To-day Nicholas and I agreed to marry. I shall try to become more dignified, as if I were partly Mary Hervey and not only Mary Hervey Russell. I must work harder—both to help him and so that Richard can have everything he needs.'

Her last thought, as she lay down in bed, was of Richard. In spite of her great happiness, two tears forced their way under her eyelids and she had to harden herself not to cry.

The next morning she wrote to Penn. She heard nothing until the end of the week, when he answered that he was coming to see her. He came on Sunday afternoon, and at first he was cold and overbearing. He accused her of having deceived and lied to him.

'You told me in July, when you came to mother's, that you were giving the fellow up. I suppose I can take it that was a deliberate lie arranged between the pair of you——'

'No, it was all mine.' She felt ashamed to say that nothing had been deliberate—at that time she had been only unhappy and uncertain. And it is true, she thought, I was dishonest—and I have behaved badly. She tried to think of an apology which would not make him more bitter.

'Why should you imagine,' said he, 'that I'm going to let you keep Richard?'

Hervey felt a flash of rage through her head. 'For one reason, you have never kept him yourself. And for another —you gave me your solemn promise—when I forgave you for Miss Hammond. You even said then that you would help me in every way, if the time came when I wanted to leave you. I don't ask you to let me divorce you, or to make any sacrifices, but you have no right to take Richard from me, and rather than lose him I would give Nicholas up even now. But that wouldn't do you any good.'

'Nothing is any good to me,' said Penn sadly. 'I shan't take the boy from you, Hervey. Anyhow I'm finished. You've done me in.' His face quivered. Hervey saw that he was going to cry: she felt sorry for him, and bitterly ashamed. Forgive me, forgive me, she thought, and so that she need not look at him she walked over to the window and leaned out.

'*Must* you do this, Hervey?' Penn said.

'I'm sorry,' she muttered. She turned her head awkwardly. 'I'm sure I don't know what I can do with my life.' He stood up and took his hat. 'I'd better take myself off. Sunday afternoon, too—it's awful, awful—there's not a thing to do and nowhere to go. I feel like shooting myself.'

After a minute Hervey said softly: 'Is there anywhere you would like to go?' She was in despair, as if she had promised to live with him again.

'When I was coming here this morning I thought—How wonderful if a miracle happened and instead of kicking me out Hervey said: Hurry up, we're going to Richmond, just

as we did in the old days.   And everything would be all
right.   And now——'

Hervey spoke with decision.   'Well, let's go to Richmond.'
She ran out of the room, downstairs, and telephoned to tell
Nicholas that she would not be dining with him.   When
she went back to her room and saw Penn waiting for her
with a smile on his face, she felt a sudden dislike: he had
no more shame than to ask her to pity him and once more
she had given way to it.   She hid her feeling, and listened
attentively when he talked to her about the book he was
writing: it was the third he had begun since he went to
Oxford.   He can finish nothing, she thought; he will not
be able to finish this, and he will always have excuses.   When
he said that his book would startle the country she felt sorry
for him again.   I have no right to leave him, he has not
more sense than a child, she thought sadly.   She made a
suggestion about the book, which he agreed to consider.

A strong wind was blowing: it sent the leaves scudding
from the trees and in the autumn sky vast clouds toppled
like snowballs.   It turned out that Penn had left the notecase with his money at home.   Hervey paid for their lunch
in Richmond and for dinner at Oddenino's.   Afterwards
they came back to her room.   She was tired out and nervous;
she sat down on her couch, her bed by night, hoping that he
would go soon.   At last, since he showed no signs of moving,
she said:

'I'm very tired.   I was working until midnight last
night.'

'You want me to go?'

'It's half past nine, my dear.'

Unexpectedly Penn covered his face with his hands.
'Don't send me off to-night, Hervey.   Let me stay.   Just
think—I'm going to be alone for the rest of my life.'   He
let his hands fall weakly and looked at her with a grave
frightened face.

There is not a line on his face, thought Hervey;   he
doesn't change: he is thirty-three and unchanged.   She felt

a confused impulse to keep him with her. The half-formed thought crossed it: after all, I have been married to him. At the same time she was ashamed, and indifferent—it is unimportant, she thought, it is nothing; it would be unforgivable.

'I haven't anything with me, no luggage, no money to go anywhere.'

'Why is that? Where did you mean to spend to-night?' she asked coldly.

'I was going home.' He looked at her with an awkward smile. 'The last train left an hour since.'

'Why didn't you tell me?'

'I couldn't face it. I kept hoping that something would happen. Even now I can't believe you're getting rid of me. How have you the heart to do it, Hervey?'

She was stirred by some feeling which belonged to the past, to the days when he had been part of her inner life. Without the least wish to do so—but only this weight of the past and its memories—she was about to say to him, Very well, stay. At this moment she heard Nicholas's voice in the street—'Hervey.' She sprang up and went over to the window. Nicholas was looking up at it; she received an extraordinary impression from this glimpse of him in the dark street—as if a number of unimportant items, his straight rather stiff back, his gloves, silk muffler, the stick pressed against his side, had been invested with a symbolic dignity. She felt the deepest respect for him.

'Wait for me—I'll come down,' she said. She was more ashamed of herself than she had ever been. 'No, no,' she said quietly, 'walk to the end of the street. I'm not quite ready.'

She turned to Penn. He was standing with his back to the fireplace, a look of disdain on his face. She scarcely saw him; he had become rubbish to be cleared out of the way. 'Please go now, Penn.'

'Very well,' he said haughtily.

'You will need some money for an hotel.'

She held out a note. Penn took it with the same stern and haughty expression, and put it into his pocket without looking at it. ' I'll return it to you in a day or two.'

' Please don't feel that you need repay me.'

' Well certainly you owe me some money,' he said in a curt voice.

' Yes, yes.'

' I had you and Richard on my hands for more than three years.'

' The three years after Richard was born.' Hervey nodded. She found his gloves and gave them into his hand. He pushed them in his pocket; a piece of paper fell out on to the floor: he stooped for it quickly but not before Hervey had noticed that it was a cloakroom ticket for luggage. She said nothing. With a last smile full of meaning and irony, he went away, slamming the door.

The sight of the ticket had completed Hervey's self-scorn. To think she had so little discipline that she had been ready to take him back. She had no time to reproach herself. She washed her hands, took a coat, and went down. Penn had gone, and at first she could not see Nicholas. Then he came towards her from the other side of the street. She went to meet him. ' Who was with you ? ' he asked.

' Penn.'

' I thought so.' He made no other comment. He began to talk of his mother, who was half reconciled to his divorce; Hervey listened and looked at his face in the darkness, and felt happier. It seemed to her that she had been ill and had recovered. The cool air on her cheek and the pressure of Nicholas's arm in hers were both so close and real that the disaster she had just escaped retreated to the edge of her mind. I don't understand it, she repeated: but in fact, with one part of her mind, she understood it very well.

Two days later, Penn and Nicholas met in her room. Penn came in a few moments after Nicholas, said ' Well, Hervey ? ' in a cold voice, and greeted Nicholas with what deserves no better but to be docketed stately courtesy. The two men sat at opposite ends of the couch. Nicholas was grey in the face: he felt that this meeting was sordid and thoroughly false. Moreover he had taken an instant dislike to Hervey's husband. Everything about Penn, his voice, his attitude, his coarse nostrils, exasperated Nicholas; he could scarcely look at him with civility. He felt ill, as though he were inwardly bruised.

Hervey knew, from the grey tinge in his face, that he was in pain. She felt nothing, however. Her mind was cool and observant, almost amused. She had taken a number of papers and bills from her desk and when neither Penn nor Nicholas seemed willing to speak, she half turned her back and began to sort them, tearing up some and folding the rest into a neat bundle.

At last Penn said: ' I understand you wish to marry my wife, if it can be arranged.'

' Yes,' snapped Nicholas.

Hervey broke into a fit of laughter. Both men looked at her, Penn gravely, Nicholas with surprise and disapproval. She controlled herself and went on sorting papers.

They made a few other as meaningless remarks, then Nicholas left. She did not move to see him out: she felt it would be embarrassing and useless. When he had gone she went over to her desk and looked for a rubber band to put round the bills.

' I suppose you want me to go too,' Penn exclaimed.

' Yes,' she said gently.

' It's all over.'

Hervey opened a drawer, felt in it; it's all over, she thought dreamily: she closed the drawer and turned round.

' I never thought you would let me down, Hervey,' Penn said quietly. He looked at her.

Her throat felt as though it would burst. I will *not* cry, she thought, disgusted by her weakness. She looked into another drawer and said hurriedly: ' There are no rubber bands.'

' What did you say ? ' asked Penn.

'I said, there are no rubber bands, I ought to buy some, it's necessary,' she said loudly.

'Why?' Penn asked, taken aback. He waited a moment, then seized his hat and walked slowly and stiffly from the room.

Hervey sat down, and began to laugh. Her mind mimicked for her the affected voice Penn had used. 'I understand you wish . . .' This is terrible: how can I laugh at it? she thought. She jumped up and walked about the room until she could control herself. She felt terribly ashamed, but as soon as she thought of their faces and of Penn's words her lips twitched. No, no more, she scolded herself, in her mother's voice; think shame now.

In one corner of the room lay four cases of books and a tin box which had arrived from Danesacre the day before. She borrowed a tool from her landlady and prised open the cases. When all the books had been unpacked, dusted, and set on shelves, she unlocked the box. She knew that it was crammed floor to top with the letters Penn had written to her before their marriage. He enjoyed writing letters.

Half my life is here, she thought. Obeying a strong impulse, she carried the box to the basement, where there was a furnace for heating water (sometimes it did). She filled the boiler with quires of words that had cried, laughed, and suffered passion while they were alive. Now it is really at an end, she thought. Grief choked her and she fought to quiet it. Forgive me, dear dear Penn. It was my fault— I was the stronger and harder of us. She threw in the last bundle, pressed it down with the rake, and drew the damper. Mrs. Vera Wood, meeting her on the stairs, thought she looked almost ferocious. A madam, that's what she is, she said gleefully, and why shouldn't she be? Life's hard on women that are too soft: no mercy. No going back to begin again. She looked at Hervey's retreating back, and thought confusedly of to-night's veal, of the petersham for her skirt, and the photograph (like and unlike a million others, the face smooth and immature, eyes without thought, leather strap crossing the tunic) that stood in an imposing frame—she would rub off the tarnish—on her dressing-table. In her mind the photograph had replaced the original, and when she thought of her husband the living image wavered and faded out, leaving its glossy shadow with her. Who's there? she cried, thinking of someone who had come in, but it was eight years ago, and now hurrying into her room she pushed behind the photograph a half-empty jar of cream and the curling-tongs.

CHAPTER XXXIII

PARTY IN A FOG

THE next day—it was October 9th—Evelyn Lamb telephoned to Hervey to invite her to tea. She felt a momentary sickness when she heard Evelyn's voice. She was too cowardly to refuse to come—her usual cowardice in an awkward meeting. She would say anything to avoid an unpleasant scene.

At four o'clock she was waiting, nervous and irritated, in Evelyn's workroom. Once more she looked with grudged pleasure at its simplicity. What spirit—the same?—in Evelyn, wrote her essays, with their directness and precision of judgment. Hervey frowned. It vexed her intolerant mind (and years) not to be able to place the other woman, to be forced to distrust, dislike, admire, feel sorry for her. Evelyn came in and walking quickly to her took both her hands.

'It's heaven to see you, Hervey. You can't know how I've missed you and thought about you.'

'I was very glad to come,' Hervey said, with the conviction she could put into a lie of this order. She was acutely embarrassed.

'Don't let us quarrel again,' said Evelyn. She looked at Hervey with an imploring gaze. It was impossible to be either comfortable or believing, and Hervey could only smile in answer. She had a smile which deceived most men and women into supposing she loved them: did it deceive Evelyn? But that I shall never know, she thought helplessly.

'Sit down, Hervey. Shall I ask them to bring you some tea here? Or would you like sherry?' Hervey declined both. 'The usual dreadful people are coming this afternoon. I know you'll help me with them. People like you—it's your trick of persuading them all that you love them. Hervey, you could become a figure in the writing world, if you would take trouble. Perhaps you don't want that. It's ghastly, I know—but then what else is there to do? what *do* you want?'

'Peace, quiet, and a little fun,' Hervey said quickly. She was thinking, So you fetched me here to make use of me? I don't mind that.

'I have scarcely a single friend—among the hundreds of people who come to the house and stay for hours,' Evelyn whispered. 'You're one of the two or three people I love and can trust. I have no one else.'

Can she possibly be sincere? Hervey wondered.

Hearing voices, they went downstairs to the drawing-room. Hervey had come dressed in a knitted coat and skirt, with a hat made of silk ribbon, now shapeless and faded by the sun. She was supremely indifferent to her clothes, but she looked with envy and liking at Evelyn's dress, the rough black silk fitted closely round her body. It had been designed for her —and Worth it, Hervey thought, delighted with her small joke. It carried her through the first awkward moments, before she had turned herself outside in to face the company. She went through this curious process each time again. There was no shortening it. The self which emerged to do duty for the living original was not in the least inhuman: Hervey had no social grace but she had kindness and gentleness and she had come to have a certain authority.

Before long there were at least forty people in the room. It could hold sixty in comfort—a room running from back to front of the house, perfectly proportioned. Tall windows faced towards the river. All the lights were lit. The October afternoon, thickening to fog, crept to the windows. When a servant approached to draw the curtains on it someone had protested: gradually the light inside the room took a strange aqueous quality; it changed colour imperceptibly, until it was opaque; in the corners of the room, and above the cornice, it began to flow into thin eddies like water swirling round a stone. Hervey was entranced. None of the others seemed to notice it; they had separated into groups, talking against each other, with here and there a solitary, out of place and unfriended. Hervey wandered about the room, talking to these outcasts. It was not so long since she herself had been an outcast. As she went, she caught echoes of the talk, streaming back like seaweed, in the current of excitement flowing between minds and bodies. A room full of writers, musicians and what not, must (she thought) be closely like the tank of electric eels at the Zoo. She smiled nervously at the reviewer who also wrote poetry and was said to have excellent taste. Although Hervey was afraid of this woman, she could not help despising a gentility that is held aloft like a buckler. Another elderly and beautiful woman was saying as she passed: ' My dear, at that time she was sitting at my husband's feet all day: he wrote her first novel for her. Many critics, I am told, consider it her best.'

Evelyn presented her to a prosperous fellow-novelist, but while he talked to her his face was half averted and his eyes searched the room for a mark better worth his powder: Hervey tried valiantly, but soon fell into disconcerted silence and crept away from him.

A young very stout man was leaning against the wall. He was alone and neglected, but seemed happy. He was as tall as he was stout, and by his smooth cheeks could be twenty-five. His smile was kindly and good-humoured. Hervey talked to him for several minutes before she learned that he was the benefactor providing money for a new monthly paper, born so much before its time that it was forced to live in an incubator. He said that he was not a writer. I have found, thought Hervey, the true patron. She looked at him with respect.

' How good of you to give money in these hard times.'

' All times are much the same in my business,' he answered.

' Yes ? '

' I own a shroud factory.' He looked at her with a fond
smile. ' It's a family business—do you know, I found out
that in winter the girls caught chill after chill through
coming in wet? Now we provide dry stockings on the worst
days. Result—fewer colds, more and better work. Oh,
we're thoroughly modern in our methods. I'd be pleased to
show you round the workrooms any day.'

' Thank you,' Hervey said gently.

She withdrew. But now she could only see people
standing about in their bones, gesticulating with glasses and
cups of coffee. It was a nightmare. Almost with relief she
saw a new-comer approaching her. No bones visible here.
William Ridley was solid flesh—you could imagine it set
cold like a bladder of lard, but not dissolved. His small
shrewd eyes gleamed with ironic humour.

' You here again ? ' he greeted Hervey. ' I thought you
were dead and buried in the country.'

' So I was.'

Less than a month ago, Ridley had published his first
novel. It had every quality of a great novel except great-
ness; every excitement except the mysterious excitement of
literature, the shock of a new birth, a spiritual exultance
which springs between the word and the idea, and derives
from both and wholly from neither. The book had been an
instant and overwhelming success.

Hervey stared at the writer of it without envy, but not
without sharp interest. She had tried faithfully to read the
book and had broken down after fifty pages, wearied by so
much jovial noise and bustle. It seemed to live in much
the same relation to literature as Tannhäuser to music.
She even thought that the time was past for such books,
crammed like sausages with the beliefs, irrelevant or fraudulent,
of comfortable people. She confessed that she was wrong.
Fifty thousand readers in a month cannot be deceived.

' Your novel is a success,' she said, smiling.

Ridley looked at her with a derisive gleam in his eyes.

' Yes, and I told you it would be. And it's no flash in the pan, either. I have another dozen or more where that came from.'

He has reached a stage in his journey, she thought. A rich dark vapour from the farther stages rose and enveloped him.

' And I'll tell you what,' Ridley said, genially, ' that last book of yours is as dry as sticks. You want to get more life into them, see? Don't overdo it, though. All you women writers, you're either too careful or else too violent. What you want to do is to strike out something for yourself, don't keep on hashing up old stuff, and don't try to be clever. Look at me now—I have tons of new ideas, but I take care to put them in the vernacular, so that everybody can enjoy it. That's the road to do well. I told you—and I told Evelyn Lamb the same.' He had begun to look about him. ' Here, who's our Evelyn got with her?' he asked slyly.

Hervey turned to look. She recognised Julian Swan at once; but with a sudden feeling of uncertainty, she held her tongue. Evelyn, she knew, had been Ridley's mistress for a short time. It was clear that the intimacy between her and Julian Swan had reached the stage where Evelyn wished everyone to believe they were lovers. The very way she laid her arm on Swan's was an avowal.

Ridley struck Hervey lightly with his elbow. ' Looks to me as though our Evelyn has to make the running herself.'

The impulse to protect the other woman was too strong for Hervey's prudence. ' Writing popular novels has blunted your mind,' she said pleasantly.

She left him. Walking round the room to the window she saw there a young woman dressed as unsuitably as herself. It was D. Nash, whose first book was on the step of coming out: she was pressed against the wall, hiding her thick country shoes. Hervey saw that she was in agony, hating every one in the room and vexed with herself for having come. Why had she come? Probably Evelyn had written to her one of her lying impulsive letters.

Hervey watched her for a moment, and then crept to her side. 'Why are you here?'

'I was invited,' D. Nash said gruffly. Her dark eyes were as expressionless as stones. Simply she is not here, Hervey thought: she was sorry that the other young woman was not enjoying herself and began to try to make it up to her.

'I have reviewed your book for the *Daily Post*—it is worth a thousand dull clever novels.'

'Thank you,' D. Nash said, quivering. A little appeased, she looked Hervey in the face. 'I never thanked you for taking it to Mr. Frome. I suppose he is publishing it because you told him he must.'

Hervey corrected this illusion about the nature of publishers. 'Even so,' D. Nash said brusquely, 'you did everything for me. I know I'm a fool, but I'm not stupid.'

'It was a privilege,' Hervey said; she did not add 'to serve genius,' but had meant it. In D. Nash's first novel there was the simplicity, directness, and exaltation of the *Songs of Innocence*. 'Have you begun another book?'

'Not yet,' D. Nash answered. 'There's so much to do in the country in summer. There are the jams to make, fruit to pick and bottle, and then cooking for the harvesters . . .' Sinking her voice she began to talk of what was familiar to Hervey, the clear beauty of the Hampshire downs, blue-green in summer and grey-green in winter, and the lines as cleanly sharp as if God had stretched down his compass to make them; the smell of bread baking; the jogging gait of a fat pony along the roads; the call; the return call—she cupped her hands here as if the image of a room, a warm cell, had entered her mind; the movement of the seasons. Her hands were large, and the fingers lay apart on her knee, as if resting between labours.

'At one time when I was living on a farm in Hampshire,' said Hervey, 'I helped to make the cheese for the winter. It was warm in the dairy, warm and still, and the floor cool stone. I stirred the cheese with my right hand—it turns the nails soft—and held a book in my left.'

'What was the book?' interrupted D. Nash.

'It was a translation of the Book of the Dead.'

'A queer book to read then,' said D. Nash, with her deep short laugh. She stretched herself, forgetting the shoes.

'I had it from a library,' Hervey said.

D. Nash looked at her closely. 'You should be living that life now.' She stood up.

'Would you like to speak to anyone?' asked Hervey. 'Mr. Squire is over there, and Mr. Edmund Gosse, and several novelists. Mr. Middleton Murry is here somewhere, and Mr. Wolfe, a poet. That plump old man is an editor pregnant with his leading article—Doomsday and After.

'For heaven's sake—no,' cried D. Nash. 'Besides, I have no more time. But I'm less sorry I came,' she finished simply.

Hervey walked with her to the door, because it is unpleasant to walk alone through a great many distinguished people who do not know you and would not be pleased about it if they did. She returned, meaning to find Evelyn and say good-bye. There were now fewer people in the room but those that were left made more noise. Julian Swan had attracted eight or nine listeners. He was boasting himself that he had helped to bring down the Labour Government. It had resigned that day: Swan's part in this event was not clear, but he was jubilant and presently flushed. 'Now they're on the run we know how to keep them there,' he exclaimed. 'Do you know what—there's too much of this equivocal damned liberalism loose in the world, except Italy. Time it was hit hard over the head and given a pauper's funeral. The difference between a liberal and a Red is only a degree of smell. The one with his snivelling conscience and chattering about liberty opens the door to his nastier brother, and so we shall go on until someone has the decency to kick them both out. Freedom for the scum of the earth! We need a Mussolini. I can tell you——'

One of his listeners was William Ridley. He was watching Swan with the sly shrewd derisive look in his eyes which vexed people at whom he looked in this way. They supposed he was jeering at them. Very often he was—but with the almost impersonal malice of a peasant.

'Here now,' he said, nodding his big head at Swan, 'what do you know about freedom? You don't know much about mine, do you? Try telling me what not to do with my own tongue and brains and you'll hear about it from both. I'm not any man's jack.'

The jibing note in his voice pricked Swan. 'Don't be too sure you'll always be able to save your skin,' he said with open contempt.

'I don't see anyone in this room big enough to reach me,' Ridley answered soberly. Swan turned away with care not to drag his foot.

Leaning towards Ridley, Hervey whispered: 'Well done. It was very fine.'

'Are you off now?' he said heavily. 'I'll come with you.'

They stepped into the fog. It caught at their throats and so wrapped them round and bemused them with prickings in the eyes and nostrils and rolled past them in sluggish waves of dark acrid vapour that they were only aware of walking by the feel of the pavement under their feet. Hervey, the country-bred, was afraid. It was all she could do not to seize Ridley's arm. He saved her from disgrace by taking her elbow. His voice grumbled away in her ear like water underground.

After they had walked for almost ten minutes the fog lifted ahead, and they could walk without groping. She found he was still talking of Julian Swan.

'A jackanapes,' he said, 'a pup of the ride-'em-down school. Like to dock him with my own hands. I hate tyrants, whether they wear helmets, top hats or red shirts— it's all one to William Ridley. If I had my way I'd give every man in the country free bread and beer and every woman free a good house and to every child free milk and schooling and a doll or an engine or something.' He chuckled.

'Yes, I approve,' Hervey laughed.

'What was your father?' Ridley asked.

'A sea captain,' Hervey said. 'All mine, the Russells and the Gartons, have had to do with the sea for five centuries.' She thought, without speaking about her, of Mary Hervey. Why should I own her? she thought drily. For another reason she would not tell him about the Hansykes, landowners before the Gartons were heard of—how did these forgotten master mariners make their voices carry out of the past? Only by their headstones in Danesacre old churchyard on the lip of the east cliff.

'Middle-class, with more wants than pence,' Ridley exclaimed. 'Mine too. It's us that have given England the most and best of its teachers, writers, managers, experts, together with its certainties and its excuses for doing nought but go on in the same way. Don't talk to me about Mussolini—nor the dictatorship of the proletariat either. I can do m'own dictating.'

He released her arm, and they walked side by side in silence. A profound intimacy sprang between them, and because of it, since they were unlike in everything except their hard stubbornness, at the same birth an equal enmity. Why, thought Hervey, I know him as well as I know myself. But what in her was a spirit, in him was no riper than the seed buried in the ground. He had, though, a dignity with his gross conceit. Hervey felt it; and liked him no better for it. She would have preferred him to be all gross, so that with an easy conscience she could despise him. As it was, for two pins she would have liked him because she knew him.

'You'd better come in: I'll make you a hot drink,' she said when they had reached her street. 'Something to put you on, we say in Danesacre.'

'You and your Danesacre!' Ridley jeered.

He came in, snuffed about the room a little, and approved it. They went on very well together. In the middle, there was a single knock at the door. Nicholas walked in. Hervey

had given him a key to both doors.   He came forward
smiling, sat down as if in his right, and made himself pleasant
to Ridley.   In a few minutes Ridley stood up to go.   He
had observed that Nicholas walked directly across the room
to lay his hat and stick on a chair in the far corner.   Master
here, he thought smiling.   Time I went.

He was scarcely out of the room before Nicholas exclaimed:
' I can't stand that man.'

' You don't know him,' Hervey said: she was half irritated,
half pleased by his violence.

' Thank God I needn't.'

He built a great fire, and sat shivering over it.   The fog
was in his bones.   To spare his going out into it Hervey
made an omelette and coffee in Mrs. Wood's kitchen.   With
bread and honey they sat eating it before the fire, and afterwards talked, and then were silent, feeling the inadequacy
of words or kisses to express love.   Making one of his sudden
movements Nicholas knelt beside her.   ' Do you ever hate
your body ? ' he asked.

' If I thought of it at all I should only be sorry for it,'
Hervey said.   ' It's been cold and hungry, it used to ache
washing clothes and carrying Richard upstairs; I couldn't
hate anyone who has known me so long.'

' I hate mine for failing me so often now,' Nicholas said
under his breath.   ' A wretched instrument,' he said.

She knew this mood of his, an impatience which fastened
on her, expecting she would ease it.   Another woman
prepared it for me, she thought.

' The body's enjoyment counted for everything in my marriage.   When I came back in 1920 I wasn't so—adequate.'

' You're hurting yourself to no good,' Hervey said.

' For a time I believed that Jenny had only left me
because of it.   Even now, although I've realised that she
had a score of reasons for leaving, I sweat when I remember
some things that were said.   I'd made up my mind not to
risk hearing them again.   Suppose you came to feel in the
same way about me, Hervey ? '

'Will you never forget her?' Hervey said sadly.

'What do you mean?'

She chose words with blind care. 'Only that you, Nicholas, are the most marvellous experience I have had in my life. To lay your hand to mine gives me pleasure.'

'Oh my poor dear,' Nicholas exclaimed. 'There are better pleasures.'

'I know,' Hervey said. 'You have had them with Jenny, and so you are sorry for me.'

'You'll have to forgive me,' he said anxiously. He put his hands over her knees. 'Don't tremble. I didn't mean that. My beloved Hervey. I wanted to say—if I were not always tired——'

'I am perfectly happy,' she said, with a faint smile. 'Perhaps my senses are too childish—or too subtle—but I find that a light touch like this gives me all the pleasure I need or can bear.'

'Oh Hervey, Hervey, you are beautiful,' Nicholas said.

He laid his arms round her, and covered her knees and hands with kisses. He felt that she breathed more quickly when he touched her. 'You do everything for me, bear with me, and approve of me,' he said. 'I should like to spend the rest of my life here in this room. If I could stay to-night——'

'Why shouldn't you?' Hervey said quietly. 'The couch you gave me in place of my old one is wide enough for us both. You wouldn't have to walk through this fog.'

'Your landlady——'

'Isn't up before eight o'clock—you could leave earlier.'

Nicholas stood up. 'Are you sure? You want me to stay?'

'Yes of course,' Hervey said. She rose, and kissed him. 'Why are you afraid of the simplest things? Now I must make our bed.'

He watched her take sheets and blankets from a cupboard. He enjoyed watching her so much that he forgot to offer his help until it was too late. Then she took off her dress and hung it away in the same cupboard. He remembered watching Jenny make precisely that gesture of lifting and smoothing—for a moment his mind was cold with the past. He closed his eyes. When he opened them the present swung back, with the quickening shock of blood in his wrists and temples; he felt a sense of warmth, joy, and exquisite relief.

Hervey glanced at him and lay down against the wall, trying to take up as little room as possible. Nicholas was surprised to feel her thin and weak in his arms. He felt a sudden shamefaced pity. I ask too much from her, he said to himself. Moving a little, she put her mouth against his ear and whispered: 'Have you room?' He answered by holding her still closer until it seemed that they had one heart and one breath, and Nicholas thought: This is the meaning of my life, the circle of quiet at the centre—oh, let me not forget it, not fear again.

CHAPTER XXXIV

PRICE IN THE OPEN MARKET
OF A MESS OF POTTAGE

HERVEY listened patiently for an hour to Nicholas's mother. Clara Roxby scolded and lamented as though Hervey were to blame that he had married Jenny. Her words, too rapid and incoherent for ordinary sense, took first one shape and then another in Hervey's mind, as a cloud is at one moment an eagle and in the next a castle with ramparts and in the next a hound. One of these images, a young dreaming Nicholas in love with his young wife, was no pleasure to her. She would have been glad to run away from it. But Clara would not allow this: an unwilling cruelty drove her to tell Hervey all she could remember about Nicholas's love for his first wife. It was partly because she had not been able to tell anyone what she suffered in seeing her only son waste himself on a loose woman. And then, too, she had to talk about the horror in which she held divorce. Neither Georgina nor Nicholas had any patience with her shrinkings. It scarcely crossed her mind that Hervey was the last person she should have expected to listen to her with kindness.

Insensibly she began talking of much older griefs. Again Hervey's mind was opened to ghosts who had scarcely a shadowy claim on her—a young lively Clara poked her toe through her flounces; dropped her wedding bouquet; bore her first child (Nicholas) without help but that her husband and a native woman gave her; opened the letter telling her of her husband's cruel useless death.

'And then,' Clara Roxby said, 'my mother—*your* grandmother, Hervey—came in like a great key in the lock and took charge of Nicholas. She did everything for him—and to tell you the truth, Hervey, you remind me of her too strongly, and I suppose I shall have to sit shaking and groaning in my room while you do exactly what you please with him—just as *she* did . . . No, don't soothe me! I'm extraordinarily agitated and I'm enjoying it.'

'You know that Nicholas will always do as he likes,' Hervey said gently.

Clara's face altered swiftly. 'Yes, he will,' she said. 'Nicholas is very selfish—the only person for whom he was unselfish and kind and thoughtful was Jenny.' She looked at the young woman with belated surprise. 'Why are you so kind to me, Hervey?'

Hervey shook her head. She had left the slight smile on her face for so long that it seemed grown there—did the wind change? she thought. Now if she said: Because in the last resort I am indifferent—it would be true—but she was not likely to say it. You could count on much kindness in her before you came on the last resort.

She left Clara at last, and hurried away to meet Marcel Cohen. She put out of her mind Nicholas, Nicholas's mother, and his wife, and thought closely what she must say to bring him to give her work. He had invited her to lunch with him at the Carlton. As always, walking into one of these places, she felt she had no right to be there. She was too soon. She sat down and looked morosely at the flunkeys; because she was shabby she despised them.

Cohen was especially kind to her when he came. He admired in Hervey Russell something he had not himself, a polite heart. He would have admired it less had it not been joined with a shrewd powerful mind. It was always in his mind that he could use her: so much shrewdness, energy, intelligence, tempted him to set it to work, as if she were a valuable tool lying idle.

He wondered whether she felt awkward sitting here in a tweed coat. 'The first time I was invited to dine with a rich man,' he said, smiling and nodding, 'I had no money

myself at that time—I got the better of him very simply—
I made a point of not agreeing with anything he said.   I
didn't disagree.   But if he suggested that claret would be
a good drink, I said Yes, but burgundy will be better—and
when he praised Baden as a handsome place I, who had
never been out of London, cried up Aix-les-Bains—all with
the greatest politeness and simplicity.   To this day—when
some great man who mustn't be disobliged asks me to do
this or that—I say to him: Certainly, my dear sir, but you
must allow me to do it in my own way, which is not yours.
It never fails to impress.'

Hervey looked at him with so vivid a sympathy that he
talked for another quarter of an hour about himself.   He
then realised that for the eighth time (the number of their
meetings) he had not succeeded in learning more about her
than he knew at first.   He was more surprised than offended.
It was long since he had had anyone to whom he could
speak of his hard youth.

Hervey had not forgotten for a single moment that she
needed work.   She had no chance to speak of it until the end
of the meal.

' Ridley has given up his reviewing for the *Evening Post*,'
Marcel Cohen said.

' Yes ? '

' You have reviewed two or three books for the paper, I
see.   Do you like reviewing ? '

Hervey did not like it.   One in a thousand novels had
some beauty that was worth pondering.   Of the rest you
could say only that they were worth a week or an hour, or
worth nothing.   To spin two hundred words off that was
torment.   She looked directly at Cohen.

' Yes.'

' Well enough to do it every month ? '

Ridley had been writing a column every week in the
Evening Post.   She was silent for a moment, then with an
air of candour said: ' Every month ?   You wouldn't mind if
in addition I wrote weekly for another paper ? '

It did not enter his mind that she had not been asked to write for some other paper. It did not enter Hervey's that this leap of her wits, this almost instinctive parry, was a cheat.

Marcel Cohen's eyes, lustreless, protruded. And now you could see by how much a brutal temper had helped him to his prosperity. An unimportant detail, if once he concerned himself with it, could spring a mine under his staff. He had once sacked an entire department for putting to other use a shelf labelled Files.

'Another newspaper? Certainly I should object,' he said with energy.

Hervey put her head down. 'Naturally I would rather write for the *Evening Post*,' she said. 'It has a better standing than—the other paper. But in the beginning, sometimes money is as necessary as reputation.' She looked at Cohen with her dazzling smile.

'Well,' Cohen began. He tapped the edge of the table with his fingers. Hervey watched them, thinking how strong and yellow they were, like the separate limbs of an animal. She was silent.

'You'd better take over Ridley's column and write once a week.'

After a moment Hervey said calmly: 'Yes I could do that.'

'We paid Ridley too highly. You can write twenty-six articles at ten guineas. If we're both satisfied, you can go on with it. We'll see.'

'I shall do as well as I can,' Hervey said.

'Of course you will,' Cohen answered genially. The trace of his annoyance vanished. He was pleased with her, with his bargain. There was nothing in her looks to tell him that she would have been content with five guineas. Now she was already adjusting her mind to a new level. If he wanted her to go on after the first six months she would ask fifteen.

'We'll have fresh coffee,' Cohen said. He sent a waiter

off to bring him a copy of the *Evening Post*, and unfolded it.
'Well what do you think of a government that lets itself
be thrown out on behalf of a gutter rat of a Socialist agitator?'
With bleak contempt—he knew the smell of gutters—he
quoted: '*Soldiers, Sailors, Airmen, don't shoot strikers*. Now,
if it had been Don't shoot Ramsay MacDonald, it would
have meant something,' he sneered.

Hervey strove with herself in anguish. To tell him that
she was a Socialist and to lose by the word all she had bought
and paid for with lies. What business has he with my
beliefs if I do his work for him? Then bitter shame overcame her. She said nothing, sullen and inert, looking down
at her hands and at the worn edge of a cuff.

Cohen's working car, a Daimler, had waited outside the
restaurant. In the chauffeur's hearing he said: 'Now,
young woman, mind what you're about and I'll see to it
you get on.'

Hervey turned red. She hurried away, shamefaced and
unseeing, towards the Circus. In her absence of mind her
eyes rested on the figure of an elderly man huddled in a
doorway. Some moments later, her mind came back to the
place and remembered that it knew him. Fretting at the
waste of time, she turned and walked back. The man had
a few sprigs of heather in one hand. They were his passport to an existence of sheltering in doorways and the angles
of walls. He did not recognise Hervey. Of another life
he had had he retained only the memory of a wrong done
him, and the names of his enemies, the enemies of all
simple trusting men. 'Where are you living?' Hervey
asked.

There was no answer to that. She waited a moment,
half seeing the disturbance, as slight in itself as the final
tremor of a life, started in his brain by her voice. She had
spoken hurriedly, ashamed to be overheard, if anyone should
see her speaking and getting no answer. His eyes filmed
over.

Hervey looked covertly in her purse. Our food and

drink, she thought, cost two pounds. She had less than the
sum in her purse: she put all she had into his blind hand,
but that did not help her. She was angry with herself,
because she had given away her money, and because she had
lied, and because at some moment, in some place, she had
made the wrong choice. There is still time to go back, she
said. She knew that she would go on, until she lost herself.

.   .   .   .   .

Hervey writes. ' At that time I believed that I should
be a poet. I did not realise the fatal inadequacy of my
mind, which neither sees nor hears, but feels in the dark.
I feel everything, even the different pressure of light and
darkness on my eyeballs. Now I am in a narrow street
between walls. When I emerge from it shall I be old and
exhausted or young still and of use?

' The truth is that I have no courage. I have the gross
strength of hunger. If you beat my fingers off at one edge
they will grip the other. But I hate above all violence
and cruelty; when it comes to killing I can feel no difference
in the agony of a dead striker and a fat dead rich woman
who while she was alive believed that the poor are animals
and foul their beds. I am not ruthless enough to endure
violent revolution. I shall argue myself into a fever and lie
awake to-night if I think along this road. And the road
ends in a bog.

' Do you remember the patch of black spongy ground in
the middle of the moor, with the stumps of trees sunk in it,
like rotten teeth, crumbling under our feet to powder?
How long since the trees were green? Fifty years, two
hundred, a thousand? There are too few trees and too
many people in this country. I should like to revisit it for
a day when the Black Country has gone back to grass, the
wild horse stamps on Parliament Hill, and the Strand is a
marsh shaded by trees seeded from the forest that has folded
over the stones of Park Lane and Oxford Street.'

CHAPTER XXXV

"THE RATS ARE UNDERNEATH THE PILES"

COHEN leaned back in the car. When he was alone, without need to talk, to show himself to an audience, his face was older, yellower, almost tragic. He was unaware of tragedy. It sprang in him from an older root than his early poverty, older than the boy of nine slaving to support his mother and sisters, older than the infant swaddled in a clean rag in a room without light or air. It underlay the brutality in the lower part of his face and the generosity in his mouth with its fine womanish curves.

He thought of the young woman during the moment it took him to settle closely into his seat. Why did he take trouble with her? That she was finally intractable, because of the cross grain in her, he knew. It might be her likeness to her grandmother—the old woman had spoken to him once, with unnoticing rudeness, in the score of times he had seen her. Under-lip thrust forward, he hoped, without rancour, that she had heard in her grave change coming to her beloved firm: what had been one body, strong, shapely, now embraced eighteen more, and the whole swollen and dropsical with added water. I should get out clear, in good time, he thought—now, this week. Another man seated in his skin argued that what he risked if he stayed was worth the peculiar pleasure of being in at the death of Garton's. Pleasure? Cohen retorted, turning upon the other his yellow outraged face: maybe you want I should ruin myself for your pleasure? Feeling in his pocket he drew out a small shabby notebook, the kind with a leather cover which takes refills (his staff supposed he carried it because he was too mean to buy another, but there was another reason), and his pen, and began writing a note to remind himself to order his brother-in-law, who was also his broker, to sell the rest of his holdings in Garton's. He paused with the note half written, crossed it through, and returned the book to its place. Maybe Garton's would ride it out, in the end. He addressed the overbearing and indomitable old woman. 'If you'd been alive to look after your business it wouldn't be the shape it is.' Hervey Russell was politer to him than Mary Hervey had been. Would she be so, he wondered, if she were not poor? Or had her upbringing tamed her? He wished briefly that he had asked her about her beginnings. There was a story, a harsh one, about her mother, Mary Hervey's daughter. A sudden and devastating coldness swept round him, a lick of wind. No one can relieve himself in words of his burden of memories. To no one could he bequeath the deeds and thoughts, the truly horrible and despairing knowledge of life acquired by a boy of nine.

He walked very slowly up the stairs to his room in the offices of the *Daily Post*. One or two queries awaited him. The next day's issue contained, with a savage attack on the draft treaty with Russia, another castigating certain Tory papers for treating with respect the views and activities of Russian émigrés, former officials of the old régime. The draft treaty, with its provision for a loan, had only been signed two days—the ink was still wet when the Government took its fall. Both Cohen and Thomas Harben had lost money in Russia, and Harben had a special interest in blocking sales in England of Russian timber. The attacks in the *Daily Post* seemed to defeat each other. Cohen passed both articles. He was surprised by the question.

' Use both? Why not? ' he said, in his harsh peremptory voice.

' It seemed contradictory——'

' Nonsense. Why help Russia out of her mess? But to trust these White Russian riff-raff—they with their Diplomatic Representatives—I'd as soon jump out of this window. They're rotten—rotten through.'

He brought his strong white teeth together with the sound that made his editor think of a rat. He knew Cohen's pleasure in destruction. That rodent mind of his picked holes in every old building that came its way, and made a profit of the pickings. It had other pleasures—there was, for instance, Cohen's understanding of music, certain music. And he gave freely to obscure charities. How do you account for a well in the desert? There must be rock somewhere in the dry ground.

Cohen dined at the club. He went home to find his daughter, Mrs. Groelles, waiting for him in his library. She was vexed, he saw that, her body erect and still in the chair by the fire, hands gripping the sides. When he came in she made a movement with them which he recognised. It was his dead mother's very gesture of impatience, whenever a child (she had eight) wearied her. He thought what rage Fanny would feel if he told her that. When she married Groelles she had cast off, by a deliberate act, from her race. She had had friends of her own age, Jews; from one day to the next she denied them. Even her mother and father had not eaten in her house. All this Marcel Cohen had seen and he forgave it to her. He loved her as Jacob loved Benjamin, so that he put her faults outside her, like elder brothers for whom she could not be held responsible. So. And yet to-day, and as willingly as a good steward, the savage part of his mind regarded in her not only her wilful alienation but the measured growth in her of the thing she denied. It seemed that, as she denied her race, with an equal force it invested her delicate body, and whom she had put outside spoke from within.

' Well, my treasure,' he said, hurrying to her, ' it's very pleasant to see you.'

' It's not pleasant to sit here two mortal hours waiting for you,' Fanny said. Her voice had a harshness, unless she took pains to soften it, which came strangely from her young rounded body. She was thin without sharpness, tall, and white-skinned.

'Two hours!' Cohen repeated. He seemed confused. 'I'm very sorry indeed. If you'd only told me you were coming. Have you had any dinner?'

'I didn't want any,' she said curtly.

Her father made a sound of distress. 'No, it shouldn't be, Fanny. If you don't eat properly you'll fall ill, and then what should I do? I'll have sandwiches sent up— and a little glass of burgundy, eh? Makes blood—as nicely as port, and you don't like port.'

'I don't want anything,' Fanny repeated, her voice quick and unloving. 'Do let me alone, father. I didn't come to eat.'

'Well, never mind why you came, the great thing is you're here.' Cohen touched her hair gently—it was red, darkened and smoothed to her head with essence, one finger-size bottle of it costing two guineas. It was no wonder the large allowance Cohen made her covered less than half her needs. She and her husband were always in debt. John Groelles had nothing, and did nothing.

A man like Cohen is only deceived by himself. He knew—but without knowing it, since the thought never formed itself in his mind—that his daughter, his treasure, was hard without reason for it. Everything, every softness, had been given to her. She took all that was given. As a child, she gave back something, a sudden rough caress, a word. You could think her roughness a pretence, as if she had rebelled against the slack easy endearments poured over everyone and everything by her mother, by Sophie Cohen. She would say sometimes to her mother, even then, when she was a child: 'I don't like you, I don't care if I never see you again.' Then, when the mother complained, crying and scolding, Cohen would say: 'Now, mother, the child doesn't mean it.' Secretly, he delighted in her rebellious temper. She is like me, he thought proudly: she doesn't want she should be treated like a pet animal, like a baby.

When she grew up, and when he knew her better, he admitted nothing: he gave, gave, gave; she took it all, and now even caresses were withheld unless what she wanted from him was so hard to come by or costly that she was half afraid—not ashamed, never for an instant ashamed, only afraid he would not give her what she must have.

When he saw her come towards him he wondered what it was she wanted, and when he felt her hand pressing his shoulders. He put an arm round her small waist—it was as if his arm enclosed nothing—and drew her on his knee. She yielded. Her cheek touched his lightly.

'What do you want, my darling?' he said softly. He pinched the lobe of her ear. 'New ear-rings? A narrow pearl, eh? Or maybe another emerald? Or you have now a bill you can't pay, like last March, it was March, or February. Tell me.'

'I always have bills I can't pay,' Fanny sighed. She leaned suddenly and sharply forward, as if her thought jerked her upright. 'Do you know what, daddy, the way we live is wrong. Johnny should work at something. All he does now is spend, and that's not right, is it? A man should do something. If I were a man, I know I would be at something to make money.' She looked at him, a little breathless, so that he knew she was repeating a speech she had prepared. She was not complaining of her husband. Only from her voice he knew that she was still absorbed in Groelles as in the first weeks, admiring and approving of him with a passion she had not wanted to control. He waited.

'Can't you give him some work to do, daddy?' Fanny said. She stroked his face.

'You want that I should make him an editor or something?' Cohen laughed.

'No!' Fanny said. He felt her body jerk and relax. 'You know he isn't clever in that way,' she said, controlling her voice. 'He's wonderful with horses—he can shoot and swim and fly—he's promised me not to fly at night again or to do any more stunts, it worried me so I nearly went mad,

I couldn't sleep and there were lines coming under my eyes, you'd hardly believe it—but he wasn't trained to anything with his mind, not like you, daddy.'

'No, not like me,' Cohen said.

'I thought—there must be something you could find for him. A friend of ours, of Johnny's, is a director of two companies. He doesn't need to speak or to write anything, when they send for him he goes to the meetings—quite regularly—and if something came up that he knew about he would speak, of course. You have to be known, your name, something about you—Groelles is one of the oldest names in England, you know that, daddy——'

Cohen listened to her voice as it went, now soft, now rasping into uncontrolled loudness. He had begun by wondering how much actual money she needed to satisfy her: after a time he realised that she was serious, she wanted money, but she wanted it to be given to her this time in this way. She must have planned it carefully. Groelles, he thought, had suggested it—perhaps pride, tired of taking money always, ask for work. Work? Fanny had ceased talking: her arms, laid round his neck, tightened their hold. She brushed his hair with her lips. He smelled the scent she used sparingly, sharp, thin: a time since he had asked her the name, not caring to repeat the mistake he had made once. 'Loneliness,' she answered smiling: 'the smaller phial costs me five pounds.'

'My darling,' he said, half groaning.

'There must be something——'

'Get up now,' her father said.

She stood up, looking at him coldly, her face hard. 'All those shipping firms you have interests in.'

'Had,' Cohen said.

'But you know everyone—I know that.'

Cohen stood up suddenly. There was a strange warmth and a strange weakness in his body, as though blood were gushing inside it—the sensation faded as he moved, leaving behind a faint pleasurable excitement. Against his judgment,

and against if it came to that his will, he said: 'Very well,
Fanny, I shall think it over and see what can be done—I——'

His head dropped forward. He was trying to think of
Groelles. Instead he thought, How young she still is—
seeing her eyes sparkle: she jumped about like a tomboy,
clapping her hands, and kissed him on both cheeks. 'Thank
you, thank you ever so much. Johnny will be so pleased.
Thank you, daddy.'

When she had gone he went into his wife's bedroom to
speak to her. Sophie Cohen had been in bed for a fortnight
—longer—he barely remembered on which day she had first
told him she felt ill. She went to her bed there and then,
and since she refused to see a doctor—she who so enjoyed
calling the doctor for a pain in her little finger—he did not
believe in her illness. He supposed she wanted a rest—or a
trouble made of her.

She was propped up, wearing a quilted jacket and three
lace shawls over her nightgown, and the room like a furnace
house. Nearer the bed the air felt hotter than anywhere
else and with the smell of cloves and another faint un-
identifiable odour, acrid, stealthy, he could scarcely breathe.
He moved to open a window at the top, but she protested
and he came back good-humouredly to the bed. Her arms,
lying along the sheet, were bluish white and very thick.

'Well, Sophie,' he said, and smiled at her.

'I heard Fanny was here,' she began at once, and fumbled
at the sheets, 'and I said for her to come up to talk to me,
and she sent word No, she wouldn't come, she didn't like
sick-rooms. Sick-rooms! Me, her mother, and she calls it
sick-rooms. Is it a way for a good decent girl to speak of
her mother? Lying here, ill and in pain, and she is in the
house and she won't even speak outside the door, and not
to come in, to say Aren't you better? like any girl would
who had a living heart in her or any milk of human kindness.
She's a stone. That girl is a stone.'

Cohen took hold of one clawing hand and patted it. 'She
was thinking of the boy, of David. You know at eight

they get sick very easily. You don't want he should catch something from you, Sophie.'

'Is it scarlet fever I have on me? or influenza, or the plague, or what is it? Can I give David this pain I have, if she was only to stand inside that door and speak a few words, only one word, to her mother? No—she's hard, like a stone. I tell you.'

Sophie began to cry weakly, her body, fat, and shapeless as a bolster when it was unstayed, swelling and falling under the clothes. Her high arched nose, strong and beautiful, was pinched. Her grey curls were disordered.

'How do we know what you have when you don't see Farbman,' Cohen said gently. 'Let me speak to him on the telephone. Now. I'll just say you're not good and he's to step round in the morning. Now, Sophie, you like him, you know you like him. What worries you in seeing him, eh?'

His wife ceased crying at once, as if some warning had been conveyed to her in his words. Her expression as she looked at him was reserved, sunken. 'No,' she said.

'No what?' Cohen humoured her. 'No doctor? Or no pain?'

'I can look after the pain myself,' his wife said. She drew her hands under the sheet and clasped them over her slack heavy breasts. She began to complain again about Fanny. At last she ended. 'No kindness. David now was kind. He was the only one cared about me what I was feeling,' and flinched back, catching her breath.

For an instant, in self-defence only, Cohen pretended to his mind that she meant the second David, her grandson, Fanny's son. But it was the other she meant. And thinking that she had refused to go to him when he was dying, his mother, a Jewish mother afraid to look at and cherish her son as he died, he felt anger swelling and pressing in him against the walls of his body. He was outraged. When he looked at his wife again she had shut her eyes.

'You should try to rest,' he said heavily.

He pulled her door to and went downstairs to his library. Before he turned the handle he heard the telephone; he moved slowly, still obsessed, and listened for a full minute without hearing what Harben said, although each word was as loud and distinct as if he were in the room. 'I can't hear,' he said.

'Something wrong with your instrument. I hear you very well. I said, Did Swan come in to see you about the Russian letter?'

He had to make haste now, hurrying along the corridor of the hospital, into the hall, to his car, leaving David alone behind the screen. Despair, and then grief, left his face with the upward motion of his lips. He felt the edge of the desk under his hand. 'Yes, of course. The letter. No, he didn't come.'

'I told him this morning to see you at once.'

'He didn't come.'

'Well. You'll know what to do with it.'

'Yes.'

He had scarcely taken his hand from the instrument when it began to ring again. He listened again. The difference in the two voices amused him, Thomas Harben's peremptory, too assured to need emphasis, and Swan's resonant, at moments hard, eagerly self-assured without ease or certainty. Cohen flattered himself that he would have known all this only from listening to them. Swan spoke of 'the Russian First Secretary': Cohen realised after a moment that this gentleman had taken the title from a former post in the Tsarist Embassy; he paid no attention, feeling with his free hand in the drawer below his knee to reach his cigars, until Swan said: 'Well, that's that, there's no need to recapitulate. I was to report to you that the shell was delivered at the Foreign Office to-day.'

'The letter?'

He could feel that Swan smiled. 'Call it what you like. It has a time fuse on it, so I call it a shell.'

All this romanticising—of an incident which to Cohen

seemed less important than the decisions taken by other, quieter men, the price of gold, for instance, or the interpretation of a clause in the financial provisions of a treaty, or even the bill of sale on a cargo now being unloaded in a South American port—wearied him, and he frowned with displeasure and growing anger. He could not light his cigar with one hand.

'Yes, yes,' he said. 'I understand. You want the *Daily Post* to print in about a fortnight. You have not sent me a copy——'

'I shall bring it to you myself, for safety,' Swan said.

'The post is quite safe,' Cohen observed. 'I once lost a parcel of socks, but it was a long time ago and I think my wife had forgotten to address it. She might.'

He listened to an exasperated sound at the other end, waited, then laid down the telephone with relief. His teeth were bared for a second in what might be meant as a smile; then as he fitted his body more closely into the chair to speculate on the value for himself, his newspapers, Thomas Harben, and a number of other people for whom he had less respect, of the news he had been given, his face altered again; it was now engrossed, patient, alert.

CHAPTER XXXVI

EARLHAM IS SUCCESSFUL AGAIN

RACHEL EARLHAM looked round the room from the chair into which she had dropped, only for a minute. That was a mistake—she would never be able to get up again. The counting of votes had been going on for three hours. It must be nearly over. Yes, there—they were emptying out the last boxes. She saw the checkers bend forward again a little, relief, eagerness, banishing for a time longer the fatigue they were all feeling. She knew. Her shoulders felt now as though her body were hanging from them and had been hanging for hours, days. She leaned forward. When she straightened herself again she saw that Louis was talking apart to the agent; helping herself out of the chair, she went over to them.

'Are we losing?' she whispered to Kean.

'I don't know, Mrs. Earlham. I don't think so. It's very close one way or the other.' Kean smiled at her, his sunken cheeks lifting with humour. His hands twitched. She remembered that his wife was ill. 'How is she?' she whispered. 'Better,' Kean said. He turned away. Rachel wondered afresh how they lived at all on Kean's wretched salary, five young children and now that the mother was in hospital (and the nurse saying to them, as if it were their own fault, 'She has been *starved*, I tell you') the eldest girl was managing—they called it that. Rachel saw her again, coming to the door with that bucket she set down, her face bewildered, surprised, streaked with dirt, as though she were lost in some childish thought in the stress of her unchildlike toil.

Louis caught her arm as she passed him. 'Go and sit down,' he croaked, his voice almost gone.

'No, I must help,' she said.

She walked slowly round the table, pausing to look over the shoulders of the tellers. Just as she reached him one of their checkers said 'No!' A voting paper had been fumbled on to the wrong heap. 'That was clever of you, Rigden,' she whispered, to encourage the checker. He was deathly tired. His eyes were bemused and heavy: he rubbed at them with the back of his knuckles like a child. There were no reserves in the Labour ranks—each man and woman of them had worked to what seemed the end of his strength, to discover then it was not the end. Even the children had run errands all that day. The man she spoke to came every evening straight from his factory to the committee rooms, to work without food until midnight. He was no more devoted than others. A passion of love and gratitude lifted her beyond her own weariness; she turned and went quickly back to Rigden and stood at his shoulder. 'I'll watch here with you,' she smiled.

'It's all right,' Rigden said awkwardly. 'I was sleepy when I come in but I'm awake now. You'd better rest yourself, Mrs. Earlham.'

'We're winning, I think.'

Rigden nodded, watching the teller's hands. 'The rigs they come in beat me,' he whispered. 'It's a party to them.'

Rachel glanced aside to the three women who had joined a group surrounding the Conservative candidate. They were all at the far end of the room, waiting: some of the women were in evening dress; covered at first in cloaks and fur coats, they were forced by the heat in the room to reveal bare shoulders, necklaces—one woman carried a king's ransom in diamond bracelets from wrist to elbow of her arms.

'Deptford nothing,' Frank Rigden said under his breath. 'They'll be friends of his, not voters.'

'They have all voted somewhere.' Rachel looked at the

women with a little contempt. 'I wouldn't show my diamonds here,' she said quietly.

With a trace of apology in his smile for speaking freely, Rigden said: 'Mrs. Earlham, you don't need diamonds to prove you're better than what they are.'

News of Labour defeats was coming in, passed from mouth to mouth. Kean hobbled across the room and touched her arm. 'That damned lying letter has done it,' he whispered, 'the one they say Zinovieff wrote. Who is Zinovieff? Maybe the editor of the *Daily Post* wrote it himself. Never mind, Mrs. Earlham. It don't matter if we lose this time, we'll win next time or the time after. Suppose we lost every fight—we'd win the last one. Bound to.' Rachel smiled at him. It's nearly the end, she thought. Her body felt quite empty. She went back to Louis and stood beside him in silence. Anything was bearable when she could be with him.

Earlham said: 'What's that man's name you were talking to?' He did not catch her answer. Then Kean spoke to him. Then one of the officials on the other side. He stood talking to Kean and the other man: he was thinking that whether he won this election or lost it nothing much would happen to change Kean's life—or the life of that fellow over there with the quiet nondescript face, whose name he had forgotten again. He felt a sudden shame because of the difference between their lives and his, and because of the poorness and monotony of their life, and because no change could be brought about in time to save either of them from living and dying in the poverty into which they were born. Then what am I? he thought. Why should they choose me rather than another man?

He was alone for a time, except for Rachel, while Kean talked with the other officials. He saw the group at the far side of the room shift, break apart, then Kean's smile, wavering, excited, stretching out wider as he limped quickly and clumsily on the leg that had been caught two years back in the machine, to be the first to shake his hand.

The defeated candidate spoke to him and shook hands, his womenfolk looking on with aloof vexed faces. Earlham made a short speech, his tongue cleaving to the roof of his mouth. He could scarcely see or stand. Kean pulled at his sleeve. 'They're waiting for you outside, Mr. Earlham.' Rachel came with him. He was aware of her at his side for a moment and then he forgot her in the familiar excitement of looking at a sea of faces upturned to him. His throat felt cracked. He saw opened mouths, eyes, a crazy-work of light and black against the street-lamps. After the warmth of the room the cold struck through him. He shivered, but his mind was alive with words: he had only to open his mouth and they poured out.

Rachel held her head up and looked at the crowd, waiting for him to stop speaking. For no reason at all she felt embarrassed. After a time, she realised that what distressed her was the falsity of Louis's speech. He has said it all so often that it no longer means anything to him, she thought. Her cheeks burned, and she hung her head. Did the others, did Kean and Rigden, hear it? Suddenly she took a step forward, and under cover of the darkness seized Louis's arm and held it. She was ashamed of her thoughts. Louis was worn out. He was speaking mechanically, scarcely able to stand up. And now she thought only of taking him away, as swiftly as possible. She felt agonisingly impatient, her own weariness forgotten. Turning her head, she said to Kean: 'Can we go now? Louis must rest.'

'Cobham has been waiting with his car in the street at the back,' Kean answered. 'We've only got to get him to it.'

'Cobham? That's, let me see——'

'The butcher Cobham. He's going to drive you home.'

'How will you get home?' Rachel said. 'There are no buses at this hour.'

'Walk,' Kean said, smiling.

She thought of him dragging his leg along the pavement through street after dingy street. And then the cold room and the empty bed, the children asleep now in the other room. She bit her lip to prevent herself crying. What would be the use of that? It was Kean who had to walk, or, rather, hobble for a mile to his spoiled house.

Louis had finished his speech. She looked at his face in profile, and her love and anxiety strengthened in her. He must rest, he must sleep, she said to herself, her body rigid, because before all these people she must behave sensibly, not to let them see what she felt. ' Round by the back,' Kean said. She hurried after them, buttoning her coat with stiff fingers. It was too long for her and she trod on it and stumbled when she reached the car. A man caught her arm. ' Oh thank you,' she said, ' —and thank you for all your help.'

' It was nothing,' he said diffidently. ' And we won. We won.' He was looking past her, at Louis.

' Good night,' Rachel said. She thought that very likely he had not heard her. He said nothing, still looking at Louis as if he expected something. Louis did not see him.

The car started and turned into a side street to escape the crowd. Louis leaned all his weight against her. ' I never can remember who that chap is,' he said.

' His name is Rigden,' Rachel said quietly: ' I thought— did you see him there? '

' Rigden. Yes that's it.' He settled back in the car. ' Thank God that's over,' he breathed. ' I can scarcely believe it. I'm fairly done, and my voice has gone to nothing. I don't suppose I shall sleep. My head feels like a furnace full of hot cinders.'

Rachel drew his arm into hers and held it as if it were a child, stroking it gently. She forgot everything in her anxiety to be at home. She felt anxiety and an infinite tenderness. I shall rest you, I shall keep you safe, she thought. Straining forward in the car, she was already in their room in bed, holding Louis so that he slept.

·   ·   ·   ·   ·

Frank Rigden pushed out of the crowd and started home. He had not far to go. When he opened the door Sally had waited up for him. She had expected him earlier and saved a meal for him, but he was too tired to eat. He tried, thinking she would be vexed, but the food was tasteless through waiting and after a minute he gave up and pushed the plate to one side. Sally moved it away. She was thinking that she had not seen him since half-past five that morning, when he went off to work. So now she stood, leaning with a hand on the dresser, while he told her about the work, how he and another had gone from house to house arguing with men and women too slack to vote, sometimes bringing them in, and then he went on to the hall and Kean took him in with him to help and—' I can't keep awake, I thought, but I did, y'see, Sally, and we won, we won. We won.' He repeated it in a dry voice, almost at the end of his excitement.

' Well, I'm glad,' his wife said.

He had had the sense of helping in a hard effort, as if he were pushing at the back of a crowd that moved forward —but it was over, or else he had forgotten it during the walk home. He looked at the familiar room, and at his wife standing there, and felt that everything was the same. But why should it have changed?

' I hope he thanked you for working like you have.'

' Mrs. Earlham did. She was getting into the car and she a'most fell, she was that done. Joe says to me, he says, How old d'you think she is? She could be sixteen, but there's a kid, she must be over twenty. I don't know, I said.'

' Oh, they had a car to go home in, did they? '

He was vexed by her wordless disapproval. He sat still a minute. Then Sally began to move about the room, raking the ashes and setting his breakfast ready. He remembered something.

' What did they tell you at th'hospital this morning? ' he asked. After the birth of her second she had been at the hospital twice a week: neither of them knew very clearly what was wrong with her—'It seems I'm not right,' she had said vaguely: she said her back ached.

'You went, didn't you?'

'I'm not going no more,' his wife said.

He looked up at that, lifting his arms from the table, where they had been stretched out as if they had nothing to do with him. 'Are y'better?'

'I'm not going.' She raked needlessly in the hearth. 'They mean it all kindly. I know that. But there's always something said—and the students—I know they're only young and merry—but it makes you feel you were some kind of animal, and they were leaning over watching you. I wasn't brought up to do like it, and I'm not going again. I s'll come right in time.'

She had turned a dull red. Without understanding he knew that her country decency had been outraged in some way. A sense of bewilderment, familiar and heavy, woke in him. It's like th'army, he thought at once, not knowing that the thought had been there a long time.

His wife was crying quietly, her face in the bend of her arm; he went over to her and put his arm round her shoulders, and he stood stroking them without finding a word to say. Let her cry it out, he thought. The last trace of his exultance in victory had faded. He felt sorrowful, as sorrowful and helpless as that day when their livelihood in the country was taken from them, and they had to leave. We aren't no one, he thought; they could do anything to us. He and she were of no importance: at any moment they might have to struggle again, only to live. A little warmth came to him, from Sally's quivering shoulders. 'Poor lass,' he said gently. 'I'm all right,' she answered, leaning against him for a moment.

She dried her face with her hands. 'We must go to bed, Frank, you'll never wake.' He stood still, his head bent—there was something he wanted to tell her. He waited, frowning—with his look of withdrawn patience, as though he were waiting for something he had long ceased to expect and yet he waited. 'We're still—we're still here, y'know,' he muttered. That was not it. He gave up trying to tell her what had troubled his mind: there was no victory in his heart now, nothing but weariness, and pity for her. He turned off the light over the table and followed her upstairs. In their room the child stirred and whimpered. Sally stooped over the cradle. Her shadow on the wall seemed to him something he remembered: he pondered it for a moment while he took his things off, then lay down on his side of the bed and fell asleep.

CHAPTER XXXVII

GARY AND GEORGINA ROXBY

THE fog had stretched over the city all day, at the level of the highest roofs. It formed a black ceiling, and wisps and tentacles of it, drifting lower, caught at eyes and throat like salt in the air. Now in the late afternoon it lifted, but it was still as dark as before, the light had waxed and waned unseen at the other side of the fog. It was like a fairy-tale in which the lost child falls down a well and finds a new country with fields and flocks grazing there below the water. On November 6, in London, he would have had to fall *upwards*, to find himself once more under a clear cold sky, in which, believe or not as you like, there were birds—chiefly gulls from the estuary—flying and calling, and white clouds.

Gary looked up at the sky as he stood in Piccadilly Circus, waiting to cross. For the first time in months he was restless. He thought of Spain, of Africa. Three years ago he would have booked his passage without a thought. He had been free. That was before he had decided to understand his business, to find out where the money came from, to take his proper place at the head of his own affairs. He had soon learned that money, in active hands, breeds money faster than it slips through idle ones; but in learning it he had put his neck in a yoke, and here he was, his eyes smarting after the fog, his mind as restless as an electric sign—wings and feet in the web.

He walked on. In a florist's shop it was high summer. Even a beggar in Spain is happier, he said to himself. He remembered a wine shop in Bayona in which when they were young he and Nicholas had purchased what in their

286

poor Spanish they thought was white wine. It turned out
to be Spanish rum, smooth as honey, as though they had
drunk the night sky.

When he put the key into the door his servant opened it.
' Miss Roxby came, sir.'

' When ? '

He felt a flash of rage behind his eyes. It was from his
body, not in his mind. Moving quietly, he controlled it;
in a few minutes he was able to face her, not as if he were
divided between impatience and pity.

' Why didn't you tell me you were coming ? '

' Because you would have made excuses.'

It was impossible for Georgina to make an awkward
movement. Her joints were as flexible as a dancer's, and
when she raised her arm the line flowed from her shoulder
to the ends of her fingers without an angle.

' Now that you are here——' he began.

' Now that I am here,' Georgina interrupted, smiling,
' I am going to speak and you have only to answer. How
many times have I seen you since May ? '

' Twenty ? '

' Five.' Georgina looked at him with courage. ' If
I had not made sure that you had no other woman I
should have given you up. I have three questions. Before
the War you were in love with me, weren't you ? '

' I was,' Gary said.

' And during the War ? '

' Yes.'

' Last question. What changed you ? '

' My dear Georgina,' he said, ' you want to know the
impossible. There are stages—one grows, drops an interest
—it isn't possible to say when or what happens.'

' Why are you lying ? ' Georgina said, a little sadly. ' If
I didn't love you I shouldn't know you were lying. As it
is—each word is flat and dead in my ears.' She stood up
quickly and walked towards him. ' Will you tell me the
truth, my darling ? '

' I don't love you,' Gary said.

' The truth, the truth. I love you with all my heart and mind.' She wrung her hands. She was haggard and flushed—less beautiful than she was scarcely a month since. What can I do? Gary thought. He was in torment—yet part of his mind remained cold and accurate. He noticed that one finger of her right hand was stained slightly with smoking: she smoked too many cigarettes, at least fifty in the day.

He decided to tell her the truth, but the decision made him sweat over his hands and forehead. This annoyed him and he felt disgusted by his body.

' Very well, I'll try,' he said. ' But sit down.'

She seated herself at once, and again, although he was sorry for her, he controlled a spasm of impatience. Something in her attitude, the shape of her bent neck or her waiting hands, rose against him, like a womanish cloud. He saw that she was preparing herself to hear anything; that in itself irritated him. He felt the injustice of his thoughts.

' Apart from a doctor and a nurse or two, no one knows this about me except Nicholas.' He saw her hands move one in the other. Now what does she imagine? he thought. She was looking down.

' Some people find certain words shocking,' he went on. ' Words that are in ordinary use, I mean.'

' Nothing shocks me,' Georgina said.

A thought took away his breath for a second. ' You don't know already what is wrong with me? '

' I think you are—ill.'

' You can call it an illness.' After all, this is hard, he thought: he endured. ' You know that I came through the War unhurt until nearly the end,' he said as gently as he could. ' Then I was wounded in such a way that I am impotent.'

Georgina moved her hands. ' That doesn't seem important.' She went on: ' I mean that I can see—that it would be important to you. It is not to me.' She spoke a little too quickly and without thinking.

'You're in that state when women enjoy sacrificing themselves,' Gary said.

The blood rushed into her face. She looked at him with fear and entreaty. 'How little you respect me!'

'What has respect to do with it?' he said. 'I've told you'—he was on the point of losing his head—'I've told you that I'm only half a man, and you want me to explain something else. I can't discuss my state. If you want to do anything for me—you'll go away.'

'Please tell me one thing more,' Georgina said.

'What is it?'

'Does marriage, does love, mean nothing more to you than a part of it?'

Gary looked at her without kindness. A woman, he thought, is more insensitive than a savage. He began to walk up and down the room. At one moment he thought she was going to lay a hand on him, and his skin crept. Then he felt sorry for her again; and he knew that as soon as she was gone he would remember the past and he would think of her wit and courage, yes, and her love. In her absence the last would change its shape and not repel him: he might even wish for it; but not for it as it was. He could only wish for it as a warmth, a relief denied to him because it could not be separated from a human being. But he must say something to help her.

'It is not a question of marriage meaning this or that. Intimacy of a kind that means living with, touching, thinking of another person, being obliged to them, perhaps depending on them—in a word, marriage—has no longer a *meaning* for me. It is as though you invited me—but no, I have no right to horrify you. Try to think that the idea of marriage —if you can think of marrying a man in my state—would be detestable to me if it were ever in my mind. It is never there.'

He saw that although she was listening with hard effort she scarcely understood him. It came to him to wonder how much or little of what we say reaches another mind.

This thought widened for ever the area of silence between himself and the rest of the world.

He made one more effort for her, talking with cold vehemence. 'You have tried very many things, Georgie—war work, dancing, a lover, love—none of them has satisfied you because you did not give away your self to one. What did you want from me? A satisfaction——'

'To be with you and to help you,' Georgina said in a low voice.

'There are things better worth having,' he said, smiling. 'You are half asleep. You should wake up and find an exacting thing to do, and try that. You have a good quick mind. I could help you; I know someone who——'

'No, no, Bill. I don't want your help. I wouldn't encourage your awful pride.'

He was silent.

'I am sorry,' Georgina said, looking at him so that he knew she was not.

'But you're wrong; I'm not proud,' he said calmly. 'I have found something to do.'

Georgina smiled for the first time, and looked at him so eagerly, so frankly, he found he could talk to her. He told her about his work; about his schemes, his great ambitions; about Thomas Harben: she listened with an air of intelligence, not looking at him. When in the excitement of it he turned to stride about the room she looked at him, but he did not know that.

She interrupted him. It was six o'clock. He walked with her to the lift, and as she stood there he thought that she was much thinner. There was a deep line like a shadow on her cheeks.

He felt exhausted; but the relief which flooded him when he went into the empty room was overwhelming and marvellous. For a time he was conscious of nothing else.

He remembered that Thomas Harben expected him to dinner. On the way, he thought with love and impatience of Georgina, and the one feeling was as passionless as the other. He would like to help her, but he knew that nothing he could say was of use. In her eyes the substance of living was all: no woman, he thought, was ever intoxicated by a shadow. Before he reached the house he had forgotten her for the time, and his feeling of relief had changed to calm self-confidence.

He was no longer uneasy with Harben. For one thing, he had penetrated the other man's liking for him and this had had the strange effect of lessening his respect without giving it any warmth. On the whole he disliked Harben.

To-night he was too tired to enjoy a discussion of the Economic Council. He agreed it had made a good start and that Swan was turning out well. After that he listened in silence. He seemed to be two persons, one watching the other as he ate, drank, and nodded his head. The watcher had darkness at his back; he was in a trench at night, with a fire-bay near at hand in which he could just see the shape and features of a middle-aged sergeant, untidy, bulky, sardonic, a lecturer in economics in civil life, the most willing and intelligent soldier in the company. This man was talking in an undertone to a very young soldier and Gary listened. From time to time he kept an eye on his other self, at the table with the heavy Victorian silver and the thin-stemmed glasses. All at once he heard Harben say:

' At that time her grandson, your friend Nicholas Roxby, was marked down as the future head of Garton's.'

He had no notion what had been said. An instant of complete darkness followed, during which he fell horribly, with a sick jerk of his body, as in half-sleep. The feeling lasted less than a minute, and made an end of the division in his mind. It had seemed so natural that, until it was over, he had not given it a thought.

He said nothing. Harben too, was silent: then as if he were at a loss he began to talk of another matter. He spoke of Louis Earlham. ' Your notion of making friends with him was as good as any,' he said smiling. ' There was no need for it—nothing was simpler than to quash the talk of an inquiry—there was no real risk—but I can see a possible use for your friend. He *is* your friend?'

'He's very pleasant and intelligent,' Gary said, with sincerity. 'I like him.'

'Does he need money?'

'I imagine he does,' Gary answered. 'He has one child and will soon have another. His wife is very simple—young, shy, kind. She takes care of him.' He recalled a glimpse of the shabby dining-room when he came to call one evening to take Earlham to dinner. Rachel Earlham had charmed him. 'She is a Jewess.'

'You could do something for him,' Harben said.

Gary jerked his shoulders. 'They're both completely honest.'

'Oh, honesty,' Thomas Harben said. 'I wasn't implying that you should bribe him! There are more ways of killing a cat than choking it with butter.' His mouth twitched a little. 'I had something to say to you. Yes. Swan tells me that one of your secretaries, a man called David Renn, has friends in the Communist Party. He may even be a member of the Party.'

'I have friends in the Labour Party myself,' Gary laughed. He was not inclined to discuss his employees.

'Not quite the same thing,' Harben retorted. He said nothing more, but he was satisfied that Gary would look more sharply at his secretary for the future. Over the coffee Harben became almost eloquent. The company of this one man stimulated him, so that he talked to him more freely than to anyone else, except Lise. With her he talked to himself.

'We need to safeguard ourselves on every front,' he exclaimed. 'Japan, America, Russia. In my belief Russia is as much a rogue nation as Germany and sooner or later will have to be crushed. We ought to keep on hammering at that through Swan and the E.C. The Americans are only at the beginning of their troubles . . . Japan . . .' He began to tell Gary how much money he had invested already in Japan, and to discuss labour troubles and the inevitable defeat of labour by economic pressure applied from this side and that, and the future of shipping—Gary listened, with a suppressed passion.

He was now certain of one thing—the width of the gulf between himself and Harben. Harben cared first of all for his money and the power it gave him. He enjoyed power for its own sake. When he looked into the future he saw it alive with the same triumphs and struggles as in the past, but magnified to infinity. In this vision (if one choose to call it vision) England was no larger than a trench marked on a map, the war map laid on the table of his mind.

He is after all an anarchist, Gary thought. He has no idea of order, or of discipline; he does not know from experience that hunger and bad staff work can ruin the best troops in the world. He is as much out of date as any of our old generals in 1914. This country, this England, is going to be cleansed and rebuilt, but he will not be the architect. I must doubt if he will even live in it.

He no longer felt tired, though his body ached; he listened, and agreed where he could: now and then a quiver of excitement and pleasure ran through him. He was certainly happy.

CHAPTER XXXVIII

ONE ROXBY IS LIKE ANOTHER

He had known she would return but he had not expected her so soon. He was drinking his morning cup of coffee when the hall porter telephoned from downstairs that Miss Roxby had asked for him. Without thought he told the man to bring her up and he opened the door to her himself.

She walked into his sitting-room as though it were the most usual thing in the world for her to come to breakfast, dropping her coat on one chair and her hat and fur on another. She was wearing a black dress, in which she looked older than her twenty-nine years. She is pale, he thought, and so thin that her shoulder-blades stick out.

He sent for fresh coffee; she sat facing him at the table, talking in a low voice, with a gaiety that reminded him of the past. She smoked all through the meal, lighting one cigarette from another: she had reached the seventh when she told him why she had come.

'I was awake half the night. Everything is clear and simple, if you will only listen to me. We enjoy so many of the same things, the country, and foreign cities, and walking.' She looked into his face with an air of simplicity and candour. 'Let us live together, Bill. I won't be any trouble to you, I'll keep out of your way when you're hard at work, and appear when you need rest and amusement. We should have to marry—if only because my mother would be unhappy if we didn't. But that is only signing one's name. Don't run away from me—I promise I shall be good company and never a nuisance.' She laid her hands, palm upwards, in front of her on the table.

'My poor Georgina,' Gary said, 'you have nothing to give me—not any more than I could give you, or another woman. I don't feel any need for company; if I did, I could get it without spoiling your life.'

'You are spoiling my life by not taking me at my word.'

Gary shrugged his shoulders, without speaking. After a moment, tears came into her eyes: she turned away from him, and controlled herself so quickly that only three or four tears fell on to her cheeks. They dried there, since she hoped that if she kept still he would not notice anything.

He was looking at her closely: he saw the tears, and he noticed at the same time the dark skin under her eyes. She was certainly living too hard, and wearing out her beauty sooner than need. The rare texture and whiteness of her skin was very slightly dulled, her lips were thinner. Gary felt a profound grief, even love; yet he could voice neither. Moreover, he felt impatient; he wanted to finish this for good and all. At the same time even her imperfections seemed to him touching. But he had a great deal to do and not enough time. Argument was useless, as well as rousing in him that feeling of revulsion which destroyed his calm.

'You can't dedicate yourself to me,' he said drily. 'It's not an interest for life, and that is what you now need. Do rouse yourself, my dear, and find something worth your doing. Your intelligence is running to seed; it would be less important if you were less intelligent. You could have a good life.'

Georgina stood up. She looked at him with a calm face. 'Then it's no use. You don't want me.'

'I would give five—ten years of my life to make you content.'

'Nonsense,' she said: 'you won't give me even your spare time.' She turned to look for her coat. When she was going, something in the way she held herself, in the look of her shoulders, reminded him so sharply of Nicholas that he felt a temptation to keep her. He had lost Nicholas.

What if he found him again in his sister? His head swam, and he opened his mouth to call her to turn back, to let him look at her face. But keeping quiet; the impulse died in him as quickly as it had arisen. Georgina went out without saying good-bye: she smiled at him, and touched his hand, but did not speak. Perhaps she could not, or perhaps she was now only playing a part. She had a vivid sense of the right and dramatic gesture.

Gary went back into his room and closed the door. His hands jerked upwards and he muttered: 'Nonsense. That's nonsense,' without knowing what he had said. He sat down, and at once his mind grew quiet, and he remembered what he had been thinking before she came in.

He went into the next room and asked the telephone operator in the building to put him through to the offices of the *Daily Post*. He had no respect for Cohen and felt it would be impossible to argue with him politely. To avoid argument he spoke in a hurried voice.

'Do you remember that we discussed the advisability of giving Louis Earlham more regular work on the paper—and so more money?'

'That was in the autumn,' said Cohen.

'Yes. I think the moment has come. In the first place, he needs money.'

'So do a great many other people,' Cohen laughed.

'You asked me for my advice,' Gary said coldly.

'Oh, no doubt you're right. I'll consider it.'

'Thanks.'

He stretched himself, and felt hungry. He thought with pleasure of the long day in front of him, and hearing David Renn in the next room called him, and began directly to read over a report and to dictate notes on it. He remembered hearing that Renn was a Socialist—or a Communist, was it?—and decided that some day he would question him. It did not seem important. Certainly it mattered less than his vague feeling of hostility to Renn—which he knew to be unjust.

CHAPTER XXXIX

NO ONE KNOWS THE TRUTH

ONE Thursday evening in November, T. S. went to see Hervey. He found that she was going out, but Georgina was with her and he could not bring himself to leave. He sat down. At a loss for words, he said:

'I had a letter from your husband this morning. He wanted to borrow money.'

'Don't lend it to him,' Hervey said sharply. 'He won't repay you. He's leaving Oxford without finishing his work —only out of laziness.' At once she felt ashamed. Why am I so disloyal to Penn? she thought. She said quickly: 'I had no right to say that. The truth is—people see that Penn does no work, and that I work very hard, and they are sorry for me and despise him. It's false and idiotic to compare us in that way. I'm not better than Penn because I work harder.' She added: 'No one knows the whole truth about anyone.'

'Why can't you forget Penn?'

'I shall forget him in time,' she answered. She looked at him with an embarrassed smile. 'Do you know, last week I invited Georgina and Nicholas to dinner at the Carlton. I never did such a thing before. I ordered the dinner, even the wine, beforehand—and when I was discussing it with the head waiter I was thinking of Penn. It seemed a shame he was not going to be there. He would have enjoyed it more than any of us.'

T. S. laughed at her. 'You are as mad as a hare. Why don't you promise him a pension?'

Hervey felt she ought not to let this pass, but she could

not find an answer. Moreover, Nicholas was expecting her. She smiled at Georgina and went away without speaking again to T. S. As she shut the door she heard him say: ' May I stay a short time? ' She did not hear Georgina's reply.

For a minute T. S. sat with his chin sunk, trying to control his thoughts. He was as acutely aware of Georgina as if she were standing at his side. This sensation confused him and made him feel stupid and light-headed at once. He had nothing to say. He lifted his head at last, and glanced at her. She was half lying on the couch, her head held back so that her long white throat with its faint swelling was stretched out to its length. Tendency to goitre, he repeated to himself, trying to destroy her beauty. His hands felt large and awkward and he pushed them out of sight.

' You're silent,' Georgina said. ' What's the matter? Are you anxious about Hervey? She can look after herself.'

But you needn't say so, he thought. ' I was wondering why I had stayed.'

' Upon my word, you are very polite,' she said softly. ' Have you a match? '

He got up to look for a box. ' You smoke too much,' he grumbled. Holding the lighted match for her, he felt her hand steadying his fingers. His body trembled like a schoolboy's. He looked at her face. She was smiling, with something sly and mischievous in her glance. He thought she was laughing at him and he felt wretched and angry. I'll go, he thought. He went back to his chair instead and sat there with arms crossed, so that she could not see that his fingers were squeezing his flesh. ' You must smoke more than thirty cigarettes a day.'

' Fifty,' Georgina smiled.

' You'll ruin your stomach.'

' Are you a doctor? No—I remember—you're a research chemist. I always wanted to be a scientist.'

' Nonsense,' T. S. said. ' You are talking for the sake of talking. If you were interested in science there was nothing to stop your working at it, was there?' He relaxed his arms and looked severely at her. I want her, he thought. She must be laughing at me again—I want her, I want her —he felt exhausted, and sorry for himself, and very clumsy. It was the last that kept him still in his place. He felt sure that if he stood up to go away he would trip up or in some way make a laughing-stock of himself.

'Why do you dislike me?' she said mildly.

'I? Dislike you?' Then he realised that she was trying him. She knew quite well that he did not dislike her; it was a trick: she wants admiration, excitement, he thought with contempt. He was about to speak when, turning her head, she looked at him simply.

'No, you don't dislike me. But you are angry with me for some reason—or you are unhappy about something else.' She stooped sideways to crush out her cigarette, and at once lit another. 'I know all about unhappiness and how it makes one dislike other people.'

'You?'

'I'll tell you something else. Unhappiness, when it has to do with another person, isn't fatal. There's even a certain lasting satisfaction in it. You know where you are.'

T. S. saw that she enjoyed talking about herself. She is impressing me with her tragic and complex nature, he thought, and at the same time he felt a tremor of pity. Her unhappiness might be genuine—as genuine as the impulse to make the most of it. The light falling on her face from above deepened the lines beside her mouth. In a few years she will be almost haggard, he thought. He felt a deep tenderness and love in the thought that she would be less beautiful.

'What is it? What is the matter?'

Instead of answering him directly, Georgina smiled, with the same half-sly half-inviting expression. She altered her position on the couch so that both knees were uncovered; and she seemed to glance with pleasure at her long slender legs. 'They say that women's legs are too short for real beauty,' she observed: 'mine are certainly long.' She raised one an inch or two from the couch to prove her words.

T. S. felt that he was smiling, a wide foolish smile; it had spread to his face from his body, which was shaken with inaudible laughter. He looked at her more closely, at the delicate bones of her head and wrists, her thick smooth hair, her eyes, the lines of her mouth, in which, for the first time, he saw something lax and gross. He stood up and shuffled across the room to her, feeling his knees scarcely able to support him, and halted staring at her.

Her face had become serious, but the sensuality, the hint of grossness remained: he saw now that it was due to the deepening of the shadow round her mouth. The line, curved like a bow, which followed the inner contour of her cheek and as it were enclosed her mouth in brackets, was copied from an old portrait, some male ancestor, no doubt. In time it would deepen to be a cleft. With the bewildering swiftness which was at the least half her beauty—as a field is more beautiful when sun, wind, and shadow, are changing it every moment—she dropped her grave air, and made a space for him to sit with her on the couch. 'Don't stand there; sit and tell me how to improve my mind. Look at all these books. Do you imagine Hervey reads them?'

He shook his head. 'I don't know, she's capable of it.' He sat down on the edge of the couch and began to stroke her arm. 'You don't like me especially, do you?'

'What can that matter?'

'I should like, just this once, to know the truth.'

'The truth,' Georgina said solemnly. She burst out laughing. When she laughed her expression was deliciously droll and childlike. About everything she did, every movement, there was the same air of individuality, as if she were the first person to move her arm in just that way, and every gesture she made was expressive not only of hand or arm but of her whole body, her self indeed. T. S. watched her for a moment. He did not know whether she was laughing at him or at something which was in her mind, but he found it unpleasant. His heart was not lightened by it; he felt as though he were watching the destruction of some delicate, fine object, the only one in existence.

' I must go,' he said. He stood up and took his overcoat on his arm.

Georgina ceased laughing but made no move to keep him: before he left the room she had stretched her hand down to the floor, to her half-empty cigarette case. He wondered how long she would sit there—probably not long, since she liked an audience. Where would she go?

CHAPTER XL

THE next afternoon—Friday—Hervey was at work in her room when Georgina came in, carrying what at sight Hervey supposed was a typewriter. It was a gramophone. She had brought with it one record, and with that she offered to teach Hervey to dance. 'Since you learned to dance when you were at school—(' I danced once during the War,' Hervey said. The exquisite edge of Salisbury Plain divided her mind; aeroplanes from the T. D. S. droned overhead; dust thrown up by military lorries whitened the hedges—they rushed through country roads past farm carts drawn into the ditch; American voices blended with English, with the unstressed Hampshire speech. Now I am happy, she thought—this rushing in American lorries, this dancing, this lying awake to remember a voice, this rapture, these hours spent in idle waiting, are life. Now I am living)—you will find the new steps quite easy. You must make Nicholas take you out. We'll have parties. . . .' She started the gramophone, and began her lesson. She made Hervey follow her across the room, and as soon as she knew the steps turned facing her and said: 'Now, I am your partner. Now dance . . . No, let yourself move with me. Don't try to lead, *I* am leading. Don't stiffen your back. Can't you hear anything?' She began to sing in a roughened thread of a voice: '*Swa*nee River, *Swa*nee River, la-h la dee *da*-dee,' and broke off to laugh and shake Hervey gently—'oh, you're impossible. You don't even trust anyone enough to dance with them. Or else you're too domineering to give way. You can't dance well unless you're willing to

302

surrender yourself to someone, either your partner or the
musician. Try again. No, no. Then simply watch me
for a moment.'

She freed Hervey, re-started the record, and began to
dance alone. Hervey leaned against the door to watch her.
Her mind delighted in sharp images, turning even sounds
into marks of varying thickness. As she looked, she thought
of a wave in the instant before it breaks: shining threads of
foam run across the skin of the water; to look at it is like
looking at glass which by a miracle is throbbing with life.
The green is opaque, faint shivers run through it under
and across the foam, the edge thins, rears backward with
spumy locks, then rushes down in a welter of green and
indigo, with broken flakes of light from the dissolving
plumes.

The merry silly tune ran up and down, like the sound of
heels on a bare floor. It entered into the dancer's swaying
body and took back a mould of it, so that years after Hervey
heard it with despair, joy, and tears, as if it had been the
greatest music in the world.

Georgina stood still, out of breath. She silenced the
gramophone, and sat down. Hervey began to think of her
work and to turn the pages.

'Enough for to-day,' Georgina said. 'I came here on
purpose to ask you—and don't answer if it vexes you—has
Nicholas talked yet to his wife? I must ask, because Jenny
has written inviting me to see her—the first time for a year,
two years.'

'Why didn't you ask Nicholas?' Hervey said. Regretting
her coldness, she said more than she would willingly have
given away. 'He hasn't said anything to her. He hasn't
asked her to divorce him, he hasn't been to see her.
Yesterday evening I took my heart in my hands and
spoke to him about it. He said—he agreed—he would
see her this evening, tell her, and ask her to divorce him
at once.'

Georgina listened and realised that Hervey was not sure

of Nicholas. She feared his uncertain temper, and feared
to lose him. I knew that anyone who fell in love with
Nicholas, as he is now (she thought), would suffer. Hervey
is too much in love with him. Looking again at Hervey,
she thought: All the same, she is harder than Nicholas,
she will keep on her road whether he stays with her or
not.

For some reason she remembered that, when she was
dying, Mary Hervey had sent for Hervey. The message
came too late. A sad pity, Georgina cried, seeing the
despotic old woman face to face at the end with her marred
image.

'Well—you are luckier than I am,' she said, looking down
and smiling, 'I made the most humiliating mistake—
William doesn't care for me any longer. I offered to live
with him on any terms.'

Hervey did not know what to say. She felt that pity
would only be another humiliation. Something harder and
stoical was in better taste. 'Do you mind seriously?'
she said.

'Of course. There was something I didn't know.
He is impotent. Nicholas knew, and ought to have told
me.'

Hervey jumped. 'I wish you hadn't told me,' she said.
'My mind is a graveyard of secrets already.'

It explains, she thought, his settled contempt for women
—which he would not admit in words, and which I
felt: Georgina ought to have held her tongue; she has
no discipline. Looking at her friend, she forgot everything in her love for her. Georgina was smiling. Her
hands, which she held in front of her on the table, were
steady. I shall never see her tears, Hervey thought. She
said nothing for a time, but moving from the door to the
bookcase she paused long enough beside Georgina to give
meaning to her next words. 'Your dress is new, I like it
so much,' she said, smiling. Georgina knew that it meant,
I like you and I am sorry for you. She touched Hervey's

hand for a second. ' I buy too many clothes. Your friend
T. S. is right about me.'

' T. S. is very eloquent about social wickedness,' Hervey
said. ' He won't do anything except talk. He is very
bitter in words, but he leaves action to the others, the
vulgarians.'

' Do you call yourself a vulgarian? '

' I can do vulgar things. I tricked Cohen into giving me
more than he meant.'

' You'll die rich,' Georgina mocked.

' No. I was born under an awkward planet, and honesty
will keep breaking in,' Hervey said drily. ' Have you ever
thought,' she said, with sudden energy, ' how confused our
life is compared with Mary Hervey's? She knew precisely
what was right to do and what wrong. If she did wrong
she knew it—her life was simple and precise.' Her mind
leaped forward. Mary Hervey (she thought) would have
known certainly that she had no right to leave her husband,
that it was a self-indulgence—where I turn this way and
that, giving new meanings to old words. Freedom, I say,
is a human need; I protest that Nicholas needs me, I dismiss
Penn. I reject the old values and set up new ones forged
by my own mind.

She had seated herself on the floor, and now in her
excitement she jumped up and making an awkward movement, the pain gripped her suddenly. She stumbled forward,
with a groan, biting her lip. Georgina was horrified by her
look.

' What is it, Hervey? ' she cried, running to her.

Hervey's face quivered, but she had controlled herself.
She wiped her forehead. ' It's not of the least importance.
Now and then I have a pain—here.'

' How long have you——? '

' I don't know. Five or six years,' Hervey said, indifferent.

' You must have it looked to at once,' Georgina exclaimed.
She felt afraid and angry. ' Promise me.'

Hervey nodded without committing herself. She did not mean to do anything. Her mother had taught her that illness is shameful, and she had as well the feeling of a poor woman towards her body—that it must do its best without help, until the moment when it surrenders unconditionally. She evaded her friend's sharp words.

CHAPTER XLI

HERVEY waited throughout Saturday, expecting that Nicholas would come to her. He did not come and there was no letter from him in the last post. On Sunday morning she awoke on the thought, I shall see Nicholas in an hour or two. The hours passed, until ten o'clock at night. At that hour and only at that hour she faced the certainty that he was not coming. This was the first time after she came to London they were not together that day.

She thought, Of course there will be a letter in the morning. On her tray in the morning were four. Spreading them swiftly to find his—it was not there. At the shock her heart seemed to drop in her body.

A curious apathy followed. It was as if a safety curtain were lowered in her mind, and she paid no attention to what was going on behind it, but did her work: she finished the weekly article for the *Post*, then turned to the endless typing out of her novel. Ten minutes before the usual hours when letters were delivered, at twelve, five, and last of all at nine, she took her stand in the doorway of her room and listened. After a time she heard the fall of letters into the box, two floors below, then her landlady's running feet along the passage, then a faint sound as the letters were spread out on the table in the hall. After the woman had shut herself in her back room, Hervey crept downstairs; there was one letter for her on the last post but it was not from Nicholas.

She worked until past midnight, then prepared herself for bed. In the moment before sleep overcame her, one thought separated itself from the darkness. It was a shadow that becomes a man—If he has gone back to her—then again a shadow, nothing, the darkness. She thought dimly that she would understand it if he had. This moment of comprehension was ended by a foretaste of agony. Then again she shut her mind.

On Tuesday morning there was no letter. Towards noon she forced herself to ring him up. His voice was dry and uninterested. 'Hervey? Yes?' She lost her courage, and muttered that she had been thinking . . . He did not wait for her to go on. 'I'm going up to Scotland to-night,' he said shortly.

'Scotland?' she echoed.

'Yes. I've been asked to value some furniture.'

'When are you coming back?'

'I'm not certain.'

She waited another moment, then, since he did not speak, she said 'Good-bye,' and turned away. The silence after the light tap of the receiver on its hook was like a hand covering her ears. She steadied herself with the thought that he would write before he went.

The letter did not come that night. In the morning, then.

There was no letter on Wednesday morning. She began to reckon the time taken by letters from Scotland, but though she knew it was no use she still watched for every post that day. Towards evening Delia Hunt came upstairs to invite her to go out with her.

They went to the Trocadero and Delia chose a table near the orchestra. She was in rare good humour and ogled the conductor and the waiters until Hervey's cheeks burned and she wished herself in her room. 'How old d'y'think I am?' Delia demanded.

'Forty?'

'Out by fourteen years,' Delia chuckled. 'I'm four and fifty—I swear I don't feel more than eighteen. I'm as lively as a flea under all this.' She smacked herself on the thigh with gusty approval. 'Do you know what—I haven't spared m'self, I've had m'fill and more than once. Eh?

who says we're made for anything else? If you've been filled you know you have, and no mistake. Dear knows how many men I've brought up in the way they should go. And all for pure sport. Ho, I don't say I haven't done pretty well for m'self, I say I never did anything but it was more for the sport of it than for money. Ho me, if it was my last word I'd swear down I never denied m'self when I was warm—not like that animal over there—see her?— pretending, nasty wretch, she doesn't know what she's about. Shall we drink?'

She ordered a bottle of claret, but drank it herself. Hervey was ashamed to be seen drinking with her—she was not old enough yet to ignore the glances her companion drew on them. Delia thought she was tired, and talked the louder. At last a phrase she used caught Hervey's inner ear—'the suck of the tide.'

'What do you know about tides?' she said, smiling.

'Enough to last me,' Delia retorted. 'It was a manner of speaking, if that suits you. What I said was, the tide's turned since I was your age, that was and God save the old Queen 1900—it's on the go-back and you and me and all this raffery is going with it. Time was London was darker at night, but you knew where you were. What I say is, and mark you, if the lights was to go out now, or it might be to-morrow, you wouldn't sing sweet and low. Ho no! Hark, hark, the dogs do bark, the you don't know and you won't like it when you do is coming to town. Now the day is over, Night is drawing nigh. Even cheese isn't what it was.' She beckoned the grinning waiter. 'Haven't you got a Stilton? You can remove this, I don't want to wash m'hands, and I certainly can't eat it.'

Hervey looked at her with renewed liking. Delia Hunt's indifference was superb: she did not care whether she was disapproved or liked. She had lived as she pleased, and that alone gave her a laugh at the expense of the fastidious and scrupulous. There might be no place for her in an orderly world—a pity, Hervey thought. She kept her head down when she had to walk the length of the room behind Delia. Delia had her own gait. She held her head high and rolled her body below the waist. She leaves a furrow in the air, Hervey thought.

There were no letters spread out in the hall. As Hervey opened the door of her room she saw the letter laid there under her feet. Her heart made a sickening movement in her side. She stooped for it, turning it over on the floor. The writing was unfamiliar.

She worked hard the next day, her mind numbed. During the afternoon the telephone jarred her into life. Georgina spoke to her, and Hervey's voice was such that her friend paused and said doubtfully: ' Is Miss Russell there? '

' No,' Hervey said.

At ten o'clock, after the last delivery, she went to bed and fell asleep. She heard nothing, and what wakened her was awareness of another person in the room. Opening her eyes she saw Nicholas at once, without shock. He had seated himself at her side on the bed. The fire had died down as she slept, and the room was almost dark. ' It's all right, Hervey,' he said softly. She sat up and looked at him without speaking. Nicholas did not move.

' Yes.' She felt no surprise or joy.

' I can't live without you.'

' Where have you been—what has happened? '

' Nothing. Nothing I want to talk about.'

' Have you been with your wife then? '

' I saw her. It's over and I've come back,' he said quietly.

Is it over for me? Hervey thought. The strangeness of this moment held her. She was divided from the woman in the bed, able to watch her and the stooping figure of Nicholas with curiosity and a little pity. It was as though she looked on at the meeting, in the half-light of the underworld, of two for whom light would not quicken.

' You'll take me again, won't you? '

' Yes,' Hervey said. She put her hand out and touched him. ' You should have written to me.'

' I know,' Nicholas said. He stayed with her a long time, half lying on the bed, his arms across her knees. She could scarcely keep awake, and slept as soon as he went away.

Her mood of acceptance had gone when she awoke, and she began to think instead that Nicholas was treating her with no respect or kindness. He ought not to leave me (she said) for a whole week and then have nothing to say. Doesn't he realise what he did to me? No, it is too much.

During the morning she wrote a long letter, which she did not mean to send him. She meant to say most of it, and she wrote it as a rehearsal.

He came in the evening. In the moment he came towards her, she knew that what she had written was wrong. The account did not balance. It was useless to make a sum of his deeds, to write ' It is too much,' when he had only to come himself for everything to appear different. After all he is better than I am, she thought. An independent quarter of her mind held out and demanded to know the truth. The truth, the truth.

' You must tell me what you have arranged,' she said gently.

' Jenny has agreed to divorce me,' Nicholas said.

' You didn't write to me. I suppose you were—unhappy.'

' Very.'

Hervey moved away from him. ' You had better tell me what happened.' At this moment she felt implacable. She felt it shameful beyond all that he should keep back anything that had to do with the other woman.

' I told her that I wanted to marry again,' Nicholas said. He frowned nervously. ' She cried—She agreed to everything; at first she was friendly and said she hoped it would turn out better—But she began crying. She couldn't stay in the house. We went out and walked about the streets for an hour and came back. If she had flown into a temper —but to see her hurt and defeated—humiliated——'

' How long is it since she left you? ' Hervey asked in a low voice.

'Nearly five years.   Oh I know, I know—She said herself she had no claim on me: she kept repeating that she was thirty-five and had nothing to live for.   I couldn't argue with her.   I felt as though I had been beaten on the head. I didn't want to see or talk to you, Hervey, I wanted to get away—forgive me.'

'She was not crying only because she is thirty-five,' Hervey said.   'When you told her, she remembered that she had once been twenty-three and very confident and happy.'

Nicholas looked at her with a smile and said humbly: 'Let me talk to you about her, Hervey.'   He talked a great while.   As Hervey listened, her hands folded on her knee, the image of Jenny Roxby slowly took shape before them and Hervey willingly lent her her own blood.   She saw a vain, greedy, healthy, youthfully pretty woman, for elegance a peacock, cut off from life by an insensitised spirit and by her self-love.   She saw her inventing for herself an unreal lying world.   She fancied that any man must find her irresistible.   It was only right that she should be courted for her charm, her seductive smile, which she rehearsed before the mirror, her soft hands, her wit, her voice, her short graceful figure.   As soon as she saw the door opening to a brilliant life with another man, she left Nicholas.   She even despised him.   Again when the man jilted her she ran back to him, because her husband was the right person to help her.   She fancied he must still love her and wish to come between her and unpleasant moments.   How could he feel anything else?   Since he was moody and tired, she no longer wanted him as a lover.   Simply she depended on him, for more than money.   Her self-confidence was not boundless.   He it was who kept alive the legend of the enchantress.   And so when he went to her and said, I want you to divorce me—the legend collapsed in a moment, she with it.

Hervey saw all this with as infinite a clarity as if she loved Jenny.   She felt no sense of triumph.   She saw that

Nicholas was sorry for his wife. She saw, too, that touching his pity was a little pride in having been generous to her. Other impulses worked in him. It was not for nothing that he had loved Jenny with a single mind and with the whole of his younger self, and with that part of it which survived the War. His love and pleasure in her were finished; but it is no use pretending that a passion of this kind will not leave marks.

She tried now to be gentle and pliant with Nicholas, so that he would know he could trust her. She loved him completely and there was nothing she would not do for him.

CHAPTER XLII

HARBEN LEARNS SOMETHING ABOUT JULIAN SWAN

HARBEN had too much sense to deny that there were women with much the same intelligence as himself. But he had never met one. The minds of such women as his wife and her friend Evelyn Heywood (he insisted on giving her her married name, because it annoyed her) seemed to him useless, like the catalogue of a museum which is closed to the public; and respect paid to them for their taste, sensibility, and what not, excited his hatred. Evelyn especially made him think of a fish, proud of its scales—his wife at least had the stiffening of her feudal tradition, which had once been real. He had never yet known a woman to whom he could speak of his affairs with as much certainty of being understood as if she were a junior shipping clerk. He did occasionally talk to Lise, but it was a monologue, in which he pursued his thoughts aloud. There was one way in which she was useful to him. He had the greatest respect for her insight into character and would at times arrange for her to make the acquaintance of some man only in order to have her judgement on him.

It was for this reason that he had asked her to seek out Julian Swan and had made it easy for her. He had his own opinion of Swan and he expected she would confirm it. And except in one detail, she had done so.

'You tell me he has a grudge against life,' Harben exclaimed. 'What do you mean?'

'It was his poverty at first—and now his lameness,' Lise said softly. 'To be poor and ambitious—at school—at the university, and when he had so many important relatives—

must have been like a thin rope round his ankle. It is very appropriate that he should have lamed one ankle for life. And it has not improved him! '

' You're telling me that I shouldn't trust him.'

' Oh yes, trust him,' Lise said. ' It will be years and years before he feels able to do without you.' She smiled lightly. ' He will be reckless only according to plan, as your old generals used to say. He is what you call a realist —that is, he does not believe in change, except for the worse. He accepts the society he sees and tries to turn all to his advantage. . . . He is very greedy,' she went on. She looked into Harben's face. ' He ate six macaroons and all the *friandises*! ' She did not tell him that Julian had wanted to seduce her. The young man had attracted her, immediately, and it was only her prudence—she knew he was unreliable and would talk of the adventure—that withstood him. She sighed.

Harben rose to go away. He had lunched with her. He did this three times a week and always ate an apple charlotte made in the German way and with a quantity of black Barbadoes sugar. ' You keep your rooms too hot,' he grumbled.

Lise smiled at him lazily. She was as warm as a cat when he bent over her to kiss her. He breathed in the scent of her clothes and body—she would not tell him the name of the scent she used; it was not in the least exotic but again it reminded him of his boyhood and of something that he thought of as foreign, as if foreign were only another word for youth. It was strange that it should be so with him, since now there was no country in the world to which he was not bound.

Outside the icy December wind cut into his lungs. He hailed the first cab he saw and shut himself into it, thankfully. ' Those rooms! ' he groaned to himself. He could not help smiling a little. In a moment he had forgotten Lise.

Julian Swan was waiting for him at Garton House. Three

years ago Harben had pulled down the old offices of Garton's and put up a vast new building which could house all his allied interests. The financial house of Harben & Co. occupied the ground floor. Shipping and shipbuilding firms, including Garton's, were on the first and second floors; iron, steel, bridge-building, blast furnaces, plate mills, and so forth, had the third; coal and oil the fourth. The fifth and top floors held accountants, together with the offices of the Stokes Chemical Works. Everywhere there was plenty of room. Some rooms could have been divided again and some were even empty. Room for growth.

He let Swan wait for three-quarters of an hour. When he came into the room at last, Harben stood up to shake hands with him, a thing he had never done before. He spoke, too, in a friendly affable way. Swan hardly knew what to make of it. He was too acute to believe that his merits had been recognised at last, and too innocent, in spite of his vanity and his ambitions, to think that Harben was paying out rope long enough for him to hang himself. He sat down and plunged into an account of the growth of the Economic Council. A campaign had been planned and was on the way, with the help of leaflets and articles in the press, and arrangements for public meetings, to combat the new move to nationalising the mines. He laid a copy of each of the leaflets and articles on Harben's desk. 'I found the most difficulty where I least expected it,' he remarked. 'I was not able to get a line into either of Marcel Cohen's papers.'

He waited. Harben only grunted, and to overcome a feeling of discouragement Swan added quickly: 'The money is coming in well. George Ling has sent us a personal subscription of two hundred and fifty pounds!'

Harben's face quivered with a sarcastic joy. 'He's frightened to death!'

'Of what, sir?' Swan laughed.

'Of dying poor and in misery. He has only half a million invested.' For an instant he saw the madman standing beside the street lamp, and he saw too something he must unconsciously have noticed at the time, that the old fellow had long very sensitive fingers, and a gold keeper ring on the fourth finger of the left hand. Let him sell that, he thought, surprised.

' There's one other question,' Swan said. ' In the beginning you told me to watch one of the Labour members of Parliament, Louis Earlham—and I understand now that he's become almost friendly with William Gary——'

' You can leave him alone,' Harben interrupted. ' He's not of any importance. He may even be useful—but you'd better leave that to Mr. Gary: he's the best judge of it.'

' The question of the World Shipping Company is closed ? '

' Long since,' Harben said.

When Swan had left the office, Harben glanced through the articles and leaflets. He was not thinking about them. The ridiculous words, ' Six macaroons and the *friandises*,' jumped into his mind. I'll keep an eye on him. The opening paragraph of an article caught him. He read it with approval and thought, He's meeting people who'll be useful to him later—but what does he want, what could he do for himself? He gave it up, and rang for a secretary to whom he handed the papers.

' Mr. Ling would be glad if you could spare him a moment.'

' Talk of the devil,' Harben said. ' Very well. Bring him in.'

He looked at George Ling with a cold interest. A year younger than I am, he thought, for the hundredth time. It gave him a keen pleasure to contrast his vigour with the other man's senility. The sight of Ling never failed to irritate him, but to balance it the feeling of pleasure was always there too. If he did not see Ling for several months he began to think of him and to look about for him in the club.

' Well. What can I do for you ? ' he asked, with a

frightening geniality. He was least to be endured when he was affable. 'Do sit down.'

Ling continued to stand, pressing his arm against a chair. His face, which had been smooth and rosy only so short a time ago as the War, had shrunk surprisingly, and at the least shock his chin trembled for several minutes.

' I don't like it,' he began, and stopped.

'Come. What is it you don't like? Eh?'

'The way Garton's shares are going,' Ling muttered. 'Do you know that yesterday—yesterday—a block of a hundred of the ordinary shares were sold for less than they stood at before the War. Oh my God, where will it end?'

Now he sat down and placed his hat and gloves under his chair, as he still did in drawing-rooms when he went calling: he had never liked the fashion of leaving them to a servant. His old man's scraggy knees showed under a layer of thick wool and one of broadcloth. There were tears, of cold or terror, at the edge of his lids, and for some reason this disgusted Harben. A revolting creature, he said to himself.

'What do you expect—with trade as it is. Freights, wage disputes, inflation, deflation, the whole devil's dish——'

'Yes I know, I know,' cried Ling, 'but tell me when it will change. When will the turn begin? Tell me now.'

'You'll never be as rich again as you were during the War,' Harben said brutally. 'Until there's another war.'

'No, no, don't let's have that,' Ling said trembling. He pressed his fingers over his eyes. During the War itself he had been filled with fervour, and though he wept when his only son was killed he rejoiced, too. But now he felt that the War had been a blunder, almost unparalleled in its enormity. He blamed it for everything he disliked and feared—social unrest, the price of hand-made boots, his failing health, the invidious position of his daughter, a married woman living apart from her husband, his losses, the collapse of morality. He no longer knew his way about the world. Even his food tasted less good. Sometimes he caught himself wishing for death, but he was afraid of that, too. I am all alone, he thought, a lonely old man; I shall die soon in my wretchedness.

'Then you must resign yourself to lose a little money,' Harben jeered.

'Only a little! How much is that, eh? How much? I always believed Garton's was as safe as the Bank of England.' It was safe and sound in Mary Hervey's day, he thought. He looked at the walls and the desk. This new costly building had never seemed to him so secure or handsome as the old one. He could imagine Mary Hervey's expression if she had lived to see it, the marble pillars and the stone frieze outside. Humbug, she would have called it in her harshest voice. Only to recall Mary Hervey's voice made him shiver.

' My daughter's money is in Garton's—that is to say, her husband's money, the amount his grandmother Mrs. Hervey left him—he makes her an allowance—in fact I may say he allows her the whole income from it——' but here Ling became confused. Tears now of vexation sprang to his eyes. What can I be thinking of to tell him these things? he asked himself. And without waiting for the other to answer, he got up and went away, leaving Harben staring in surprise.

In the entrance-hall he passed Julian Swan in conversation with a man who looked like an officer in mufti, large and well-built, with a brutal and overbearing cast of face. Keeping his back to this man, he drew Swan aside and asked him in a low voice about the work of the Economic Council. The young man answered him in a polite quiet manner, with a charming smile. 'Good, good,' Ling said, still overwhelmed. ' I shall let you have a further hundred pounds. I can't afford it—but something must be done. Things can't go on as they are! '

CHAPTER XLIII

EVELYN AND SWAN

To each his fear. Hervey was afraid always for her son, old George Ling lived in terror that he would lose his money, and Julian Swan was afraid of dying. He over-ate whenever he had the chance; he thought nothing but that he would be ill, or even die, if he omitted to feed himself well at the proper times. Yet he was physically reckless and cheerfully exposed to danger the body he cherished with such anxiety. As a soldier he showed no fear. After the accident to his leg he endured the probings of an unskilled doctor with stoical calm.

This was not the only contradiction to be met in his nature. Belonging by birth to the impoverished side of a family so old that it had ceased to think of class distinctions (there being no other in its class) he was snobbish to a degree. His intelligence was acute, painstaking, and logical; on the sensual side he showed neither self-control nor taste— but in a curious way he contrived that his sexual greeds should not stand in the way of his ambitions. The last were boundless. He believed that he could be in England what Napoleon was in France; he talked perpetually of a nation trained to arms and at the same time he insisted that he was a realist, a man who faced the hard ineluctable facts of human nature and progress. To listen to him on affairs you would think that Europe had turned about and was marching straight back through the Middle Ages to the Roman era, perhaps beyond that to barbarism. With his reddish hair, full red lips, and broad chest, he looked the part of a half-civilised Goth. He was affable, energetic, spiteful, self-indulgent, generous, vain. He was not afraid of hard work.

He had never been able to reconcile himself to his lameness. It was a sorer wound to him than his poverty, and he took as much pains to conceal one as the other. His more unkind speeches or acts were sometimes due only to a twinge from the damaged bone.

After the interview with Harben he was in the highest spirits. He called on Evelyn, and between mouthfuls of bread and butter and sandwiches (he pushed whole ones in his mouth as if they were sweets) he talked about himself and his future, frothing at the mouth like a mustard pot.

' I don't mind telling you that I have more and warmer irons in the fire than the Economic Council. Why—I can speak of it now—I saw the Zinovieff letter before Marcel Cohen did. What do you make of that ? '

' Are you trying to tell me that you wrote it yourself ? ' Evelyn asked, smiling.

' Not I. But perhaps I know who did.'

He watched her from the corner of his eye as he talked. She was looking very well, and her clothes satisfied his taste, which was for the extremes of elegance and sophistication. He was not in any sense in love with her, but his vanity, an emotion which usually did the work of tenderness in him, had been stirred by her quickness in surrendering to him. She was fifteen or sixteen years his senior, and that, too, was a source of satisfaction to him. Until now his appetites were better pleased by older women or by young women of the lowest class. There was something immature as well as gross in his instincts.

' Tell me,' he said suddenly, ' who is the man I quarrelled with in this house—a writer, with a complacent snout. Talking of the letter reminded me of him.'

' The novelist, William Ridley,' Evelyn answered. She felt ill at ease, as if she were being forced to confess to a mistake.

'Ah! I'm astonished that you could bring yourself to touch him.' Swan went off into a fit of malicious laughter. His right arm described an arc outwards from his body, the supposed outline of Ridley's, and with the other he gripped Evelyn's arm, shaking it to and fro in his amusement.

Evelyn withdrew herself at once. 'What do you mean, Julian?' she said smoothly, with the least hint of irony. 'Have you been taken in by gossip? I'm afraid you're too innocent for some of the people you meet here. They stuff you with tales no one else believes.'

'Oh I didn't believe it, I knew you better,' Swan said. He was abashed, and hid it under an insolent manner. His heart actually beat more quickly. He resumed his hold on her arm and this time he hurt her, sharply and deliberately. When she was forced to cry out, he loosened his grip. There were marks of his finger-tips on the soft flesh; he stroked them gently, smiling at her: slowly his hand made its way to her shoulder, then slipped underneath the dress. She quivered, lying back in her chair; her eyes were wide opened, her body arched itself, expecting, against her bored despairing knowledge of it, that it would at least feel—what? ecstasy, annihilating blind joy. She was even slightly afraid of Swan. That was perhaps her only genuine and unforced emotion at this moment.

He had scarcely left her when she rang the bell; as soon as the servant appeared she flew into an irritable rage, and scolded her for leaving two paintings awry on the wall, the curtains badly drawn, and dust—positively, thick old dust— on the edge of the table. The bewildered girl listened in silence. She saw that the pictures were straight, the curtains hung as usual, and as for dust, the room had been thoroughly turned out that morning and every inch of the table polished. She was a young country girl, without pertness or spirit to defend herself. Very soon, as she was trying clumsily to adjust the curtain, Evelyn rapped her across the arm in exasperation with her slow movements. Flushing deeply, the girl turned aside; her elbow caught a figure in black glass, knocking it across the floor in pieces: she gave a cry of terror and backed out of reach.

'Go away, go away,' Evelyn shouted. 'Get out of my sight. Go. Send someone else to clear up this—destruction. Tell Mrs. Simpson I don't want you to stay here.'

She could not wait, and began brushing the fragments together with her handkerchief. 'Destruction—wilful disorder and destruction,' she said under her breath. A tiny splinter of the glass caught her finger. Twisting the handkerchief round it she went across the landing to her bathroom: during her absence from the room the broken glass was swept up, chairs which had been moved were pushed into their right places, and the hearth swept.

She came in, sent an indifferent glance over the room, and seated herself on the couch with an air of dejection. From brooding over the awkward servant, she went on to think about the disrespect for authority which she noticed everywhere in society, particularly in the lower classes. She thought that this disrespect was growing, and that it was aggravating the frightful disorders in the world. Then it seemed to her that she herself was a victim of this disorder. If it had not been for the wrong-thinking spread by malcontents and liberals, society would never have become infected, uncertain of itself, restless, and she would not have been the mistress first of William Ridley and then of Swan: she would be enjoying the calm dignified life for which, in her heart, she had always craved.

But why not change now? she thought. A sudden joy flooded her mind. She rose and began to walk about the room with hands clasped behind her back, the gesture of a schoolgirl. At this moment she felt all the pure enthusiasm of the schoolgirl for a new faith. She would live simply and narrowly, working harder than before—a poor scholar.

The image of her husband came into her mind. She was vaguely irritated by it, as if he were one of the obstacles to her living a changed life. His big clumsy head, the eyes gleaming sardonically under his twitching eyelids, had all the air of mocking her new emotion. I must have him on my side, she thought. Impulsively, coming in her pacing about to the door, she opened it and ran upstairs to his room.

He was at work with a book open on the floor, and a paper with a half-finished graph pinned to a board. Even this exasperated her, since it was something outside her knowledge. She thought of his work almost as an affectation. What relation had graphs to life? Surely her longing to begin a new life was nobler and more valuable than these dreary exercises.

T. S. looked at her in a surprised way. It was months—perhaps years—since she last set foot in this room. He paid her rent for it, together with a sum for his food; he rarely ate a meal with her, but when he was in the house he had a tray brought to him here. In this way he tried to ease his discomfort in living in a house of which the rent and rates amounted to half his income.

He listened with bent head to the outpouring of ideas—like twigs turning and bobbing on the surface of a swift stream.

' But what do you mean to do ? ' he said at last, glancing at her with a smile. ' Dismiss half the servants, shut up the drawing-room, refuse all invitations? Inside a week, you will have grown tired of explaining to your friends that you have become a hermit. They won't believe you. They'll go on writing and telephoning. In the end you'll accept just one invitation, and one other. Then you'll invite only a few friends here. In a month you'll be living precisely the life you live now, except that you will have had to engage new servants in place of those you dismissed. My dear, why deceive yourself? If you want to live a new life, you must leave London and hide yourself in the country with no address. And are you sure you could bear that ? ' Against his will—since he had meant to be kind—his voice became ironical. He grudged the time she was forcing him to waste.

'You destroy everything,' Evelyn said.

'I'm sorry——'

'No, no, you're not sorry. Jeering at visions is one of your affectations. The frightful thing is—you kill them.'

Her mouth drooped at the corners between bitterness and self-pity. T. S. thought she might cry. He could not endure tears, and he said hastily:

'Well, forgive me, Evelyn. The fact is—you don't often take me into your confidence. I was startled. I take it all back.'

Evelyn stood uncertain. She felt an impulse to forgive him, a longing for sympathy and kindness. At the same time she was deeply resentful and wished to punish him for not listening to her with respect. But what did I hope? she thought. A mist of light nebulous images filled her mind. Out of this confusion, as if taking advantage of it to leap upwards, another impulse seized her. She said abruptly:

'Why on earth did you marry me? Please answer.'

All expression ebbed from her husband's face, as though he turned his back on himself. 'You know the reason well enough, Evelyn. Much more surprising—why did you marry a temporary officer without money, a future—or ambition?'

'I should have known it couldn't possibly last. A husband twelve years younger than his wife. Ridiculous!'

T. S. was struck by the quiver of pain in her voice. Long before their estrangement he had realised that Evelyn rarely spoke the truth about herself—either because it bored her or because she thought it would set her in a vulgar or dull light. This made living with her an exercise (of the wits) for which the War left him no energy. He had to remind himself now that an habitual liar sometimes speaks the truth.

'When I first saw you,' he said gently, 'you looked the same age as myself. Now I look ten years your elder.' He had no will to be drawn into a useless argument. He was sorry for her, for her growing fear—he had once had a curious dream, in which she was being killed in a room that glittered from the gold painted on the walls—and at the same time he could not help her. His feeling of repugnance was slight and inescapable; it sprang from the same nerve as his pity. Evelyn touched his shoulder for a moment. He made no response; he had to school himself not to move aside.

' I'm horribly alone,' she said softly. ' I'm fonder of your friend Hervey than of another woman, but she doesn't like me. Or at least she's disloyal. When my sister was alive I felt that there was one creature who would never fail me.' Her expression changed abruptly. She gave a little laugh, smothered and merry. ' Once when we were children I was going to be beaten for something. We were as alike as two peas except that she had light hair. What do you think she did? She brushed a bottleful of iodine into it and presented herself for the whipping in my place. And Papa's whippings were not a joke. He used a leather slipper, on the classic point.' She threw her head back, laughing, with her eyes turned to the past.

T. S. could not help a throb of liking. It passed in a moment, when she laid her hands on his arms. He did not move. She looked at him in silence, and drew back. Without a word, her head held on one side to avoid seeing him again, she went out of the room.

CHAPTER XLIV

MASTER AND MAN

A SIDE of his work Swan enjoyed without reserve was the choosing a subordinate. He had a feminine belief in his power to command personal loyalty. Equally characteristic was his preference for men of superb physical vitality. He would make use of men with more intelligence than strength, but such a man never drew him. Simple brutality did not attract him, but brutality—or the threat of it in reserve—overlaid by charm, by the marks of adolescence which usually accompany violence in grown men, was certain of a response in him.

When Hunt came into his room, Swan noticed at once his easy springing gait: he had a smile which noticeably softened his face, a heavy jaw, and quick restless eyes. At the moment he looked as open as a boy—Swan suspected that it would not need much in the way of opposition to turn this boyishness into something vindictive and highly unpleasant. That's what I like—a genuinely dangerous animal, he thought. He was slightly excited. He had observed Hunt send a rapid glance over the room, as one used to choosing a position.

He shook hands with him affably. 'Well, sit down. Let me see, I have your documents, and the letter from—You were in the army, you've travelled, you were selling arms from 1911 to '13, after the War you went to Ireland, you served in the Black and Tans——'

'I was responsible for a district,' Hunt interrupted.

'How old are you?'

Without hesitation Hunt said: 'Forty-three,' taking ten years off his age. 'And I don't feel thirty,' he smiled.

Swan had already decided to employ him—Hunt had applied, with letters of recommendation from two respectable politicians, for the post of outside organiser—but it flattered his sense of power to ask questions which the other man would be forced to answer.

' Where were you born ? '

' Newcastle. My father was in shipping.'

A spasm of inward laughter seized him at this account of his father, who had been a docker, oftener out of work than in; he had drunk himself out of his wits when his son was a child. That child was apprenticed at thirteen to a man who gave him an early foreknowledge of hell. Somewhere in Hunt's mind, the road to it obliterated as deeply as possible, was a cupboard under the stairs of a cellar, in which, in darkness and in pain, the child tried to forget what had been done to his mind and body. He was ashamed. His tears ran over his hands to his knees. He could not put his humiliation into words, and if he could, who would have listened to them ?

' Shipping, eh ? But you didn't go into it.'

' My parents both died early,' Hunt said. ' In any case, I wasn't interested in living a quiet life.' He passed rapidly over several years in his mind and came to the first acceptable fact. ' I went out to South Africa.'

Swan began questioning him about Ireland. ' What do you think of the Irish ? '

' What does anyone, except the Irish themselves, think of a country where a man might be murdered only for a joke ? I'd trust savages easier.' Watching Swan to see the feeling it roused in him, he described an ambush which had been betrayed by a young schoolmistress. ' One of my men was killed. I sent for the girl the next night. She was brought into the barracks and I tried her. She said she was innocent—but we had proof. Now, there's only one way to treat the Irish when you're fighting them. I kept her in the back room for a quarter of an hour, she had a nice not too thin figure, then we took her out the door into the outhouse and put a revolver to her.'

Swan controlled an inner revulsion. In spite of his firm belief that violence carried its own sanctions, he disliked the sight of death. Before he could inflict it, he would have to be in a condition of great excitement. The other man's matter-of-fact cruelty shocked him. He put the story out of his mind. True, he was going to use Hunt to do work which needed great energy and vitality, but not (not yet) any ruthless habit. It takes all sorts to rule a country, he thought.

Swan felt a quiver of satisfaction in the thought that this arrogant-tempered man, many years his senior, would take orders from him. I can dismiss him if I feel any suspicion that he is out of control or disloyal, he thought.

A curious thing happened then, as he stood up—a film of darkness over his brain for a moment, like a hand passing behind his eyes. He stumbled against the edge of the desk and Hunt caught him.

' Thanks,' Swan said, with a frown.

' All right ? '

' Yes, quite. I felt a little dizzy.' He sat down, his face flushed, and watched his new subordinate walk from the room. Although Hunt held himself stiffly, there was not the least stiffness in his movements, which were extraordinarily graceful. His body was heavy, but compact and quick. Swan surprised himself by thinking, I'm master here. He had almost said it aloud, so definite was his sense that in meeting Hunt he had passed a stage in his life.

Hunt walked easily, shouldering his way in the crowd pouring towards the tube stations. Detachments flung themselves at the out-going buses, the rejected turning away to try a new assault. It was the hour of release from shops and offices, and the city quivered like an ant-heap. Hunt was used to walking and he preferred it.

When he reached the house, he listened a moment outside the door of his wife's room. He heard a great rustling of paper. The wardrobe door groaned on its hinges. He went in. Delia was standing half-clothed before the fire, her crumpled chemise caught up on the curve of flesh below her waist. She stooped as he came in and pulled at her stockings, but as soon as she straightened herself they slipped down again below her knees.

'Hand me them,' she said, pointing towards the bed.

Hunt passed his hand about over the clothes. She must just have left the bed; a faintly acrid warmth rose from it when he moved the blankets.

'Is this what you want?'

'No. Aren't they there?' She came towards him, stretching her arms over her head. Again he reflected on the ease with which she moved herself. Below the knees her legs were those of a dancer, fleshless at the ankle, with a ball of muscle above. Her thighs thickened outwards to the two great cheeks; when she stooped he saw a groove squeezed out in the flesh beneath them deep enough to take his little finger. There was another groove under her breasts, a proper welt, looking like the mark left by a cut.

She felt about at the foot of the bed, grumbling. Her hand vanished under the quilt. 'Here all the time,' she said, with calm triumph.

She began to work herself into the corset, tugging at it with one hand while the other forced down a wave of flesh which swelled upwards. Her broad shoulders quivered. 'Doesn't half heat you,' she gasped.

'I shouldn't think you could breathe in them,' Hunt said.

'That's where you're wrong,' Delia answered. Turning herself before the glass, she passed the flat of her hands over her sides. Even so laced, it seemed that she could move each full buttock separately as she walked. 'Heavenly mentor and friend, that's what they are. We'd be ruined without them.'

She walked about the room, picking up garments where she had dropped them as she undressed, and talking half to herself. She was in a good humour. 'Who invented elastic, I'd like to know? he was a mug anyway. If it had been me I'd have invented something that wouldn't perish before you can say knife, letting everything about your legs, as like as not in the street. *For those in per-il on the sea.* I'd better take another pair. Where's that comb got?'

She dragged the comb through her hairbrush and held it up to the light with a look of concentration: ' I thought as much, it moults every winter, like some bird, yes it's the cold ': grumbling, she took the hair and rolled it with a swift movement over one finger. ' Where's that vase? It must be full of combings already. Yes it is, I'll take them round to Madame Rose in the morning, madame indeed, I'll ask her to make a plait, no, better have curls, I could pin them underneath that hat where it shows the white lining. If you believe me I've saved every hair for years, waste not want not—it's like the sparrows, nasty dirty creatures. This vase has come in useful. I've had it twenty, no, twenty-eight years. I saw it in th' window when I was working Regent Street and I said, If it isn't the image of a vase used to be at the end of m'aunt's mantelpiece when I was eight, I said I'm going to buy it, if it takes the skirt off me who cares? I said. There was a fat monkey behind the counter gaping at me: It's a guinea. To you. I was going to ask And what is it to m'—— but I thought better of it, and I felt in m'stocking and there was only twenty-two and sixpence. All right, give it me, I said. And look sharp. You should have seen his face! '

Hunt had listened to her with half an ear. It was bitterly cold outside, and the warmth of the room made him sleepy. His head felt large; the backs of his ears tingled, as he sat up to rub them he saw with surprise that his wife had taken down her fur coat.

' Where are you going? ' he asked.

' Bernberg and his friend looked in this morning and he asked me to see them both in the Monico at eight.'

She was holding her face close against the mirror; frowning, she wetted finger and thumb and worked them along her eyebrows. He saw her looking at him as she did it. To see am I on to it.

Following her with his eyes as she crossed the room and began to feel about under the pillow, he saw the edge of a letter for a second before she whisked it out and pushed it into her bag. If it had not been for this, she might have gone where she liked. But the gesture, and the white corner of the envelope, flickered in his mind like something seen at a great distance in the moments before darkness. Running towards it he found himself in a small rough-walled room, in a night as hot as the baked dust, looking at a soiled scrap of paper on the bed. The bold unformed writing was like Delia herself at that time—young, handsome, lascivious, as bold as any of the men in a town where no decent woman had yet set up house. At that time—she had been his wife for two years—he was though brutal gentler than she was. If she had gone away without that single sentence he was young enough to have followed her and tried to bring her back, but from that moment to this a line laid under the ground carried hate. He was curiously unaware of it. Events, pressing the soil down over it, seeded another country in him before ever he saw her again. Allow that he had humiliations older than that one, but they had had no meaning for him; they were the blows a child accepts without malice, learning from them only to despise softness and goodness. From that moment, he noticed every rebuff and added it to his contempt for anything that by other people was named decency or religion or brotherhood. Yet his only brothers were men, not wolves; since wolves are lacking the purely human quality of evil. If Hunt had so far been lonely, it was not because there were no others of his order.

Delia was afraid of him. Her body at present bore marks of their last quarrel. But her spirit was more than her fear: she would not give an inch before him when he was in an ill temper, she would not even hold her tongue; she still answered him when she was on her knees trying with her bruised body to reach the bed.

Now when she saw him coming towards her she made a derisive gesture. She moved back before him, smiling, and when she reached the wall she struck at his face, seeing for less than a second the upper and lower lid of his eyes move together. In falling she caught her arm on the fender and thought that it was broken, but it moved, and she brought it over her throat and breast. She lay still, looking at Hunt. She was aching all over, there was pressure at the back of her neck, much like a hot flat-iron, she thought. The bright wall of the room nearest her became grey and indistinct, as though rain were pouring between them. She was sorry for herself, and a tear or two gathered, cold and smarting, at the sides of her eyes. Glancing up, she saw the edge of the table over her head; it made her think of a stall in a Brixton street, and she was a thin starved child lying near it on her back, the stones cold and dirty, and the flaring gas jets, and women's skirts, and her fingers spread claw-wise against the light.

Hunt did not look at her, but he went over to the dressing-table, and held up the vase for which she had paid a guinea. Holding it by the lip, he broke it against the table. Delia saw it and groaned. Her fingers moved a short way over the carpet, and feeling a fragment she held it tenderly for a minute. The room dissolved about her, with the noise of wind in a chimney, and now flecks of scarlet veined the darkness behind her eyes. They mounted to a wave. It obliterated her sight, and the broken pieces of the vase. Hunt yawned, and went out of the room to the bathroom. When he returned he noticed without interest that Delia's breathing had altered. Her eyes were wide open, and they were empty, like the eyes of a newly-born infant. They did not move when he walked close past her head. Her bag was lying at the side of the bed. He stooped over it and felt in it for money. A moment later he was opening the front door of the house; as he stepped out he almost knocked over Hervey Russell. She scowled at him and hurried past.

CHAPTER XLV

On her way Hervey knocked at Mrs. Hunt's door. No answer coming, she went upstairs to her own room, on the floor above. The next morning, when she was at work, her landlady came in and told her that Delia had had a stroke the night before. She was lying in her room, dressed, pieces of a broken vase about her. ' She must have had it in her hand when she fell,' Mrs. Wood said. Clearly, she had already arranged the scene to her full satisfaction; she gave Hervey a lively account of it as if she had been in the room at the time.

' A nurse is there with her. The doctor says she may live for days or go any minute. Do you want to look at her? Funny—she can move the fingers of one hand. Everything else is dead—paralysed.'

' Ought I to go? ' Hervey said, with distaste.

' As you please. If she is alive anywhere—and how do they know when she can't speak up for herself?—she might want to see you.'

Hervey felt no wish to see Delia. ' Is her husband with her? '

' Him? He hasn't been home all night. Who knows where he is.'

It was on the end of Hervey's tongue that she had passed him leaving the house about seven o'clock. An instinct to avoid trouble, obeyed nearly without thought, kept it back. She followed the other woman in silence, and knocked gently at Mrs. Hunt's door. I stood here last night, she thought, with fear.

Delia was lying on her back in the bed. Her hair had been brushed off her forehead by the nurse and plaited, so that she seemed less flamboyant, and more like any middle-aged respectable woman. The only other change was in the shape of her nose, shrunken now, as if it had been pinched together over her nostrils. She had a high colour in her cheeks and her eyes were open.

When Hervey stood over the bed some change began in the place to which Delia's mind had retreated and, with the remnant of a company, was holding to the last conceivable moment. At Hervey's approach she felt a need, an impulse as vague and desperate as the first cry for food. Her life was with her as a burden not to be carried away in silence. Begin with the blue hissing jet of gas, the circle of light on a tablecloth of red cotton, rough to the fingers. She had a continent and an age laid up in her. Unrepentant pride filled her. A struggle began, without understanding, as in sleep. It was the wish to tell someone, before it was too late, everything that had happened to her in her life. Not for a long time did she give in. She laboured dumbly to lift the great weight. Her need became an agony; and in time that passed slowly into indifference and resignation, and so wore to nothing.

In the first moment when Hervey stood there, Delia's hand moved very slightly so that her fingers touched her friend's wrist. Hervey did not like it, but she stood quietly. Delia's eyes were at first blank, then expression of some sort came in them, it might be entreaty or grief. It was in any case hard and uncomfortable, as if the solitary watcher on a cliff at the last hour of daylight sees, straining his eyes, an arm move in the sea—is it an arm or a log of wood? Hervey tried to believe that Delia could read in her face the words she did not speak—Good-bye, Good-bye, I shan't forget you, she thought firmly. To herself and not meaning Delia to hear, she thought: It doesn't seem hard to finish, after all.

Delia was buried three mornings after this one. Hervey

was not going to the funeral, and she was in her room when the door opened abruptly and Mrs. Wood spoke to her in violent excitement.

'You must come and help me,' she said. 'The men won't nail up the coffin. They think she's still alive. What shall I do? I can't let the men go away——'

'Her husband——' Hervey began.

'Don't talk to me about him. He stands there yawning and staring out of the window. I haven't patience to look at him.'

Hervey went downstairs. The coffin lay across four chairs, men standing about it, talking. The lid rested against a chair. Hervey walked over to the coffin and saw Delia lying there at her ease. Her cheeks were as rosy as in life. It was impossible to think her dead.

'I haven't buried anyone alive, and I'm not going to,' a man said in a high voice.

Hervey's heart jumped. She glanced round and saw Hunt watching her with a guarded and overbearing look on his face. He came forward and said quietly: 'I've sent for the doctor. It was the only thing to do.'

'Yes,' Hervey said under her breath.

She walked away from the coffin and stood as near the door as possible. The room was bitterly cold, and Hunt wore his travelling coat, which came to his heels. In the silence Hervey noticed foolish details: the greenish colour of Mrs. Wood's eyes, a knot in the wood of the coffin, the jar of cold cream open on the mantelpiece. It was much better not to think about Delia.

She could not feel indifferent to Hunt. He disturbed her in a way which, if she had not deeply disliked him, would have been next door to physical desire. She knew that he was violent and unprincipled, an enemy. Looking at him she felt a weakness, a tremor that was partly fear and partly a strange recognition.

Within ten minutes the doctor came, seeming impatient and half-frozen. He looked closely at Delia, and in an authoritative voice, hoarse from much drinking of whisky, the smell of which now spread through the room, he said: ' Certainly she's dead.'

' Are you sure ? ' Mrs. Wood asked.

' I assure you she is certainly dead,' he said sternly. He spoke to Hunt. ' A most unnecessary and unpleasant delay.'

' I agree with you,' Hunt said.

' You can go on with your work.'

The men looked at each other and in silence took up the lid and placed it on the coffin. They seemed embarrassed, and stood in each other's way. Hervey went back to her room. In order not to think of Delia, and of her rosy cheeks, which were now completely covered up, she sat down and began her work. She went on with it even when the men carried Delia Hunt out, their feet heavy on each stair, their voices coming back from the turn of the walls.

CHAPTER XLVI

THE HUMBLE PETITION OF
JENNY CHARLOTTE ROXBY

HERVEY found that her salary from the *Evening Post* went
no further with her than half the sum. She was one of
those for whom money has no real value. She would never
become rich. When she had earned money she spent it at
once, rarely on herself—to her Puritan conscience, ' waste,'
' extravagance,' are only worn on the back or put into the
belly. Then finding herself penniless, at once her wit
devised ways of earning more money—so well that, this
time, she would be safe. A delusion. The more she earned
the faster she spent, and the end of a month found her as
straitened as before.

She was now anxious to finish the typing of her novel, so
that she could ask the publisher for money—to spend at
Christmas. She had no contract with him for this book,
but nothing was farther from her mind than that he would
reject it or the price she put on it.

Her back ached with the long hours copying out her
difficult manuscript. For change without relief she read
novels, and spent a day in seven groaning over her review
for the *Evening Post*, which cost her more to write than to
dig a grave, as we say.

Something strange was taking place in her. She was
displeased with herself, with her want of success, and her
instability; but never had she been happier. A decade of
disorder and bitterness was over. Now my life is beginning,
she thought; and no voice reminded her that the thought

had opened each door in her short life. At moments she was happy for no reason. She would stop work, and rest her hand over her eyes to shut out everything except this ecstasy.

Her security was suddenly and sharply disturbed. On that morning she was sent a document of which the first sight made her tremble. She read it through stolidly, from 'To the Right Honourable the President, THE HUMBLE PETITION of JENNY CHARLOTTE ROXBY SHEWETH; I. That on the 26th day of June 1915 your Petitioner then Jenny Charlotte Ling was lawfully married to Nicholas Roxby (hereinafter called the Respondent) . . . and there has been no issue of the said marriage . . . the Respondent committed adultery with a woman referred to as Mary Hervey Russell . . . WHEREFORE your Petitioner prays That her said marriage may be dissolved and that she may have such other relief as may be just . . .' to the 'Take NOTICE' addressed at the end to Mary Hervey Russell herself. She was shocked by the indecency of the document. Until now she had imagined that only certain divorce cases were obscene. Now she understood that it is the divorce law itself which violates human decency. She felt angry and ashamed. She was on the point of cutting the document to shreds with her scissors —it was too stiff to tear. A superstitious fear of the law held her back; instead, she pushed it to the back of her books and there it remained, in one bookcase or another, for several years.

Whether it was this document, or (as he said) a mistake in his accounts, or his meeting with Jenny's father, Nicholas that evening was in an unapproachable mood. Hervey listened to him for a time quietly, and said at last in a calm voice:

'The truth is, you don't want to change your life. The thought of moving your clothes and books to another house, even the thought of living with me when you have lived alone so long, is boring you. You would rather nothing changed. Do you never think I might be dreading it? You know I detest the trouble of a house, I should like to live like a poor scholar again.' She looked at him with a soft smile. 'If you are afraid to live with me, you can draw back now. *I* have been afraid.'

'Why didn't you say so?' Nicholas exclaimed.

'Because it is no use. We must go on or back; if we don't live together we shall grow tired of each other. This meeting and saying good-bye and writing letters is exciting —and a compromise. Living together may be a failure, but it is the next step and not to take it will make us ashamed.'

Nicholas smiled at her with so much liking that involuntarily she looked away. Her heart beat quickly. No one is like him, she thought; no one is so fine or so exacting, tiresome, and self-absorbed. He will take everything; and I shall usually be content. She felt an exquisite pleasure in the knowledge that her life was not going to be easy. There could be in it nothing she would resent too seriously— even when, as would certainly happen more than once, she for the time lost patience. If he disappointed her, she had not even a retreat in case of need.

'Let us go out,' she said before he could speak. 'I'm tired sitting at my desk. One of these days we'll live in the country. In another ten years London will be uninhabitable—already it smells worse every day and the people look more hideous.'

They took a bus at the end of the street. From the sound only of Nicholas's voice, she knew that his mood of self-distrust was over. Perhaps, she thought soberly, he is not in love with me as he was with Jenny, but at least he is sure now that he cannot do without me. I have grown necessary to him.

In Whitehall they left the bus and walked slowly along the Embankment. The night was open and very clear, with a sky so thickly covered with white clouds that they seemed snowfields—over part of these snowfields the moon cast a faintly yellowing glow—beyond its circle vast arctic deserts gave off a cold light. The river, Hervey said, was coming in fast, but for beauty you should see the Danesbeck sliding between its wharves. Nicholas took her arm. 'You think no place so fine as Danesacre,' he laughed.

'Why, no,' she said simply.

He was still ashamed of himself. 'You're so good to me, Hervey. I try out my spleen on you—and I don't even read your books.'

'Why should you?'

'You don't use your mind in them.'

'I'd starve if I did,' Hervey said shortly and lightly. 'Don't you know I take everything seriously except myself? That's not the spirit of a successful novelist. You ought not to despise my novels—they represent the triumph of matter over mind! My mind. Don't let's talk about them. I want to know something else—yesterday I was seeking a place where to live in quiet. I found such a one—but before I tell you about it, I must know what you can afford. I shall pay half of all our expenses—if necessary, I can pay more.' She said this as calmly as if money were not earned.

'I ought to have more money than you,' Nicholas said quickly—'in fact—I think I earn less. I have my unearned income of five hundred—left me by Mary Hervey—but Jenny must keep that.'

'The whole of it?'

'Yes. Do you mind? I have been allowing her that amount since—I'd rather not ask her to take less—in fact I——'

'Certainly don't ask her to take less,' Hervey said. He has no sense—five hundred is too much by half, she thought scornfully. She felt that his vanity would be the ruin of them. 'And your business?' she asked timidly.

'I have put into it—into the house and the stock—all the other money I had. I've been taking out eight pounds a week for myself. Is that enough?'

'Enough for what?'

'For everything you want.'

'You can't look at it in that way!' Hervey cried. 'Is eight pounds the sum the business will stand?'

'I don't know yet,' Nicholas said. 'But it's what I spend.'

Hervey was silent. She did not know how to comment on so airy a reckoning. If she said what was on her tongue, it would sound harsh and too contemptuous. Her own carelessness was one thing—she excused it and glossed it over—but not to know whether you are spending more or less than you earn—that was past belief or excuse, mad. She looked at Nicholas in astonishment. He has been badly brought up; he knows nothing about actual living, she thought. From this moment she began to think of herself as the head of the family—and she took over the responsibility for them all.

'The rent of the furnished flat I have seen is four guineas. It is the top of a house. In front is only Primrose Hill— the rooms seem suspended over the hill, a great way out of reach. You could think you were in a lighthouse. It belongs to an airman, who is flying in—or perhaps (I don't know) to Africa. For all I know he is a bird by day and becomes a man at night—anything to do with this flat is possible. Add five guineas to the four, for housekeeping —making nine—you can give me half, or four, and if more is needed I can manage the difference. Do you agree?'

'If you say it is possible,' Nicholas said. He thought she was not leaving him a great deal for himself.

They had turned back, and had walked past St. James's Park, past the Palace and through Eaton Square into the genteel shades of the past. The big houses snored a little in their sleep. From one of them—it was George Ling's town house—a fat butler led forth a fat small dog who had purposes of his own. 'The glories of our blood and state,' Hervey said. Nicholas laughed out, by which she thought she had done well.

Nicholas came home with her. Without understanding it, he had come to feel that he knew very little about her. She seemed open, yet told him almost nothing. He would like to question her, about herself, only (you understand) to draw nearer to her, but the words eluded him. He felt tired suddenly and stretched himself face downwards on the couch.

'What is it, Nicholas? Are you still anxious about the future?'

'I love you. I love you.'

'Is that all?'

Why do we talk glibly about sharing lives when we can scarcely share the simplest feeling with the being nearest to us.

If I can only be wise enough, Hervey thought now. She felt that in the last few hours she had become a reserved and experienced woman. Until this hour, for all the difficulties of her life she had not known the meaning of discipline. Now I must certainly learn steadiness, she said anxiously.

As soon as Nicholas had gone she went back to her book. Eight pages in her minute hand remained to type. Each page except the last was a labyrinth of corrections. There was work for four or five hours at least, and it was now some minutes past midnight. She began eagerly, but before long it seemed that her fingers were twice their own size. She kept stopping to rub her eyes, which closed of themselves. In spite of fatigue, these last pages of the book seemed to her very fine. The portrait in it of her grandmother was almost life size, and nothing warned her that the proper place for portraits is a gallery. This volume ended at a moment when Mary Hervey was still a young fortunate woman. In the next, she must be punished for her pride; at last she must die, the usual end to a trilogy.

At six o'clock, exhausted, already asleep, she corrected the last page of the typescript. To finish all now, she wrapped the four hundred odd pages in a good sheet of paper and addressed it with shaking hands to Charles Frome, Hamish Foster & Co. She began to fumble with her sleeve. She awoke two hours later, lying across her bed, shivering with cold, one arm still in her dress, the knuckles of the other hand touching the floor.

CHAPTER XLVII

DEATH OF A WARRIOR

Renn was summoned to his former lodging by Clive's grandmother. Clive had been away during the summer, a damaged parcel consigned to a convalescent home, after he had had scarlet fever. That was actually the end for Clive. His best hope of survival would have been to stay (without fever, of course) in his basement with his grandmother and the cockroaches. He was perhaps becoming acclimatised to it—as his sister, who was four years older, had become already and was strengthening her hold on life as Clive's weakened. Everyone knows that boys are the harder to rear, and at no time since he was aware of them had Clive been indifferent to the cockroaches, the visiting rats, and the offensively human smells of his house. He endured the two last, and fought the cockroaches with spirit. When he was in hospital he kept a wary eye open for their advance, which he constantly expected. It did not occur to him that in this building he was in safety: once, towards the end of his stay, he ventured a word or two about them with a nurse; and neither did it occur to him that he could believe her. But he had learned something, and at the convalescent home he carried out his inspections in silence, more puzzled day by day, until it came to him that if there were none of his enemy here there would be none at home— the world had moved on into a cockroach-less year.

This hope (it had not had time to become a belief) slipped from him within an hour of his return. He let it go with his reasonable smile, a flicker of lips and eyelashes, half politeness and half a childish defence, with which he greeted any familiar unwanted turn. The convalescent home had added an inch to him and even browned his skin. So far good. Alas—with a treachery he had never expected from it—it did more. Under a feint of curing him it exposed him more unkindly, and this time helpless, to all the disadvantages of living in a cellar eight feet by ten, with walls porous to damp, dark, since light and air entered by a narrow grating in the pavement, and malodorous by reason of seepings from what the landlord strangely termed a convenience, placed in the yard outside where thirty people could enjoy it. Although he did not know it, Clive was defeated in the moment he set foot in the room. At first he did not notice any difference. He had fought the cockroaches all his life, without being able once to count a victory. When he went to bed he drove them off, slept, and before morning they had brought up another battalion and were in position when he awoke. Nothing for him to do but to begin again, with fresh spirit. It was when she noticed for the first time that he had given in, Clive's grandmother sent to entreat the doctor to come. She waited a month before sending, troubled by a vague delicacy: she knew that she would never pay him. But by now Clive was too weak to think of going back to school; something must be done or she would have trouble. An official, holding his nose, would poke it into the basement, on behalf of society.

The doctor knew Clive already. He scarcely needed to turn back the coverings from his little carcase to see that there was nothing more to be done for the valiant fighter of cockroaches. It was not even worth while despatching him to hospital. He could die as easily here, without occupying a whole bed for the purpose. At the same time he was not ready to abandon Clive. He came to see him every day, and even tried on him remedies for which he raided nobler and wealthier doctors. If Clive signalled to him, even doubtfully, that he was prepared to live, he would carry him from his cellar—but it would be against his sober judgment, which contemned the folly of struggling to save a child whom society has already sentenced to death. He was spared the doubt. Reasonable and sensible as he was, Clive went on dying, without hurrying, it is true, but equally without turning back. Renn's promise to take him in an aeroplane ' the week after you can walk from here to here ' came too late. Clive's joyful smile covered a scepticism so well worn that one saw that it was part of his birthright, given to him instead of a body immune to the worst effects of tainted air and damp walls.

It was not long past noon when Renn stepped into the basement. Clive's grandmother was just lighting the gas again. ' It has scarcely been out an hour,' she grumbled, ' down here you could think you were buried.'

' It's an Esquimaux' hut,' Renn said to Clive, spreading out his arms: ' snow and ice outside, reindeer stables, penguins, bears, quite a zoo. Have you, by the way, eaten your blubber this morning ? '

Clive glanced up, pleased for a moment. Renn sat down and looked into the cup of half-warm milk and water. Blowing off the skin, which he disliked as much as Clive, he began dropping spoonfuls down Clive's throat. After a few of these Clive pressed his lips together and turned towards the pillow. That he should be disobliging was a bad sign. Now he is really leaving us, Renn thought. He noticed that Clive's glances returned again and again to the white globe of the gas, and each time he frowned slightly. ' Is it worrying you, old chap ? ' he said, in Clive's ear: ' shall I turn it down ? '

' I believe it's the only thing he can see,' the grandmother said, vexed. Clive's glance, as wavering and empty as an infant's, passed lightly over Renn's face to the globe. A noise of feet on the grating startled him, but the slight jerk his body gave under the quilt seemed to stop short of his mind, which had perhaps found a way into some space where the white globe was a sun. Leave him alone there, thought Renn.

When he left the basement room, about four o'clock, he was surprised to find it half daylight still. He drew a long breath, and looked at his watch. He had to be in Deptford, to see his friends, an hour before the meeting called at six o'clock. He set off to walk to the bus. At the corner of the street a small shop had been preparing for Christmas with sprigs of holly arranged along the front of the window, and pieces of cottonwool on threads fastened over the glass. Scarlet paper spread over the electric light bulbs threw a fine rosy glow over the whole window. At once he was a child, strolling with a forced calm beside his mother to look at the Christmas shops. How many far-fetched wiles he had used to direct his mother's eye to the tea-cosy he intended to buy for her, in hope to hear it commended. How anxiously she provoked his remarks on the penknife placed at the side of old Mercer's window—' or there's an engine, David, what do you think of that—only as an engine?' And how cunning each thought himself, while pretending out of kindness to be taken in by the transparent guile of the other. She was no cleverer than I was, Renn thought, her voice always gave her away when it came to the one thing she hoped (perhaps because it was cheap) that I should praise. He stopped short. None of that here, he said, scowling. This is not a shop, nor a street, to feel sentimental about. The houses are rotten and unhealthy, they are overcrowded, there are other Clives in the basements, the women have more spirit than hopes, and if the coloured paper rope I see festooning a window is not wicked waste of money I'll eat the next well-fed letter-writer to *The Times* I meet.

He reached Deptford, and the café where he had arranged to meet Henry Smith and Hervey, half an hour before time. To his surprise he saw Louis Earlham drinking coffee at a table alone. With diffidence—they had not seen each other since that afternoon in August—Renn went over to him and sat down. Earlham greeted him with clear pleasure and Renn felt slightly ashamed of himself.

'What are you doing here?'

'It's my constituency, after all,' Earlham said, smiling. 'Why are *you* here? I suppose you're going to denounce me at a meeting of anarchists.'

'No, only the South London Socialist Society—and why should I denounce you?' Renn said calmly. He was surprised to find that his bitterness had not diminished. He still felt that Louis had retreated from a position he should have held, and he did not forgive it. Yet who am I to blame anyone? he thought. It is a fortunate accident that I am able to earn a living without telling lies—and by the way, my employer has never asked me about my beliefs; when he does I shall probably find myself without a job. Glancing at his friend, he saw that Earlham felt embarrassed, and now he was ashamed for him too, and very sorrowful.

'How is Rachel?' he said awkwardly.

'Well and happy. Your god-daughter is flourishing too.' Earlham smiled. 'We shall have another in four months.'

'Splendid. Give Rachel my love.' And now more than ever you'll need money and safety, he said to himself. He could think of nothing to say. His silence, like his bitterness, sprang from the fact that he had not ceased to love Earlham better than any man. Henry Smith came in, followed directly by Hervey. 'My friend, Louis Earlham,' he said to her: 'Henry Smith you know already.' He waited with a little malice for the loving smile she would give each man, to cover her nervousness. Henry Smith took his eagerly. The half-starved youth she had seen once in 1919 had become a handsome and impatient young man. Four years lived in Spain and Germany as a labourer, a lorry driver, once as a waiter, had filled out his body. His mind had made wider journeys. In many ways hard and selfish, he had one unselfish passion—it was for social justice—fed by biting memories of his own and now by scenes he had witnessed in the slums of Barcelona and Hamburg. The brutality of poverty in these cities, unsoftened by our English patience and yielding ways, had shocked his mind. At twenty-four, he had the eyes of a man of thirty. For the rest he had still a country face, with high cheek bones and a fresh tint: when he smiled, the ends of his mouth turned up to form a half-circle. He was like Hervey in that he could in a few moments persuade you of his familiar kindness. Unlike her in not caring whether he pleased or did not please. As soon as he heard Earlham's name he said, indignantly:

'Oh, it's you. I've been wanting to ask you how the devil you can bring yourself to write so much nonsense for the *Daily Post*. Don't you know anything about Cohen? He's nothing but a scoundrel. Why, he hasn't even the decency to keep to his own side of the fence—he wants to pick up pennies on both. As a Labour member you have no right to help him.'

'I was a journalist before I was a member of Parliament,' Earlham said, 'and if Cohen is willing to print Labour views why shouldn't I supply him with them?' He spoke in a low voice, glancing at Renn. You could think he was appealing to his friend to support him.

'You don't understand journalists,' Renn said quietly to Henry Smith; the point of his tongue flickered across his lips. 'When Louis sees a fence, he blushes and sits on it.' His mouth was dry: his head throbbed and he raised both hands to it.

Henry Smith laughed aloud, like a schoolboy. Before he could answer, he felt a light pressure on his arm, below the edge of the table. He glanced at Hervey; she frowned without looking at him. He understood that she was warning him to talk of something not so near the bone, and since he was anxious to please her—he was impressionable and he thought her attractive—he said:

'I've just come from Munich. Do you know that this so-called National Socialist Party is very dangerous? I've never seen so much crazy excitement at a political meeting, even in Germany. When Stresemann's name came out the whole audience stood up and yelled with hate—

I timed them—for six minutes forty seconds. I tell you that country's going cuckoo. I don't give the Republic ten years the way it's being handled by your opposite numbers in the German Government.'

'Four madmen don't make a lunatic asylum of a nation,' Earlham said angrily. 'I know all about your crazy friends.'

Henry Smith shook his head. 'Maybe you know another friend of mine in Berlin, a Social Democrat, by name Kesten——'

'I've met him,' said Earlham.

'You must be the other Socialist he knows. He spends his time making friends with monarchists and officers of the *ancien régime*—he calls it practical co-operation. In 1919 he carried his principles to the point where he and an aristocratic colonel took turn about to shoot down dissatisfied workmen. Very practical.'

'A cheap sneer,' said Earlham. 'Even in a new Republic order must be maintained. Or you think not?'

'In the same circumstances you'd shoot?'

'Yes I would,' Earlham shouted. He brought down his hand on the table, so that the coffee cups rattled in their saucers.

'I must take care to keep out of your way during a revolution,' said Renn, smiling. He had grown paler than before. A powerful light fell on him from the side, so that his features appeared drawn with strength and delicacy on a colourless background, the light shining through them.

'The fatal respectability of Kesten and his colleagues has to be seen to be believed,' Henry Smith cried. 'Their chief care is never to say or do anything that might offend the other side, or frighten Conservative old women into fits. Don't imperil the elections! In place of a red flag they keep a bucket of cold water and another of sand under their tables to pour over their own followers. When democracy, call it liberty or socialism or what you like, is strangled in Germany, you'll find that the handkerchiefs round the victim's throat bear the laundry marks of the Social Democratic

Party.' He was pleased with his little joke. 'Hey? Isn't that so?' he laughed, and looked at Hervey.

Earlham tried to speak calmly. 'He's your pupil, isn't he?' he said to Renn. 'I congratulate you. But couldn't you have taught him that playing at revolutions is a nursery game—at least in this country?'

'All right, all right,' Henry Smith said. He leaned across the table, now sober and angry. 'Be clever and politic—it's your job, I know—I'm not quarrelling with you for doing it. All I say to you is, you're so busy being clever and politic, and scoring points, you forget you were put up to be a clever *Socialist*. Has someone been telling you and the rest of them that they can sneak Socialism in by a back door when the other side isn't looking? It's all my eye and MacDonald! What do you think we feel, watching you sing cradle songs in a top hat.' He looked at Earlham's face and roared with laughter. 'Come back to Munich with me in January, and I'll show you what happens when one side is afraid to sing and toss caps in the air and the other isn't.'

'Germany isn't England!'

Henry Smith agreed amiably. 'The middle classes in Germany have been through hell. And Germans have a very curious habit of looking for traitors at home when they're defeated abroad. Say to a German, Your men put up a grand fight, it took the rest of the world its time to beat you. Is he pleased? Not at all. We were stabbed in the back at home, he cries. Those crazy idiots in Munich yelling " the traitor . . . the traitor " till their throats split. Well, I'll tell you—every nation gets the traitors it deserves, and cautious leaders are the same everywhere and they make the same speeches.'

'Tell me, Louis,' said Renn, gently, 'why did the Party put up a speechless septuagenarian owner of a bakery at the by-election in November? It was a safe seat—you could have had a man worth having in the House.'

'Sometimes it is necessary to reward a faithful servant,'

said Earlham gloomily. ' I can tell you he isn't a year over sixty-nine. He's been in the Party for over half a century.'

' Serve fifty years without a single act of disobedience and you shall be given a safe seat,' Renn said smiling. ' A baker. Why, yes, he's practically a bap.'

Henry Smith looked curiously at Earlham. ' Are you here to answer questions ? ' he asked.

' It seems so,' Earlham said.

' Can you tell me which of our people will help me to get a house pulled down? It's in your constituency, not ten minutes from here. You should be the one to help. By God, if I could make it a rule that every Labour leader and member of the Executive Council and the General Council had to live in a slum—yes, live—I'd live in one myself, willingly and joyfully. I shouldn't be surprised even if it made Socialists of them! You, you'd demolish the hovels in these parts fast enough if it was the only way of getting out of them.'

' Why not describe your house ? ' Earlham said drily.

' Number 98 Smith Lane,' Henry Smith said. ' Mark it. You'll hear about it again. I'm not going to describe it. I'll only tell you that eight people live in one ground-floor room, ten in the other two. The basement, which is flooded every year, houses a man and wife and three children. The house is running with rats. They gnawed one side of a child's face last week——'

' Oh! ' Hervey said.

' All right, all right—Very well, I'm going to get it closed. It may take me twenty years—unless you'll help me.'

' We haven't time to give to one house,' Earlham said shortly; ' once we're in office we'll pull down every such slum in London.'

' I'll bet you five pounds,' the younger man answered gravely, ' that another Labour Government will come and go, and my house will still be there, and still lived in. And why? Because my work will be cancelled out by your methods——'

'But Louis Earlham will still be Labour member for Deptford,' said Renn.

'And now I think you two have baited me long enough,' Earlham said pleasantly, 'I must go back to my job, which you find so futile and inglorious.' He looked at Hervey. 'The only woman has said nothing. Is your opinion of me the same as theirs?'

Hervey blushed hotly, in embarrassment and from her feeling of shame. This was not the only time she had seen one child tormented by all the others, but she had never known it happen that one of the tormentors felt an agony more crushing than his victim's. She detested cruelty. And she liked to stand well with everyone, with no reserves. That was impossible here. All three men had turned towards her; they were waiting for her to speak, Earlham with a look of polite bitterness, the other two with assurance. She looked more closely at Earlham. He is sensitive and intelligent, she thought swiftly ; he is sincere. It was painful to her to oppose him.

'I don't know enough about you,' she said, nervously. 'I think it a mistake for socialists to pretend that socialism is not drastic, not a revolution. But as for your methods— you may be justified—nothing is simple——' In another moment she would be sunk: she grasped to save her a root of her faith—'No one knows the whole truth about anyone.'

After a momentary silence, Henry Smith jerked back his head and burst out laughing. 'Hervey, I'm ashamed of you!' he cried.

Hervey looked at him with her intimate smile. She was impressed by him, by his knowledge of events in the world, and his peasant good looks.

'Time for the meeting,' Renn said. He sent Hervey a sharp glance. 'Too much imagination,' he said in her ear. He disliked the notion that she was sorry for him.

The meeting was held in the back room of the restaurant. Not more than twenty-five persons had come. Renn was in the chair. He listened to a number of speeches on the need for a forward policy: he approved, but he had heard the speeches before, many times. That there was some thread joining this room to Clive's basement he felt certain. Otherwise he would not be here. But for the moment he could not lay hands on it—he felt only the futility of meetings in shabby rooms, and the passing of resolutions urging the need for a miracle. He despised himself for his weakness. If there is no need for miracles, why be a socialist? Immediately below him, in the first row of chairs, a woman sat half asleep, her hands folded in her lap; her fingers were cracked and shiny from years of work. Every few moments she roused herself and tried to follow the speeches, but always her weariness conquered. And again she roused herself, moving her hands, and listened. Only the hope and belief in a miracle brought her here, Renn thought; if she can believe, I can. A sudden disturbance began at the far side of the room. A man had knocked over his chair in standing to speak and he was now dealing blows with his fist on the back of another. The tenant of the second chair flinched and protested. The man bawled on. He was prepared instantly to begin a riot in the High Street, to smash shop windows, to strike and see blood flow—Renn was forced to speak.

'Don't talk nonsense here,' he said, harshly.

'We shan't get anywhere without violence, comrades,' the man said. 'Action, not words, is what Lenin has proved. Where would he be if he had sat talking instead of drilling a Red Army?'

'Most of us have seen armies enough for a lifetime,' Renn said. 'If it comes to fighting again we shall want to know what we're hoping and fighting for. Making trouble in the streets and cooling your head in jail for six months afterwards won't bring us anywhere. Where did you learn your tactics, my friend? Chicago?'

The disciple of violence sat down grumbling. When he left the chair at the close, Renn found Hervey at his elbow. She forgot to speak as though nothing she had to say were unusual. 'I know that man well. Hunt, his name is Hunt, Timothy Hunt. He was the husband of a friend of mine, she's dead, he used to beat her. I don't think for a moment that he's honest.'

'Where is he?' Henry Smith exclaimed.

They looked round. The man had already left. Renn questioned several persons; no one would answer for the man, no one knew him. He had walked in with others from the front room.

'Your wife-beater was probably an *agent-provocateur* of some sort,' Renn said, gaily, to Hervey.

'Here, in London?' Hervey protested. David likes to imagine himself a conspirator, she thought.

'Why not in London?' Smith laughed. 'His methods are crude, but are they the worse for that? He'll learn. For all he knew, he was dealing with an ignorant audience.' He looked at her and said eagerly: 'Come and I'll show you my house. You, too, David.'

'I'll come with you,' Hervey said.

She was not to see Nicholas that evening, and (without thinking it) she felt that she was on holiday. It was the feeling of before the War, when she and Philip and T. S. walked about London, three poor scholars, as fortunate as the day. This freedom she had forgotten. Now with this stranger it returned for a short time, and with it other careless ghosts, other nights, other voices, loosening the silence that lay over them no more lightly than earth. I have made a friend, she thought easily. She was always sensible of appearances and would stare until she was ashamed at any person who pleased her by being, to a degree of strangeness, beautiful or ugly. David Renn had early seen and understood this habit in her, and that it was no more personal than the artist's scrutiny of his model. He had an impulse to step up to the younger man and whisper: 'Don't imagine you will come any nearer than you are at this moment.' But Smith was not dull and not (bating his years) conceited and would discover it for himself.

'I can't spare the time,' he said absently. 'In half an hour I ought to be in Wigmore Street. I must go.'

He took a bus going to a northern suburb; half-way up Regent Street he was already ten minutes late. A second halt in fifty yards was too much for him: he left the bus and hurried off on foot. Wigmore Street was empty and nearly dark. He began to run. His wounds had been hurting him all day; now suddenly the pain spread out, like the fingers of a hand, through his body: two fingers probed his back and another searched for his heart. He stood still and breathed slowly and carefully. His forehead was damp and he felt a cold trickle starting at his temples. He dried it and walked on slowly. The pain drew back, rose, drew back. He breathed more easily. He could see the length of the street to Baring's; no one was in sight waiting, and there were no lights. Hannah had gone home, too impatient to wait for him.

He reached the door and stood close to it, leaning against a window. After all, I got off lightly, he thought: I can't complain, I might be dead or incurable in hospital. It was disquieting to think of the care taken to keep alive certain human remains of the War, bodies without minds, faces without mouths or any recognisable features, limbless trunks, suppurating pieces of flesh which had been men. Watched over and tended, they would probably survive the next war.

Renn limped towards a street lamp, to see his watch. It was now forty minutes after the time he had agreed with her to be there. He turned to go home. The side door of the shop opened, and Hannah called: 'David. Bless you —I couldn't help it. It's the Christmas orders, why does everyone spend and spend at Christmas, why can't they spend all the time? Disorderly, I call it.'

She put an arm in his, and fastened her hands over his arm like a child. 'I'm hungry and tired—could you forget your socialist principles for once, and let me have a cab? Are we going to your room?'

In the cab she almost fell asleep. His lodging was in

Marylebone Road, two rooms on the ground floor. The light had been turned off in the passage and Hannah fell sleepily against the chair, and swore aloud. His landlady was deaf and he hoped asleep.

He had set the table before he went out. 'Cheese, goose sausage, fruit, butter, bread. Is that right?' he asked anxiously.

'You remembered everything,' Hannah said. She kissed him. 'Oh Davy, how good you are. I adore you with my heart—and my stomach,' she added, sitting in to the table, with a hand already stretched towards the food. She ate eagerly, and talked the whole time. Her face was rosy with the cold, her thin brown hands moved like birds. Her eyes, bright as they were, were brighter for their overlining black eyebrows, thick, straight, like rods. Renn watched her eat, and tried to memorise her face.

'You're not eating, David.'

'I can't eat and look at you.'

'Why?'

'Looking at you fills me full to the edges,' Renn laughed.

'Sit by the fire then, my dear one.' She came over to him and seated herself on his knee. 'Are you going to send me home?' she asked, in her loud merry voice, with an air of candour.

'Can you stay?'

His heart was beating inside his throat, at the back of his skull. He had prepared, he thought, for everything, but not for simplicity. 'Oh my love,' he said quietly, 'oh my love, my love.'

When they were lying, side by side, in his bed, Hannah laid her finger across the scars on his leg. 'Was that your serious wound, David?' 'No. You are that,' he answered. She began to laugh—you could not say it was an unpleasant sound, unless a loud clear bell, rung without art, is disagreeable to your ear, but it was noisy to wake the deaf.

Renn let this tide of sound wash over him. He felt quiet

in every part of his mind and body. The gentle weight of Hannah's shoulder, the warmth flowing from her, penetrated him: even his bones felt it. From another house in the street came the sound of a piano played by an unskilful hand. *Exquisite friendly speech,* he repeated drowsily. Hannah raised herself on her elbow and tweaked the curtains, so that the light from the street fell on him.

' I like to see you, my dear. Are you happy now? '

' Very happy.'

' Content with me? '

He turned his face from the light. ' I'm better than content, but I should like it better if you were here always. The thought of your going away—as if these were four ordinary walls and not the wall of China—is very unpleasant.'

' But I must go.'

' If you were living here——' Hannah lay over him and closed his eyes and mouth with her mouth—' let me breathe,' Renn said.

' Not if you will talk of marriage. I won't be married. Not until I have triumphed.'

' Why should it prevent you? ' he asked, after a minute.

' Don't talk about it, my dear kind David,' she said gravely. ' I won't alter and I won't marry; I'll be your loving Hannah, your dear sweetheart, your wife-by-rights, *und so weiter*: does that satisfy you? '

' No,' Renn said, ' but I'll make it do for a time.'

' Turn your head.' He turned obediently to the light. ' You have the strangest face, David. It has so little colour, even in your lips, that I can think of it as transparent. It seems to have no eyebrows and yet there they are, like arches, not in the least like mine. One expects to feel the bones of your head small and delicate, but when I put my hands on it I feel it broad as broad. I do believe you're stronger than I am.'

' I should hope so indeed,' Renn said. He stroked her arm to the fingers and so down her thigh to the knee, as

round as an apple under his hand. ' And don't discuss me
to my face. It embarrasses me.' She laughed loudly again,
so that he was forced to silence her. Her thin arms round
his neck were those of a child, but there was nothing childish
in the need that strove with his.

CHAPTER XLVIII

CHRISTMAS EVE

RACHEL EARLHAM watched her husband dressing to go out
to dine. She was thankful not to be going with him, she
was tired, there was still something to do, her child's garments
to iron—half her mind was already in the warm dimly lit
kitchen—yet a feeling of uneasiness persisted. It arose
partly from Louis's unfamiliar looks—he was wearing the
first tailed coat he had had—and partly from her sense of
something, too much, unsaid between them. Thoughts,
words, were heaped in her like a month's neglected mending,
and the moment to look them over with him never came.
He was no busier than usual, nor was she—yet they talked
less freely, and sometimes at night, when Louis was asleep,
she would lie awake thinking that to-morrow she would
speak to him about their life, about changing it—in some
way not at all clear to her now, but she knew that a
change should be made. She arranged, even to the words,
what she must say, and imagined Louis's answers, but
nothing ever came of these plans, and the burden on her
mind was the same.

Louis turned from the glass. ' Does this look all right,
Rachel ? '

' It fits you very well,' she said evasively. In her
heart she believed that socialists ought not to wear
such clothes; and that she held her tongue was a
measure of the silence between them. It was nothing to
her that the leader of the Party set the example which
Louis followed.

Louis came over to her and stroked her hair. ' I wish we

were going together,' he said, with vehemence; 'without you everything is dull.'

Rachel was silenced. He really means it, she thought—yet, in that case, why go? Another thought moved so swiftly behind the first that there must have been a likeness.

'David hasn't been here for weeks—months.' As soon as she had spoken she felt her burden lighter, as though now at last she had begun to say what had so long waited for speech. She looked expectantly at Louis. Her heart beat quickly.

'He is annoyed with me,' Louis said.

'But why?'

'I hardly know—or rather—he is an idealist who has never had to make his ideals serve a working policy. A few weeks in the House would cure him. He ought to know—when you are advancing under fire—things don't always go according to plan. The longest way may be the shortest—you may have to retreat, to change direction, to——'

He is repeating, Rachel thought, phrases he has heard a great many times. As if in answer, Louis said: 'I had another talk with MacDonald last week, and if Renn thinks we compromise too much he ought to have been listening, to know all we have against us.'

'All the same, I should like to see him,' Rachel said.

Her husband looked sharply at the clock. 'If I'm going by bus, I must go,' he exclaimed. He kissed her, folded the ends of his scarf into his coat, and opened the door. 'No light, Rachel! I don't like you to go up and down stairs in the pitch dark. If you were to fall——'

'Wait, I'll light the gas on the landing,' Rachel said. Louis stood still. He watched her arm move, holding the match, and the line of her body raised straining against the wall. She seemed to him young and very small, like a child working at a task beyond her strength. He did not move to help her. The dark house, the stillness, and Rachel's lifted arm, were met in an instant as sharp-pointed as memory

—I was lovely, I am gone. When she turned, he rested a hand on her neck, stroking it lightly. 'Go to bed early, and sleep,' he said, gently.

Rachel followed him downstairs to the front door. She felt sorrowful and disheartened, as though she had managed badly; but now there was no time to improve matters. Trying at least to end well, she asked with a show of eagerness:

'Who else is dining to-night with you and William Gary?'

'Thomas Harben and his wife—some other people— I don't know.'

'Harben,' Rachel said, hearing this name—in one of those intervals when the mind seems to be thinking in another quarter of time than the present—repeated back and back from a still lengthening distance. She was shocked certainly by the notion of his talking to these people; they were enemies, irreconcilable, without goodness or scruple. To shake hands with them, to eat at the same table—her thoughts deafened her with the roar of waves. All this time the word 'Harben' was falling in darkness as a stone falls.

'Good night—don't work late,' said Louis, smiling.

Rachel nodded and closed the door gently. Earlham felt for a moment that she had closed it in his face, then he set off half running towards the main street. He had to wait five minutes for a bus; when it had carried him a part of the distance he realised that he would be late. He jumped out at once and sought a cab. If Rachel could see me she would disapprove, he thought. In his heart he felt more at his ease driving to Gary's flat than if he arrived on foot.

He was after all late. There were already eight people in the room. With a strong sense of unreality he looked into the sardonic face of Thomas Harben, seeing it as strangely large, powerful, and inexpressive, as though it were composed of a less mutable substance than flesh. It is impossible that I am here in this room as the equal of these people, he thought. But his legs and his tongue moved;

he spoke, Thomas Harben listened. The sensation of unreality passed almost at once, and he felt a new confidence,
half-intoxicating pride. For less than an instant the starved
urchin and the ambitious scarecrow young man looked with
awe and surprise at their successor—What, you here! Then
he was finally at ease. They moved into the dining-room,
and Gary, looking at him with a friendly smile, said:

' I think you sit in your usual place, Louis.'

These words gave Earlham an extraordinary pleasure—
almost he felt that he, with Gary, was the host of this dinner-
party; he turned with assurance to speak to Mrs. Harben,
seated on his right. Before this moment he had scarcely
looked at her. Now he saw a handsome woman, of middle
age, with dark hair and a noticeably white skin. She looked
back at him in a friendly way, and at once questioned him
about an article he had written in the *Daily Post*. He was
pleased and astonished; and he went on talking to her with
all the ease in the world. Lucy Harben listened, and at times
smiled thoughtfully, glancing at him with eyes as calm and
searching as his wife's, but hers were dark, almost pitch, and
Mrs. Harben's were a cool bluish grey. Earlham found
himself seeking her glances for the pleasure it gave him.
It seemed that she admired his account of the condemned
who sit in darkness in slums. He found he could agree with
her that over-much weight was laid on the personal aspects
—' the merely personal,' she said—and not enough on the
technical and practical. 'We don't need to be told how
ghastly some of these houses are, but what actual steps to take
to get rid of them—how to meet the cost of re-building, how
to compensate the landlord. All these problems which *must*
be faced and which—do forgive me—some of your colleagues
in the Labour Party seem determined to ignore. The solid
good sense with the brilliance of your article pleased me
so much.'

Earlham felt a slight discomfort. He did not want to
discuss landlords and their compensation. A crude hasty
answer would suddenly destroy the ease between them.

He felt most anxious to keep it. In time, he thought—when I know her better—there is a time and a moment for all things—time—the growth of confidence—the right time, the right moment. He made a quiet evasive answer. Mrs. Harben looked at him with a smile: lowering her voice, she began to speak of books and writing, again as though his opinion had peculiar value for her.

He saw no reason to tell her that he read nothing except works on politics and economics. He felt as though he were launched on a strong smooth current, strong enough to carry him anywhere. The dinner, more elaborate than other meals he had eaten with Gary, drew off part of his mind. The cluster of glasses near his hand, darkly reflected in the polished surface, the dulled gleam of silver, the warmth, the flow of voices about the table, formed together the walls of a cell—but that it is too lifeless an image for what was as yielding and delicate as a woman's soft arm—in which deliciously easy and self-aware, he sat with his friends. He talked, he listened, he talked again: at moments he was eloquent.

He could not imagine why he had once doubted whether he could hold his own with people whose experience of the world was a hundred times wider than his. He felt that he was growing the whole time, in decision and suavity. His mind was lucid and vigorous. When, left alone at the table with the other men, he was able to correct a statement of Harben's, the sense of his boldness gave him a stab of pleasure. In mind already he was reliving the scene before Rachel, who when he talked seriously to her inclined her heart to hear him.

The bus Earlham had left in such a hurry waited for another three minutes at the side of a stream of cabs and buses pouring in another channel. Many of the cabs had pairs of skis fastened to the roof—the nearby station was a gateway to one of the playgrounds of Europe; the few (compared with the many prisoners) passed through to be

shown the wonder of snowy mountains, sunlight, dazzling
skies: they were not always the ones in need of these
medicines. Each laden cab on its way to the station passed
at least a hundred persons in sore and urgent need of rest
and pure clear air. Fortunately it never occurs to these
unfortunates that they are a hundred to one. True, the
driver of Earlham's bus thought for an instant, If our Gert
could get out there she'd be saved—but he was a long way
from supposing that his Gert's life was worth as much as
the life of young Mrs. Carabas, whose Daimler, laden with
rugs, skis, and cabin trunks, swept past him in the last second
before that line of traffic was immobilised and his given the
signal to move. As he moved his gears, the half-formed
thought vanished: he watched the great worm of cabs, drays,
buses, in front of him, push slowly forward between the
street lamps. There was another longer wait at the Park
corner; and he had no sooner covered a few hundred yards
than he was halted again at the tail of the worm, its head
near the Ritz. To his right he caught glimpses of the deep
mist of trees; on the left he had a clear view into a high
wide room, filled with a yellow light, in which some
several persons were lolling it in elbow-chairs, like mutes
in a play: he saw a waiter approach one of them, carrying
on a tray a decanter and a tumbler ; he felt his own
mouth suddenly gritty with dryness. Once again he moved,
and this time reached the first of the shops. From here to
its end, Piccadilly was one treasure-house. Only to glance
into these rooms where the last Christmas shoppers were
handing out money in exchange for dresses of velvet, lamé,
and satin, underclothes of silk and fine wool, winter strawberries, roses, violets, silk dressing-gowns, jewels, spiced
hams, boxes of china tea, jars of caviar and pâté, skis, boots
made by hand, riding hats, top hats, books, gold-mounted
bags, was to know that this was a rich street of the richest
city in the world. Even when the doors were closed for
the holiday enough would remain within to feed and clothe
a multitude. The bus passed through this fair, and with

many halts crossed the Circus, passing by the theatres and the pavements where the typist and her friend jostled women in furs hiding their jewelled necks: the man holding up a handful of boxes of matches and a card inscribed LAST HOPE stood in the midst of the women in fur coats and all the other people, as though he were not there. But that they walked round not through him he was for them not there. The bus passed him, and passed the shadowed spaces of Trafalgar Square, with the gleaming tree between the columns of the church, and the lit windows of the shipping companies, and the great bodies without hearts of the protean animal of State. It crossed the river by a fine bridge, and now at once it was in another quarter of the city. There were crammed shops, and shoppers, but none here were rich and many were as poor as maggots, as could be known by their sunken cheeks and hands holding the lapels of coats over the garment underneath. Behind the bastion of brightly lit shops and decent houses along the route many ways led by this or that corner, with its one street-lamp, into such a house and a room as the man standing unnoticed in the Circus would enter when he came home for another night, and that this night was marked from all others—a feast to celebrate a birth—would not lead him to blaze away all his matches at once. The bus moved with the main current flowing through this old and debauched quarter of the city. It passed a big jolly woman, already a little tipsy, a young woman whose cheekbones stretched the skin of her face so that below them it was like a thin mask of bone, a negro slate-grey from the cold, a small child playing with an orange which he threw about like a ball and then fondled in his bosom. At the corner of Deptford High Street a man carrying a string bag of apples and oranges ran out from a shop and climbed awkwardly on to the bus. There was no room for him to sit, and while he stood leaning against the end rail, his bundle pressed under his arm, a faint smile came and went on his face. 'For the kids?' said the conductor, jerking his arm at the bag.

The man's smile widened and his remote patient gaze moved slowly from the conductor's face to his bundle before he nodded. 'Yes, it's here all right,' he said softly.

The bus descended a hill between a bank and a high wall. For this short space all was quiet, as if in darkness this valley became young again—like the wrinkled hag of the fairy tale. The bus drew up at the foot of this hill. Holding the bag carefully away from him, the man stepped out. He walked a short way along the road, close to a stretch of rough ground, dark; at its farther edge a few points of light marked the river, and a cold penetrating breath came from its unseen mouth.

Bent before the wind, he crossed the end of this open place; he hurried along a street of small houses, a second, a third, all the houses alike and dingy from age and soot, and came to the street where he lived. Here a light in the window of his own kitchen pleased him. He went in at the back door and at once, from being no one, a fragment of the crowd flowing through the streets, he was himself, he had a name, Frank Rigden, a wife, two children, and a house in which every chair, picture, cup, and strip of carpet was almost as near a part of him as his hands. Like his wife and his children they were so much that was safe, familiar, and personal in a world in which, without thinking about it, he knew he was of no account. Here, and only here, he could feel that he was needed. Here he counted for something.

The kitchen was gay with ropes of coloured paper. Sally had laid the children's presents, a ball, a pair of coloured slippers, a jersey, on the table, and now she added to them two oranges and the two reddest apples. She touched each thing with a curious meditative smile before filling the boy's stocking with his gifts and laying the woollen ball aside.

'Isn't she to have a stocking, then?' asked Frank. He felt aggrieved.

'Not this year. She's too little to know,' Sally answered.

'Maybe she isn't.'

His wife only smiled at him. She sent a glance round the room, to be sure that all was done, and sighed with relief. ' I'll just sit a minute,' she said, in a voice as though she were excusing herself for a bad habit.

She sat on a low nursing chair by the fire and looked at the flames, her hands crossed on her knees. Frank watched her for a moment. After the cold, the warmth of the room made him sleepy. He was overcome with drowsiness; Sally's stooping body brought to his mind a woman belonging to his other life, the three years in France in the War. He had seen this woman only once: the battalion was going into the place called ' rest ' and at dusk it marched through a silent village: the only thing he noticed in it was a yard in which a fire had been lighted, and a woman squatting on her heels in the glow, so intent that she did not lift her head to see the marching men. For some reason the sight of this woman brought his heart into his throat with surprise and delight. Now when he looked at Sally he saw beyond her the lines of swaying men and the steel-grey sky at the end of the French village, like a wall. With a start he came back to the room, and to Sally, but for a moment she seemed gigantic, crouching over a blaze with her head on her arms, and then she was small and dim, as though he were seeing her from a vast distance: he no longer saw her face; she was a woman bent over a fire, she was his mother, she was the woman in the French village, she was old or young—he was not sure.

A knock at the back door roused him. It was a feeble knock, as though whoever stood there was uncertain and timid. Sally went out, and he heard her voice coming from the dark scullery, and a muttered reply. In a minute she came back. Her mouth quivered into a smile; she looked rosy and confused.

' It was an old man selling lavender bags. At this time of night—and Christmas Eve.' She went on as if ashamed: ' I gave him something, Frank. We aren't as poor as that yet.'

She came closer to him and laid her hand on his shoulder as she did when she was troubled. Without knowing why, she felt afraid. Of what was she afraid? At times London itself frightened her, growling in her ears like a wild beast— she was still too much the countrywoman to be at home here. But she was not thinking now of the acres on acres of streets outside: her uneasiness sprang from within, from deep in her own body. She took Frank's arm and laid it round her waist. So held she felt warmed and comforted. For a moment, perhaps, she thought this was all the assurance she needed to know that everything would go well, there would be blazing coals in the grate every winter, and apples and oranges on the dresser for their Christmas. She felt very sleepy. 'Let's go up,' she said in a slow voice. The fire was now only a layer of red cinders: she raked it, straightened the rug, looked searchingly about the room, then lifted her arm to the light to turn it out.

CHAPTER XLIX

When Hervey went up to Danesacre, she and Nicholas had been living a fortnight in the flat above Primrose Hill. She left him to live his Christmas there alone. It was unthinkable for her not to be with Richard at Christmas. She was relieved that Nicholas did not protest: if he had, she would have left him just the same, but then she would have felt guilty. She promised him not to stay longer than a week.

Her mother did not know yet she was with him. Hervey meant to tell her part at a time. The first night she was at home she told her she intended to marry again. Mrs. Russell showed neither surprise nor anger.

' Who is it you are wanting to marry ? ' she asked.

' It is Nicholas Roxby,' Hervey said. She was more afraid than if he had been someone of whom her mother had never heard.

' Nicholas Roxby! ' her mother repeated. She was seized by one of her sudden rages. ' Why hasn't your aunt Clara written to me? I don't like it, I don't like it at all.' Her face crimsoned. She looked with anger at Hervey.

' I begged her not to write to you,' Hervey said. Her mother's harsh voice woke the fear that was always at the bottom of her heart since she was a child, and knew the tone and frown which meant she would be thrashed. ' I was anxious to tell you myself.'

There was a long silence. Mrs. Russell stared into the fire, her mouth working, as it did when she was upset or angry. Hervey looked at her with misgiving. A change came over Sylvia Russell's face, swiftly, softening and relaxing it. She looked older and tired.

'I haven't seen him since Clara brought him here when you were a baby,' she said. 'He and the girl were brought up with all they wanted, while you children had nothing you didn't work for yourselves. I don't suppose he was any cleverer than you were, but your grandmother never asked if *you* were getting any education or what became of you. And as for Jake——'

Hervey turned away. She could scarcely endure it when her mother relived the past with this bitterness. Her heart ached so. Don't think of it, don't think of it, she cried. Her helplessness made her rage. She felt as though a knife were being turned in her own breast.

'Nicholas isn't rich,' she said, forcing herself to speak. 'He left the firm during the War, partly because of the profits.'

Mrs. Russell's eyes started at that. 'I don't understand you.'

'He thinks—that money is less important than other things.' She bit her lip, anxious lest Nicholas should seem a fool. Mrs. Russell could fill her laughter with a searing contempt from which her children had flinched all their lives. Hervey would do anything rather than start it against herself. She looked at her mother with doubt and fear. Nothing was bettered by that in her heart she was sorry Nicholas had thrown away so much money.

'He is quite right,' Mrs. Russell said abruptly. She thought a moment, then asked: 'What does he live on?'

'Instead of a showroom he took a house in Chelsea and filled it with old furniture and old glass, which he sells. He understands everything to do with furniture.' She said nothing about the income of five hundred pounds left to him by Mary Hervey. What was the use—since Jenny had it all? It would only vex her mother to know that his first wife had so much influence over him. She might even laugh.

'Well, what is going to happen?' asked Mrs. Russell.

'I have asked Penn to divorce me, and he has agreed,' said Hervey quickly. 'I shall keep Richard, of course. Penn wouldn't want to bother with him, even if he had any money. He hasn't taken his degree, and he's living now with his mother. I don't suppose he'll ever do anything.'

She felt that she had thrown Penn to the wolves for no reason but to make things easier for herself. 'I'll be bound he won't,' her mother said contemptuously. 'He's lazy to his very bones—a good-for-nothing.' Her mouth worked angrily. 'A rare soft sit-down he's had of it all these years! I can't be anything but relieved you've got rid of him.'

Hervey did not answer. She felt a distinct sense of shame. Why had she exposed Penn to her mother's scorn? She was almost ready to think he had a better right to be protected than Nicholas—was she not leaving him? She closed her mind to these thoughts, as sharp as crab apples in her mouth.

'The divorce won't be heard until May,' she said calmly. 'And after that is six months to wait. I thought—I can't see the sense of waiting so long. I thought Nicholas and I might begin living together at once. He's not strong— the War—and it would be more economical——'

Mrs. Russell answered her as calmly. 'You must do as you think best.' Everything is changing, uncertain, she thought. She had a strange conviction—strange to her— that Hervey, Nicholas, and all the others who were young enough to have many years to live still, must be allowed to decide for themselves what turn to give their lives. No one, she thought, has the right to say, What you are doing is wrong. Since too much is wrong—and no one can say what further they will have to endure before they die. Jake was destroyed, she said, when he was nineteen, at the time when Nicholas escaped with his life—but next time he might not escape, or Richard might not escape. She looked at Hervey with kindness.

'You know that whatever you do you are my little good

Hervey,' she said to her in a softened voice. 'You always had courage for anything. And I'm sure you deserve to be happier.'

Hervey could not find words. Her love for her mother had its roots too deep in her life, and they were too hard and twisted with other things, to make response easy for her. To be forced to show her feeling made her awkward; her tongue felt as heavy as a stone. She blushed and looked at her mother with a smile.

'I shouldn't have done anything without you,' she said, hurriedly. That was the best she could say, and her heart turned in her side with love. Mrs. Russell seemed satisfied. She stared in front of her, her blue eyes less remote and cold than usual, as though for a few moments the present were closer to her than the past, in which, as in a kind and familiar country, she now lived during the longer part of the day. When Hervey had gone up to bed, her mother opened the Chinese cabinet and took out a bundle of old photographs, but she soon put them back again, and sat looking into the fire, her dress turned back over her petticoat and the palms of her hands resting on her knees. She thought for a short time about Hervey, and about her patience and her stubborn spirit. She is too careless of herself, the mother said. From time to time her lips moved, as words spoken in the past came to them. She forgot that Hervey was a woman of thirty, with a son and a lover, and thought of her as a child, whose goodness lay deeper in her than her obstinacy. It was not long from these to the time when she had no doubts, and in that brief gaiety she dreamed until the growing coldness of the room woke her. She started, and saw it was late and the fire all but gone.

Hervey spent her time with Richard. It was easy to look after him. Although he was nine years old, tall for his years, and self-possessed, he liked to be bathed every evening, and if Hervey offered to help him dress he stood still and let her pull his clothes on and fasten his shoes. He was wilfully lazy. He had filled out since she brought him to Danesacre to live; his cheeks were rosy, his lips a clear scarlet; he had straight thick fair hair, black eyelashes, and northern blue eyes, clear and very bright. She was glad that he was handsome and seemed clever. His smile, like her own, was warm and kind. But he had very little to say, to his mother or anyone, and at times she felt as though there were a blind ditch between their minds. As children do, he disliked questions. Unless he wanted to do or to be given something, he rarely began to talk. She thought it was because he had been away from her so long during the last four years, and she felt sorrowful and guilty, with the heavy feeling of wrongdoing and time slipping past, inexorable—I want him with me, she thought; he is the centre of my life, and Nicholas an indulgence and my loving Nicholas and seizing him for myself an indulgence. I am a wicked woman: four years ago I left Richard because of my ambitions and I had no patience or discipline, and now to have Nicholas I am leaving him.

Richard's room in her mother's house was filled with pieces of heavy furniture; there was a wardrobe in which Jake's airman's jacket still hung, two large chests of drawers, a desk, a rug, a monstrous bookcase. It was not a child's room, but he was pleased with it. You could see that to have a room of his own gave him a feeling of safety and dignity. Hervey felt again—It was I, your mother, who should have given you this.

Her last day in Danesacre she helped him to arrange his books and toys on the lowest shelves of the bookcase. A book fell down by the wall. To reach it Hervey dragged the heavy bookcase out; the pain started up in her body— It's like an animal, she thought, afraid. The claws moved quickly downward. She knelt on the floor, waiting. Now it has gone away, she thought. Opening her eyes, she felt round for her handkerchief and dried her face. She was giddy—But I got away again, she thought. She picked up the book and showed it to Richard. He said, carelessly:

'This room would be better if my grandfather was not in the next room.'

'Why, Richard?'

'He comes in and steals things. He stole my knife. He put it back afterwards but it was broken. He broke it. He's wicked.'

'Not wicked—queer,' Hervey said.

'He's queer, but he's bad, too,' he said quietly.

'Still, it's a nice room . . . As soon as I can I'm going to find a house for us to live in. You shall have the largest room in it for yourself.'

She watched him, and he did not answer. She felt that she had lost him again. He had begun to talk to her, and almost at once he had nothing to say, and no wish, it seemed, to listen. Ashamed of her tears, she turned her head away and kept them back.

'Shall you like that?' she asked him.

'Yes,' Richard said.

He doesn't notice whether I am here or in London, she thought. She was going back on the night train, at ten o'clock. She gave him his bath at seven, and when she was drying him he said: 'Don't go.'

'*Oh!*' Hervey said. She was seized with despair. Her thoughts were in a hopeless confusion: I can't go, I must, Nicholas is there alone. 'I'll come back as quickly as I can,' she said, lowering her voice. 'In a few weeks. I must find that house for us.'

Richard's face changed. 'You could stay here,' he said. He began to cry.

'Oh my little dear, my love,' Hervey said. A hard knot formed in her chest. 'It's to get money for us, this isn't our house, you know, I'll come back for you, I'll write letters I'll send you what would you like a train something you want very much it's only for a month——'

He let himself be comforted, and began laughing. When she was taking him upstairs he said: 'I wish these stairs would never end.' He got into bed without more words.

Hervey folded the quilt round him, kissed him, and put the light out. 'Good night, my darling.'

'Good night.'

Nothing is worth this, she thought. Thinking it did not help her. She did not send Nicholas a telegram—'Am not coming back.' It was as though she knew that not to go back to him meant she lost him, and not to stay with Richard meant hard grief but not the grief of an irrecoverable loss. She thought she could come back for Richard. She thought that since, whatever happened, he was the heart of her life she could make good any loss. We all have our illusions.

The cab which fetched her to the station was so old that it broke down at the foot of the hill. She had only one bag and she carried it the rest of the way. The station is alongside the harbour, and she had time enough to walk on the quay for a moment. It was full moon. The sky was a cold blue, as pale as the sea; above the east cliff, behind the skeleton of the abbey, were motionless white clouds like feathers. The tide was out, and in the harbour the mud with the water in it was like beaten silver.

There were other people in the carriage, and to keep herself from crying because of Richard, she wrote an exact account of the harbour with the bright thread of water, the sleeping gulls, and the mud. An old countrywoman in the corner seat, who knew her, stared at her and thought: Eh, what a black look yon has—thrash you as soon as look at you, as they say.

After a time her mind began to plan the future, which it did so readily you could know it had been along that road many times. She would persuade Nicholas to live in the country, she would write, she would make money, Richard would go to school, Nicholas to London to sell his furniture; in the evening, when Richard was asleep in his room, it would be with them as though she and Nicholas were alone. Do this, her mind said; say this, do that—you can do anything if you try.

She reached London at four in the morning. Nicholas had been waiting for her for an hour in the station. He hurried her towards a cab. She followed thinking he was angry because he had waited. When it started, he turned round and gripped her arms. 'You've been away a year—I've been only half alive. You mustn't go away again, do you hear?'

His absurd vehemence made her laugh, but it started other thoughts in her mind. He is sleeping, she said. During the day he won't speak of me, he would rather no one sees he remembers me. She pressed her lips together. So that Nicholas should not notice she was thinking of other things than his satisfaction and excitement she bent down and laid her cheek against his arm.

CHAPTER L

WITH the end of this year living in London Hervey had done with it. All earlier memories of the place, from the year before the War, were worn thin, fine gold in their day, now not the worth of a little rotten apple. But for Nicholas, she would have gone.

He was not yet willing to leave London—next summer, he said, or autumn, at present he disliked the notion of a morning and evening train journey more than he disliked the town. Hervey learned quickly that he would give up none of his unmarried ways: he dined five days out of seven at his club, easier for him on his way from Chelsea, ordered in twelve bottles of claret—she had all but sent them away when they came, supposing a mistake, but Nicholas laughed and said surely she didn't grudge him a glass of wine at dinner. To Hervey's careful soul and narrow training, wine every day and a dozen bottles of it in the house at a time was nearly dissolute. Certainly she thought the money could be better spent.

Nicholas handed her five pounds every Monday breakfast: with that she paid the week's rent and the wage of a daily woman. For all else she was responsible, and what with the need to live (as she thought) on the claret level, and haste, she spent in a week more money of her own than she used to need a month. She had Richard, too, and a not obscure impulse made her spend more money on him now—if Nicholas had so much and if living with Nicholas she spent more, Richard himself must have more. It was just.

379

She had begun another novel. When she sent the manuscript of the last to Charles Frome she told him at the same
time that she wanted an advance of three hundred pounds.
He had answered that he would read the book and tell her
whether this was possible; that was a month since and no
word had come from him. She thought about it every day
and did not speak of it to Nicholas.

He was at times unapproachable, sunk in his work, or his
dry thought. At these times, her own mind plagued her.
All that she most feared and disliked, a domestic life and
possessions, were fast about her again, and by her own deed.
She could not blame Nicholas. He had not chosen it. And
still she wished to be free, and still bound herself harder
each day to a sort of life she disliked with her bones. The
solitary eccentric living on in her, uneasily, stirred her
against it. What have you gained, and lost your clear
purpose? A jeering Yorkshire voice added, Not to speak of
the money you are spending!

One morning, less than a fortnight after she came back,
Nicholas vexed her so that she said:

'You think of nothing but your work, if selling chairs
only rich people can afford is work.'

'What do you expect me to do? Shut down the business
of N. Roxby and join you in writing unnecessary novels?'

Fool that I am to mind, Hervey thought. Quietening
her voice: 'I'm sorry, Nicholas. The truth is I don't like
living in London, it costs too much and there are too many
of these Londoners.' Then, as though it were a joke, she
said: 'It's not important—I would give up my own life,
and Danesacre, to live with you anywhere.' Nicholas did
not answer. 'Are you still angry?'

'No, I'm not angry. But it's not right. You ought not
to feel that.'

Her heart failed her a little. 'Why?'

'Because it's not reasonable—and because I don't.'

'Don't feel it?' Hervey said, smiling. 'Why should
you? Come to it, why should I? It remains that I do,

and if I do why should you mind? It's not of importance, it doesn't matter.'

' It matters that you won't accept,' Nicholas said.

' What should I accept? '

Nicholas was beside her now, and touched her. ' What is it, Hervey? '

' Will you laugh if I tell you? Promise? '

' Yes? '

' I love you completely, and that is more than you can say, and I die daily of it, which is much the same as to say I'm living it—or I think it is.'

' Nonsense,' Nicholas said. ' Nonsense, you're not dying. Think of the innumerable things you have to do, and you want to do them.'

' I'm doing everything I have time and chance for.'

' Not with your whole mind, Hervey. You don't even turn that loose in your books, you've admitted it! '

Hervey laughed at him, the numbness rising to her throat, and he kissed her and went away. Poor Hervey, she thought, smiling again at her weakness, you're hurt. Looking at her hands, she cleared the table and spread her papers on it. It's not true that I'm doing what I choose, she thought. I could be living easily with Richard, I don't care any more to be in London, or to be known—I'm clean of that green fever. And I choose this moment to lose my wits again, and for what? Well, I shall do as I can: I'll never, never again, give myself away as I did now; I'll keep quiet—what was it Philip said? *sit still in my bones.* I must.

She looked in the mirror between the windows, eyes searching eyes with self-pity, until she laughed at herself. Who'd have thought it of you? she mocked. She felt free and light, as though she were beginning life again, with no hand on her to turn her this way and that, no Richard, no Nicholas, no Penn even. For a moment she saw the road Penn led her those nights, going between trees, stumbling in the darkness over the roots of trees. How long since that irrecoverable delight, silly, up and down like a child swinging, half afraid and half out of breath with pleasure, seeing the spoiled runnel from the factory glitter like Orinoco in the moon—oh poor Penn.   She stared back at him— This new life I've chosen isn't going to be easy, you can think that, if it's any good to you.

She shook her head, clearing it—who used to say, *That was yesterday*, and laugh at her?—and began to write.

She wrote until late afternoon.   Evelyn Lamb's secretary telephoned; the bell shocked her, destroying the last flicker of energy.   She rested a few minutes, feeling the stiffness ebbing from her fingers and from the back of her head, then hurried out.   It was fine to breathe cold air, even though it was the flat dead London air.   Evelyn (she would) kept her waiting. She sat in the outer room, talking to Evelyn's harassed secretary.   The door opened at last and, of all people, Delia's husband walked out in front of Evelyn.   Hervey was so taken aback that she stared at him and blushed.

Hunt gave her a direct glance, as though guarding himself. He had an engaging smile.   ' Afternoon, Miss Russell.'

As soon as she was alone with her, Evelyn said sharply: ' Then you know Captain Hunt?'

' I knew his wife,' Hervey said.   ' But what is he doing here?'

' Julian Swan sent him to see me.'   Evelyn frowned. ' My nerves are bad to-day,' she went on.   She struck her hand against the desk.   ' You might spend this evening with me, Hervey.'

' I can't do that,' Hervey said gently.   ' Tell me what it is you want, and I must go.'

' Oh.   Is Nicholas dining with you to-night?   Quite a change.   I hear from Julian he's in the club until ten or eleven every night of the week.'

Hervey bit back a foolish rage.   ' Do you believe all Julian tells you?' she said, smiling.

When she left the office of the *Review* she thought, What next?   Her restless mind would not leave her behave sensibly, go home, think of supper, a cup of warm milk, read, and fall asleep. She walked quickly, seeing nothing. I must find my way through this to some quiet, she thought. After a time she thought, I know what I should do; I should think more of my writing, give my mind to it, so that when Nicholas is living to himself I can be safe— oh, but I can't live in this place, I must go home. She stood stock still on the edge of the pavement, seeing the water of the harbour quiet at night, the narrow streets, the road steep as the side of a house to the moors, and the sea lipping the old walls. Nicholas would never be content there, she thought. I have married a peck of trouble, and half my mind, that should be settling it, is in Danesacre still—and consider the awful rent of that flat! She groaned softly, thinking in one moment of Richard, and of her book about which Frome had said nothing yet.

She walked on. She was hungry, and going up to the first floor of a crowded restaurant, found a seat by the wall. The room gave itself up to her, forms and colours sharp and grotesque—monstrous half-globes of light dropping on gilt chains from the ceiling, the false marble of the walls, sharpened planes of flesh and the lightless surface of clothing, a boy's lifted face, blurred, and the pitiful hard impudence of the eyes, another young man rubbing anxiously a mark off his jacket with wetted handkerchief, and his young woman watching him in scorn and understanding, the trembling hands of old men, the waitress's exhausted voice, a raddled respectable woman swinging false pearls in her ears, the cold blank face of a girl, painted, and the thumb of her hand splayed back as if it were boneless. The smell of food came to her in waves. She watched the jaws moving: at one moment the room was filled with eyes, some bright, some ruminant, alive and restless in the unliving flesh. Because of all these people she had a sharp feeling that she was alone, the knowledge that she was alone, and in that like them. Nothing lasts, she thought, seeing herself with Penn, with that child Richard, with Nicholas: the lights go out—the wildness of early love, the ease of youth, the searing dryness of hate; nothing remains but this body, the least warm of friends.

So she stirred her coffee and drank it, and at last thought she had found the answer. I must learn to be quiet in myself, to ask for nothing, to keep quiet and to give Nicholas all he needs, to make a decent life from these fragments.

She went home. Nicholas's coat was lying there in the hall. She stood a moment in astonishment, then pushed open the door of the sitting-room. He sprang up and came towards her. 'Where have you been until nine o'clock, Hervey?'

'You didn't say you were coming in,' Hervey said, at a loss. 'Have you had dinner?'

'I don't want any.' He was impatient. 'I thought you were never coming, I've been thinking of you all day, of your voice and how good you always are to me.' He put his arms under her arms and held her. 'You're so lovely, *so hold und schön und rein*. My lovely Hervey!'

Hervey held him away, to ask him if he enjoyed living with her. I'm not old, she thought, I'm not tired or useless.

'I'm very happy,' Nicholas said, his face kind and for a moment warm and young.

Her heart moved. She was certain now she had done well to risk her life with him—that was in the end what she had done. In the end I have come the right road, she thought, seeing it no easier than other roads and herself unconfident. Standing so, with Nicholas's arms on her, she felt her life drawing to another edge, as a stream quickens to the fall. It is better to feel too hardly than to be old and quiet. Days slide under the hand like coins, and if shortly you will have only enough left to buy quiet, why think about it before time?

CHAPTER LI

Mein Herz gleicht ganz dem Meere,
Hat Sturm und Ebb' und Flut

NICHOLAS ROXBY knew more than any other dealer (except at once his former master, the Jew Salamon) about old furniture, but he was a bad salesman. If a customer vexed him he walked off and left him standing there in the room, before the table or the cupboard he would perhaps have bought if Nicholas had not lost his temper. And like Salamon he disliked parting with certain things and would hide them away, but unlike Salamon, who always sold them in the end, and at a great price, Nicholas contrived to insult would-be purchasers so deeply that in their turn they walked out and never came back. He had no head for figures. His accountant and faithful secretary, Mrs. Hughes, was cheating him all this time, and he did not suspect her. With folly he would give her a blank cheque to fill in, to send out to someone from whom he had bought furniture; more than once or twice she drew this money herself and destroyed the bills and letters sent by the angry creditor. That there would be a disagreeable end to this form of stealing she knew, but preferred not to think about it. She may have believed that her thefts would be hidden among the inextricable knots she was tying in the accounts. Or Nicholas's carelessness about money may have infected her so that she scarcely thought of herself as a thief. A curious truth is that she was very fond of him, willingly worked late, and endured his vile tempers.

In January when she brought him the figures they were worse than his fears. Certainly he expected losses in the first year—but not this heavy loss. The sum of the money owing to him was large, too, and he scolded Mrs Hughes for not sending her accounts out regularly.

'You needn't think I don't send them,' she retorted. 'It's them don't pay up. *I* can't go after people and force them to pay, can I? I'm a secretary, not a debt collector.' In her indignation she forgot certain sums, paid in cash, which had found their way into her pocket. They showed in her books as still unpaid.

'You'd better bring me your books to look through,' Nicholas said irritably.

'I haven't finished yet,' she answered. 'I got out the totals because you asked for them. I can't work quicker. I'm doing two men's work already, and last week I was here till nine every night. You ought to have another secretary.'

'Or another accountant,' said Nicholas. He would have enjoyed shaking her. Hurt by his ingratitude and over-bearing voice, she cried noisily. 'Go away, go back to your room,' Nicholas shouted, waving his arms. Afterwards he was ashamed of his loss of self-control. He spoke to her kindly and told her to take a day's holiday. For the time he forgot to ask again for her books. He disliked figures only less than he disliked answering letters. One drawer in his desk was called the Mortuary, because it was filled with letters, not easy to answer, which had been left to die slowly of neglect.

He gave himself all the more trouble to be certain that nothing he showed in his rooms was less than perfect in its kind.

Hervey could see he was becoming anxious. She looked with dismay at the figures when he showed them to her, and asked at once for details. That vexed him sharply, as if she were accusing him of neglect. He gave her an evasive answer. Hervey did not choose to ask a second time. In her heart she expected only that he would lose his money: the Nicholas who had refused to succeed Mary

Hervey in Garton's was capable of anything—except of earning any money!

In her judgment there was a trace of contempt. It did not alter her respect for him as an honest mind, but it was enough that she would not trouble herself with his business. Why waste energy on what is certain to fail? She had too much work to do. Now more than ever she thought of herself as being the person on whom their living depended.

Nicholas had another splinter in his heel these days. Since the evening he told her, Jenny had written to him every day, letters filled with bitter malicious phrases. She recalled all their past to him, reminded him of his passion for her, quoted his words, his letters, in those years, and reviled Hervey, speaking of her as ' the common Yorkshire servant girl,' ' the woman Vane,' or shortly as ' Vane.' She took the trouble to learn everything she could about Hervey, and in one letter she asked Nicholas whether ' the servant-girl's brat is legitimate? ' ' I am told,' she wrote, ' that Vane's husband treated her badly and I congratulate her on finding another and more gullible protector.'

These letters irked Nicholas unbearably. He carried them about unread for days, then opened four or five together and looked rapidly through them. In spite of everything he was sorry, bitterly so, for Jenny; he would be glad to help her, and the long incoherent foolish letters made him ashamed for both of them. His feeling of responsibility for her strengthened—she must be ill or unbalanced to pour out this nonsense. He recalled the streak of melancholy in the squalid old man, her father. Twice she wrote to him in the third person—' the beautiful Mrs. Nicholas Roxby presents her compliments to the woman Vane and trusts she will learn the ways of decent society in time to prevent public disgrace.' Nicholas found it excusable that she hated Hervey. At the same time he shuddered at the notion of seeing his wife again. His pity for her became marked with distaste for a diseased mind.

In a weary moment he showed Hervey a letter, not the

most ridiculous. Her expression when she was reading it startled him quicker than the biting words she used. This was the first time he saw in her face what he came later to call her 'Yorkshire look,' shrewd, sneering, stubborn and kind in one moment. The kindness now was overlaid by contempt. He saw the likeness to Mary Hervey at her worst. For a few minutes he disliked her. He regretted strongly that he had betrayed Jenny to her.

Thinking of this, he said coldly that she looked discontented—but why? Hervey felt confused. She had been considering that he ought to be more angry with Jenny for spreading lies about her. She could not bring herself to say this. Instead—' I was wishing we could go out more,' she said hastily. ' It would be a change to hear some music.'

' I'm sorry. I know you find me dull,' Nicholas said.

' No, that's not true.'

' True or not, I haven't time to go out at night,' he said.

There was a long silence, while Hervey tried to overcome her feeling of bewilderment and humiliation. At last she said slowly: ' You're not fair, Nicholas. If you left Chelsea a little earlier one or two evenings—or spent a shorter time in the club—we could go to a concert. It's not that.' She looked at him. The blood ran to her cheeks. ' You don't take any trouble for me as you did for your other wife. *She* expected you to please and amuse her, and you thought about it, and were careful of her. Of me, you think that I can look after myself. I can—but you should not think it. You want me to be Hervey Russell, who is hard and can look to herself, and yet you want quite another Hervey to live with you. How can I be both?'

' You can be a great many things when it is to please yourself,' Nicholas said. He spoke calmly. The bitterness he felt had scarcely anything to do with her.

' What do you mean, Nicholas?'

' You speak of my self-thinking. But you are not in the least frank. You keep more from me than you like me to know.'

'You shut yourself away so much that in self-protection I have to keep back part of myself,' Hervey said, with a smile. 'You break my heart.'

Nicholas looked at her softly. 'I know I do. If you want to, you can draw back now.'

'No, I chose it,' Hervey said.

'I warned you, Hervey.'

'I know that—but sometimes you talk as though I were necessary to you.'

'I love you more than anyone, and more, in a different way, than I have loved—anyone.'

'Not more than your work,' Hervey said.

'I can't put you before my work, even if it is, as you said, hardly to be called work.'

'Why not?'

'For a very simple reason. You may become tired of me.'

'No, never,' Hervey said. She looked at him and said: 'I would rather live with you than with anyone. But so long as I am alive I shall always regret that you give so much thought and time to what is not alive and so little to living. We shall die, and what good will your work have been?'

Nicholas was at the other side of the fireplace. A few yards seemed a wide space between them. Hervey saw that by giving herself away again, risking another humiliating snub, she had gained something.

'It was a mistake for us to become lovers,' Nicholas said. 'Since we came here I've realised that. After all I can't feel what you want me to feel, I'm too tired to enjoy complicated emotions, and you, my dear, are too good to rouse easy ones.'

Hervey had to wait a moment to speak.

'Why have you told so many lies?' she said quietly. 'If you had no passion, why did you make a pretence of it?'

'It wasn't pretence.'

'Well, then, if it's over now, why not tell me? I'm not childish, I can live an ascetic life as well as the next man.

I have only to practise the thought that you're not pleased with me in this way.'

With sudden energy Nicholas came across to her and knelt leaning against her chair. 'You know exactly why my first wife left me after the War,' he said with emphasis. ' My new wife might come to feel the same things about me. How can I help expecting it?'

Hervey looked at him and smiled with joy. 'You were afraid,' she said : 'don't you know me yet?'

Next morning a letter came from Charles Frome asking her to come to see him about the novel. The letter, which was a long one, went on: ' I think I had better say at once that I don't feel this fourth novel is very satisfactory. My chief feeling is that you are trying to do something for which you are not fitted. I don't know why you have chosen to experiment in this method, which contrives to be dry and violent in the same moment. Your natural romanticism suited you better, and if you'll forgive me for writing bluntly —after all, the question of money does enter into it, since you are asking us to pay half as much again as we paid for your last book—it had a much better chance of succeeding ...'

There were three pages, with examples from the book itself. She was at first ashamed that her book was not liked. She felt disgraced. She forgot this in thinking of the money. A sickness of fear seized her at the thought that she was going to be refused. She put the letter away after one reading, with an air that it was nothing.

At two o'clock this afternoon she, with Nicholas, was to appear at the office of Penn's lawyer in Lincoln's Inn Fields. They were to be served with the Petition for divorce and— this puzzled her—they were to be identified. Identified? It smelled too much of the keyhole. Only to think about it angered Nicholas. In ten minutes he went off to work, and Hervey took out the letter again.

During this short time she had thought what she must do. Without hesitating, she rang up another publisher who had spoken to her about her books. ' I should like,' he had said, ' to publish them,' speaking in the boyish and amiable voice he used when he was trying to corrupt his neighbour's author.

' Do you still care to publish my next book? ' Hervey asked this voice, her own noticeably flat.

' Certainly I do,' she heard. She felt relief and no surprise.

' If I tell you it is better than the last, are you willing to pay me three hundred and fifty pounds? I should like to know this now, but if you can't tell me without considering, I'll wait.'

' Are you offering the book to me? '

Hervey could not help smiling. ' I'm th-thinking about offering it to you.'

There was a short silence, then the voice said: ' Three hundred and fifty pounds sounds almost reasonable.'

Oh, does it? thought Mary Hervey Russell, it sounds extravagant to me. ' That's very kind,' she said gently. ' I'll write to you or come and see you.'

She did not take it that she had sold the book, but she felt strengthened to face Charles Frome.

Waiting in the outer room, in company with two haughty young women typing letters—one of them had long nails, which tapped the keys of her machine like a woodpecker— she was aware of fear in her belly and of cold hands. At last she was summoned upstairs. Charles Frome gave her a chair beside his desk and said:

' Well, Hervey, what about this book? '

Frome was her age, but because he had known her when she was poor and very shabby he was able when she talked to him to spoil her self-confidence. Thinking of the money stiffened her. At the same time she was grieved and stubborn.

' I can't alter the writing,' she said. ' Or the book itself.'

' What do you want us to do? We'll publish it, of course. But I don't see how we can begin your new contract at three hundred. I think we should pay two hundred on this book, two hundred and twenty-five on the second, and two- fifty on the third. What do you feel about it? '

'I feel that I'd rather you didn't publish a book you don't like.'

The argument went forth and back for the most of thirty minutes, Frome vexed, patient, cool, Hervey uneasy and determined to take her book away at once. Even the money, although it was important, became less to her than her wish to escape. Charles Frome was surprised by her hardness and disobedience, and vexed with himself for having thought she would behave well under criticism. He failed entirely to see her as for the moment she was, a Yorkshireman with something to sell.

At last Hervey stood up to go. By offering to look it through again, she had without awkwardness got her manuscript.

'Don't decide now,' Frome said. 'Frankly, we'd rather publish the book as it stands than let you go to another firm.'

'Thank you for being patient, Charles,' said Hervey, smiling. She felt so much satisfaction at having the book safely in her hands that she forgot to be awkward. For this man who had been kind to her she felt affection and no gratitude. Why be grateful, when you are poor, to one who is safe and well-off and has spoken slightingly of your handiwork? She was far from supposing that she would ever fail. As she went down the stairs and out past the human woodpecker, she thought, Three hundred and fifty pounds from an uncritical publisher is better than two hundred with good advice. But in fact she no longer respected Frome's advice: she thought he knew very little of life.

She met Nicholas, and went with him to the lawyer's. He was almost speechless with anger at being compelled to this legal mummery. Truly it was worse than Hervey had expected. After the papers had been given to them by an elderly solicitor, this sober gentleman asked them to stand close against the window of his room. It looked on to a narrow yard, below the level of the street. Four figures, in single file, walked at a funeral pace across this yard, faces over their shoulders, looking in at the window. Penn first, in the overcoat Hervey had given him on his last birthday; a large displeased woman, the chambermaid from the hotel at Stockbridge; a bully in a navy suit, who was an inquiry agent; and a wizened young man, the solicitor's clerk. This extraordinary procession passed.

Hervey turned to Nicholas. He was no help to her. He hurried her from the house; on the doorstep he said: 'I shall go straight to Chelsea,' and fairly ran from her. She walked across the square, looked back on some impulse, and saw Penn. She waited for him. The wind flattened his overcoat against his long thin legs; with his narrow head he looked tall and boneless. He spoke to her in a jaunty voice. And now she was no longer sure that he felt nothing very deeply.

'Well, Hervey, what are you doing this afternoon?'

'Nothing,' Hervey said. She had been going to call on the second publisher, the amiable and well-meaning, but now she thought: I can't disappoint him.

'Would you like to have tea somewhere and dance?'

'That suits me,' Penn said.

'Let me see whether I have enough money. Yes. I have.'

The ballroom in the Piccadilly Hotel is below the ground —that always made Hervey think of the pressure of stone and earth on the walls of this lighted room. A dozen of couples were dancing and she wondered whether among them was another wife entertaining her husband who was divorcing her.

'How is your book going on?' she asked him.

'Slowly,' Penn said. 'I don't intend to hurry myself. Luckily I can afford to take my time over it—mother's only too happy to have me living with her. For the matter of that, I can get a job any day in Fleet Street—I know plenty of the right people. Trust Thomas Penn Vane for that!'

Hervey felt the old impulse to encourage him, because his bragging was little likely to be filled. 'You shouldn't

delay too long with the book.   After all, you need to live.
You won't be content always to live in the country with
your mother, and with no money.'

'Speak for yourself, my dear.   I daresay I have a better
time than you do.'

He told her about his new friends, one man who owned
a yacht, and another who had invited him to stay a year in
Scotland.   Hervey listened and nodded.   He is pleased with
what I consider rank folly, she thought: which of us is
right?   I to work and struggle, he to live an idle life on
his mother's small income?   She felt uncertain.   I shall
not be at peace, whether I make the best of my ambitions
or do not.

'Well, and are you happier than you were, Hervey?'

'I work very hard,' Hervey said, lightly and evasively.

'If you don't like it, you can always change your mind.
I shall welcome you back with cheers.   No doubt when
I'm sixty I shall give up feeling.   At present I still think
of you.'

Hervey looked down at the table where they were drinking
tea.   It came to her that Penn the unreliable and useless
had never wished to explain to her that she was less necessary
to him than other things.   He is not more selfish than
Nicholas, she thought.   I neither like nor respect him, but
it will be a long time, many months, before I feel free.
She was trying to find words to please him—suddenly she
felt impatient and scornful.   Much use it is what I feel at
this moment, or in a year's time!   Since I could not endure
Penn any longer, I ought, if I had any self-control, to put
him out of my mind.   All this fuss comes of imagining oneself important.   In my life Richard is the one person to
whom I am bound and no pretence about it.   Thinking of
Richard she saw Danesacre, as it would be at that hour:
she looked at the frost-bound winter hills; in the early
dusk the cold air blowing from them drove back the sea
wind; the rocks circled the house.

She came back to the overheated room with distaste.   Now

glancing at Penn's face she remembered part of the bitterness of her life with him. Even if the fault was not his—I brought out what was evil in him, she thought—why pretend that it was endurable? And why think of it?

Her mind was stirred as though, looking on the ground, she had seen by its shadow a bird moving swiftly out of sight. There is still time, she thought. One year or the next I shall learn not to be afraid, and not through cowardice make myself all things to all people.

The dancing ended at six o'clock. She said good-bye to Penn and hurried back to the flat. She had thought Nicholas might come in early, wanting a meal. He did not come until ten, but he was vexed with himself for staying away.

'I meant to dine and come straight home. Then I began talking—it was all of no importance, talk about nothing—and I ought to have been here.'

'Something more than that is worrying you,' Hervey said. 'You're vexed about this evening only because something else is going wrong, and you think it's your fault.'

Nicholas was walking about the room. He stood still and looked at her. 'What do you mean?'

'I don't know,' Hervey said. 'But I know that when I make a fuss about wasting two or three hours it is because I'm not working at all. Why are you dissatisfied?'

'I believe I'm a fool,' Nicholas said, with vehemence. 'I can't sell things. I know for certain when a thing is good and genuine, but when it comes to selling it I'm useless. Useless, Hervey.'

'Are you losing money?'

'The worst is I don't even know how much.'

'Who does your books?'

'Mrs. Hughes is weeks, months, behind with them.'

'Why not have an accountant in to look at them?'

'I resent spending any more money—I can't afford it.'

Hervey smiled. She saw that he did not wish to know how badly his affairs were going. He will lose every penny, she thought calmly. ' If in a year's time nothing is better, will you have an accountant ? '

' I'll see. Very likely.'

Hervey said nothing more. He had spent the day over the books, writing down the chief items, and he meant to make out a rough balance-sheet now. He told Hervey to go to bed.

She tried to keep awake there, but she was already half asleep when he came into the room. She stretched her arm over the pillow. Nicholas sighed and lay against her with his whole weight. She felt an exquisite joy. Her heart did not beat more quickly—this happiness was of her whole self.

After a few moments, he said: ' Are you asleep ? '

' No,' she said, ' I was thinking. I wish I could give you all the things you want.'

' I shall never have any of them, and in the end I want you more than the rest.'

When it is too dark to see the lips moving, words live in a life of their own.

' I can't see the end—and we have so little time left,' Nicholas said.

' One begins badly, and afterwards it's not easy to live without double-thinking. I wish I had known you when I was young and just beginning. I should have made fewer mistakes.'

' I wish I'd known you ten years ago.'

' What are ten years ? ' Hervey said.

' Without you I should always have been alone—now whatever happens I shan't have to face that. But what is the use of talking, it doesn't tell you what I feel. So many words, so little time. Do you know what the time is?— after half-past one. It was that when I came to bed.'

Loving Nicholas and wishing to help him, thought Hervey, I have left Penn to do the best he can for himself. Nicholas fell asleep. When she thought it safe she drew away her arm. It was stiff and she rubbed it gently. Noticing that the curtains which had been hanging motionless across the open window were blowing out, she moved the blankets stealthily on one side and stood up. She fastened the curtains back.

Primrose Hill seemed a great way beneath. Lines drawn by the street lamps crossed it this way and that: she noticed the circle of pale grass round the nearest lights; it became smaller and smaller until of the farthest lamps only a point of light remained. At night, this ghostly hill was beautiful beyond praise. Hervey looked at it and said, I can't endure the thought that I shall forget what living here with Nicholas was like when it was happening, and am angered to know that all this will remain here unchanged after I have been driven out of life. I'm bound I shan't go willingly or easily. She had not lived long enough to think that death like the collector of taxes calls again and again at the same house. Even her young London had now died a score of times. The ghosts it had given up were three poor merry scholars, and then a harassed young wife, and then young men in an earth-coloured uniform, a boy clumsy in his airman's jacket, with shamed tears in his eyes, and then Philip who should have died sooner. She scarcely thought of these. She thought of Nicholas, of her home, of the houses between the cliff-edge and the harbour, of pools in the road crossing the moors, of her present life, uncertain, without quiet or security, of her own uncertainty and ignorance, of the need to overcome them, and of her son. For him at least she had only single thoughts and heart—that another year would not go by until he was with her, and what he needed, now and so long as he needed it, that he should have.

THE LOVE CHILD
by Edith Olivier
New Introduction by Hermione Lee

At thirty-two, her mother dead, Agatha Bodenham finds herself quite alone. She summons back to life the only friend she ever knew, Clarissa, the dream companion of her childhood. At first Clarissa comes by night, and then by day, gathering substance in the warmth of Agatha's obsessive love until it seems that others too can see her. See, but not touch, for Agatha has made her love child for herself. No man may approach this creature of perfect beauty, and if he does, she who summoned her can spirit her away...

Edith Olivier (1879?-1948) was one of the youngest of a clergyman's family of ten children. Despite early ambitions to become an actress, she led a conventional life within twenty miles of her childhood home, the Rectory at Wilton, Wiltshire. But she wrote five highly original novels as well as works of non-fiction, and her 'circle' included Rex Whistler (who illustrated her books), David Cecil, Siegfried Sassoon and Osbert Sitwell. *The Love Child* (1927) was her first novel, acknowledged as a minor masterpiece: a perfectly imagined fable and a moving and perceptive portrayal of unfulfilled maternal love.

"This is wonderful..." — *Cecil Beaton*

"*The Love Child* seems to me to stand in a category of its own creating...the image it leaves is that of a tranquil star" — *Anne Douglas Sedgwick*

"Flawless — the best 'first' book I have ever read...perfect" — *Sir Henry Newbolt*

"A masterpiece of its kind" — *Lord David Cecil*

THE SHUTTER OF SNOW

by Emily Holmes Coleman
New Introduction by Carmen Callil and Mary Siepmann

After the birth of her child Marthe Gail spends two months
in an insane asylum with the fixed idea that she is God.
Marthe, something between Ophelia, Emily Dickinson
and Lucille Ball, transports us into that strange country of
terror and ecstasy we call madness. In this twilit country
the doctors, nurses, the other inmates and the mad vision of
her insane mind are revealed with piercing insight and
with immense verbal facility.

Emily Coleman (1899-1974) was born in California and, like
Marthe, went mad after the birth of her son in 1924. Witty,
eccentric and ebullient, she lived in Paris in the 1920s as
one of the *transition* writers, close friend of Peggy
Guggenheim and Djuna Barnes (who said Emily would be
marvellous company slightly stunned). In the 1930s she
lived in London (in the French, the Wheatsheaf, the
Fitzroy), where her friends numbered Dylan Thomas, T.S.
Eliot, Humphrey Jennings and George Barker. Emily
Coleman wrote poetry throughout her life — and this one
beautiful, poignant novel (first published in 1930), which
though constantly misunderstood, has always had a
passionate body of admirers — Edwin Muir, David
Gascoyne and Antonia White to name a few.

"A very striking triumph of imagination and technique...
The book is not only quite unique; it is also a work of
genuine literary inspiration" — *Edwin Muir*

"A work which has stirred me deeply...compelling" —
Harold Nicolson

"An extraordinary, visionary book, written out of those
edges where madness and poetry meet" — *Fay Weldon*

PLAGUED BY THE NIGHTINGALE

by Kay Boyle
New preface by the author

When the American girl Bridget marries the Frenchman Nicolas, she goes to live with his wealthy family in their Breton village. This close-knit family love each other to the exclusion of the outside world. But it is a love that festers, for the family is tainted with an inherited bone disease and Bridget discovers, as she faces the Old World with the courage of the New, that plague can also infect the soul...

Kay Boyle was born in Minnesota in 1902. The first of her three marriages was to a Frenchman and she moved to Paris in the 1920s where, as one of that legendary group of American expatriates and contributor to *transition*, she knew Joyce, Pound, Hemingway, the Fitzgeralds, Djuna Barnes and Gertrude Stein: a world she recorded in *Being Geniuses Together*. After a spell living in the bizarre commune run by Isadora Duncan's brother, she returned to America in 1941 where she still lives. A distinguished novelist, poet and short-story writer, she was acclaimed by Katherine Anne Porter for her "fighting spirit, freshness of feeling." *Plagued by the Nightingale* was first published in 1931. In subtle, rich and varied prose Kay Boyle echoes Henry James in a novel at once lyrical, delicate and shocking.

"A series of brilliant, light-laden pictures, lucid, delightful; highly original" — *Observer*

"In delicate, satirical vignettes Miss Boyle has enshrined a French middle-class family...The lines of the picture have an incisiveness and a bloom which suggest silverpoint"— *Guardian*

If you would like to know more about Virago books, write to us at 41 William IV Street, London WC2N 4DB for a full catalogue.

Please send a stamped addressed envelope